The Brightest Star in Paris

Also by Diana Biller

The Widow of Rose House

The Brightest Star in Paris

DIANA BILLER

ST. MARTIN'S GRIFFIN
NEW YORK

This is a work of fiction. All of the characters, organizations, and events portrayed in this novel are either products of the author's imagination or are used fictitiously.

First published in the United States by St. Martin's Griffin, an imprint of St. Martin's Publishing Group

www.stmartins.com

Designed by Devan Norman

Library of Congress Cataloging-in-Publication Data

Title: The brightest star in Paris / Diana Biller.
Description: First Edition. | New York : St. Martin's Griffin, 2021.
Identifiers: LCCN 2021016072 | ISBN 9781250297877 (trade paperback) | ISBN 9781250804969 (ebook)
Subjects: GSAFD: Love stories.
Classification: LCC PS3602.I4368 B75 2021 | DDC 813/.6—dc23
LC record available at https://lccn.loc.gov/2021016072

First Edition: 2021

10 9 8 7 6 5 4 3 2 1

To Bonnie Billings
1983–2011

AUTHOR'S NOTE

This is a story about love and healing, but it is also a story about trauma. For a list of content warnings, please visit my website at dianabiller.com/books.

The Brightest Star in Paris

CHAPTER ONE

Paris, October 1878

The Palais Garnier was three days away from dress rehearsals.

Magnificent and vast, built of gold and marble atop a dead arm of the river Seine, the theater was the most celebrated and reviled building in all of France before its first stone was even laid. To the pious folk of the countryside, it was a symbol of the opulence and sin that had plunged France into years of war and civil strife, surely a punishment from God for the decadence of Paris during the Second Empire. To the rich and fashionable of Paris, it was also a symbol of opulence and sin—which, as every aspiring sophisticate knows, are the crucial ingredients of a good time.

No one asked what the poor of Paris thought. They had caused rather enough trouble over the last decade, after all.

While the ornate marble rooms and plush red velvet seats stood empty, backstage was a hive of activity. The smell of fresh paint and turpentine mingled with the sounds of workers pounding away with hammers and the string section warming up for rehearsal. Young girls, the *petits rats* pulled from the hills of Montmartre to be background dancers, ran through the halls laughing, the excitement of an upcoming performance suffusing their thin faces with pleasure. Opera singers ran through their scales; seamstresses hemmed costumes until their hands ached and their fingers were red; even the horses in the underground stables stomped their hooves in excitement.

Amidst all the noise and joy and life, Amelie St. James, *étoile*—prima ballerina—of the Paris Opera Ballet, sat still and silent, thinking about how hungry she was, and how much her hip ached.

"Just one more pose," the photographer said, his assistant hurriedly moving the equipment. "Hold the bouquet like that—yes. Stay perfectly still—" *Click*, flash. Amelie blinked the stars from her eyes as the photographer nodded in satisfaction.

"Now, Mademoiselle St. James has time to answer a few more questions," the Director of the Opera Ballet said to the dozen or so journalists gathered in the small room. He had chosen the Salon de la Lune for the meeting with the press, just one of the many jewel-like magnificences of the Palais Garnier. Dark, ominous birds and bats soared across the ceiling, surrounded by sharp rays of silver paint and glowing golden constellations. Platinum leaf lent the room a feeling of being surrounded by actual moonlight, the mirrors lining the walls magnifying the effect. Amelie caught her reflection through the dark-suited men. She looked too pale—the hours of sitting and answering questions had taken a toll.

"Mademoiselle St. James," one of the reporters began. "You'll be dancing the title role in the upcoming revival of *Giselle*, but your piety is well-known. Giselle, of course, disobeys her mother and falls in love with a man far above her station. What would you say to young, impressionable girls who might find Giselle's decisions romantic?"

Considering she goes mad and dies before the second act, I'd suggest they avoid princes. In disguise or otherwise.

Amelie's slow smile had its own reviews—"St. Amie's melancholic, graceful expression of goodwill elevates all who are privileged to see it"—and she deployed it now. "I consider *Giselle* to be very proper viewing for young women," she said. "Giselle makes a grave mistake and pays an enormous price for it." Again, madness and death. "But it is ultimately a story of redemption, sacrifice, and the purity of love. Given the chance to take revenge on the lover who betrayed her, she protects him instead. She puts his needs before her own, and in that way, I believe, attains salvation."

The journalists diligently dashed her answer down in their notebooks. The Director nodded, pleased with her performance. St. Amie, the people of Paris called her: beloved, pious, and kind.

For years, the Paris Opera Ballet had faced scandal after scandal. Most sprang from its association with members of the notorious Jockey Club, who treated the company like their own personal high-end brothel. Since the Club was made up entirely of the wealthy and powerful, those in charge of the Opera Ballet had no desire to *actually* sever ties with it—rather, they preferred to roll out half-hearted "morality" measures every few years, hold regular press conferences with the company's resident saint, and leave the men of the Jockey Club free to raid the company for as many mistresses as they liked.

So long as they maintained a few scraps of propriety, the public turned a blind eye. Amelie was the scraps.

Seven years ago, she made a decision out of hunger and fear. That decision had changed everything. Now, she lied every day of her life, but she wasn't hungry. She only danced with propriety, her heart not quite in it, but her sister never had to worry about where she would sleep that night.

This was how she earned her safety. This was how she protected her sister. And even if every last one of these interviews chipped away at something inside of her, it was not too high a price to pay.

"One more question, gentlemen," the Director said genially. "Mademoiselle St. James is preparing for a very difficult role. We mustn't keep her too long."

Would that you had said that three hours ago, before I missed rehearsal. She would need to hurry to fit in enough practice before Honorine's bedtime.

"Monsieur Charpentier, go ahead."

A thin young man near the back leaned forward. "Mademoiselle St. James, you're well known for your charitable works. Is there a project you'd like the public to know more about?"

Irritated mutterings met her ears from the other journalists, who obviously considered it a wasted question.

"I'm currently working with a foundling hospital in Montmartre," Amelie said. "They're in desperate need of donations—clothing, food, money, really anything would help—"

"She lives up to her nickname, doesn't she, gentlemen? I'm afraid that's all we have time for." The Director stepped neatly in front of her. "A pleasure to see the press, as always."

She hadn't given the name of the hospital yet. She stood, a stab of pain racing from her hip down her thigh, and tried to catch the young journalist who'd asked the question, but the Director grabbed her arm.

"Must it always be Montmartre?" he murmured. "Couldn't we help the less fortunate somewhere more fashionable?"

"It will always be Montmartre," she said calmly.

"It reminds people of your mother."

"She's not a secret."

He frowned. "I suppose it could be something like 'daughter atones for sins of mother,'" he said. "Yes. That's what I'll tell them. Good work today." He patted her avuncularly on the shoulder and hurried to join the journalists. As he led them from the room, he made some joke, resulting in uproarious masculine laughter.

Alone in the room, Amelie avoided her reflection. This sparkling, extravagant room wasn't for her. This was for the rich and powerful, those who shone as brightly as the platinum on the walls. She gathered her things and made her way backstage.

This was her place: behind, and above, and deep, deep below, in the parts of the enormous building that made the Palais Garnier one of the most magnificent theaters in the world. The seven stories plunging underground included the large stables and a costume atelier roughly the size of a railroad station (as well as a cistern that legend had already turned into a lake). The soaring heights above the stage allowed scenery to be dropped in and out with all the ease modern invention could provide. Everything about the Palais Garnier was large and lavish.

The ballet rehearsal room was at the very top of the building, directly beneath the roof. She paused when she reached the stairs.

The hip had been a problem for a year. Before that, it had been . . . not a problem. A concern, perhaps. A mere irritation, beginning four years prior. And before that, a mild, constant discomfort she'd chalked up to the normal pain of being a ballet dancer.

It will be fine, she told herself as she began the seven-story climb. Two more years and she'd have enough money so that she and Honorine could be secure for the rest of their lives. She could retire. The hip would last that long. It would have to.

By the time she reached the top, the pain had spread down her entire leg. There was no one around, so she leaned against the cool plaster wall, taking deep breaths until she could think around the enormous, radiating ball of agony filling her body. Slowly it shrank, and shrank, until it was just barely manageable. She took another breath and walked into the studio.

It was a beautiful, curved, sun-drenched space with huge oval windows overlooking all of Paris. The room still *felt* new, the wood floor barely scarred, the iron beams arching toward the ceiling, freshly painted. It was like a bonbon held out for an unruly child: *See what happens when you're good? See what you get when you behave?*

She dropped her bag next to the wall and placed her hand on the barre. Three more hours, she decided. Two more years.

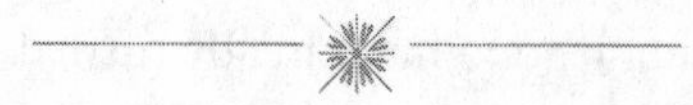

When Dr. Benedict Moore stepped out of the Gare du Nord, eyes bleary from hours of train travel, the first person he saw was the girl he'd left behind.

Amelie St. James, ethereal and perfect on a dingy train station poster, balancing impossibly on her toes, a wreath of white flowers resting atop her auburn hair. The illustrator had taken some liberties with her face—her nose wasn't quite so dainty, and the smile was altogether too sweet.

Yes, but she's been elevated to sainthood in your absence. Saints probably couldn't afford smiles that hinted of mischief and devilry. Still, he doubted sainthood had changed the nose.

The artist had captured her eyes, though. They were the color of the Seine in the summer—deep blue green, eyes you could lose yourself in. Eyes of summer.

Twelve years. She'd saved his life, and she'd changed it, and now he was back in her city and he hadn't decided if he should even visit her.

"Benedict!"

Dr. Victor Durand pushed through the crowds outside the station, his mild, bespectacled face illuminated with an enormous smile, his thinning blond hair blown askew by the October winds.

"Victor," Benedict said, briefly embracing the smaller man.

"Welcome to Paris," Victor said, opening his arms expansively. "Or I suppose I should say welcome back. It's an exciting time here, very exciting. I've already made a list of what you'll want to see. It's going to be difficult to fit it all in; I don't see why you couldn't stay for a few months. You've already gone to the difficulty of crossing the Atlantic Ocean, after all—well, I suppose you have to be back to set up the institute, but only a few extra weeks—"

"I know," Benedict said, struggling to follow the rapid-fire words through the haze of his travel fatigue. "It's too short."

He'd be in Paris for a month and a half, a business trip culminating in a major congress of brain scientists from around the world. He was there to learn, to collaborate, to present his work, and as the head of the brand-new, not-even-open United States Institute for Brain Research, he was there to recruit. Several promising young candidates would be present at the conference, and he hoped to come home with one or two of them. Before the conference he was scheduled for a number of meetings and tours, and now that he was finally standing here, a few feet from Amelie's image, he had the terrible, sinking suspicion it had all been one enormous excuse.

He stole one last glance at her before Victor led him to the waiting carriage.

They piled into the brougham, pulled by two beautifully

matched dark bays, and Victor's coachman shut the door behind them. The carriage was new, its seats perfectly sprung and upholstered in a soft, comfortable fabric. It wasn't an opulent vehicle, but it spoke of quiet wealth and absolute security, reminding Benedict that Victor might be a doctor, but he was, by birth, a member of an illustrious French banking family.

He relaxed back as the carriage rumbled into the road and promptly slowed to a crawl. Victor scowled out the window. "This I imagine you did not experience the last time you were here," he said. "It's the construction, you see. Traffic has become impossible."

Benedict laughed. He'd traveled across an ocean and a country, only to get stuck in traffic.

"Oh yes, laugh all you want, but you won't think it's so funny when you've been here a few days," Victor said, but his irrepressible smile returned. Bad moods had trouble sticking to him. "At least we'll have time to decide upon our itinerary before Camille has a chance to interfere—" With a flourish, he produced a folded piece of paper.

"Oh my god, you actually have a list," Benedict said. "Be honest. It's just a list of Impressionist studios, isn't it?"

"Of course not," Victor said, indignantly. "There are also *several* galleries. I knew you would want to expand your art collection while you are here—"

"Oh, you did, did you?"

"—and besides, there is no better way to experience Paris than through the eyes of the artist—"

There was no resisting Victor's recent obsession with the so-called Impressionists, in defiance of almost every art critic in Paris. Benedict found himself resignedly considering the logistics of shipping paintings across the Atlantic and could only hope he wouldn't have to purchase a painting from *every* painter they visited. Going by Victor's shining face, the odds didn't look good.

Well, his parents had a large house. They could find some wall space. And his brother and sister-in-law, Sam and Alva, could be counted on as well.

He listened politely as Victor gave exact descriptions of the work of every indigent artist in Paris, watching the streets roll by. They were wide and magnificent, almost martial in their straightness. For the last twenty years, Paris had been engaged in an aggressive urban transformation, one that rolled ruthlessly onward no matter the government in charge of it. Twelve years ago, the project had only been beginning; now it was nearing completion, or so he thought. He didn't recognize the city outside the carriage window, and thus he didn't notice anything odd about their direction until the carriage turned abruptly down a side street and he found himself back in old Paris, with its bumpy streets and laundry lines and somewhat decrepit-looking cafes. The driver stopped, and Benedict stepped out, thinking of a hot meal, a bath, and a soft bed.

"Shocking transition, isn't it," Victor said, following him. "This street is scheduled for demolition next year, or perhaps the year after. You find pockets like this everywhere."

"You sound very calm for someone whose home is about to be torn down," Benedict said.

"Oh! We don't *live* here, dear fellow," Victor said, linking his arm through Benedict's and pulling him along the grimy sidewalk. "There's someone I knew you'd want to meet! A genius, an absolute genius. I discovered him! I'm his patron, you know, although you mustn't tell Camille. . . ."

Benedict had been traveling for fifteen days straight. He only barely stopped himself from weeping.

Victor led him down the street, through a cafe, and up a rickety set of back stairs.

"Victor . . ." Would it be rude to beg for sleep? Somewhere in this city, there was a bed with his name on it. He was sure of it. His trunk, which had vanished along with the carriage, was probably well on its way to it. *That trunk doesn't know how good it has it,* he thought bitterly. *No one's making it meet an impoverished artist before a nap. It's unreasonable! No one should be expected to make small talk with Impressionists without proper sleep.*

The door opened, and a tall young man with a receding hair line peered out, blinking his eyes against the light.

He looks like he's *had a nap.*

"Monsieur Durand," he said, his voice high and surprisingly beautiful. He turned, leaving the door open, and Victor pulled Benedict inside, introducing him in excited tones.

He was surrounded by ballerinas. The room was full of them—sketched on paper and scattered over a sofa, a series in hazy pastels piled against the wall, a half-finished oil locked into an easel in a corner. Girls in white, women *en pointe,* all beautiful, sylph-like—ethereal, unreal creatures flying from the walls and chairs and the staircase in the corner. They floated, they balanced on impossibly small feet, they were free of physics in a way no human could be. They weren't people, and in his increasingly delusional state, he felt something malevolent in the display.

He chose a chair facing away from the bulk of the canvases and sat without waiting for an invitation. It seemed unlikely the artist would issue one; he was focused on explaining his most recent work to Victor and itemizing the many ways his work differed and surpassed that of someone named Degas. Occasionally Victor would turn to Benedict and explain something. Benedict really did try to listen, but it was warm in the little studio, and the chair, though old, was quite comfortable. . . .

When he was pulled out of slumber, a disappointed Victor shaking him, night had fallen and the gaslights outside had been lit.

"Sorry," Benedict mumbled, sleep clinging to him like a warm coat he was loath to discard.

"No need to apologize," Victor said, but Benedict detected a hint of stiffness.

"Yes, there is," he said. "This is fascinating, but I'm afraid the journey caught up with me."

Victor's brow cleared. "Oh, thoughtless of me. I ought to have taken you right home, I was just so excited. Well, it's good you rested—André must go to the opera house immediately, there's a corner he didn't get a good sketch of when he was there earlier, and he's realized it's the only thing that will do for the oil he's working on. You brought your coat, didn't you? It's a quick walk."

"Err—"

"Yes, here it is. Alright, André, we're ready."

The artist nodded, having apparently lapsed into a creative fugue, and Benedict found himself holding his coat and being pushed out the door.

It was cold outside, the October wind nipping at Benedict's ears. He hurried into his coat and followed Victor and André down the narrow sidewalk, fatigue clouding the edges of his vision and lending the Parisian evening a touch of the fantastic. They emerged from the little side street onto a wide boulevard, brand new, with short, empty fences where trees should be. Traffic appeared not to have moved, the same smart carriages and shouting drivers giving Benedict the impression of having stepped momentarily out of time. He was lost, completely lost, and concentrated on not losing Victor and André in the abruptly fashionable throng traversing the sidewalks.

When they stopped in front of the enormous building at the end of the boulevard, Benedict's senses took a moment to catch up with him. It was . . . well, it was tall. And wide. And covered in more embellishment than Benedict had ever seen. There was some Roman influence, some Byzantine, and some . . . well, frankly, some sheer bad taste, and it all accumulated in a monument to stun the senses.

"The Palais Garnier," Victor said, next to him. "Takes the breath away, no?"

Benedict nodded.

"The crowning achievement of the Renovation. Fourteen years and thirty-six million francs." Victor sounded pleased by these facts. André stood nearby, shifting anxiously from foot to foot.

"There's an opera opening next week, we'll come back then and do things properly," Victor continued, his voice lowering as they bypassed the grand front entrance and headed toward a small side door, barely visible in the shadows. "This isn't precisely by the book."

He knocked on the door. A man answered, and some paper francs changed hands before all three men were ushered into a dark, narrow hallway. André scurried down it, showing more life than he had since the Degas conversation, and Victor and Benedict followed.

That hallway led to some stairs, and then another hallway, and another staircase. The way was barely lit, and completely empty.

"Where are we?" Benedict whispered. It seemed like the kind of place one whispered in.

"Backstage," Victor said, a lone lamp momentarily illuminating him. His face was tense and excited; he was having an adventure. "These halls were used as a prison for Communards once."

The Franco-Prussian War began four years after Benedict left Paris. It quickly became a disaster for the French, ending after a four-month siege of Paris during which thousands died of starvation and disease. A few months later, the city, furious about the mishandling of the war, rose up. They chased the government out and created the Paris Commune, a socialist government that survived three months before the French government marched back into the city with the strength of the French Army behind them. What followed was a massacre, later called *Semaine Sanglante*—Bloody Week. When it was over, the French government had retaken the city, and twenty thousand Parisians were dead.

He thought about those Communards, imprisoned in a half-built opera house, as he followed Victor, down this hallway, up those stairs, around this corner, past that costume shop. . . .

He stopped, backtracked.

There were tutus in the costume shop.

"Victor," he said, forgetting to whisper.

"What?" His friend, several meters down the hall, turned. "Benedict, what are you doing falling behind? You could get lost."

"You said this was the opera house."

Victor looked impatient. "Yes?"

"Those are ballet costumes."

"Yes?"

Benedict made a sort of bewildered, helpless gesture. "Why are there ballet costumes in an opera house?"

"They perform together," Victor said, as if this were perfectly obvious. "Come on!"

"Victor."

"Benedict!"

"I can't be here. I have to go."

"What are you talking— André! Wait a moment. What are you talking about?"

"I just—I can't be here. There's someone I know, who works here, and I don't want—" He didn't know what he didn't want. He wanted to do things the right way, to reach out properly, not creep into her place of work at night. He didn't want her to think that after all this time, he would barge in on her. He wanted to give her the option to ignore him.

Victor sighed. "It's ten o'clock at night, Ben. I had to bribe the doorman to let us in. There's nobody here. And we're almost there anyway. Ten minutes for André to sketch and we'll be on our way. Stop dawdling."

Ben took a breath. He was being ridiculous. Amelie had gone home hours before, and this rather asinine little adventure had nothing to do with her. He would follow, watch the artist sketch, leave, and never get in Victor's carriage again.

"And I would *love* to know how you've already managed to become entangled in a love affair with a dancer, considering I picked you up from the train station not three hours ago," Victor continued as they started walking.

Not quite a love affair, Benedict thought. *A friendship, a kiss, a goodbye.*

They turned down another endless dark hallway.

He would send her a letter tomorrow. He didn't know if she'd want to see him, if anything had changed in the years since she'd sent him away, or if it mattered. But he'd been back in Paris three hours and all he could hear was her voice. He wanted to know what she thought of all this, of the Impressionists, the Palais Garnier, of the wide new streets and the abrupt old pockets. To leave without trying to see her, just once—that was more than he could do.

Another hallway, another steep wooden staircase, another hallway, a door with light coming from underneath it, Benedict's warning coming too late—

André pushed the door open, and there she was.

CHAPTER TWO

Amelie suppressed a sigh of irritation and smiled politely, prepared to remind the men that this area of the opera house was off-limits to the public, particularly at this hour. Of course, they knew that, since the doors were locked promptly at seven on nights there wasn't a performance. The only way they could be here in the first place was if they had bribed some doorman or stagehand to let them in.

The polite reminder never left her lips.

Before.

That was all she could think. *Before* was standing in the doorway, six feet tall, fifty pounds of muscle heavier than the last time she'd seen him, thick dark hair shiny with good health, all wrapped up in an expensive cashmere coat.

She took two steps toward him. He took two steps toward her. She stopped.

Flickers of memory. A thin boy. Ice cream. The feeling of freedom in her chest, how it felt like laughter—

A small apartment, curtains drawn. Her mother's hair, tangled and messy, tears drying on her face.

After.

Panic pressed thick and humid against her lungs. She couldn't get a breath.

"Not open to the public," she said, or thought she did. Some combination of those words.

His face, stricken, like the last time. Hurt.

Some man with spectacles was talking, apologizing, probably. She didn't care, she needed them—him—to go. If they didn't . . . she didn't know what she'd do.

"Please leave," she said.

Ben didn't say anything. He simply turned and pushed his companions out the door. Made them go away. Shut the door behind him.

She sank to the floor, pressing her cheek against the cool familiarity of the smooth wood boards.

Ben from the lake, Ben from before, Ben, Ben, Ben . . .

Too much. The memories crashed into her like waves, one after another, so she couldn't catch her breath between them. She couldn't do this. She would drown.

So, she didn't. She closed her eyes against the memories, the good ones and . . . the other ones . . . and pressed her hands into the floor and *felt* a tight, furious, panicked ball go past her, through her chest, through the top of her head, and away.

And like that, she could breathe again.

She pushed herself into a sitting position. She smoothed her hair back from her face with a slightly shaking hand. Sighing, she pulled her water toward her and took a long, deep draught.

Ben's back in Paris, she thought, and like her hand, the thought only trembled a little. There was a long pause after it, though, where she stared at the wall.

He hadn't come looking for her, she decided. He'd been as shocked as she was.

He'd looked well.

The thought filled the emptiness in her chest. She let herself smile, just here, alone at the top of the city. Oh, he'd looked healthy and rich and happy, everything she'd wanted for him. She put her hand to her throat and closed her eyes, feeling the gladness for him. He was alright. Someone was alright.

That was good.

Amelie pulled herself to her feet, letting her hands linger on the wooden barre, grasping at the comfort of it. She moved into first position and resumed her barre work, letting the motions numb her. She wouldn't think of him anymore. She had to finish and get home to Honorine.

Her *tendus* were a little stiff, her feet not articulated as beautifully as they ought to be. She turned her head toward the mirror, watching her foot go in and out, forcing herself to use every centimeter of the motion until *before* was simply a word, and the *tendu* was correct.

She was finishing her *frappés* when the door opened once more. She froze, her breath stopping as she watched in the mirror, but it was only a vaguely familiar girl from the corps. Lena or Leisl or something like that. The girl nodded politely—why was she here so late?—and took a place at the barre on the other side of the room. She was wearing her *Giselle* costume, a long white silk tutu and tightly fitted bodice with small, silly wings attached to the back. Amelie hadn't realized the costume department had finished any of the fittings. She supposed the girl was making sure she could move in the thing, although the costumes were so expensive and precious it was unusual to practice in one before dress rehearsals.

What had she been doing? The girl was distracting. Oh, what was her name? It bothered her, not remembering. She made a point of knowing the names of the dancers in the corps—after all, she'd been one, and she remembered how hard it was. Unlike the principals, the dancers at the top of the ballet hierarchy, the corps had to dance in everything. It was exhausting and invisible work.

Louise? Lisette? No, *Lise,* that was it. She remembered her particularly because another dancer had remarked that they looked somewhat alike—a little taller than average, with auburn hair and straight, muscular builds. Amelie had noted casually that they had different eye colors: hers were a kind of blue green, and Lise's were some shade of brown.

And now she was wasting time thinking about the eye color of a corps member when she was only halfway through her warm-up. She glanced behind her at the girl, who was into her *tendus. Focus, Amelie. The longer you dawdle, the later you'll be.*

She took a deep breath. *Fondus.* She'd been doing *fondus.* She sank into them, bend and out, bend and out, bend and out, focusing on the straightening of the leg and the turnout of her hip muscles. The pain was there, but it, too, had been slightly overwhelmed by the events of the evening.

Really, the girl—Lise—should have waited until Amelie was done with the room. Amelie wasn't usually the type to enforce hierarchy, but she was being *so* distracting. . . .

How is she being distracting? She's just doing her barre, perfectly quietly.

Oh, hurry up.

She went into her *grands battements,* the high kicks that marked the end of a barre routine. When she finished, Amelie wiped her brow, drank some water, and began a series of hip stretches that kept the worst of the pain at bay.

Alright. She needed to run through at least part of act 2. By this point in the ballet, Giselle had died and come back as part of a pack of female ghosts, called Wilis. The ghosts had been wronged by men in life and were now out for revenge, enacted by dancing their targets to death. As a method of killing people, the guillotine seemed cleaner, nor was Amelie precisely sure *how* someone could be danced to death, but it made for a couple of pretty good scenes. In the end, Giselle saved her love from such a horrific fate, and he presumably went on to enjoy his life.

She, of course, stayed dead.

Amelie moved to the center of the floor and ran through the music in her head until she found the part she wanted: Giselle begging Myrtha, the queen of the Wilis, to spare the life of the man who betrayed her. Forward and back she danced, pleading with the imaginary queen, running to her lover to protect him. She was a little behind the music in a sequence of steps near the end, so she focused on making them smaller, tighter, more precise. The entire section she was rehearsing would last no longer than two minutes in the production—but she went through it until sweat ran down her brow. When her hip ached too much to go on, she walked to the barre where she'd hung a towel and wiped her face.

"I always thought you'd make a good Myrtha."

Amelie took a long drink of water. She didn't know what to say to that. She danced girls who died, not queens of vengeance.

"You're tall," Lise continued. "And you look kind of fierce."

Amelie laughed—no one had thought her fierce in a very long time. "I'll take that as a compliment," she said. "It's a good role. You're as tall as I am. Perhaps you'll dance it one day."

She saw a flash of white teeth as the girl smiled. "Perhaps," she agreed. Amelie laughed again.

"Well, I'm done for the day," Amelie said. "The room is yours."

"Thank you," Lise said. "It was an honor to watch you."

Amelie nodded briefly and gathered her things. It never failed to make her feel awkward, the younger girls looking up to her. As she headed for the door, glancing at the clock to see how much time she had before Honorine's bedtime, Lise began work on the corps section of act 2—the Wilis, emerging from a cemetery, dancing a man to his death.

CHAPTER THREE

"That was St. Amie," Victor hissed, as Benedict marched him and André down the stairs. "Right? That was her."

"She was *sweating*," André said, in a tone of mild revulsion.

"Camille is never going to believe this! Ow, Benedict, stop pushing me! You're going to make me trip! I should have asked for an autograph—she wouldn't mind if I went back and—"

Benedict tightened his grip on his friend's shoulder. If necessary, he would throw the man over his shoulder and carry him out.

You.

That was what he'd thought, standing in the doorway to the studio. She'd been dressed in white, standing before two enormous, arched windows. Framed by the night sky and the lights of all of Paris.

You. She'd always been Benedict's *you.*

For two glorious steps, all he'd felt was joy. He'd seen it reflected in Amelie's eyes, those river-goddess eyes. And then he'd seen it turn to terror.

Leave, she'd said. So, he had.

He had caused that terror. The thought made him cold and sick. He was ashamed and mortified to have pushed himself upon her, when she obviously had no wish to see him. No, it hadn't been intentional, but he should have turned around as soon as he'd seen the tutus.

Then, too, he would have been spared the hurt spreading through his chest. She didn't want to see him. Why had he thought she would? They hadn't parted well. The joy she'd left him with, the . . . peace she'd given him, would always outweigh the pain. For her, it was clearly otherwise.

They reached the bottom of the stairs. André tried to pull out his sketch book. Benedict took it away from him.

Finally, they stepped out onto the wide, busy sidewalk. Benedict walked to the street, hailed a hansom cab, and bundled the men—protesting—inside.

As the cab rolled slowly into traffic, he glanced out the window at the opera house. She was there, at the very top of it. Still dancing. Still *her*.

And beneath his shame and hurt and mortification, he heard the word *you*, beating with steady, glowing joy.

By the time they let André off, he'd recovered his composure. Somewhat. He was preparing to spin some faint excuse for his behavior hurrying the men out of the building when Victor spoke.

"Here we are," he said.

The lamps were new and bright in the neighborhood they drove into. Tasteful gray-white apartment buildings reared above them, muffling the sounds of the city and creating a strange sensation of absence, like when you dipped your ears just beneath the bathwater. Staring out the window, Benedict felt his fatigue return. How could Victor tell the buildings apart?

Apparently, the driver could, because the carriage stopped in front of one, and Victor hopped out. "I've been thinking," he murmured. "Perhaps we don't need to mention the St. Amie business to Camille."

Benedict lifted an eyebrow. "You just remembered she doesn't know about André," he said.

"I just remembered she doesn't know about André," Victor said.

Considering the debacle that had just occurred, Benedict did not feel he was in a position to comment on someone else's marriage. He simply nodded.

The paint on the outside door was bright and smooth with newness; the lobby smelled of fresh wood and lacquer and placid, modest wealth. The Durands' apartment was at the top of the four-story building, the only one on the floor. Victor pushed the door open, calling for his wife.

"Camille! We're back!"

"You've exhausted him," Camille Durand said, entering through a side door and smiling at them. "Hello, Benedict. You look like the dead."

"Camille," Benedict said, shaking her hand. She was a tall woman, with kind, brown eyes, a wide, laughing mouth, and all the pragmatism her husband lacked. Benedict liked her enormously.

She ushered him into the sitting room, a comfortable, fashionable room with walls lined floor to ceiling, salon-style, with paintings. The windows looked out on other windows. His sense of disorientation increased. Where were they? How did they know where they lived?

He really needed that nap.

Maybe he'd hallucinated her. In his memory she looked like

a hallucination—a painting a thousand times better than the implausible creatures in André's studio.

He forced himself back to the moment, exchanging the usual pleasantries with Camille. He'd met the Durands five years ago, in Austria, when both he and Victor had spent a year at the University of Vienna. Victor had visited him three years later, staying in America for two months, but he hadn't seen Camille since Vienna. He remembered she loved riding and asked after her horses.

"They're fat," she said, in a tone of fond disapproval. "We'll go riding while you're here. They're getting lazy. Oh! There are some letters for you."

That snapped him awake. One of his hopes for this visit was to meet the legendary, reclusive anatomist Emile Bonnet. He'd sent several letters to the man begging for an audience, but so far, they had gone unanswered.

And apparently, they had remained so. Camille handed him three letters: one from his sister, one from his sister-in-law, and one from his father.

He tried not to be disappointed. Not everyone had such a caring family, after all.

"I already looked at them," Victor said. "Bonnet didn't reply."

"Victor!" Camille hissed. "You can't just look at other people's letters."

"They were on our console table," Victor said, in his most reasonable tone. "It's not like I steamed them open. Besides, I knew he was waiting for Bonnet. He's not going to write back, Benedict. He hates people."

Benedict tapped the letters against his palm. Bonnet's reputation as a misanthropic hermit was well known—as were the rumors about his research. He'd spent three decades studying the cerebral cortex, and it was rumored he had developed the most detailed, accurate map of the brain ever made. A map like that could change the field. It could also finally, *finally*, make brain surgery possible.

Benedict wanted that map.

"You can think about that after you've rested," Camille said decisively. "I'll show you to your room."

The guest room was pleasant and airy, its walls noticeably bare.

"This room has yet to be invaded," Camille said, nodding at them wryly, "but I can't vouch for it remaining that way during your stay."

Benedict smiled and looked out the window. "I can't figure out where we are," he said, trying to orient himself by the unfamiliar streets.

"When was the last time you were here?"

"Twelve years ago."

"Mmm. A long time, in the history of Paris."

"Yes," he said.

"But we don't dwell on the past here," Camille said briskly. "The future is what matters, I am told. And when the future is too much to bear, I leave for my family estate in Burgundy." She pointed out the window. "There is Montmartre, of course."

He had already picked out the hill, dark against the sky. The only recognizable sight in view. Pinpricks of light were dusted across the top like sugar.

"And if you tilt your head, you can see the corner of the Gare du Nord, just past that building." She pointed, and he followed her finger until he made out a blaze of light that could be the enormous train station. He imagined himself as the third point of a triangle with the two landmarks and came up with a rough idea of his location.

"It's . . . it's very nice," he said, remembering his manners. "But different."

Camille was still looking out the window. "The trees died," she said.

"I beg your pardon?" He glanced out, understanding what she meant. There weren't any trees, not one on the entire street. "Why?"

"The air killed them," she said. "It's too dirty. They couldn't breathe it."

While Benedict blinked in surprise, she shook her head and smiled ruefully. "Supposedly, they're finding a kind of tree that *can*, so I'm assured it's only a temporary affliction. Now, let's see, the footmen brought your trunk up, there it is, and the washroom is down the hall and on the left. If you need anything, ring for it. I'll have a plate sent up for dinner."

She nodded and left the room, closing the door neatly behind her. Benedict turned toward his trunk, and then back to the window, her words running through his mind.

Twelve years was a long time, in the history of Paris.

Amelie dreamed of angry women dressed in white and awoke to her sister poking her in the ribs.

"Amelie," Honorine whispered, stabbing her finger into her side. "Wake up."

"No," Amelie said, pulling the sheet over her face to hide her smile. No one could cheer her up faster than her sister. Honorine made everything worth it.

"Can I borrow your hairpin?" Honorine said, still in a whisper.

"You can't be serious," Amelie said from beneath the sheet. "You did not wake me up at the crack of dawn for this."

"I didn't wake you up all the way," Honorine said. "You can go back to bed right after you lend me your hairpin."

"Which one?"

"The one with the pearl on the end?"

"You're living in a fantasy world."

"The one with the little brass bird."

"I should not reward this behavior. You will turn into a monster child."

Correctly interpreting this as permission, Honorine squealed and bounced off the bed. Amelie pushed the sheet down and sat up, resting against her simple wooden headboard as she watched her sister rummage through her jewelry box.

Honorine was eleven years old, almost twelve. Her birthday was in two months, and Amelie already had plans for the celebration. She had thick, dark hair, almost black, worn in the simple regulation braid of St. Mary's Academy. Her school uniform hung loosely on her—every year Amelie bought it a size too large so she would have room to grow. Amelie was proud of that uniform. It was the uniform of the best girls' school in town; every year Honorine had three sets, and every day she went to school clean and pressed and neat.

"You were home late," Honorine said. "Was it the press?"

Amelie had barely made it before Honorine had gone to sleep. She suspected her sister had dawdled while getting ready for bed, allowing her more time.

"Yes," she said. *And old memories, suddenly reappearing.* "And I had to run through a section I'm struggling with, after."

"You always say you're struggling, but the papers talk about you like you're the best dancer in the world. You're being dramatic."

Amelie laughed. "The papers don't get to see that part."

More important, the papers wouldn't like that part. Oh, they loved hearing about how disciplined she was, how many hours a day she spent in the studio, but they didn't want the real story: how some days she had to clean the blood from her pointe shoes off the floor, how sometimes she vomited after dancing too long, how she hadn't had a waking moment free of pain for four years.

How all of it was so she could dance in the polite, fairy-like manner the public loved so much. So she could dance madwomen with restraint and sylphs with domestication. So she could die, over and over, and the audience could sigh in satisfaction, because she had died correctly.

In the beginning, she had missed *dancing*. Those moments when emotion ran through your body, turning you into the emotion itself. The laughing, soaring freedom of speaking the things words couldn't say.

"There," Honorine said, calling Amelie abruptly back to the present. "How does it look?"

She'd stuck the pin down through her braid, so the brass bird sat at the top in a little nest of hair.

"Charming," Amelie said. "Don't lose it."

Her sister rolled her eyes. "I'm going to go get breakfast."

"I'll be out in a minute."

She lingered in bed, her hands suddenly shaky. Seeing Ben again was bringing up dusty old thoughts—wishes and resentments long forgotten and best forgotten again. Regrets were dangerous.

She swung her legs out of bed and stood gingerly, hissing as her weight landed on her hips. It was *bad* this morning. For five minutes she did nothing, thought nothing, as the pain found places to settle.

She'd made those choices so she could survive and Honorine could thrive—and look. It had worked.

Two more years, she told her hip. *Two more years.*

When she could walk, she headed down the short hallway to the dining room. The first steps of morning and the last steps of night were always the worst.

Three years before, Amelie had pulled together the funds to buy an apartment in a smart new building, only a few minutes from the Palais Garnier. The building was white, four stories, pleasantly elaborate, and identical to the buildings adjoining it and those being erected at breathless speed all over Paris. Entire neighborhoods were razed almost overnight, their residents forced up and out, to Belleville and Montmartre and other working-class neighborhoods still accepting refugees from the City of Light.

But St. Amie was a creature of new Paris, and so in new Paris she lived.

The apartment wasn't large: a sitting room, a connected dining room, a small kitchen, a bath, and two small bedrooms. It had fine wood floors and white plaster walls unmarred by scratches and scuffs. The high ceilings were adorned with plaster roses circling the light fixtures. Amelie had furnished it in polite style—everything in good taste, restrained, perhaps two years out of date.

The windows were the apartment's most notable feature. They were huge, taller than Amelie, and opened onto small ledges with black iron railings. Many of the residents of these new buildings had flowerpots on the ledges, bright red geraniums and cheerful orange nasturtiums, even domesticated roses in larger containers.

Amelie's ledges were empty.

She put a smile on her face as she entered the dining room. Honorine sat at the head of the glossy wooden table, thoughtlessly devouring an enormous breakfast as she leafed through a textbook.

"What are you reading?" Amelie asked, easing into a chair as their maid, Suzanne, put a cup of coffee in front of her.

Honorine pushed the open book toward Amelie, changing seats so she was sitting next to her. "We're studying the travels of Marco Polo," she said. "He was an explorer in the thirteenth century. He traveled all the way from Italy to China."

The book was open to a map, beautifully illustrated, of Europe and Asia. Honorine pointed to Italy—that one Amelie knew well enough—and traced a line to the section labeled China.

She'd heard of China, but she'd had no idea it was so large, or so far away.

"Did you know there are people who do nothing but make better maps?"

Amelie had not known that, and she frowned as she considered the question. "How would one go about . . . making a map?"

"Sister Agathe says it's a lot of complicated measurements. I'd like to learn about it, though. Maybe I could make a map of Paris! It's always changing, they must need new maps by now."

"I'm sure they do," Amelie said with a smile. The grandfather clock chimed the half hour, and Amelie shut the geography book reverently. "Time for school."

Her sister nodded, drained the last of her tea, and stood. There was the usual hectic search for a misplaced notebook and a quick kiss dashed on the top of Amelie's head before Honorine was out the door, Suzanne trailing behind.

Amelie was left alone with her thoughts and the ticking of the clock. As neither was pleasant company, she pushed herself to her feet and walked to the short barre she'd installed in the sitting room to begin the lengthy process of warming up her hip.

By the time she was in the studio for morning class, her hip was in tolerable working order. She sat alone in a corner, stretching her calves as the rest of the company trickled in. Light rain spattered the enormous windows, and several girls ran in with wet hair and harried expressions.

There were thirty or so there that morning. They stood as the ballet mistress, Madame Renard, entered, thumping her cane imperiously against the floor. The room smelled of sweat and damp and beeswax.

"We will begin," she said, nodding at the pianist. "*Pliés*."

Madame Renard had no need of the cane: she used it to keep time, to punctuate her irritation, and occasionally to poke with. She'd been a student of the great Marie Taglioni, and though she was in her sixties now, she could still sketch out movements as her idol had once taught them. That was ballet—a constant chain of dancers, passing tradition and style and choreography from one generation to the next. No successful paper notation had ever been created.

As the company flowed into their first *pliés* of the day, a young girl, no more than sixteen, ran in late and breathless. She dropped her bag by the door, rain still dripping down her face, and took her place at the barre behind the other younger corps members. Madame Renard scowled at her, and Amelie winced internally. The girl was in for an impressive scolding after class.

"*Tendus*," the ballet mistress announced sharply, sketching out the combination in the air.

Sometime around the *ronds de jambe*, Amelie noticed a shift in the mood of the class. *Ronds de jambe*, which involved circling the leg from the hip, were painful for her, so by the time she was aware of the change, it was well advanced. The occasional hurried whisper. The muffled gasp. Hasty glances when dancers thought Madame Renard wasn't looking.

Someone's pregnant or someone's dead.

One of the younger girls peeled off and ran from the room in tears. Madame Renard's face was approaching apoplexy as she announced the *développés*.

Alright, either that was the pregnant one or . . .

Another girl ran from the room. Madame Renard banged her cane in fury against the floor. The pianist stopped playing, startled or terrified or both.

"The next dancer who leaves the room without permission will be leaving the company," she hissed. "Am I clear?"

The remaining company members nodded. A sharp pain stabbed Amelie's forehead. Something was wrong.

They finished class in silence. The moment the *révérence* was over, the dancers streamed out the door, talking over one another in such a hurry that, though Amelie was straining to hear, she couldn't make anything out.

As she took her pointe shoes off, the Director entered the studio and took Madame Renard aside. They spoke quietly for several minutes, the old woman's face impassive. At the end she nodded and walked away.

Amelie hurriedly tossed her shoes and towel into her bag and stood. The Director nodded at her as she approached him.

"I assume you've heard?" he said, his tone equal parts annoyed and resigned.

"No," she said. "What happened?"

"They fished one of the corps girls out of the river this morning," he said, sighing.

"My god," Amelie said, crossing herself. "Who?"

"Lise Martin," he said. "It's a terrible time for it, right before the opening. If the press gets wind of it—well, we'll have to hope they don't. I wish we'd held off on your interview round, that could have held their attention awhile."

His words buzzed around her, tinny and high-pitched. "But I just saw her," Amelie said.

"I'll have to pull in a girl from the school to fill her part, I suppose," the Director continued. "At least she was only a corps member. Easy enough to replace."

"I *just* saw her," Amelie repeated. "She must have—my god, she must have fallen in right after—"

The Director stopped and looked at her. "I never took you for the sentimental type, Amelie. Did you know the girl?"

She shook her head. "No . . . no. But I talked to her last night, before—"

"You can't have," he said bluntly, looking at his watch. "She's been absent from rehearsal for days. From what the morgue says, she's been dead about as long. You're thinking of a different one. I mix them up all the time, too."

"I— You said Lise— Is there another—"

"Pull yourself together for the dress rehearsal tonight, won't you? Some of the subscribers are coming, unofficially of course, but it wouldn't do to give them less than what they're paying for, would it?" He patted her on the shoulder and wandered away, leaving Amelie alone in the studio.

"It's not an uncommon name," she said aloud. "There's another Lise. Oh, but that poor dead girl."

She couldn't stop thinking about it for the rest of the day. It bothered her that she couldn't place the girl—a member of her company had died, and Amelie didn't even know what she had looked like. Someone she had danced with, taken class with. She wondered about the dead girl while eating lunch, during a short afternoon rehearsal, walking back from dinner.

When she returned to the Palais Garnier to prepare for the evening's dress rehearsal, she found the Jockey Club littering the hallways.

The members of the Club were the Opera Ballet's most enthusiastic supporters, buying out the boxes every year. They went to dinner during the first act of the opera, arriving in time to watch their favorites onstage during the second-act ballet. Depending on the mood and the opera, they might or might not stay to watch the opera finish.

Once, in the early 1860s, when Amelie was at the Opera Ballet School, the composer Wagner had arrived to mount a production of his opera *Tannhäuser*, specially requested by the Emperor himself. He allowed a ballet to be included, but insisted it occur in act 1, to better augment his opera. When the members of the Jockey Club arrived for the second act, they were furious to realize all that awaited them was . . . singing. Being wealthy aristocrats, they had no difficulty making their displeasure known, disrupting the performance with whistles and jeers.

Wagner pulled *Tannhäuser* after three performances and returned to Germany.

Seventeen years later, the Jockey Club still reigned supreme, and tonight there they were—sprawled over the red velvet seats, wandering backstage, embracing their current mistresses, recruiting new ones. Amelie tried to ignore them. They were interchangeable, these men in soft clothes who treated dressing rooms like cattle markets.

As she passed the door of the large dressing room shared by the young girls of the corps, she heard the sound of crying, and hesitated.

They've lost one of their own, she reminded herself. And like it or not, as one of the company's prima ballerinas, she had a duty to the younger members.

She stepped inside. She'd never been inside the room before—the corps dressing room she'd gossiped and laughed in had burned down long before the Palais Garnier had neared completion. This one smelled the same, though—of cheap perfume and laundry needing to be done. Memories rose, threatening to choke her. Girls she'd laughed with, friends she'd loved, long dead. Giggling as they'd stitched pointe shoes and compared blisters and told secrets. Whispering to her friend Jean-Louise, with her delicate fairy face and light blue eyes, telling her about the boy from the Bois de Boulogne. Jean-Louise, who hadn't made it past the first month of the Prussian Siege.

This was a bad idea.

"Mademoiselle St. James?" The young girl's voice was hoarse. The other girls in the room looked up, red-eyed.

They were all so very young.

"You came," another said, with the touch of worship that always made Amelie feel as though her skin was shrinking.

"I—I heard about Lise Martin," she said, hating the stiffness in her voice. "I'm sorry. I imagine you were her friends."

"That's so nice," the first one whispered. "I can't believe she's dead."

"Do you—um—do you have a picture of her?"

The girl hastened to the back of the room, where a little memorial had sprouted. "Here," she said, holding out a copy of the corps annual photograph. "Back row. Third from the left."

When she took the frame, she knew what she was going to see. She'd known since that morning—perhaps since the moment she'd seen her in the rehearsal room.

Lise Martin, third from the left, tall in life as in death.

The girl in the *Giselle* costume.

The girl from the night before.

"Thank you," Amelie said, handing the photograph back. Her voice didn't tremble. She nodded and left.

Seeing her first love wasn't the most extraordinary thing to happen to her in the last twenty-four hours. She'd spoken to a ghost.

Amelie walked down the hall to her dressing room, breathing carefully. She had a friend in America who'd been haunted once. Or had it been the house that was haunted? And you couldn't live in a city as old as Paris and not, once in a while, have a *feeling*. Amelie believed in ghosts. But there was a large difference between believing in them and talking to one.

Perhaps ghosts were one of those things people experienced but didn't talk about that often. Like bedbugs.

She entered her dressing room, shutting the door behind her and leaning against it. "God have mercy on her soul," she said, crossing herself. "May she find peace. God have mercy on her soul."

"He *might* need more convincing."

Amelie's gaze slid toward the back of the dressing room.

There was Lise Martin, tall, auburn-haired, still in her *Giselle* costume.

And she was standing next to the body of a dead man.

CHAPTER FOUR

God forgive her, her first thought was *I can't be found with a man in my dressing room. Dead or otherwise.*

"Before you say anything, I'm sorry." Lise bit her lip. "I didn't mean to. I *swear.*"

Amelie opened her mouth. And then shut it.

Her ears were ringing. Her dressing room, so familiar, suddenly seemed foreign and overly bright.

One thing at a time.

Crossing the small dressing room, Amelie placed two shaking fingers at the man's neck. He was still slightly warm, but no pulse rewarded her search.

He couldn't be older than thirty, perhaps not even that, despite his thinning brown hair. His skin was pale and gray in death, his eyes open in glassy horror. He was dressed richly, even ostentatiously: the wings of his collar so high they cradled his face, his cravat secured with a ruby-and-diamond-tipped pin likely worth more than Amelie's apartment.

She recognized him, not one of the more popular Jockey Club members. A hanger-on. There were no obvious wounds.

He was simply . . . dead. A corpse. This was an important detail, as it now seemed one could be dead and *not* a corpse.

She straightened. Looked at the body. Looked at Lise.

"He's dead," she said, staring at the girl, who was also, undoubtedly, dead. Not that she looked it—her complexion was pink and bright, her body seemingly solid. She wore the same costume as before, the white bodice and long tutu of the Wilis in *Giselle*. She looked like a healthy nineteen-year-old girl getting ready for a performance. But now Amelie knew what had so distracted her when she'd seen her in the studio. She knew, without any question, that if she reached out and touched Lise, there would be nothing there. She was no longer a person inhabiting a body.

In her daze, Amelie calmly noted the ways in which this new bodyless state manifested. There was something wrong about the way she was standing. Gravity should play some part in it, for one. Instead, Lise was standing like a person who had a vague memory of what standing had been like.

"I'm sorry," Lise said. "I'm so sorry. I *swear* I didn't mean to kill him. How could I! I didn't even know I *could*, and then he just . . . fell over."

Amelie nodded. This was as good a place to start as any. "May I ask how you . . . er, killed him?"

Lise muttered something.

"I'm sorry, I didn't hear that."

"I said, I danced him to death."

"I see," Amelie said. "That was a little derivative."

"I know," the girl said miserably.

"I'm sorry to be so slow," Amelie said. "But if you could, perhaps, explain how you did so? I've never felt *Giselle* was very clear on the mechanics."

Lise twisted her hands together. Could she feel herself doing that? The warmth of one hand against the other? Or was it simply a memory?

"I . . . He came in here. On a bet," Lise said. "Some of his friends thought it would be funny if he propositioned you."

Amelie nodded encouragingly. That happened sometimes.

"I was waiting for you," Lise continued. "And he came in, and I saw . . ."

"You saw?"

"Into his head. I saw what he was thinking. Oh, Mademoiselle St. James—"

"Please," Amelie said faintly. "Call me Amelie."

"Really? Oh, thank you—but Amelie, I'm dead, aren't I. I'm a *ghost*."

Amelie hesitated, but nodded. Lise put her hand to her mouth, and then quickly crossed herself. That seemed like a good idea, so Amelie did it, too. What *was* the Church's stance on crimes committed after death? Amelie didn't imagine it would help the whole purgatory thing.

"I knew it," Lise said, slumping against the wall.

Should she comfort her? "I'm sorry," Amelie said.

Lise sniffled a little. "It's not that I'm sad about dying," she said. "That seems a little different from this side. But why am I a ghost? I don't want to be. Is it— Amelie, did I kill myself? Is this my punishment?"

Suddenly, the room looked darker, the shadows more . . . alive. "I—I don't know," she said. She wanted to say that heaven wouldn't be so cruel, but what did she know? Her experience had only ever led her to believe in a harsh God.

"Oh," Lise said. "Why can't I *remember* anything?"

Amelie's gaze landed on the body on the sofa again. She couldn't be found with it in her dressing room. She might believe in ghosts, but as an explanation for dead bodies they were lacking. The room was so bright—she rubbed her hand over her eyes.

One thing at a time.

"Lise," she said, her voice as calm as if she was telling Honorine to finish her spinach. "Tell me what happened. With him."

Lise sniffled again. "I saw his thoughts," she said, slowly. "I saw one of his memories. He'd . . . he'd hurt a girl he knew. And he was thinking about it. I took—I took revenge for her. Oh, Amelie. I didn't mean to. One minute I was seeing what he did, and then the next I was barely myself anymore."

Amelie considered the dead man. She was vaguely aware she was not reacting as she should. St. Amie would be distraught that a man had been murdered. After hearing Lise's explanation, Amelie St. James thought he'd probably gotten what he deserved.

An ugly thought. She pushed it away.

"But *how*, Lise?"

"I think I can make people see things," the girl said. "I made him see . . . me. Like I was Myrtha. Is that what I am now? A vengeance ghost?"

"So you made him *think* you were dancing him to death," Amelie said, ignoring questions of ghostly classification. "And somehow he died from that."

"I think I frightened him to death," Lise said.

They sat in silence. The corpse let out a noise. Both women jumped.

"It's the body settling," Lise said.

"Yes," Amelie said. She'd seen enough death to know what happened afterward. She looked at the small clock on her dressing table. "I have to finish warming up," she said.

She walked to the short, makeshift barre mounted against

the wall and began a series of leg swings. "Were you wearing that when you died?"

"Um. No?" Lise said. "I don't think so. We should probably do something about the body—"

"So, you just, what, imagined it?"

"What?"

"The costume," Amelie said doggedly.

"Oh," Lise said. "Yes. I believe so. Anyway—"

"You should lose the wings," Amelie said.

"Um—"

"I've always thought they looked ridiculous," she continued. "Did they just steal the ones from *La Sylphide*? Why would vengeful ghosts have sylph wings? Or wings at all? It makes no sense. Especially Myrtha. She *definitely* wouldn't have a pair of stupid sylph wings. I bet they wouldn't even support your weight enough to fly. Although ghosts probably don't have weight. Do you? It doesn't look like you do. Does that mean that you can fly?"

"I don't know," Lise said. "Amelie, we have to do something about the body. If someone finds him here—"

"Can you see into my thoughts? Can you make *me* see things?"

Lise looked down, then away. She bit her lip. "I'm making you see me," she said quietly.

"Oh," Amelie said, stretching to the side. "Right."

"I won't look into your head if I can avoid it," Lise said, her words coming quickly. "Only—I think I live there now."

Amelie straightened abruptly. "What?"

"It's you," Lise said. "I think I'm haunting you."

The murmur of voices outside the door interrupted them. Both women froze.

"Pretend you aren't here," Lise hissed.

"No, I don't need to see her," a man said, in a deep voice that was terribly, dreadfully familiar. "I just . . . I have a note for her. I was hoping to give it to someone—"

"Oh, go ahead and leave it on her dressing table," someone replied. "Doesn't look like she's in."

Time slowed. She heard Ben thank the man, heard him step toward the door, heard him turn the door handle—

Then the door opened, and for the second time in two days, she was face-to-face with the man she used to love.

Benedict took one look at the scene before him, then quickly stepped inside the room and locked the door behind him.

Amelie's lips were parted, her eyes wide, hand extended as if to physically stop the door from opening.

And it made no sense, given the possible crime scene in front of him, but all he wanted to do in that moment was stare at her. She'd changed—he'd been too struck by the reality of her presence the day before to notice. The girl he'd left behind had been softness and smiles around the edges. This woman was clean lines and hidden strength. The girl had eyes that reminded him of sunshine, the woman had the eyes of a wolf. Wary.

Also, there was the body. The Amelie he'd left behind hadn't kept bodies in her dressing room. Of course, she hadn't had her own dressing room then.

He put the bouquet of flowers and the apology note on her dressing room table. "I don't know why this keeps happening," he said. "Believe it or not, both times I was actively trying to *avoid* running into you."

She looked at him, at the dead body, and back to him.

"So," he said, and fell silent. He couldn't think of a single thing to say to encompass the present circumstance.

Amelie cleared her throat. "I— You—" She shook her head. "Yes, I know him, didn't you *just* say you were going to stay out of my head."

This was addressed to the air behind her.

Odd. But there was quite a list of odd developing.

"You came back," she said, this time to him.

"I . . . I wanted to leave this note. Explaining yesterday. I didn't—the man said you weren't in. I understand that you don't want to see me."

"It's not—yes, I know we have to do something about the body—it's not personal," she said.

"Right," he said. The man hadn't been dead long. An hour, maybe. "Either way, I owe you an apology."

"You don't," she said. He stepped closer, looking into those river eyes. Her pupils were wildly dilated.

"You're in shock," he said, and looked around the room. She needed to lie down, but the body was currently occupying the only proper lying-down furniture in the room.

The floor would have to do. He took off his coat, folded it neatly into a pillow, and set it down.

"Lie down while I find something to elevate your feet with," he said. Maybe that box would work—yes, he thought it would.

"What?"

"This will help," he said. "Also, if you have a blanket—"

"I can't lie down. I have to warm up. And—" She looked at the body, back to him, to the body, and finally landed on him. "You *do* see it, don't you?"

"*Of course* I see it," he said soothingly. "And you can warm up in a minute, but if you go perform like this, you'll probably do yourself an injury."

She stared at him with a bewildered expression. "I don't have *time* to humor him," she said, this time toward the costume rack.

"Only a couple of minutes," he said coaxingly, and she threw her arms into the air and moved to settle on the floor.

He put her feet on the box and found a long piece of silk that would do excellently for a blanket. Once she was properly situated, he sat down cross-legged next to her and put his hand on her forehead. Not the most scientific method of checking someone's temperature, but it would do.

"No fever," he said, satisfied.

"I know I don't have a fever," she sputtered. "I might be going mad, though. What time is it?"

"Six thirty."

She groaned. "Why couldn't you have murdered him *after* the show?"

"I—"

"Not you." She took a deep breath. "Ben—"

Hearing his name on her lips, in that delicate French accent, was startling. It had been so many years. Once, a smile had dwelled within it; now, there was only caution.

"Am I going to report this mysterious body and ruin your career forever? No, I am not. I admit to some curiosity, however."

"Would you believe me if I said a ghost did it?"

"More readily than you might think," he said. "Why?"

She shrugged, looking up at him warily.

"Oh lord," he said. Grimacing, he crossed the room, performing a perfunctory examination of the body. A young man, late twenties or early thirties. No external wounds, no obvious cause of death—and yet dead he was.

"Were you here?"

"You believe me," she said.

"And I will tell you why, when we have fewer pressing matters on our hands. Were you?"

"No," she said. "But I think it happened quite recently."

He nodded. "That seems right, going by the temperature and the rigidity of his muscles." He stepped back, considering the problem. "He needs not to be found here."

She looked away, pale-faced, and turned to that same portion of air. "I know you're sorry," she whispered. "But it won't do any good to keep repeating it."

He filed that away for later consideration. "How about the hallway outside? Would there be any reason to connect it to you?"

She sat up. "My god, how simple. Why didn't I think of that?"

"Perhaps you have less experience with dead bodies," he said, bowing modestly.

"Unlikely," she muttered. "The hallway is perfect. People are up and down it all night."

"Excellent," he said. "Problem solved. I'll simply move the body while you're onstage."

"You'll . . ." Amelie shook her head. "What are you doing here, Ben?"

"I'm here for a conference," he said.

"A conference," she repeated, and then laughed, sharp and sudden. "You just . . . happen to be back in Paris, the day before a ghost murders a man in my dressing room. Do you know, I believe you may be bad luck for me."

"I'm sorry to hear that," he said evenly. "You've only ever been good luck for me."

"I'm sorry," she said. "I'm sorry. That was a horrible thing to say." She rubbed her hands over her eyes. "You are as lovely now as you were then. And I—I'll have to ask you to keep my secret. But please go."

He frowned, shaking his head. "No," he said.

"N— My god, this night. No, he was much more biddable when I knew him last," she said to the costume rack. "Ben. This doesn't concern you. I'm not going to implicate you in a murder you had nothing to do with."

He shrugged. "You didn't have anything to do with it, either."

"Unfortunately," she said, "it took place in my dressing room. And I've been informed that the haunting is personal."

"You're talking to it, aren't you," he said. "The ghost. You're having a conversation with it."

She closed her eyes for a long moment before nodding.

"That's . . . incredible," he said. "And worrying. Do you have any pain?"

"I— Ben—"

"You have to get onstage," he said, taking her pulse. Elevated, but nothing more than one would expect from the circumstances. Even her eyes were returning to normal. "I agree with the ghost. You should humor me."

"I— Oh, fine. No, no pain. Nothing new, anyway. Yes, I *know* he's handsome, I have eyes. Oh—*merde*." She lapsed into exhausted silence.

He bowed in the general direction of the ghost. "Thank you," he said, and then moved the arm Amelie had thrown over her face to check her temperature again. Normal.

He sat back and considered her.

In his years as a doctor, he'd developed a good sense of when a patient was going to listen to medical advice and when they weren't. She shouldn't perform in this state—but if he told her that, she was undoubtedly going to ignore him. Casually, he put his finger in front of her eyes and moved it back and forth. She tracked him successfully.

Physically, she was fine. She just had a ghost in her head.

To Benedict's profound regret, this was not the first time he had conducted a haunting exam. His brother Sam was both a famous inventor and the world's foremost ghost expert. Until a few years ago, Benedict had classified the latter as a misguided hobby. Then Sam found himself a real-life haunted house, with a ghost who had a nasty tendency to sneak into people's heads and make them see nightmares straight from a book of ghost stories.

Well, Benedict thought it was a nasty tendency. Sam thought of it more as a charming quirk—until it happened to the woman he was in love with. Then Benedict found himself rousted out of bed at three in the morning and making a very cold, very unpleasant early morning train journey to conduct an impromptu medical exam.

Alva—Sam's now wife—hadn't been fine, though. She'd collapsed after the haunting. And Sam had only experienced it for a few minutes. Amelie seemed to be hosting it continually, without apparent physical distress.

"Can you see it?"

"Ben—"

Right. It wasn't time for science. It was time to move a body. He nodded and helped her stand.

"I know," he said. "You have to get ready to go on. I am going to move the body, and I'm not interested in further argument. You can't move it now, and you can't risk leaving it unattended while you're onstage, because apparently the stagehands here will let anyone into your dressing room. I am the practical solution."

"But—"

"And furthermore," he continued, "I owe you, and I take my debts very seriously. So, I'm going to do this for you, and the faster you accept that, the faster you can be onstage."

"You don't owe— What are you talking about?"

"That sounds like further argument," he said.

She twisted her hands together. "I can't believe you're standing here in my dressing room fighting with me about who's going to move a body."

"It wasn't how I planned on spending my evening, either," he said.

She glanced nervously at the clock.

"You saved my life, Amelie," he said softly. "This won't pay back what I owe you, but please, let me do it for you."

"I didn't— Yes, I see the time, Lise—" She took a deep breath. "Alright. Yes. I hate that I'm saying it, but yes."

"Good," he said. "I'll wait here until the coast is clear." He looked around, sat down in the dressing table chair she'd vacated, and extricated his notebook. He had observations to record and a telegram to draft.

Watching him, she flitted around the dressing room, getting her shoes, adding a pin to her hair. She hesitated by the door, obviously torn.

"It's all in hand," he said.

"Are you . . . dismissing me?"

"Yes," he said, finding his spectacles and putting them on. "You are *de trop*, I'm afraid. Completely unnecessary."

She hesitated but seemed to decide something. "I'll be back after act 2," she said. "But . . . I suppose you won't be here. Um, you could come to my apartment later? After ten?" She dashed an address down on a scrap of paper and handed it to him.

"Wonderful," he said. "We can talk murder and hauntings over tea."

She blinked, startled, and hurriedly left the room.

Benedict stared at the closed door before standing to lock it. He leaned against it.

Amelie St. James, ladies and gentlemen.

He felt like he'd run five miles and drunk five cups of coffee after. His hands weren't shaking, but they wanted to.

It was all one hell of a coincidence.

He'd never known a ghost to kill anyone before, but it was probably only a matter of time. Amelie hadn't seemed afraid of it, so he'd have to assume for now the murder had been accidental rather than premeditated.

He sat back down and started composing the telegram to Sam. He had a while before it would be time to move the body. Maybe by then his heart would stop racing like he'd just kissed his first girl.

GHOST KILLED MAN STOP WILL SEND DETAILS SOON STOP

He leaned back, squinted, and thought that pretty much covered it. Sam didn't know about Amelie.

No one did.

CHAPTER FIVE

June 1866
Twelve years earlier . . .

The guidebook had been waiting by Benedict's bed the third morning they were in Paris. He didn't know who'd left it for him, although he suspected his mother. It was in English, used but recently published, bound in brown leather and a little too large to be convenient.

The thoughtfulness of the gift chafed at him. It had been months since he'd woken up in a military hospital with his father beside him—woken up in a different world, like Rip Van Winkle before him. He'd lost weeks of his life, and the Civil War was over. His father looked as if he'd aged ten years in one.

He didn't know who he was in this new world. At first, he focused on physical recovery—there was an ease in that. But eventually he could walk, and he was home, and so much was the same, and yet everything was different.

Benedict had always liked his family. This was different from loving them—plenty of people loved their relations but wouldn't choose to spend time with them if they could avoid it. But Benedict's family was the best thing in his life. His brother Sam was his best friend. His sister Maggie was too smart for her own good, and she made him swell up with pride like a toad. And his parents . . . they were each magic, in their own ways. His whole family was magic.

And he . . . wasn't. Not anymore.

He pulled the book onto his lap, and with a heavy sigh, opened it. There was an inscription on the first page—*To Edmund, Bon Voyage, New Year's Day, 1864.* A young British man of means, Benedict assumed. He turned to the table of contents, idly perusing it.

After the war, he tried to be the Benedict he'd been before. He tried to feel better. He tried to laugh. Each time he failed he saw the worry in his family's eyes. Not that they ever pressed him—he wished they would. Perhaps then he could protect them from it.

The last two months had been slightly better. Sam had bought some boxing gloves, and it felt good to move and sweat. Benedict had boxed in the army—the new sport was a common distraction in camp. But the magic didn't come back, and now he was in Paris, and his family was buzzing around the city like the glorious gadflies they were, and all he could do was . . . walk.

It had been malaria, the doctors said. His parents filled in the rest later, when he was stronger. An incompetent field doctor—there were a lot of them, since medical training in the States consisted of one year of training, repeated twice—knew arsenic was used for treating malaria, and had applied it enthusiastically. Benedict would have recovered from the malaria, but he almost died from the arsenic poisoning.

Sitting a world away in Paris, his eyes caught on the word *hospitals.*

He shut the book.

Two days later, after a totally normal dinner filled with love and chatter and the pressing, choking weight of his family's unspoken worry, he opened it again. He flipped past the first few pages, landing somewhere in the middle of the table of contents. He closed his eyes, stabbed his finger at the page, and opened them. The Bois de Boulogne, whatever that was. Tomorrow, he'd go to the Bois de Boulogne.

The next morning dawned clear and bright, and he set out on foot, following the map he'd memorized the night before. He didn't look around as he walked, focusing only on putting one foot in front of the other. After about forty minutes, he passed the Arc de Triomphe, stopping briefly to stare up at the massive monument, so inhumanly large.

Another forty minutes saw him to his destination, a large, well-designed pleasure park. He stared blankly at the cottages built to look like small Swiss chalets, at the well-dressed Parisians driving smart open-air carriages down the wide, shaded avenues. There was a large lake, obviously man-made, the sweeping lawn in front dotted with picnickers.

He didn't know why he'd come. There was nothing for him here. But he was tired from the long walk, and so he decided to sit and rest beneath an old, gnarled tree, watching the rowboats on the lake.

"Hello," a voice above him said. He looked up, startled, to find a girl looking down at him. She was pretty—very pretty—with auburn curls and merry green-blue eyes that turned down at the ends. Her expression was caught between curiosity and concern.

"Hello," he said, for lack of any brighter ideas.

She sat down next to him, landing in a pile of cheerful pink skirts. He regarded her nervously.

"Um—"

"Are you American? I've never heard that accent before." Her accent was uncomfortably adorable, it gnawed at him.

"Yes," he said.

"I've never met an American before," she said.

"But you—you knew I spoke English."

She shrugged. "You obviously aren't French. My name is Amelie."

First names, then. "Ben," he said.

"Ben," she said. "Like Ben Franklin."

"Er—"

"But you are not wearing a fur hat. He was our ambassador, you know. There are many portraits of him here. Are you named for him?"

"No," Benedict said, happy to have a firm answer at last.

She sighed sympathetically and stood again. She moved almost uncannily smoothly. "Come with me, please."

"Ah—" Yes, he was really distinguishing himself in this conversation.

She lifted an imperious eyebrow at him, and he stood obediently, slinging his leather satchel over his shoulder.

"Where are we going?"

"The rowboats," she said, already walking away. "It's too pretty to stay on shore, don't you think? And I can't take one out alone."

He hurried after her. She was tall for a woman, the top of her head reaching easily to his shoulder. Her curls bounced as she walked.

"Sorry," he said. "You want me to . . ."

"Row," she said, impatiently. "I want you to row. Hurry! I want the pink one, and someone else might get it."

She pointed to a rowboat tied up to the rental dock, pastel pink surrounded by blues and greens. His brain gave one final protest and surrendered. He walked quicker.

The pink rowboat was achieved with minimum fuss. She paid for the rental, pushing aside his wallet with another impatient look. He didn't object, mostly because there didn't seem to be any chance of success. The man on the dock gave him two oars and brief instructions in French—he was suddenly grateful for the years of French he'd had in school—and then they were pushing off, with Benedict behind the oars and Amelie arranging herself on the seat facing him.

She was wearing a lovely confection of a hat, which she immediately removed, tilting her face to the sun and closing her eyes. She stayed like that, a faint smile on her lips, while Benedict assessed his situation. There were three key facts.

One: he didn't know how to row. It required a level of coordination and balance he did not possess, and occasionally the rowboat rocked worryingly from side to side.

Two: it was possible—even likely—he was in said rowboat with a madwoman. Who else but a madwoman would commandeer a perfect stranger to row her about a lake, without even verifying whether he could row? They could both drown because of her poor decision-making.

Three: she was even prettier in the sunshine.

There was something magnetic about the way she soaked in the sun, as if she could think of nothing more decadent than to feel it on her skin. Benedict began to be conscious of it as well, of the pleasant feeling of warm cloth against his skin. His arm and back muscles were loosening, and he thought he might finally be mastering the rowing motion. The oars made a pleasant sound as they slipped in and out of the water.

He rowed them to the middle of the lake. Amelie's eyes stayed shut, so apparently no guidance would be coming from that direction. A gray heron swooped low over the water, landing lightly on some reeds at the water's edge. Benedict decided he might as well row over to investigate more closely—Sam, at least, would be interested in hearing about it.

They were away from the rest of the boaters, in a little pocket of lapping water and sunshine. He tried to row as quietly as possible, letting the boat coast for the last several meters. The heron didn't move, tilting its head to observe the newcomers. A tuft of dark blue or black feathers at the top of the bird's white head lent it an officious air, as though it were a high-ranking military officer come to inspect the troops.

The boat drifted to a stop, and Benedict and the bird stared at each other, before its wings stretched out in one magnificent gesture; the bird taking to the air. His throat tightened as he watched it fly away, those huge wings hardly needing to work to keep it aloft.

When he looked down, Amelie's eyes were open. She'd been watching him with consideration, but her expression quickly emptied. She yawned.

"Your rowing improved," she said. "I thought certainly you would sink us."

Her impertinence brought him back to the moment. "Really? Because it seemed more like you were sleeping."

"I am very calm under stress," she said. "And now I am hungry. Let us have lunch."

She gestured toward the dock, reaching down for her hat.

"Look here," Benedict began.

"Yes?"

"You can't just kidnap someone and order them to row you about a lake and escort you to lunch," he said.

She smiled at him. "Were you engaged in something more important?"

"Well—"

"In that case, there is no reason at all you should not row me about a lake and escort me to lunch," she said, complacently setting the hat atop her head and tying the ribbons in a fetching bow around her chin.

Definitely a madwoman, he decided, picking up the oars. A madwoman who was also a master of argument.

They reached the dock and he helped her alight, noting the softness of her hand in his. She led him to a nearby stall and procured two ham and butter sandwiches, wrapped in paper. He tried to pay—it was one thing to let her pay for the rowboat (although his father would have said differently) and an entirely different thing to let her buy his food—but when he tried to insist she simply looked at him as if he was being impossibly difficult and foolish.

"Why wouldn't you let me pay?" he asked, piqued, as they walked away.

By way of response, she let her eyes wander down his clothing. He frowned and looked down. Normally he was extremely punctilious—his brother Sam was the one who would wander out of the house in his pajamas if nothing stopped him. But today (and if he was honest, most days lately) he'd simply tossed on some rumpled clothes and left. Black, for the sake of ease. Uncomfortably, he wondered when the last time he'd shaved was. He resisted stroking his chin to find out.

"I have money," he said, aware as he spoke that he sounded petty and ridiculous.

"I'm sure you do," she said. "But since when do kidnappers make their victims pay for food? It would be . . . ungracious of me."

She looked pleased to have remembered the word, and suddenly further complaint seemed curmudgeonly. And he was hungry.

"There," she said, pointing to a pleasant-looking tree. He didn't know what about that specific tree made it stand out to her among the other trees, but she made her way there with great determination. He followed her—the pattern of his day, apparently—and they sat together and unwrapped their sandwiches.

She took a large bite of hers, the crusty bread crunching between her white teeth. "Mmm." She nodded, chewing. He took a more measured bite, but her enthusiasm was contagious. The sandwich was delicious—the bread somehow light and substantial and moist and crunchy all at once, the butter smooth and rich. And it turned out he was hungry. Extremely hungry. Hungrier than he'd been in a long time.

When they were done with their sandwiches, Amelie stood, dusting the crumbs from her skirts. "I have to go," she said, and Benedict suddenly felt utterly and absurdly bereft.

"Oh," he said. "Well, it was nice—"

"What are you doing tomorrow?"

CHAPTER SIX

October 1878

The body was gone by intermission.

She hadn't thought about it while she danced. When she was onstage there was no room for the outside world; only her body, her character, and the music. But when Giselle had gone mad and died, the last vibrations of the brass section dying with her—well, she was Amelie St. James again, lying on a stage behind a heavy red velvet curtain, thinking about the corpse in her dressing room, the man from her past, and the trouble in her future. As she'd pushed herself up, joining the crowds of dancers racing to their dressing rooms, a gnawing, anxious pain had appeared in her stomach, settling in as if it had always lived there.

But then—nothing. The body was gone. Ben was gone. Lise was gone. The hallway was filled with dancers and stagehands, everyone engaged in the twenty minutes of costume-change panic. Makeup had to be redone. Dead pointe shoes had to be replaced. Tights were discovered to be torn, crucial costume pieces were located in other dancers' dressing rooms, occasional accusations of sabotage were leveled. Everything was completely normal; a world where ghosts and murder had no place.

There was a second of sheer, guilty relief, all she could spare before she, too, had to change and rush back onstage.

Then, like that, the dress rehearsal was over, the bows made, and Amelie was back in her dressing room, blessedly alone. Her hip throbbed and her makeup was cut through with sweat streaks. Easing herself onto the dressing room chair, she reached for the pads she used to remove it.

She was still behind the music in two places in act 2, once in the second scene and once in the finale. That would have to get sorted before Friday's opening. And she didn't like her extensions in the second *pas de deux*. Oh, and she'd need to make sure she had enough pairs of pointe shoes prepared before the weekend—she could dance through two pairs in a night, and each pair took about an hour of ribbon-sewing and darning and breaking in before they were ready to be performed in. And her pancake makeup was running low. She'd need to run out and get some new . . .

And the ghost of a dead dancer had killed a member of the Jockey Club, and the boy she'd once loved had moved the body, and now, in mere minutes, she was going to meet that boy—man, now—and what do you say to a man who's just covered up a crime for you—and was it even a crime if no court in the land could convict the culprit?

No. She couldn't think about that right now.

She wasn't sure she liked the fit of her bodice. She might need to ask the costume department to take a look at it before Friday—she'd come in early tomorrow morning to talk to them about it—

Lise's costume fit perfectly. Had the ghost simply . . . imagined it? Had her costume ever been fitted to her, or had it been reassigned to the body of another girl before Lise's imprint had even been left on it? Which of the women she'd danced with tonight had been the new one? She should know. It was the least she could do—know where Lise would have danced, *noticed* her—but she couldn't even give the girl that. Why was she haunting Amelie, who could barely remember her name?

And where was she? Where did ghosts go when they weren't haunting someone?

"Enough, enough," she muttered. She looked at her reflection carefully, removing the last bits of white paint clinging to her skin, and stripped out of the sweat-soaked costume, hanging it to dry. Steadfastly refusing to think, she stepped into the simple dress she'd worn to class, reassembled her hair into a neat bun, and slipped her coat on.

The hallway smelled of paint and dust and sweat when she stepped into it. Most of the dancers were still in their dressing rooms. She could hear a din of voices coming from the corps room, mingled with the distant sound of singing. The opera had begun once more. She walked quickly, smiling mechanically at anyone she passed.

"Amelie!" the Director called out. Fixing a smile to her face, she turned, finding him beckoning to her from a group of three other well-dressed men.

The Jockey Club. The gnawing sensation returned.

"Monsieur Joubert, Monsieur Thibault," she said. She took a breath, forced her smile wider. "Monsieur de Lavel."

"Amelie."

Her mother's former lover—at least, the most prominent among them—was the de facto leader of the Club, and an extraordinarily handsome man. His hair was perfectly black, despite being well into his fourth decade, his clothes exactly right. His features were strong, masculine. He looked like the kind of man you could rely on. A powerful man. One who'd protect you.

His unusual amber eyes flicked over her, and, as if surprised, lingered. Her jaw was tight from the smiling; her teeth suddenly ached.

"There was an unfortunate incident," the Director was murmuring. "A young man had a heart attack. A friend of Monsieur de Lavel."

"I wouldn't say a friend," de Lavel said, his eyes roving over Amelie. "He was more like an irritating country mushroom with aspirations to fashion. But he was a member, so obviously I must take an interest in his passing."

One of de Lavel's friends—Thibault—snorted.

"I understand completely," the Director said, managing to walk a perfect line between de Lavel's mocking tone and the sincerity required of a social inferior. It was this, rather than any particular artistic talent, that qualified him to be the Director of the Paris Opera Ballet.

"I'm so sorry to hear it," Amelie heard herself saying. She sounded insipid and genuine, the ideal St. Amie tone. It was so ingrained that it could support her even in extremis.

"Please don't trouble yourself over it, my dear," de Lavel said. "You were lovely tonight."

His friends looked surprised, and, to be frank, so was Amelie. St. Amie was the people's darling, not the Jockey Club's. She was more of a necessary evil to them, a vacant, pious fool to be mocked behind closed doors.

"Thank you," she said. "Forgive me, gentlemen. My sister is waiting for me at home."

The men nodded and she turned to walk away. She hadn't gotten more than two meters when she felt a hand on her shoulder.

"Monsieur de Lavel," she said, forcing herself not to wince away from his touch.

"You're looking well tonight," he said.

"Thank you."

He tilted his head. "Different, somehow. Have you changed your hair?"

"No."

"There's something different," he mused. "Something . . . better."

"I've done nothing," she said. "If you'll excuse—"

"I know what it is," he said, reaching out to push a loose strand of hair from her face. "Suddenly you remind me of your mother. Strange. You never have before."

Her eyes flew to his, hot words on her tongue. He watched her playfully, taunting her. Like a cat, waiting to see if the mouse would come to the trap.

She swallowed. Hard. "Excuse me," she said, and walked away. She felt his gaze until she rounded the corner, out of sight.

The night was cold and overcast when Amelie stepped out the stage door. Fashionable *boulevardiers* strolled the sidewalks arm in arm, looking for their next entertainment, or sat at cafe tables watching their fellows go by. The smell of tobacco and absinthe was thick in the air. People nodded to her as she made her way through the evening crowd; rather than draw attention, she nodded back politely.

You remind me of your mother. . . .

As she approached her building, a dark shadow peeled off from the wall.

"It's me," Ben said, before fear had time to permeate the cotton in her brain. "I didn't know if you wanted me waiting where people could see." The corner of his lips twitched. "I've never had to sneak around before. It's quite stimulating."

"Yes," she said. "No. I mean, quite right. Good decision."

The low lamplights cast a warm glow onto his face, and for a moment, she simply looked at him.

He'd always been tall, but when she'd seen him last, he'd been only a few months out of a hospital bed. More than a decade later, his shoulders and chest matched his height. His thick, wavy, dark hair was shiny and healthy enough that the lamplight glinted off it, and when he smiled at her blatant perusal, his teeth were white and strong and straight. He was the picture of a healthy American, tall and vital, the line of his jaw clean and sharp enough to cast its own shadow. Strong muscles and strong bones.

He looked so different. Even his eyes had changed—twelve years ago, they'd been sad and haunted, with only flashes of joy shining through. Now, joy had the upper hand. He looked happy.

She shouldn't have recognized him the day before, but she wasn't surprised she had. There had always been something about him that had called to her, something inalterably *Ben*.

"Are you going to invite me up?"

She looked up at her apartment window, three stories above them.

"I can't," she realized. "I'm sorry. I should have—"

He shrugged, big shoulders in that expensive-looking coat. "Is there a place we can sit?"

"Yes," she said. Surely there was somewhere—yes, a little park two blocks away, surrounded by construction. There wouldn't be anyone to recognize her there. She started walking.

"Oh," he said. "I forgot."

He rummaged in his coat pockets and produced two waxpaper packages. He held one out to her.

"Crepes?" It was warm, the steam making a faint cloud in the cold air above it.

"I passed a vendor on my way here," he said. "You're always hungry after rehearsal." His brow furrowed when she hesitated. "Or, you used to—"

"I am," she said, taking it quickly. She bit into the warm, sweet crepe, a delicious shock of sugar meeting her tongue. He nodded, satisfied, and took a bite of his own.

They walked in silence for a block, eating their crepes and sneaking sidelong glances.

"I don't know what to say to you," Amelie said. "This all seems impossible. You, here. Ghosts. Murder. What am I supposed to say: How did the corpse removal and fake discovery go?"

"As good a start as any," Ben said. "It went well, thanks for asking. I waited until the corridor was clear, moved him out—it wasn't far—and raised the cry."

"Lise said it was revenge. Not for her. For someone else."

"Lise is the ghost? So you really *can* talk to her." He looked around. "Is she here?"

"I don't think so," Amelie said. "She was a dancer in the corps. I didn't know her. They found her in the river."

He looked as if he'd like to ask more, but they'd reached the little park. It was a dark oasis surrounded by shadowed piles of rubbish and stone. She led them to a bench and sat down, pulling her coat close around her neck.

"You believe me so easily," she said as he sat next to her, his shoulder brushing hers. "Why?"

There were no streetlamps in the park. Their bench was illuminated only by the reflection of city lights off the low clouds above. She tried to make out his expression but couldn't quite interpret it.

"We never exchanged last names," he said, slowly. "I was going to ask, our last day together, but—"

She nodded.

"Yours was easy to find. You're the only Amelie at the Paris Opera Ballet. But I don't think you know mine. It's Moore."

Ben Moore. His name.

For twelve years she'd only possessed half of it. She turned it over in her mind, careful, lest the realization turn the hazy past into something sharper.

"Amelie?"

She cleared her throat. "Moore," she repeated politely. "Like the scientists."

There was a very famous family of American scientists. Her friend Alva had married one of them.

"Yes," he said.

Something in his voice made her look at him. Surely not. It would be too much of a coincidence—

Like walking into your dressing room the very night you acquire a ghost. Like appearing in your rehearsal room after twelve years.

"Your full name," she said. "It's Benjamin, isn't it? Like Benjamin Franklin."

His lips twitched. "It's always Benjamin Franklin with you," he said. "No, my full name is Benedict."

"Benedict Moore," she said, slowly. *Sam's brother, Benedict,* Alva had written. *He's a doctor.*

"Benedict Moore," she repeated. "Dr. Benedict Moore. Son of John and Winn Moore. Brother of Samuel Moore, recently involved in the haunting at Rose House."

He blinked at her. "I admit I didn't expect you to know my entire genealogy," he said.

"I'm friends with your sister-in-law," she said blankly. "Alva Webster. We correspond."

They stared at each other.

"Sorry," he said. "You're saying that for over a decade I've been thinking I'd never see you again, and meanwhile, you've been corresponding with my sister-in-law?"

"Not the whole decade," she said faintly. "Only the last few years. We met after she left her first husband."

They fell into silence, something like inevitability in the air between them. It was quiet in this little pocket of a Paris still in-between. The neighborhood that had once curved around it sat in piles of rubble, and in turn, that rubble blocked the noise from the beautiful new boulevards just two minutes away.

"May I ask an impertinent question?"

A smile tugged at Amelie's lips. "Any man who's disposed of a body for me within the last twenty-four hours is entitled to ask anything he wishes."

"You didn't want me to come up to your apartment. Is there someone—"

"My sister."

He absorbed this information with a thoughtful nod. "I didn't know you had a sister."

"She's after your time."

"What's her name?"

It was odd to sit here and talk about life when there was so much death looming over them, but her mouth curved, as it did every time she talked about her sister.

"Honorine," she said. "She's eleven. She's . . . oh, she's funny, and brilliant. I think she's brilliant, at least. She's always reading. She's top of her class at St. Mary's," she added, pride swelling in her chest.

Benedict smiled. "She sounds wonderful," he said.

She waited for the next question, the one about her mother, but it didn't come. She wasn't sorry.

"So, you're being haunted."

She sighed and leaned back against the wrought-iron bench. "So," she said. "I'm being haunted."

"You're taking it very calmly."

"I'm not," she said. "At all. But I learned a long time ago there's little point in fussing over things once they've already happened. You simply have to pick yourself up and make the best of it."

He stared at her, like if he looked at her face long enough, he could see into her thoughts. She looked away.

"Alright," he said. "Tell me about the ghost."

Amelie stared at the enormous pile of rubble in front of her. It was hemmed in by a fence, with posters advertising events from months gone by pinned on it, their edges curling with age. The pile itself was buildings and clothes and the occasional child's toy or kitchen pan. Similar piles crisscrossed Paris, all that remained of a very different kind of city.

How had she gotten here? How was she sitting with this man, whom she hadn't seen since she'd lived another life, close enough to feel his warmth?

"Ben," she said. "Seeing you healthy and happy and successful—it's like a happy ending I always hoped for but never thought I'd see confirmed. But . . ."

"Ah," he said, stretching his long legs out in front of him. "Lovely to see you, don't let the door hit you on the way out?"

"That sounds rude," she said. "The thing is, I've . . . gained a reputation."

"St. Amie," he provided. "You're quite well known."

"Yes," she said. She supposed someone had told him about her. It wasn't a comfortable thought. "That reputation doesn't allow for handsome Americans from my past."

"More flattery." That smile again, slow and confident.

"St. Amie pays my bills," she said. "She sends my sister to a good school and makes sure we eat every night. So, I . . . I . . ."

"Can't afford handsome Americans," he said. "What if no one knew we'd met before? Even St. Amie is allowed gentlemen callers, right?"

"Certainly," she said. "If they're from a good family and marriage material."

"I'm from a good family," he said.

For some reason that little sentence hurt. She remembered him talking about his family, all those years ago. The love in his voice was still there. *They* were still there, while she and Honorine were alone.

She forced herself to smile. "Are you proposing marriage? Because I warn you, I'd be concerned you were marrying me for my ghost."

"Not marriage," he said. "Courtship."

"I don't— What?"

"I haven't been here long," he said. "But it seems to me you're in bad need of a friend."

Friend. The word was an oasis that swiftly became a mirage. It was something she hadn't thought of for herself in many years. It was loss.

"Don't," she whispered.

"I know I'm leaving," he said softly. "But I could be your friend, at least for this. I have expertise, I won't tell your secrets, and I owe you. I'll pretend to court you, so the papers have a story. I'm perfectly respectable, there won't be any scandal. We'll find a way to let Lise move on, your reputation will be safe, and once we figure everything out, we'll part ways. You can leave me after discovering my morals are not as they should be, or something like that."

She shook her head. He was so earnest, so genuine. He saw she was in trouble, and so he wanted to help her. It was simple for him.

How could she tell him she didn't want him in her life because the last time she'd only barely survived the leaving? For twelve years, that had been how she'd counted her history. The bad times hadn't started with the Prussian Siege. They'd started the day Ben No-Last-Name had walked out of that park for the final time.

No, she couldn't tell him that.

"I can't think," she said.

He slouched easily against the bench. "There's no rush," he said. "Sleep on it."

She nodded hazily, aware of his body next to hers, of the ease of his muscles compared to the stiffness of her own.

"Tell me something," she blurted. "Something real. If I don't see you again."

He tilted his head toward her, a slight smile on his lips. "How about a trade? A truth for a truth."

"You know most of my secrets already," she said.

"Maybe it's not your secrets I'm interested in," he said. "Although I admit I'm curious about your newly acquired sainthood."

She winced, embarrassed. "It's amazing how the people of Paris can be so devout one minute and so casually blasphemous the next," she said. "Alright, a truth for a truth. Me first."

Amelie watched his face in the low light. A badly rendered but enthusiastic version of "La Marseillaise" drifted over their wall of rubble. Only a few years before it would have seen its singer arrested.

A few years before that, it would have seen him dead.

Things changed so quickly in Paris. Now a drunk could sing "La Marseillaise" in public. Would he be able to tomorrow? Next year?

"Tell me about where you live," she said.

"I guess there are two places, really," he said. "I have a house on my family's land in Ohio—that's a state. Both Sam and I do, although obviously he and Alva live in New York. It's only a couple of rooms. My father and I built it together, the fall after we returned from Europe. And now, I have a flat in Manhattan, because that's where the institute I've been put in charge of will be located."

"Institute? That sounds rather important."

Another slight smile. "It is," he said. "The United States Institute for Brain Research. The first of its kind in the States. We know so little, still, about the brain. We can amputate a limb or repair a tendon or even remove a tumor—but if someone damages their brain, there's almost nothing a doctor can do. Maybe the institute can be part of changing that."

"You did it, then," she said softly. "You went back to medicine."

"Thanks to you," he said.

She shook her head, pushing his words away. "Tell me about the flat." She wanted to be able to picture him there after he was gone, safe and happy and well-fed.

"It's the second floor of a townhouse," he said. "I've only barely moved in. I have a sofa."

The pride in his voice made her lips twitch. "It must be a very nice sofa."

"It's . . . not, actually. It's quite uncomfortable. Someone put it on the side of the road, and I brought it up."

"I see," she said. "Do you have other furniture items? A chair, perhaps?"

"Well, I don't spend much time there, you see. I did just order a beautiful new microscope for the lab, though, it should be there by the time I get back—"

"Are you telling me the only item of furniture in your flat is an uncomfortable sofa that some brighter person was trying to get rid of?"

"I was exaggerating," he said. "It's not really that uncomfortable. It's a matter of sleeping on it the right way. If I lay curled up on my side, I can get my feet on it. And only my knees stick out."

"I see," she said. "Ben."

"Yes?"

"Your sister-in-law is one of the most famous writers on interior decoration in the world."

"Yes."

"So . . ."

"So, I obviously can't invite her to my home. The shock might kill her."

"Ben."

"You're missing the point," he said.

"Which is?"

"The sofa was free?"

She laughed. The sound startled her. It echoed uncomfortably in their little hideaway, lingering a split second too long.

"My turn," Ben said. "What do you do for fun these days?"

Amelie looked at him sharply. His expression was mild, an old friend asking a simple question.

"I—" It wasn't that she didn't get asked this question. She even had an answer ready and press tested. When she wasn't dancing, St. Amie enjoyed embroidery, reading scripture, and devoting herself to her charitable causes. If the reporter looked too bored by this answer, or was from a lighter publication, she admitted a secret vice: sometimes, she'd tell them, with a hint of a mischievous smile, she enjoyed curling up in bed with a cup of hot chocolate and a fashion magazine.

"I talk to my sister," she heard herself say. "It's the best part of my day. Sometimes she tells me what she's studying, the worlds she's learning about. This morning she showed me where China is, on a map. Do you know where China is? Do you know how big it is?"

Benedict nodded, watching her.

"Of course, *you* do," she said, laughing at herself. "I didn't."

"I find sisters are a great source of education," he said. "The last time I had dinner with mine, she explained a new chemical formula to me and then lectured me about the grievous unstylishness of my boots."

Amelie looked down at them. "It's dark," she said. "But they look stylish to me."

"Yes. I found them on my doorstep three days later. What else?"

"Hmm?"

"For fun."

She shrugged. "I don't have much time," she said. "I go to class in the morning, I eat a healthy and well-rounded lunch, I have rehearsal, and if I'm lucky, I get home in time to have a healthy and well-rounded dinner with my sister. After she retires, I do exercises at the barre in my sitting room, I pay bills, I return correspondence, I do all the things that keep our little life up and running and safe, then I bathe and go to sleep. Repeat."

"And what about the dancing?" he asked, putting his hands in his pockets.

"It is what makes that little life possible," she said. "It is what keeps us safe. In two years, I'll be able to retire with the money I've saved. We'll be secure."

"Two years, huh?" There was a sharpness to his gaze that made her look away, like he was calling a bluff she didn't know she'd been making. She shifted, suddenly aware of the stiffness in her hip and the ghost in her head.

"It's almost midnight," she said. "I have to go. My sister is waiting."

He stood, helping her to her feet with practiced grace. The boy she'd known had been clumsy and awkward.

"Think about my offer," Benedict said. "Here, my address."

She accepted the card.

"Also . . ." He smiled sheepishly. "This is mildly embarrassing. My friends—the ones I'm staying with—they're coming to your opening tomorrow night, and they invited me—I can make an excuse—"

"No," she heard herself saying. "You should come."

He looked absurdly gratified, and something in her chest thrilled. Why had she said that?

"I will, then," he said. "I'll walk you back to your building."

She'd been walking the streets of Paris alone after dark her whole life, but she was tired, and she didn't want to argue, so she simply started down the street with him beside her. He didn't say anything more, and after a few exhausted seconds wondering whether she needed to make conversation, she decided he wasn't expecting her to. There was a comfort in his presence, an ease.

He saw her back to the front of her building, smiled, and said good night. She watched him disappear into the night through the window of her lobby, and for one absurd moment, she missed him.

She turned and began her slow journey up the stairs, the sweetness of the crepe he'd brought still clinging to her tongue.

CHAPTER SEVEN

The next day was opening night.

Amelie went through her performance-day routine like an automaton: sending Honorine off to school; going to morning class; resting in the midday; conducting her lengthy warm-up in her dressing room where no one could see how long she had to take with her hip, or how gentle she needed to be. Nothing unusual happened, and by an hour before she was supposed to go on, she was exhausted from waiting. The evening before seemed like a dream, or perhaps a hallucination.

Opera rang through the hall beyond as she started her eye makeup. Was Ben already in the audience? It would be unfashionable of him to arrive on time, but he wasn't the sort to be late. That summer he'd always arrived before her, waiting. . . .

She set the stick of kohl down with a snap. Enough. At this rate she was going to go onstage and forget half her steps. She couldn't just keep waiting.

She cleared her throat. "Lise," she whispered. "If you're there—if you can hear me—"

A polite cough made her turn.

Lise was still wearing the *Giselle* costume, but she'd lost the wings.

Amelie let out her breath. "Real, then. Not a hallucination."

"You've only done one eye," Lise said, then glanced at the clock. "Amelie! You have to get ready! You don't have time to be talking to me."

"I— Right," Amelie said, obediently picking up the kohl.

Lise fluttered anxiously behind her. "How's your hip? Oh, I'm sorry, I know it's a secret, but it's hard to ignore. You think about it *very* loudly. Is it bad today? Are you going to be able to dance?"

"Yes," Amelie said, her words coming slowly. "Of course."

"You're *very* good at hiding it," Lise said. "I never even suspected. Did you eat? Get enough rest? You must have been so shaken yesterday. Oh, if I hurt your performance I'll never forgive myself."

"I'm fine," Amelie said. She looked in the mirror. Lise left no reflection. "I'm fine," she repeated. She was going to have to be. This was manageable. At least, it would be so long as—

"Lise," she said.

"Yes?"

"You have to promise me. No more killing people. We'll—we'll figure out the haunting. But we only barely got away with the murder." Might as well call it what it was. "If someone had found that body in my dressing room—"

She couldn't even finish the thought. Everything would have been over.

"I know," Lise said. "I'm so sorry."

"And? You won't kill anyone else?"

Silence. The ghost worried her bottom lip.

"The answer I'm looking for here," Amelie continued, after several seconds had passed, "is *Yes, of course I won't kill anyone else, I wouldn't dream of it, that was an accident.*"

"It *was* an accident," Lise said.

"And?"

"But how can I know if it will happen again?" Lise said, her words tumbling over one another. "I don't want to promise you something I'm not sure of. What if someone else, what if someone *worse* walks in? I might . . . I might not be myself again."

"Lise. You can't just go around murdering people, even if they're very bad! It's not your job to administer justice. The courts—"

"The courts wouldn't have done anything to that man," Lise mumbled.

Amelie closed her eyes. No, they wouldn't have. Justice was for the rich and powerful.

"Fine," she said, slowly. "It puts me in a dangerous position. I can't afford it."

Lise stood very still. "I'll *try,*" she said. "I can't promise I *won't,* but I'll try my very best not to."

"I suppose that will have to do," Amelie said, lifting the kohl and beginning to work on her other eye. She felt the ghost behind her, an odd feeling when she couldn't see her in the mirror.

"You said you were haunting me. Why me? We barely knew each other."

Lise drifted to the little wall-mounted barre. "I don't know," she said, thoughtfully. "But the only moments that are clear are when I'm with you. And I can't . . . It's like I'm on a string, and you're the pole I'm tied around. I tried to leave the theater yesterday, and I couldn't. The farther away from you I got, the . . . the less I was me, I suppose. Until I couldn't move at all."

Somehow that made sense, like some part of her had already known it. "So, it's not a grudge," Amelie said, to be absolutely sure. "You're not haunting me for revenge. Something I did to you that you resented."

Lise's brows scrunched together in something like panic. "Oh no," she said. "How could I? No. You've always been wonderful to me. Kind."

I didn't even remember your name.

"You know me so well," Amelie said, finished with her eye makeup and examining it in the mirror. "And I don't know anything about you."

Lise began a set of *tendus*, staring down at her feet. "There's not much to say. My parents are dead. I lived in Montmartre."

Amelie nodded, beginning work on her hair. It was a common enough biography—until she'd moved, it had been Amelie's.

"Where?"

"Near the cemetery."

Lise switched to *développés*, slow leg extensions that ended with her leg next to her ear. "I could never get it this high before," she said, before letting her leg fall with a sigh. "Too bad no one will see it now."

Near the cemetery. Montmartre Cemetery, home to poets and paupers.

Amelie's mother was buried there, somewhere. During the Siege and the Commune, things like funerals and individual graves had become luxuries—there simply had not been enough grave diggers. Mass graves had been opened all over Paris, and not only in the cemeteries. Plenty of new, fashionable squares and parks sat six feet above the dead.

"Amelie?"

"Hmm?"

"Do . . . do you know how I died?"

She spoke softly, addressing the question to the floor. For several seconds Amelie could only look at her, a sudden pain in her chest.

"You can't remember anything?"

Lise shook her head slowly, still not meeting Amelie's gaze. "I remember being in my apartment," she said. "And I remember waking up in the rehearsal room. I thought I must have died of a heart attack or something. But I heard—when you first saw me. I heard you think about the river. Amelie, you can tell me. Did I kill myself?"

"I don't know," Amelie said, forcing herself to speak calmly and steadily. "I'm not protecting you, I promise. The Director said you were found in the river. That's all I know."

"I don't think I would have," Lise said, nibbling her lip again. "Wait. What if that's it? What if I'm here because you're supposed to find out what happened to me? Like a quest."

Amelie considered this, nodding slowly. It seemed . . . very reasonable. Ghosts often came with a request, according to the stories. Lise was upset she didn't know how she died, and that was keeping her here. The more she thought about it, the more likely it seemed.

"Alright. That's good. I can—"

A knock on the door interrupted her. Amelie glanced toward it, and when she looked back Lise was gone.

She opened the door, still thinking about their new plan, only to have her thoughts fall away like dead leaves. "Monsieur de Lavel," she said.

Her mother's former lover stood on the other side, a bouquet in his hand. "Good evening," he said.

Why was he here? Had he discovered the murder?

He smiled. "Aren't you going to invite me in?"

"Of course," she said, stepping aside.

He held out the flowers to her. "Congratulations on your opening night," he said. "I'm sure you'll be as charming as always."

"Thank you," Amelie said, taking the bouquet automatically. The roses looked oddly . . . dead.

"They're from a graveyard," he said.

She dropped them.

"Isn't that right?" he asked. "Graveyard flowers for good luck?"

She stared at the bouquet. "On closing night," she said, quietly.

"Oh dear," he said, picking the flowers up and dropping them casually in her trash bin. They were too tall, and the dying blossoms nodded wearily over the edge. "Have I done something terrible?"

"Of course not," she said, swallowing.

"Good," he said, wandering to the back of the room. "I'd hate to think I accidentally doomed the production."

She made herself stay still as he stood by the fainting couch where the body had lain, idly flipping through her costume rack. He was a tall, broad man, and her dressing room was not large. His presence filled it up, leaving no room for anyone else. He pulled a costume out, looked at it appraisingly, and hung it back on the bar. She watched him touch the bodice of one, the tulle skirt of another.

"Your head is in the clouds," he said. "You haven't offered me a drink."

He had such a distinctive voice, de Lavel. Rich, like chocolate and cigars. Her mother's had sounded like birdsong layered above it.

"My apologies," she said, crossing to her drinks tray and pouring two fingers of cognac. "Here," she said, handing him the glass.

"You remembered," he said.

That word—remember. *Remember.* It was a slap. Words rushed up her throat, choking her. Suddenly, after all these years of pretending polite indifference, she wanted to tell him what she *remembered.*

Keep it down, keep it hidden, you can't afford it. He'll be fine, and you'll be dead.

Dead? Where had that come from?

"You really do look like her now," he said.

She was so hot. There was no air in the little room, only the smell of expensive cologne and the hair pomade he wore. It was thick, all around her—every inhale was him, he had stolen her breath—

"Well," he said, his voice buzzing in the background. "I suppose you need to finish getting ready. What is it they say? Break a leg."

Amelie didn't know if she said anything in reply, if she nodded, if she acknowledged him in any way. But she heard the click of the door closing behind him, the sound cutting through the tension in her body, releasing her.

She was shaking.

Why was he doing this? Why now? He wasn't adhering to their unspoken contract, the one pretending there was nothing between them, no years of acquaintance, no emotions, no—

Hatred.

And because that was another word she simply couldn't afford, she pushed it away. She sat down at her dressing table. She put the finishing touches on her hair. She thought about the steps she'd been struggling with, that she'd spent yesterday perfecting, and when she'd run through those, she started from the beginning of the ballet, step by step.

And she kept thinking about them. Down the hallway, smiling

at the dancers who passed her, through the final warm-up backstage at the temporary barre, while the orchestra played the first notes, while she waited for her entrance. And then, finally, blessedly, her cue came, and Amelie St. James fell away.

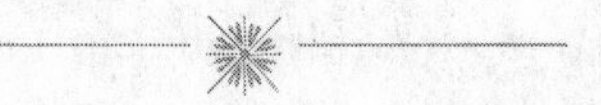

The Palais Garnier sat fat and contented after its opening night. The final trickle of theatergoers making their way from the building had stopped, and women with scarves tied around their heads pushed brooms and mops across the front steps. The light from the theater, which had poured golden and fizzy like champagne at the beginning of the night, was slowly being extinguished, one window at a time.

On a cold, iron bench, Benedict stared up at the single room at the very top of the building. It was still lit—a pale, watery light that spread mere feet across the domed roof beyond its windows. She wouldn't be there. He doubted she could even climb the stairs after tonight's performance, with her hip in that condition.

She'd danced perfectly tonight. No one would have noticed the injury—even he had sensed rather than seen it. He didn't know how she was dancing on it. The pain must be unimaginable.

Perfect. A strangely unpleasant word.

He shivered and pulled his coat closer.

After the performance, he and Victor and Camille had gone to a late supper, and then to a bar. After the three had drunk several bottles of champagne (and two rounds of absinthe at Victor's insistence) the couple had gone on to a second bar, while Benedict had announced his intention to go to sleep.

But instead of hailing a cab and returning to the Durands', he found himself on a bench outside the Palais Garnier, long after Amelie must have departed, staring at a room high above him simply because he'd once seen her there.

Amelie. For twelve years the name had meant the smell of grass in the sunshine; the sound of laughter; the feel of a hand pulling him onto a dance floor. For twelve years he'd held her in his memory, while good thing after good thing had happened in his life. He'd studied in Austria; he'd helped improve medical education in the United States; he'd seen his brother married. His health had never left him again. His beloved institute had been approved and funded. He'd saved lives and he'd laughed with his family. A thousand good moments, so many he no longer noticed them.

She'd given him that. And in return, he'd given her nothing. He had tried once—and failed. Maybe meeting her again was fate, giving him a second chance.

The light at the top of the Palais Garnier went out, casting the roof into darkness. He needed to make his way back to the Durands'. He needed to stand up.

He leaned his head back, the cold metal biting into his neck. The sky was overcast. In his imagination, Amelie stood before windows full of stars, but there were no stars to be seen. Just the lights of the city, reflected above him. Maybe he'd sleep here, with the clouds as a blanket.

"Ben?"

He lifted his head. She was there, not in white, not dancing in the heavens, but right there, standing on a dirty sidewalk, her dress a serviceable gray, lines of fatigue on her face.

"Pretty," he said, because she was.

"What are you doing here?"

A brain wasn't very heavy on its own, but once one added in the skull and all the muscles—and the teeth, one couldn't forget the teeth—not to mention two glasses of absinthe and at least a bottle and a half of champagne, the human head could become very heavy indeed. He leaned it back again, but then found he couldn't see her. He compromised, resting the side of it against the bench. There.

"Ben?"

"Hmm?"

"Are you—are you drunk?"

"Mmm," he said.

"I see," she said. Her eyes were so serious these days. Serious or wary. He didn't like it. Now she was serious and a little unsure. And—frightened? "I'll hail you a cab."

"What's wrong?" he asked, tugging on the sleeve of her coat. It was far too thin for a night this cold. He didn't like that, either.

Just like that, her expression changed. She smiled—pleasant, sweet, impersonal. "Nothing," she said. "Ben, you shouldn't be out this late, in this condition. Someone will rob you."

"You're so good at that," he said.

"Robbing people?"

"Is it the ghost? Are you experiencing physical symptoms?"

He stood, swaying a bit, and took her wrist to feel for her pulse.

"No—Ben, I'm fine," she said, pulling her hand away.

He stepped back to look at her. She wasn't fine. He couldn't say how he knew—the same way he knew she'd been pretending onstage that evening.

Hiding.

Wasn't his business. Maybe his business if he was her friend? But she hadn't said he was. He'd offered, and she'd looked like he'd handed her a live fish. But—

He sat down again. But he'd never stopped being in love with her. In his current state that was embarrassingly, emphatically clear. He hoped he'd forget it in the morning.

"You should go home," he said.

She looked down at him, worry lines between her brows. "Are you going to get a cab? Or are you planning to sit there for the rest of the night?"

"Sit here," he said, smiling up at her, because she was pretty, and because she was her. "Go home. It's cold."

"Mmm," she said, looking in the direction of her apartment. After a moment, she sat down next to him, her hands in her pockets.

He frowned. The bench was freezing. "What are you doing? You're not even wearing a scarf." He pulled his own off and draped it over her shoulders, and then, on further consideration, struggled out of his coat as well.

"Ben, I don't—"

"You can't sit here if you don't wear it."

A little spurt of laughter bubbled from her lips. "I'm St. Amie," she said. "There is no bench in Paris upon which I cannot sit."

"Huh," he said. "Just wait until you visit Ohio. I am *a very important person* in Ohio. There are chocolates in the right pocket."

There—a real smile. "Well, if you'd just said that in the first place," she said, pulling the coat around her shoulders and rooting around in the pockets until she produced the paper sack of chocolate caramels.

"Why are you here so late?"

Amelie took a moment to answer, chewing the sticky candy. "There was a change in the choreography," she said. "I needed time alone to practice."

"They changed it this late?"

She shrugged. "It happens."

She popped another chocolate into her mouth, offered the bag to Ben. "What about you?"

"Victor wanted to drink absinthe."

A fit of coughing overtook his companion. He patted her on the back.

"Ben," she said, when she had recovered.

"Yes?"

"Don't drink absinthe. It's not good for Americans."

He smiled, staring up at the sky again. When he looked down, she was watching him. He cocked his head.

"You saw me dance tonight," she said.

"Mmm."

"It was the first time," she said. "All these years, and it was the first time you saw me dance."

"That's not true," he said. Her face was close to his. The lamp above them shone golden on her face, reflecting in her eyes. "I've never forgotten you dancing."

She took a little breath in, so faint he shouldn't have even noticed it, before that sweet, fraudulent smile reappeared. "I mean professionally," she said, her voice suddenly quiet.

A few strands of hair fell across her face. He wanted to sweep them away. He didn't.

They stayed like that for a few frozen moments. She recovered first.

"I should—"

"I'll walk you home," he said, standing. "It's too cold for you."

Amelie's apartment was only five minutes away from the Palais Garnier. He imagined that was why she had chosen it. The streets were largely empty now, though occasionally they passed a bar or restaurant where the party had yet to end. A thin fog descended as they walked, turning the streetlamps into hazy golden moons.

She walked close enough to him he could feel the heat of

her body. When they were younger, he might have offered his arm—now he kept it loose at his side.

Perfect. She'd been perfect tonight. She was an astonishing athlete—no one could defy physics, but she certainly did a good job of pretending she could. He'd held his breath with the rest of the audience at every impossible balance, marveled at her stamina, gasped at her leaps.

But . . .

But this woman, the one next to him, made of muscle and bone and strength and feeling, had not been onstage that evening.

The woman onstage had been perfectly sweet, perfectly kind, and when the time had come, perfectly broken. Even her madness had been perfect—the understandable regret and horror of a young woman who has been led astray. She had died properly and politely, and when she rose from her grave, had only done so out of fidelity.

She had reminded him of André's ballerinas. Amelie, the Amelie who loved to dance, for whom movement was emotion, was nowhere to be seen, and it felt like violence. Like someone had taken something beautiful and smothered it.

He stole a glance at her profile, the sight of her comforting him. He didn't know what had happened to her—twelve years ago, she'd made it clear it was none of his business. But she was here now, next to him, and that was good.

"You said you can't repair a brain," she said suddenly.

"Yet," he said.

"So you think it's possible."

"I think we're extremely close," he said. "It's— Do you know much about the brain?"

She laughed. "No."

"Different regions of the brain control different things," he said.

"Like phrenology," she said.

He winced. "Yes. But also, very importantly, no. And that's an entire lecture I won't give. The important thing is that until we know what controls what, we can't operate on it. We could be taking out a tumor and accidentally remove someone's ability to speak. Actually," he said, feeling the pleasure of talking about something he loved with her, "that's one of the things I hope to achieve while I'm here. There's a Parisian anatomist, rather famously reclusive, who's rumored to have developed the most accurate map of the brain ever made. I very desperately want that map."

If only Bonnet would answer one of my letters.

They arrived at her apartment building. She turned to him, handing over his coat and scarf. "I hope you find your map," she said.

"Thank you."

"Now go home," she said sternly. "No more sleeping on city benches in the middle of the night."

"I wasn't sleeping," he said. "I was stargazing. Amelie, have you thought about—"

"Don't," she said.

He nodded. It was the live fish expression again.

She must have seen something in his gaze, because she hesitated before turning away. "It's not you," she said.

"You don't need to explain yourself," he said. "Go in. I'll walk back to the main road and hail a cab."

"I'm on a tightrope," she said quietly. "And when I'm with you, I'm afraid I'll suddenly jump off."

He wanted to say something stupid like *I'll catch you.* He didn't.

"I understand," he said, because she looked unbearably sad, and the least he could do was not make her worry about him. "Good night, Amelie."

She paused a moment, and then walked into her apartment building. Benedict waited until he saw her vanish up the stairs before walking away, shrugging into a coat that now smelled of rosemary.

CHAPTER EIGHT

Amelie walked up the staircase until she was out of Ben's sight and then sagged against the wall, closing her eyes. Slowly, she sank onto the stairs, wrapping her arms around herself.

Briefly, under the cloudy night sky, she'd forgotten. He'd had that smile on his face, the one she'd always remembered, until she'd forced herself to stop remembering him at all. It was a smile that said there was no one else in the world he'd rather look at. It said, *You're my favorite.*

She'd wanted to kiss him. She almost had.

Why was he back? Why now?

Taking a long breath, Amelie pushed herself back up. She needed to see Honorine.

The apartment was quiet when she pushed open the door. On performance and dress rehearsal nights she paid Suzanne to wait until she returned, so Honorine wouldn't be alone late at night. She thanked the woman quietly, giving her cab money for her journey home, and then peeked into Honorine's room.

Her sister was deep asleep. Amelie leaned against the

doorjamb, watching her sister's face in the narrow triangle of light cast from the hall. Her dark hair had escaped its braid—it would be badly tangled in the morning. She seemed so small when she was sleeping, so young. It would be so easy for something, or someone, to hurt her.

Not while I'm alive.

She closed the door softly and padded through the apartment turning off lamps. When they were all extinguished, she stood in the dark sitting room, staring out her windows toward Montmartre.

This was why she'd chosen this apartment. St. Amie might be a creature of new Paris, but Amelie St. James never wanted to forget where she'd come from.

She traced the familiar line of lights until she came to the empty darkness where the new basilica was being built. A scar and a warning.

"*Maman*," she whispered. "You should be here. You should see her."

For years she'd kept the memories away. After her mother died, she'd been so busy keeping herself and Honorine alive she hadn't had time to grieve. Later, it hadn't been safe. To remember her mother—to remember how she died—it was too big. It threatened to drown her.

But ever since Ben had returned, the memories had pressed close, circling like wolves on a snowy night. She had to be on guard, lest she find herself thinking of summer afternoons, lazing on the grass next to a boy she liked before running home to have supper with her mother, safe and happy in their little attic apartment in Montmartre. Her beautiful mother, laughing as she set some bread on their table, a bit of blue paint smudged on her cheek.

The last good summer.

"I miss you," Amelie said, her lungs tight with pain. "My God, *maman*, I miss you. Honorine must barely remember you. She should know you. She deserves to *know* you. And I deserve—"

To see you again. To see my mother. To talk to you one more time.

She realized she was still wearing her coat.

She didn't feel her hip as she went back down the stairs, or the cold of the night air as she walked to the large road a block away. She didn't think about where she was going. Instead, as the cab she hailed rolled smoothly down empty streets, she found herself thinking about the Salle La Peletier, the theater she'd grown up in, the home of the Opera Ballet before it had burned and the Palais Garnier had replaced it.

Amelie had known everything about that theater. The slight smell of mold that thickened on a rainy morning; how the third window along the back wall of the rehearsal room had lost its sash and needed to be propped up with a wooden block; the way you had to jiggle the door to the indoor toilets. She'd memorized the dust along the edge of the hallways and in the crevices no one visited; she knew the old, faded pair of pointe shoes living on a hook in the corps dressing room, left behind by some dancer long ago.

And then, one night two years after the end of the Paris Commune, the fire came. It raged for twenty-seven hours, and at the end, nothing was left but two sections of wall.

Two years after that, she and Honorine left the apartment in Montmartre. Now there was nothing left of her childhood in her life. She went from her new apartment to her new theater, along streets and sidewalks that hadn't existed a decade before. The only time she saw her past was when she looked out her window toward Montmartre Butte.

They were climbing the hill now. She didn't need to look

out the window to know where they were—the pitch of the slope told her. Halfway home.

They weren't going to the old apartment building, though. A few minutes later the coach took a left turn, and then another, and then stopped. Amelie paid the coachman and climbed out, ignoring his curious gaze.

The iron gates of Montmartre Cemetery stood closed before her.

A franc handed to the night watchman opened them easily enough, and she slipped through, pulling her coat close. The moon was nearly full, lighting the path before her. The lane was wide and lined with the tall, black outlines of elaborate tombs, standing like trees on either side. It was a grisly parody of a boulevard—Amelie imagined skeletons strolling leisurely along it, with top hats and fashionable walking sticks, stopping occasionally to exchange crushing witticisms.

Eventually she left the path, walking over grass and graves turned silver in the moonlight. She stopped at the outer walls, standing before the long stretch of earth she believed her mother was buried under.

And then, God forgive her, she closed her eyes and tried to call Leonie St. James back from the dead.

She tried for a long time. She reached out as best she knew how. She thought of her mother's laugh, her smile. Her paintings.

A long time later, she stopped.

Her mother's bones lay somewhere beneath her, six feet of utterly impassable distance.

That pressure in her chest was back. The other memories, the bad ones, were back as well.

Leonie St. James wasn't a ghost, and her daughter would never be able to talk to her again.

There were so many people she knew in this cemetery, and

so few of them had died after a long, happy life. Her friend Jean-Louise was buried a two-minute walk from here; dead at twenty-one from the smallpox that had torn through the city during the Prussian Siege. Jean-Louise, another person Amelie didn't think of. They'd danced together their whole lives. She'd dreamed of being an *étoile,* like Amelie was. Maybe, with a few more years, she could have been.

She hadn't deserved to die, a casualty of a stupid war between stupid people. A casualty never recorded, just a girl who'd died. Lise, her mother, none of them deserved—

Amelie bit her lip until the pain registered, cutting through the weight of the past. Enough. If she let herself think that way . . .

She felt the graves around her, all the people she'd once known. It wasn't right, but it was done. It was done, but it wasn't right.

No, that was the wrong way around.

She couldn't keep acting like this. She had responsibilities; she had her sister—

Honorine. She'd left her sister at home, alone, in the middle of the night. She hadn't even thought about it.

Enough.

She put it away. All of it. The memories, the unknowable, unthinkable, unbearable emotion that came with them. She closed her eyes, forcing it all *away,* far away, until there was nothing left inside her but the clean, calm Amelie who took care of her sister and danced politely and paid her bills on time.

When she opened her eyes, the only thing she thought about was how to find a cab in the middle of the night by Montmartre Cemetery.

"Amelie?"

Lise stood by her shoulder, looking worried.

Right. The clean, calm Amelie was also being haunted. That was fine. She just needed to stop letting herself be shaken. She would approach this issue rationally—

"I hate to bother you," Lise said. "But we have a problem."

Any problems could be overcome. It would all be fine—

"Well, Amelie," said a voice behind her. "Why the hell am I here?"

Amelie whipped around. "Oh *merde*," she said.

Two women stood before her.

Rachel Bonnard, summarily executed at the end of the Commune on suspicion of arson, leaned casually against a tomb. She was young, in her early twenties, with severe black hair and dark, burning eyes.

Standing next to her was a familiar-looking woman in her later years, wearing heavy stage makeup and the most extraordinary wig Amelie had ever seen. It was bright gold, with birds pinned in it and a gilded cage resting on the top, tilted rakishly to the right. A pre-Revolution opium dream.

Dead. They were dead. Staring at them, she faintly realized she could *feel* them, just a slight pressure in her head.

"Rachel?"

"So it would seem," Rachel replied, in a familiar, sarcastic tone.

That was right, Amelie remembered slowly. They'd always fought.

"No," Amelie said, after a pause. "No. One ghost. One. *One*. I can do one. One is manageable. It's an aberration. An exception. Do you know what I cannot do?"

"Handle stress, apparently."

It was all so *very* familiar, this quibbling. It was just a decade out of date. Something they had done once, a long time ago, and then Rachel had died, and now she was *here*, and—

"A pattern," Amelie said. It was hard to breathe. "I cannot do a pattern. I do not have time for a pattern. I cannot add *ghosts* to my permanent problem list. Do you understand me? *You will not fit.*"

"My god, the living are exhausting," Rachel drawled. "You lot are dead, though. Who are you?"

"Who are *you*?" Lise snapped.

"You can call me Violette," the bewigged woman said. "It's not the name I was born with, but it served me well—"

"*Violette*?" Amelie said. "I didn't recognize you. Er, you look so different."

"Oh, thank you," Violette said, preening. "I fixed a few things up, coming out of the grave. It wouldn't do, returning to Paris all out of sorts."

Rachel rolled her eyes, and Amelie stared. Violette had briefly lived down the street from the Montmartre apartment building Amelie and Honorine had lived in. The sisters had brought her dinner sometimes, and in return, she regaled them with stories of her time on the stage as a famous cabaret singer, each one more ludicrous than the last. She had died of a heart attack in 1875, shortly before they had moved.

"You look beautiful," Amelie said faintly. Violette had fixed up more than a few things. She was dressed in a bright pink silk dress that would have paid her rent for six months when she was alive, and she was draped in extravagant jewels.

The day Lise had murdered that man, Ben had said she was in shock. Now Amelie knew she hadn't been. *This* was shock; this ringing vision and muffled sound. She was standing above her mother's grave with three dead women.

She wished someone would tell her to lie down.

"Oh, stop feeling sorry for yourself," Rachel said. "Always so emotional."

"She's had a terrible shock!" Lise retorted hotly.

"You've known her for two seconds," Rachel said. "I grew up with her."

"Yes, and you've been *dead* the last eight years," Lise said.

"You're just as dead as I am," Rachel said.

Rachel Bonnard. Rachel Bonnard had indeed grown up with her. She had lived in the same building, in fact, with her entire family—mother, father, and three brothers. All four children had died between 1870 and 1871, the three boys fighting the Prussians, and Rachel a few months later. Through the gray cloud of grief blanketing those months, Amelie couldn't remember if she'd visited the Bonnards or not. Four children. Had she gone? Had she brought them something? She couldn't imagine what there would have been to bring.

"Now, girls, fighting's not going to solve anything—"

And there was Violette—

They're going to keep coming.

"Excuse me," she said, over the arguing ghosts. "Excuse me!"

They stopped and looked at her curiously. "I hope this isn't impolite," she said. "But do any of you know *why* this is happening? You didn't die at the same time. Why come back now?"

"I think it's because I admired you, when I was alive," Lise said.

Rachel snorted.

"Yes, we can assume that doesn't apply to all of you," Amelie said. "Rachel? Why now?"

The ghost shrugged. "I would tell you if I knew. One minute, nothing, the next, there you were, tromping around like an elephant. I didn't seem to have a choice in the matter."

"Alright. Violette?"

"Well, I wouldn't say *tromping,* my dear, but there was an undeniable . . . *presence.* Not at all elephant-like, really, what a thing to say, but perhaps . . . heavy. Not that I'm calling you heavy! Stage presence, that's what it was. I don't know what would have happened if I hadn't followed you. Didn't fancy staying in the dark and finding out, to be honest."

The three dead women looked at one another, and in that silent exchange there was some knowledge that made Amelie feel every inch of her living flesh.

"So, it's me," she said. "I'm the reason. I'm doing something that's . . . calling you."

That wasn't like Alva's ghost, she didn't think. A lot of people had seen Rose de Boer. That haunting hadn't been . . . personal.

"Have you been thinking of us, dear? We did all know you."

She wished she could say yes. All three of these women had touched her life for a time. But she'd danced next to Lise for years and hadn't known her. She'd grown up with Rachel, but she couldn't even remember if she'd visited the woman's mother after her death. Violette, at least, she'd missed. She and Honorine had been sad when she'd died, but she'd been older, and death had been so familiar in those years . . . In honesty, Violette had simply faded to a pleasant memory.

"The dark," Amelie said. "You said you came from the dark."

The women looked at one another, Lise and Violette shifting uncomfortably.

"Not sure you're meant to know about that," Violette said. "It's—"

"It's not where we came from," Lise said. "It's more where we woke up. Where we heard you. Think of it like . . . like a waiting room—"

"It's the grave," Rachel said, cutting through the other

women's hesitation with an irritated expression. "What? She asked."

"And . . . before that? Were you—"

"You wouldn't understand," Rachel said.

"Oh, love," Violette said. "I'm afraid she's right, though she could have put it more kindly. Wherever—not sure that's even the right word, really, which should give you a hint as to the trouble—wherever we were, I can barely remember it, now that I'm back in the living. I'm not even sure I was an *I* there. Your brain is a thing of flesh, you know. It's constrained. This . . . isn't. Do you understand, sweetheart?"

"Maybe it's heaven," Lise said quietly, and Rachel snorted again.

"What? It could be!"

"Yes, because you and I were so likely to get in," she said. "I might not have burned the buildings they said I did, but I killed three people that week. And from what I see in this idiot's brain, you—"

"Maybe it's not about that," Lise snapped.

"And maybe religion is a bedtime story told by powerful men to keep the people sleeping," Rachel said. "But keep on dreaming, I suppose."

"Why are you so mean?"

"Why are you so naive?"

"Well maybe I'm naive, but you still haven't figured out how to change the clothes they shot you in—my God, are those your *brains*?"

Rachel looked blandly at the gore scattered over her shoulders, and shrugged. "I'm not the one who wanted to come back," she said. "Why should I get dressed up?"

"Amelie, people can't just be showing up all the time—"

"Oh sorry, I didn't realize this was such an exclusive club,"

Rachel said. "You think I want to be stuck in *her* head? So maudlin! *Oh, everything's my fault, the whole world rests on my shoulders, I have to be perfect, all the time.* I see you've turned yourself into the perfect doll for the bourgeoisie, Amelie. How proud you must be."

It started to rain.

They're going to keep coming.

"She doesn't like you to listen to her thoughts," Lise hissed.

"It's not like I want to listen to them!"

It doesn't matter why. They're going to keep coming.

"Stop it, you two," Violette said. "Just—hush for a minute."

The rain was cold and hard. It soaked her coat in seconds. "I need to go home," Amelie said. "I'd like you all to leave, please. I don't mean to be rude. But I need to be alone. We'll figure this out tomorrow."

"I understand," Lise said, in an authoritative tone. She'd clearly elected herself ghost leader, simply by virtue of being first. *My God,* Amelie thought. *She's Queen of the Wilis after all.* "Come on," she said to the others. "We'll see you tomorrow."

And they were gone, somewhere Amelie probably couldn't fathom. She'd have to ask about that. Had she just asked them to go wait in their graves?

She looked at the rain-soaked, muddy grass beneath her feet one last time, and then walked out of the cemetery.

Somehow, she found a cab. The driver looked even more concerned than the last one—in her rain- and mud-soaked state, at least she didn't need to worry about anyone recognizing her—but he stopped for her.

She felt empty, slouched in the corner of the carriage. Her hip ached. She'd been foolish with it today.

She was cold.

The driver stopped in front of her apartment building. She

paid him and stepped out onto the empty sidewalk. A well-dressed man was vomiting in a bush a few meters away, his friend holding an umbrella over him and murmuring sympathetically. It was still the middle of the night; there was no sign of dawn.

They're going to keep coming.

She thought about Ben's offer. No, *Benedict*; she should think of him as Benedict. Dr. Benedict Moore, illustrious American doctor. Not Ben from the lake. Ben from before.

He'd offered to be her friend. She couldn't afford that. But—she needed help. Yes, she was on a tightrope, and yes, he made her wonder about jumping off, about the free fall. But if she did nothing, if she let these ghosts keep coming with no way of stopping them, that tightrope was going to get cut into tiny pieces while she was still dancing on it. He was smart, and discreet, and he knew about ghosts.

By the time she reached her dark apartment and checked on Honorine—still soundly sleeping—she'd made her decision.

She just needed to be careful.

CHAPTER NINE

Benedict walked out of the Salpêtrière, one of Europe's largest asylums, into a pleasant autumn day. He'd just attended a lecture given by Jean Charcot, the man credited with bringing order to the hospital, and he was feeling somewhat grim. Charcot was undeniably important: among his many contributions to medicine, he'd identified disseminated sclerosis, known here as *la sclérose en plaques*, and then had gone on to differentiate it from Parkinson's disease. His work on both diseases was seminal.

But he had recently begun an investigation into hysteria. Benedict was doubtful of any disease that originated from a belief that the uterus could just get up and walk around (a highlight of any Moore gathering was Maggie's impression titled "The Wandering Womb," in which a uterus went to various events, greeted important personages, and then commented upon them) and had been used for hundreds of years to imprison women deemed objectionable by those in power. Nothing about the lecture he'd attended had convinced him there was anything salvageable in the diagnosis. Many of the symptoms Charcot identified were easily explained by alternative diagnoses, and frankly, he doubted the validity of the rest. The man was a showman, his lectures half circus with dramatic conclusions and comedic interludes, and he seemed to be creating an environment designed to elicit symptoms, rather than faithfully observe them.

Benedict had woken to a hangover and a thousand-word telegram from Sam, filled with ghost questions he didn't know if he'd be able to ask, let alone answer.

I'm on a tightrope, she'd said, with that look in her eyes. He was beginning to think she'd been on one since she'd sent him away. The thought brought pain and sorrow and thick, black guilt that bubbled up like oil.

Some colleagues approached him, wanting to talk about the spectacle they'd just witnessed. He was mid-argument when he saw a familiar pale lavender dress out of the corner of his eye. He shifted circuitously, careful not to draw attention to where he was looking.

Amelie St. James was standing a few meters away, looking down at the sidewalk. From the lack of interest exhibited by those around her, no one had recognized her yet, but it could only be a matter of time.

Benedict excused himself calmly from the conversation and began walking toward her. When he had almost passed her, he took her wrist, quickly whisking her into a small nook on the side of the building.

He placed her carefully against the wall and looked around. When he was satisfied that they hadn't been seen, he turned to her.

"What are you doing?" he whispered. "I thought we couldn't be seen together in public."

"I—" She cleared her throat. "I suppose that depends on if your offer is still open."

"What?" He heard some footsteps approaching and angled himself to shield her from sight. This was a mistake, he realized as soon as he looked down and found her face mere inches from his own.

He eased back.

"Your offer. Of . . . help."

"I will always help you," he said plainly.

This did not seem to please her. "I want to negotiate."

"Alright," he said. "I'll give you anything you want."

"Ben. Benedict, I mean."

"You can keep calling me Ben."

"Benedict. That's not how a negotiation works."

"No?"

She frowned at him. He smiled back. He couldn't help it—he was slowly realizing she'd come to see *him* and a slow tide of joy was rolling through his body.

"I can't accept your help for nothing," she said. "I need to give you something in return."

"I like sandwiches," he said.

She huffed at him. It was a familiar huff. It meant he wasn't doing what she thought he ought to, that he wasn't seeing reason—he was being pigheaded. He'd loved that sound. He still loved it. "You said you wanted to meet with a reclusive anatomist while you were here," she said, clearly deciding to ignore him. "By chance, were you talking about Emile Bonnet?"

That stopped his teasing. "Yes," he said. "But how did you—"

"He's the only reclusive anatomist I can think of. I will arrange a meeting."

"What?"

"He was one of my mother's lovers," Amelie said. "He wasn't quite as hermit-like then, although the tendency was there. He was . . . well, I wouldn't say nice. But decent. If I write to him, he'll agree to meet you."

She spoke matter-of-factly. In America the statement would have been shocking, unspeakable. Things were somewhat different here.

"That's something I want very dearly," he said seriously. "I won't pretend to decline. Yes. *Yes.*"

She looked pleased, and relieved. "Good," she said. "Then we agree? Aid for aid?"

She extended her hand. He took it. "Aid for aid," he said. "But how did you know where to find me?"

"I called at the address you gave me," she said. "The maid told me where you were. I took a risk."

"So whatever changed your mind," he said, "it's urgent. Tell me?"

She did. The joy left his body.

"And perhaps I could still manage it," she said. "But what if they all have accidental murder streaks? Or more appear while I'm onstage? Or I start talking to them in public, and people see—"

"Amelie," he said, slowly. "You're being haunted by a steadily increasing stream of ghosts. You don't need to justify wanting help."

"Oh," she said. "Well."

"By now you should know the routine," he said. "Wrist, please."

She looked around, making sure that the crowd from the lecture had finally dispersed, and held out her hand.

Her pulse was normal. Her eyes were normal. Her coloring was normal. Her speech was normal. He'd need his tools and a little more privacy to conduct a proper exam, but there was still no sign she was being physically affected by the hauntings, unlike every other person he knew of who'd come in prolonged contact with a ghost.

"I tried to bring my mother back from the dead," she said.

Oh, Amelie.

"Alright," he said, releasing her hand. "Did it work?"

"No."

He nodded.

"I don't know what to do," she said. "I don't know what I think you can do. But there has to be something. I've worked so hard—I'm so close—my sister—"

"—will be fine, and so will you," he said. He'd make sure of it. "If this were a problem at my institute, the first thing I'd do is gather information. I'd like to do an exam, and I have a lot of questions. Some for you, and some for the ghosts. Oh, and Sam sent an epic novel by telegram. I imagine he and Alva are probably bankrupt now. We should go somewhere we can talk—"

"I can't," she said. "I have rehearsal in—oh, in an hour. I should already be warming up. I— What you proposed—"

"I'll appear to be courting you," he provided, speaking calmly, as though it were a perfectly normal thing to propose. "We should be seen together publicly, then people won't wonder if we spend a certain amount of time together. We can at least be in carriages and go on walks. Places where people can see us but not hear us. You don't have a performance tomorrow night, yes? You could go out in the afternoon?"

She blinked once, twice. "No. I mean, no performance. I can go out."

"I'll meet you after your morning class. It still finishes at noon?"

"Yes."

"At half past, then. I'll meet you outside the front entrance."

They stood for a moment, still too close, before she nodded curtly, and he turned to hail her a cab.

She needed help, and this time, he could—he *would*—give it. Beneath his fear and relief beat a warning: he was still leaving, she was still staying, like it had always been. But this time he wasn't nineteen. He was a grown man who could control his feelings.

Alright, that was nonsense. He was going to be pretending to court the woman, for god's sake. There was absolutely no chance of him making it out with his heart intact.

A cab slowed for him, and he helped Amelie inside, bowing politely and shutting the door.

He might not be able to protect himself, but he *could* protect her. He would do what he hadn't been able to do before—he'd make sure she was safe. And once he was an ocean away, he'd pick up the pieces again.

CHAPTER TEN

July 1866

Twelve years earlier . . .

They didn't see each other every day—she'd recently been accepted into the company of the Paris Opera Ballet, so there were days she danced from sunrise to long past sunset. She never seemed to tire, though. Four weeks after their first meeting, Benedict met her at the Marché aux Fleurs, on the Île de la Cité. The Marché was an open-air flower and bird market, the stalls tucked under four rows of stately trees, dwarfed by the stone buildings bordering them on two sides.

The sun was high overhead. This was the routine they'd fallen into: Amelie had class with the company every morning, and afterward, on the days she didn't have rehearsal, they'd meet for the afternoon. He only saw her in sunshine—they always parted before nightfall.

They strolled through the market, nibbling on apricot tarts (he'd managed to solve the finances argument, at least partially—now they alternated payment). Amelie laughed at a stall of brightly colored parrots spouting bon mots, her whole face alight. She experienced joy so completely, this girl. It was impossible not to laugh along with her.

"Why did you kidnap me, that day?" he asked, when they continued walking.

She took a thoughtful bite of her buttery tart. "You looked sad," she said. "Like a lost puppy."

The matter-of-fact way she said it robbed the words of their sting. His lips curled into a rueful smile. "You decided to adopt me."

"Fleas and all," she said.

He laughed, but the word brought on memories he didn't want, ones that had no place in the sunshine, among the flowers. He pushed them away.

Amelie stopped, putting her hand on his arm. "I said something wrong."

"No," he said. "Of course not. I'm fine."

She cocked her head. "You're not."

He didn't know what to say, so he looked down. He didn't talk about those days, not with anyone. There had been a time, in the summer, when the fleas—

No. That couldn't touch this.

They walked in silence for a few steps.

"Do you want to come to a dance tonight?"

Benedict looked up in surprise. "Don't you have class in the morning?"

"They're reflooring our rehearsal room," she said. "I have the day off."

"Alright," he said.

Later, he stood in the hotel room he shared with his brother, staring down at his bed, which was currently draped with every piece of clothing he'd brought with him. Sam and eight-year-old Maggie sat on Sam's bed, watching in something like awe.

"I like that blue vest," Sam said, helpfully. "The bright one."

Benedict and Maggie ignored him.

"What about this one, Mags?" Benedict held up a sober gray waistcoat.

"Where is this dance?" she asked.

"Outdoors," he said. "Some cafe."

"Not formal, then," she said, her expression serious. Maggie took only two things seriously: chemistry and clothes. She surveyed the wreckage on the bed.

"Keep it simple," she declared. "Black morning coat, tan trousers, white shirt. The blue necktie, for some fun. It's too bad you don't have a straw hat; I've seen those everywhere here."

"Should I have one? I can go get one—"

"Your black felt will be fine," she said, exchanging a quick glance with Sam.

"So," Sam said, "who's the girl?"

"Sam!" Maggie squeaked, swatting at his arm. "We agreed to be subtle."

Sam shrugged, his big shoulders straining his shirt, and looked so helpless that Benedict's lips pulled into a grin. Sam was only the oldest by a year—twenty to Benedict's nineteen—and sometimes it felt like eight-year-old Maggie was the boss of them all.

Or—it *had* felt that way, before. Benedict waited for the chasm to reassert itself, but for once it didn't, not exactly. Things *were* different. He was different. For the first time, though, he realized his family was different, too—and not just because of the suffering he had put them through. Sam and his parents had spent most of the war designing increasingly effective weaponry. Maggie had spent half her life in a country torn apart by war, with a family actively involved in the war effort.

None of them were the same as they had been before. But maybe they could still . . . fit together.

Embarrassed by these sentimental thoughts, Benedict threw a sock at Sam.

"But seriously, Ben," Maggie said. "Who's the girl?"

"None of your business," he said, but even as he spoke his head filled with questions. His family would like Amelie. She would like his family. Why couldn't he—

Because he was leaving in three weeks, and she was staying. He hadn't even thought about it before, and the oversight sunk into his stomach with the weight of lead. For a moment, the flatness was back.

His siblings sensed something was wrong. He could feel the worry coming back around him—he hadn't even realized how much lighter that burden had been over the last few weeks.

"Hurry up, Ben," Sam said. "Whoever she is, you can't keep her waiting."

It was the exact right thing to say. He couldn't keep her waiting, whether their time together was limited or no. Perhaps it was even more precious because it was.

"You're sure I don't need the straw hat?" he asked Maggie.

"Quite sure," she said. "It would probably look funny on you anyway. It might only be a French thing."

He nodded decisively and picked up the pants. "Well?" He eyed his siblings. "Get out!"

Amelie met him at the train station, dressed in bright, cheerful colors. They each bought a ticket—he rolled his eyes in frustration but didn't press the point—and boarded a loud, crowded car filled with other people dressed to go dancing. The sun was dipping toward the horizon, bathing the merrymakers in that perfect golden light that only occurs on a summer evening, when care is at least a day away and pleasure is the only pursuit.

There were no seats available, so they stood close together in the narrow aisle. Amelie clutched one of the posts and Benedict held the overhead rail, so she was tucked against him, not exactly touching, but close enough that he could smell the herbs she used on her hair. He wished he knew what they were called—they were bright and spicy and sun-drenched. He tried to commit the smell to memory. He couldn't see her face because of the hat she wore, only her curls and the tip of her nose.

Almost the entire car got off at their stop, the platform flooded with bright dresses and laughter. The crowd walked together toward the Seine, Benedict and Amelie along with them. He didn't even ask where they were going, the evening already like a cherished memory, a fairy tale. He just laughed, at nothing and everything.

La Grenouillère was the kind of place that should only exist on summer nights. It was a sort of bar-cum-dance hall, scattered absurdly over the river on an assortment of plank bridges and barges and islands. Painted wooden boats bobbed pleasantly nearby, made magical by the reflection of lanterns on the water. Amelie took Benedict's arm as the crowd from the train merged with the crowd already on the dance floor, laughing as she was shoved close against him.

"Come on," she said, taking his hand and pulling him through the throngs, already moving to the cheerful brass sounds of the band. He trailed behind her, happy simply to follow. Somehow, she found them a spot in the middle of the crush, and without really knowing how it happened, she was in his arms, and they were spinning madly with the rest of the revelers, laughing until their throats were dry and sweat ran down their backs. Her movements were impossibly light and fluid, her face alight with striking, uncomplicated joy. She danced as if she were at a fairy revel, like she never wanted to stop. She danced like it was her truest movement, and every moment spent walking or standing or sitting was merely intermission.

Benedict was not a natural dancer. Before the war, his mother had dragged the family to one of the local assemblies, and he'd dutifully escorted the girls he'd grown up with around the dance floor, feeling stiff and too tall and rather crane-like, especially compared to his ebullient brother (it should be noted that Sam was not a natural dancer, either, but no one noticed because he had such a good time while doing it). With Amelie in his arms, he didn't *feel* stiff, and she was tall enough that he didn't feel *so* gawkish, and they were laughing so much none of it mattered anyway.

When their throats were dry, and the sweat slick against their faces, they wound their way to the bar. Benedict procured two glasses of beer and managed to pay before Amelie noticed, thrusting one into her hand with a distinct feeling of smugness. She glared at him playfully but tipped it back, taking a long draught of the golden, foamy liquid and wiping her mouth with the back of her hand.

"You're wonderful," he shouted. She laughed, and the heat rose up his already over-warm face. "I mean, you're a wonderful dancer."

"Well, I should be," she said, taking his arm and leading him farther out of the crowd. The din quieted. "I've been doing it my whole life."

They walked across a narrow plank to the shore, dimly illuminated by the lights from the bar. Couples were scattered on logs and rocks, and Benedict felt his blush return as he averted his eyes. Amelie smirked at his discomfiture. She found an unoccupied log underneath a willow and sat down, fanning herself with one hand. He sat next to her.

There was a slight breeze off the river. The sound of music and laughter drifted toward them, but here, a willow branch draping in front of them, they were in their own pocket again. Without all the distractions, he was painfully aware of how attuned he was to her. When had that happened?

She sipped her beer and sighed contentedly. Suddenly he was filled with so many things he wanted to say to her, things he couldn't articulate to himself that felt vaguely like promises.

"Amelie—"

"Don't, Ben," she said, softly. She gave a small, wistful smile. "I know."

"I'm leaving." It came out as a lament.

"I know."

They sat together silently, the muted sounds of the dance hall drifting across them.

"Maybe I don't have to," he said, wildly. "I don't know what's back there for me, anyway."

She turned to him, her lips curved in a rueful smile. "Ben. You're nineteen years old. Your family is there. Your whole life."

He looked down at the dirt, tufts of grass rising black against the river. "I don't know how to be that person anymore," he said quietly. "I'm different than I used to be."

She sighed, a thoughtful puff of breath. They watched the whirl of the colorful dancers across the water.

"You were in the war," she said. "In America."

He hadn't told her, but he wasn't surprised she'd guessed. "I was an assistant surgeon," he said. "In the Union Army."

"You're a doctor?"

He shrugged. "It's not like it is here. You take two years of courses. The second year is a repeat of the first."

"But you're so young," she said.

"I started when I was sixteen," he said, remembering for one painful moment the certainty of his younger self. Sixteen-year-old Benedict had been so disturbed by the reports from the front. He'd known there was something he could do, something he *had* to do. He wasn't allowed to enlist, but he could prepare.

How little he'd known. There was nothing that could have prepared him.

He could feel Amelie's considering gaze on him. He didn't know why he was telling her this—tonight of all nights, when it had begun so magically—

"What does an assistant surgeon do?"

"We went ahead, into the field," he said. This was an easy answer, a mere description. "With as many supplies as we could carry on our backs. The senior surgeons stayed in the rear, where it was safer. They were too valuable—we never had enough—"

No, too close to danger. He cleared his throat, retreated.

"Our job was to set up a field hospital, closer to the action. We saw the wounded first, patched them up as best we could. Tried to keep them alive long enough to be transported to the senior surgeons in the back."

Sometimes they were pinned down by the fighting and couldn't even reach the men who needed them. They had to sneak out at night to drag them in, if they had lasted the day.

There were days he alone must have treated hundreds. At the beginning, he'd tried to keep count—it was the Moore way, after all. But there were too many, and never enough time. They blurred together, no longer men, only a series of diseases and wounds.

"There was a new kind of bullet," he said quietly. "The Minié ball. The wounds it left . . . there were better guns, too. And . . . no one knew how to deal with that. Generals used the same tactics their great-grandfathers had used in the revolution, but they didn't work anymore. So many people were dying. Some days all I could do was give them whiskey."

He'd never said that out loud before.

She didn't say anything, only pressed a soft hand over his. He focused on her hand.

"And then I got sick," he said, trying to find the end. "When I woke up, the war was over."

"But it's not over for you," she said, her voice quiet.

Suddenly there were tears on his face. His body was shaking. It took him a long time to answer her. His throat wasn't working the way it should. "Everyone else is moving on," he said. "It was better when I was still sick. At least then I had an excuse."

"I didn't know you before," Amelie said. "And I can barely imagine what you're describing. But I know you now, and I don't think you have to be anybody except who you are."

He laughed, the sound cracking as it escaped. "Who's that? A physician who isn't practicing, who only knows how to patch up bullet holes? A son whose parents barely recognize him?"

"A Ben," she said. "Who makes me laugh. Who brings me walnuts after my morning classes, because he knows I'm always hungry then. Who smiles when he talks about his family, even if he doesn't know it."

He stared at her, and then he blurted out the thought he didn't even know he'd been harboring. "It's my fault they're dead," he said. "If I'd been a better doctor—"

"No," she said. "It's not."

Her certitude was startling.

"Did you ever do less than you were capable of?" she asked, her voice crisp.

He thought back to the edges of battlefields, to the small churches and schoolhouses surrounded by the dead. "No," he whispered.

It wasn't a miraculous moment. The weight heavy upon him since his first battle did not evaporate. But briefly it lightened, and he realized it was not for the first time.

"You should talk to your parents," she said.

He shook his head. "They've been through enough," he said. "I don't want to burden them."

"Nonsense," she said. "They love you. I know that, and I've never even seen them. You're not going to crush them by telling the truth."

The way she said it, in the same bossy, arrogant tone with which she'd ordered him to row her around a lake, permeated the way a kinder voice might not have. *Perhaps*, he thought, *she is right.*

"I'll think about it," he said.

She nodded, and as if she sensed he couldn't dwell in those memories any longer, stood. "Let's walk back," she said. "I'm getting cold."

CHAPTER ELEVEN

October 1878

The downpour began Monday morning. Amelie watched the dark clouds roll in over Paris from the rehearsal room at the top of the Palais Garnier. The drops of rain began to hit the windows near the end of the barre section, during the *grands battements*.

Would he come? Perhaps not. Traffic would be impossible.

"Amelie, inside leg," Madame Renard said, with an irritated *tap tap* of her cane. Amelie startled and corrected, hearing some muffled giggling from the young corps members behind her. She hadn't forgotten a combination in years.

During the short stretching break that separated barre work from center work, she overheard the whispers. "*An American doctor . . .*" "*Claudine says . . .*" "I *heard . . .*"

Her face flushed as she bent over her leg. The gossip was embarrassing but necessary. It was a funny quirk of public opinion that a concealed relationship was scandalous but an announced, discussed, and analyzed one was perfectly respectable. To this end, she'd mentioned her afternoon plans to Claudine Brun, a soloist widely known to be the biggest gossip in the company.

The middle of the night had brought doubts, but several sleepless hours spent searching for another solution had left her tired and with no new ideas. She didn't know if Benedict could help her, but if anyone could, it was a brain researcher with a ghost hunter for a brother. And if he couldn't . . .

She wouldn't think about that.

The ghosts had attended class with her. All three had appeared over breakfast at the apartment, while Honorine was still in the room. Amelie had been trying to pay attention to her sister's morning chatter, ignoring the turmoil inside herself, and in a blink, Lise had appeared at the wall-mounted barre. Amelie had dropped her spoon in surprise. When she picked it up, she saw Rachel and Violette talking at the window, Rachel still with her ruined clothes, Violette in a wide, pale-blue wig embellished with rhinestone-encrusted pastel macarons and a coordinating pink silk dress.

Now Lise was stretching in the corner, out of place more because of her Wilis costume than her deadness, near several girls Amelie thought had been her friends. She sat slightly outside their circle. Perhaps two weeks ago there would have been space for her within it. Violette and Rachel had drifted away sometime during class, bored.

Madame Renard stalked toward the center of the room. "*Tendus*," she snapped, rattling off a combination, and the company assembled away from the barres, preparing for the second half of class.

The work in center was hard, and for a few blessed minutes, Amelie was able to forget Benedict and the ghosts and everything else other than how to lift that extra centimeter in her *arabesque*, how to hold her balance for a tiny bit longer, how to make her *pirouettes en dehors* a little cleaner. How to smile as her hip throbbed, how to bracket the pain off in her brain.

Nothing but her body, her hip, the piano, and the rain.

She waited for the other dancers to leave the room once class ended, busying herself with her shoes and her bag as usual. Her hip often hurt after class, and while she could conceal the limp, she preferred to wait until no one could see her slow pace down the stairs.

All it would take was one person. One slipup. The Director wouldn't fire her immediately, of course. She had a yearly contract. First, he'd express concern. Then, he'd suggest, ever so delicately, that she dance fewer performances. Next, it would be smaller roles. And finally, when it came time for contract renewal, the words *graceful retirement* would be floated. She'd find herself without a job, without prospects, and without sufficient savings.

Everyone knew dancers didn't come back from hip injuries.

But she *could* still dance. She did it every day. She could do it for two more years.

When she was sure no one would see her, she stood carefully, using the barre. The clouds were heavy over the city, and people below hurried by beneath black umbrellas.

Lise came back into the room. The ghost had left at the same time as her friends, drifting behind them like a buoy caught on the rudder of a boat.

"It's clear," she said. "The others went to wait in the dressing room."

Amelie picked up her bag. "Those girls," she said, as they started down the stairs. "They were your friends?"

Lise nodded. "Sarah and Marie-Louise," she said. "Sarah's very good. You should pay attention to her. Marie-Louise is probably going to leave to get married soon. She's sweet, but she's not really one of us. Her family has money. Her father doesn't want her to keep dancing."

It was rare for a girl from a well-off family to join the ballet—there was still that air of the scandalous about it. Amelie wondered how Marie-Louise had persuaded her father in the first place.

They walked down the rest of the stairs in silence. There was no one at the bottom, so Amelie took a respite to rest her hip before continuing down the corridor.

"Have you remembered anything else?" She spoke quietly, in case someone was nearby.

Lise shook her head. "I keep thinking about it, when I'm . . . when I exist. Maybe I drank too much and decided to go for a walk. Maybe I fell in. Maybe someone pushed me."

She stopped, her head down, and kicked at the wall with her pointe shoe. "Maybe I did kill myself," she said softly. "Maybe I stood on the Pont Neuf and decided this was all there was for me, that I'd never go further, that I'd always be hungry Lise Martin from Montmartre and that maybe, if I were dead, I wouldn't be hungry anymore."

Amelie's hand was halfway extended before she remembered Lise wasn't corporeal. The ghost looked so young. She was reminded again that Lise was closer to Honorine's age than her own.

Lise looked up. "I'm not, you know. Hungry."

Well. That was something.

"Being Lise Martin from Montmartre is nothing to be ashamed of," Amelie said. "After all, how many people could boast such an interesting afterlife?"

Lise laughed and kicked the wall one more time.

"Come on. We have to meet Benedict," Amelie said. The ghost nodded and they walked down the hallway together.

Just before the dressing room door Amelie paused. "Lise, were you seeing anyone?"

"No," Lise said.

Amelie nodded and pushed the door open.

"You cheated!" Rachel shouted, and Amelie quickly closed it. "You can't just invent cards! We agreed, a fifty-two-card deck—"

"I don't know what you're talking about," Violette said, patting her wig with dignity. They sat in the middle of the dressing room floor, a pile of slightly hazy playing cards between them.

"I'm talking about your cheating," Rachel said, throwing her hand of cards onto the floor. "You've played five kings this game. You're not even hiding it."

"Count the cards then, if you're so certain," Violette said.

"You'll just change them again!"

"You know, this wouldn't happen if you could invent things yourself," Lise said a little smugly. "You *say* you can't be bothered to change your clothes, but *I* think it's because you aren't able to."

"Does this look like your business?" Rachel stood up and crossed her arms. "No? Then stay out of it."

"It's not like you're even playing for money," Lise said, putting her nose up.

"Now, now, it's not worth the fuss," Violette said, disappearing the deck of cards up a pink beribboned sleeve. "I *may* have taken a liberty or two—"

"*Five kings*," Rachel snarled.

"But it's in the past," she continued merrily, waving a plump hand. "We have much more important matters to discuss. Amelie! Stop standing there like a statue! We have a *gentleman* to meet."

This is life now. You have to get used to it.

Rachel rolled her eyes.

"What are you wearing, dear?" Violette continued. "You

should wear your hair looser than you usually do—men like a little muss, you know—"

Lise passed a hand over her own perfectly smooth hair, transforming it to something curled and romantic.

Amelie peeled out of her rehearsal clothes and washed quickly in the basin. "I'll wear what I usually do," she said. It's not like she had anything else. "He's not really courting me, you know."

"Well, you never know, my girl, you never know. A doctor, and he's rich—"

"Leave her alone," Rachel snapped, surprising Amelie. "Are we going or not? The faster he does whatever he's going to do, the faster I can leave."

"We're going," Amelie said, changing quickly into the same plain gray dress she'd worn to class. She brushed her hair and wound it into a simple bun.

Her gaze fell on the pot of rouge sitting on the dressing table. It had been so long since she'd worn anything but stage makeup. St. Amie didn't use it.

She looked at herself in the mirror. A woman in her thirties, tired. A few lines around her eyes and mouth. Hair too severe; skin too pale. Her hand floated toward the rouge, and then fell. He wasn't really courting her. That was over. He didn't care what she looked like.

"Let's go," she said.

They hurried out the side entrance, only to be greeted with sheets of rain. She'd remembered to send Honorine with an umbrella but had forgotten her own. Through the blueish haze she saw a carriage waiting. He'd really come.

She was halfway across the plaza, arm held uselessly over her head, when an umbrella appeared above her. She glanced up, waterlogged.

"For heaven's sake, you could have waited for me to reach you," Ben said, his voice raised over the din of the raindrops.

The umbrella was large, with room enough for both of them. He was wearing his beautiful coat, and the rain had curled the edges of his hair.

She didn't know what to say. He was smiling, like they were having fun.

"The carriage is this way," he said, offering his arm. She took it.

They hurried across the plaza and into the coach, the three ghosts crowding in next to them. He shook the umbrella off before closing the door, and grinned at her through the raindrops falling from his hair.

"Oh, Ben, now you're soaking," she said. "I was already wet—"

He lifted an eyebrow. "I was supposed to let you run through the rain without an umbrella?"

"It's what I would have done if you hadn't been here—"

"No, no, no," he said, waving a hand to cut her off. "You've got this all wrong. Your line is something like, *Oh, Ben, how wonderful and gallant you are, coming to my rescue like that*—"

"Well—"

"*Without you I probably would have been swept away in the flood*—"

"Ben."

"*Thank you, most handsome and chivalrous Ben, for rescuing not only my life, but my frock*—"

She saw the flowers sitting on the seat. "Did you bring these for me?"

That stifled him immediately. "Er, yes."

They were delicate pink roses, the kind that had used to grow on the fences in her childhood neighborhood. The kind that didn't have many petals but smelled so sweet they were their own *parfumerie*.

"I never see these anymore," she said, burying her face in them. "I didn't know they still grew them. I get so many roses—after a performance the girls have to take my bouquets straight to the hospitals, or there'll be no room in my dressing room. But I haven't seen these since I lived in Montmartre. Thank you."

He cleared his throat. "You're welcome," he said.

She put the flowers carefully in her lap, stroking one hand along the fragile petals, and he spoke to his driver.

He didn't need to bring her flowers. But it would be rude not to accept them. And they were so beautiful.

As they swayed into motion, he pulled out a black leather bag and opened it. Violette, who was sitting next to him, peeked inside.

"Oh, he has all kinds of things in here, all kinds," she said. "And he looked handsome in your memories, but I must say, he's quite something up close."

"Violette," Amelie hissed. "Please."

Benedict looked up. "Are they all here?"

"Er, yes," Amelie said. "Um, Violette is sitting next to you. She doesn't use a last name. And Rachel Bonnard is to my right, and Lise Martin is next to her."

Benedict bowed politely. "It's nice to make your acquaintance," he said. "My name is Benedict Moore. I hope I may be of service."

"*Hello,*" Violette said.

"Hello," Lise echoed, a little nervously.

Rachel sighed and slouched against the seat.

"Amelie, first I'd like to conduct a basic examination. I've never done it before in a moving carriage, but—" He shrugged.

He produced a stethoscope, and after some awkward rearranging he was able to listen to her heart and lungs. He made her track his finger up and down, and then turned her face to the light, looking at her eyes. After a few more tests he leaned back.

"It's a marvel," Ben said. "Physically, you're fine. At least with regards to the ghosts. Your hip obviously is terrible."

He said it offhand, thinking of something else. Amelie froze. *Someone had noticed.*

She was opening her mouth to say something—anything that would make light of it—when the carriage slammed to a sudden halt.

Benedict caught Amelie as she was jolted forward, easing her back onto her seat as the partition window opened. "There's an accident up ahead," the driver said in rapid French. "These stupid drivers—"

"Is it serious?" Amelie asked.

"Three carriages," the driver said, in a tone of disgust. "We'll be here all day at this rate—"

"Ben—"

He was already grabbing his doctor's bag, grateful that he'd needed to bring it for Amelie's exam. "Stay here," he said. "I'll see if they need help."

He stepped out into the rain, jogging along the line of stopped carriages. He could hear the cacophony of voices that usually accompanied an accident, and his jog turned into a run.

When he reached the accident, he was greeted with chaos. One carriage was tipped over on the sidewalk, its horse caught in the traces, wild with fear, and moving the body of the coach in its panic. Two other carriages were tangled together in the street—those horses had been released and the drivers, apparently unharmed, were getting them under control.

He ran toward the carriage on the sidewalk. "I'm a doctor," he shouted in French. "Is anyone hurt?"

The first thing to do was to cut the horse free. A frantic draft horse was approximately one ton of panicked destruction, and if there was anyone in the coach, he wouldn't be able to help them until the situation was stable. "You," he shouted in French to a couple of brawny-looking men in the crowd. "Come help me."

Without waiting to see if they heeded him, he took his knife from his pocket and slowly approached the horse.

"There now," he murmured. "I'm here to—"

The horse reared, kicking out frantically with its hooves and narrowly missing Benedict's head. He took a breath. "Preferably not be kicked in the head," he continued. "Come now, there's a good horse." He got one hand on the bridle, putting all his strength into it. He felt someone next to him. "Take my knife," he said, handing it off. "Cut the traces."

A few moments later, the traces fell away. The horse, free, backed up with eyes rolling in fear, pulling Benedict with him. "It's alright, it's alright," Benedict repeated. "You're alright."

The horse kept backing up until it ran into the building behind it. Startled, it began to rear again, and realizing its head was trapped by Benedict's weight, turned toward the street. It was about to bolt when Benedict's hands were joined by several more.

"We've got him," a man Benedict recognized as one of the drivers from the other carriages said. "There's someone inside there that needs help."

Benedict let go, glancing quickly to make sure the horse wasn't going to cause further destruction, and hurried toward the carriage on its side. A man—the driver, Ben assumed, was partially trapped beneath it, either unconscious or dead.

Another man, quite conscious by the noise he was making, was inside.

He needed to assess the injuries. He stopped by the driver's side, checked his pulse. Alive. Leg crushed. Would certainly die if the bleeding was left unchecked. He opened his satchel and pulled a tourniquet out, applying it quickly. He glanced at the man in the carriage, who was holding his obviously broken arm and screaming. No other obvious injuries, other than some scrapes on his face. Benedict darted quickly to the window of the carriage. "Do you have injuries other than your arm?" he asked.

"What? It's broken, man. Are you a doctor?"

"Yes," Benedict said. "Are there other injuries?"

The man looked at him like he was insane. "My arm is broken!"

He would take that for a no. "Your driver is badly injured," he said, then turned to the crowd. "Someone help this man out of the carriage!"

"My driver— Do you know who I am—"

His shouts faded as Benedict returned to the driver.

The carriage needed to be lifted; he shouted at someone to organize it, and they must have, because as he tried to assess the extent of the injury, a man shouted, "Careful, we're about to lift!" and soon the carriage was off and he could see the whole leg.

It was going to have to come off, that was immediately clear. There was no saving the mangled mess that lay in front of him. For the next unknown stretch of time Benedict was completely absorbed by the man in front of him. He was vaguely aware that someone from the crowd had come to help him, handing him scissors and bandages when he asked. The driver had a second dangerous wound on his chest, and once Benedict was convinced that he wouldn't bleed out from the leg, he focused entirely on that. He was grateful someone had thought to hold an umbrella over them.

"When is the damned ambulance going to get here," he muttered. There was only so much he could do from a city sidewalk.

"They're here," a woman said, and when he looked up, sure enough, they were. He helped them load the man onto a stretcher and into the back of the wagon, giving the hospital trainees staffing it a quick rundown of the injuries and hopping onboard. The man with the broken arm was loaded in as well; several trainees clustered around him, setting the arm.

The hospital was thankfully nearby, and almost as soon as they stopped, an important-looking man in a white coat approached the wagon.

"Good afternoon, Doctor, I'm Doctor Benedict Moore. This man has a crushed leg and a deep wound to the—"

"Thank god. My arm is broken, and this man wouldn't treat me," the man from the carriage said.

"Monsieur Fallet," the doctor exclaimed, rushing to the man's side immediately. "Nurse! Attend me. Find a room for Monsieur Fallet at once, he must be made comfortable—"

"Excuse me," Benedict interrupted. "This patient will die if he is not operated on immediately."

"You—" The doctor turned to him. "Do you know who this is? I will deal with your patient once Monsieur Fallet is comfortable. I don't know who you are, but you've made a very grave mistake, a very grave mistake indeed—"

Benedict took a deep breath, forcing his voice to remain calm. "If you are not willing to perform the procedure, I must ask you to provide me with an operating theater—"

The doctor turned away without another word, accompanying the man from the carriage inside the hospital along with the entire ambulance staff. Benedict was left alone with the unconscious driver.

Or not quite alone.

"Excuse me!"

Amelie—Amelie?—hopped down from the back of the wagon. "*Docteur*—"

"Yes?" The doctor snapped, turning back angrily. He startled when he took in Amelie, her wet hair plastered against her face, blood staining her dress.

"St. Amie? I mean, Mademoiselle St. James?"

She nodded. "Please, *Docteur*, this man is in very grave danger." She clasped her hands together and looked upward in what could only be described as a beatific way. "You have the power to save his life." The words coming from her were not an accusation. It was as if she was passing on a very important message, the same kind Joan of Arc had once received.

The doctor looked torn. On one hand, he had a prestigious patient with a non-life-threatening wound. On the other, he had a working man who would die if not treated and was possibly blessed by God.

"I can spare a theater," he said, apparently deciding this was a good compromise. "Monsieur Bernard, Monsieur Valle." Two of the young men from the ambulance peeled off away from the wealthy man's stretcher. "You will assist him."

Obviously deciding he'd done enough to be right in the eyes of both God and man, the doctor hurried inside the building.

Alright then. "You," Benedict said to one of the men. "Do you know Dr. Durand? On the Rue de Rivoli?"

The young man nodded.

"Good. Fetch him immediately, tell him Dr. Moore requires his assistance for a surgical operation."

Benedict and the remaining trainee picked up the stretcher

and headed into the hospital, Amelie following close behind. He put the mystery of her appearance out of his mind. He was only grateful she'd been there.

Once in the theater, he hurriedly cleaned his hands before preparing the man for surgery. He'd operate himself if he had to, but he hadn't performed an amputation in years—

Benedict let out a sigh of relief when Victor hurried through the doors. "Ben? What's going on? St. A—"

"I need your help, Victor," Benedict said, quickly outlining the situation. Victor's specialty was complicated surgeries, and Benedict was barely finished speaking before Victor was shrugging into a borrowed coat and examining the driver.

"Just tell me what to do," Benedict said, and they got to work.

Two hours later the man was stable, if missing most of a leg. The trainees transferred him to a waiting hospital room.

"I think he'll make it," Victor said. "Lucky for him you were there."

Benedict looked around the room, at the blood and wreckage an amputation left behind. The limb had already been removed, but it was all brutally familiar.

"Thank you," he said. "For coming."

Victor nodded. "Now, do you want to tell me what St. Amie is doing waiting outside?"

"I— We—"

Victor's eyes widened. "She's the dancer you were avoiding. You know her. You *know* her!"

"*Shhh*," Benedict said. "It's . . . damnit, it's hard to explain."

"Oh, wait until Camille hears about this!"

"I—" He wasn't going to lie to Victor, but so much of the truth wasn't his to share. And he wasn't thinking his fastest. The adrenaline that had animated him was gone, leaving him abruptly empty and surrounded by old memories. "I promise to tell you what I can," he said. "Later."

"Oh, fine, I can take a hint," Victor said, going against all available evidence. "But there's a juicy story here, and I'll get to it one way or another. Oh! There's an exhibit tomorrow with some of the young painters I was telling you about, maybe she'd like to come! André will be there. I'm sure she'd like to see his ballerinas!"

The idea of showing Amelie those dainty, impossible creatures felt like harsh wool scratching across the surface of his brain. "We'll see," he said. "Again, thank you, Victor. You saved his life."

Victor shrugged and waved his hands. "They're magic whether I do anything or not," he said carelessly. "I have my carriage here. Do the two of you need a ride?"

Benedict nodded. "Thank you."

"I'll meet you out front," Victor said, and stepped out of the room.

Benedict stayed where he was, the heavy quiet of the room descending around his shoulders. There'd been no quiet the last time he'd done an amputation, only shelling and screaming, the smell of gunpowder and decay in the air. That man had died a few hours later, and several hours after that, Benedict had fallen ill, waking up in a different world.

He heard the door swing open.

"You shouldn't be in here," he said. "There's blood everywhere."

"Yes," Amelie said. "It would be a shame if I got any on my dress."

The wry humor in her voice made him look up. She was covered in blood. Her skirts were caked in it; one particularly gruesome spray went all the way up her bodice. Someone had obviously given her some water, because she'd cleaned her face and hands, but there were still pinkish-red streaks.

Slowly he pieced things together. Amelie, cutting the traces of the frightened draft horse. Amelie, organizing men to lift the carriage. Amelie, handing him instruments from his bag and holding an umbrella over him as he worked.

"I told you to stay in the carriage," he managed, sounding like an absolute fool.

She confirmed this impression with a slight lift of her eyebrows.

"I . . . It must have been quite gruesome."

"I lived through Bloody Week, Ben," she said, walking around the room curiously. "There isn't much that can happen to a body that I haven't seen. Are you alright?"

"What?" He was the one meant to be asking her that.

She picked up a surgical knife that had fallen to the floor and carefully placed it on a tray. "You were far away, just now. And not somewhere pleasant."

He opened his mouth to deny it, but she rolled her eyes.

"You forget I know you," she said. "I can guess where you were. We don't need to talk about it. But we do need to leave, and bathe, and put fresh clothes on, and eat. Most certainly we need to eat."

That was a very sound plan. He made himself nod.

"Good choice," she said. "You were very impressive with that horse earlier. You have very strong muscles."

"Amelie," he said slowly, a flicker of amusement sparking through the fog of memory. "Are you flirting with me in the middle of a blood-soaked operating room?"

"Of course not," she said. "That would be very inappropriate.

I'm distracting you. You may think of this as professional interest—you're a doctor, not a dancer, or a dock worker. You must work to maintain your physique."

He found himself laughing as he washed up. "Forgive me," he said. "Of course. Er, I box. We all do. Sam and Maggie and Henry, our—well, he's our brother, too, but not officially."

"You let your sister box?"

"First of all," he said, drying his hands and arms. "I could never *let* Maggie do anything. No one could; it is a feat beyond humanity's abilities. Second, when we started, we didn't *mean* to teach her. It—it was after my illness. She couldn't have been more than seven or eight. But once she saw the gloves nothing would do but that she learn. Of course, it makes complete sense. She lives to cause me pain."

"Is she good?"

Benedict shrugged. "Enough that she can land hits on all of us," he said. "And they hurt, too."

"I've never met a woman athlete outside of ballet," she said. "I know there are rowing teams, and I've heard of women croquet players, but I've never heard of a boxer before. She sounds impressive."

"She is," he said. "But if you ever tell her I said that—"

"Don't worry," Amelie said, smiling. "I have a sister, too."

Benedict watched her from the corner of his eye as they walked down the hospital hallway. She did know where he had been. It had been a long time since someone had . . . caught him like that. Discomfort was streaked through his gratitude—these days, he was the one who did the catching.

"Victor—that's the doctor I called for, who led the surgery—"

"Dr. Durand. He introduced himself as he was leaving."

"I'm staying with him and his wife," he said. "He offered to drop you off at your apartment."

"An offer I'll gladly accept," she said. "I was not looking forward to explaining the state of my clothes to a cab driver."

"I'm sorry our outing was delayed."

"Yes, it was rather inconsiderate of that man to get himself crushed by a carriage," Amelie said. "I suppose we'll have to make our public debut at a later date."

As they stepped out the front doors of the hospital, Benedict was blinded by a bright flash, and another. He stepped back, reflexively pushing Amelie behind him, before he realized the flashes were accompanied by a clamor of voices.

"Mademoiselle St. James! Dr. Moore!"

"St. Amie!"

"Amelie, over here! Amelie!"

"Or now," Amelie whispered, moving beside him once more.

"Gentlemen," she said, in what Benedict was coming to think of as her saint voice. The journalists crowded closer.

"Mademoiselle St. James, is it true that you and Dr. Moore were involved in a grisly carriage accident? Are you alright?"

"We were not involved in the accident," she said. "Dr. Moore was escorting me to lunch, and we were stopped in the traffic behind the collision. When he realized what was happening, Dr. Moore immediately ran to the scene to help the victims. He saved a man's life."

Benedict looked at her as subtly as he could. She was so smooth, so composed. It was like listening to a statue in a church.

The journalists were shouting again, having obviously gleaned the important piece of information Amelie had just fed them.

"You were going to lunch together? Mademoiselle St. James, is Dr. Moore courting you?"

She blushed. Or rather, she gave the impression of blushing.

No color entered her cheeks, but she looked down, and fluttered her eyelashes just so, and anyone who didn't know her would have sworn she had blushed. He could almost hear the journalists writing the description.

"Gentlemen, you're embarrassing me," she said, smiling ever so slightly and nudging him with her boot. He took that to be his cue.

"Perhaps we can spare the lady these questions," he said. "We've had quite a day, and though she hasn't mentioned it, Mademoiselle St. James acted like quite a heroine at the scene of the crash. I'm sure she's exhausted."

"Dr. Moore! Are you and Mademoiselle St. James romantically involved?"

"You're really putting me on the spot here," he said, becoming more invested in his role. "I'll simply say I hope to see much more of Mademoiselle St. James while I'm in Paris."

They took that as the confirmation he'd intended it to be, and there was more shouting.

"I know you'll all understand if I see her home now," he said, placing a protective hand around Amelie's waist. "Good day."

He pushed his way as politely as possible through the crowd, shielding Amelie with his body. Another round of the flashbulbs was going off and he was almost blinded by the time they reached Victor's carriage.

"What the devil was that?" Victor asked as they piled in and shut the door.

"The press," Benedict said, feeling a little dazed. "Are they always like that?"

"Good lord, no," Amelie said. "We've just handed them the story of the month."

"What story?" Victor asked.

"Later," Benedict repeated, and Victor shrugged, rolling his eyes dramatically, and asked Amelie for her address.

"Fine," he said, when he'd conveyed it to the driver. "But you're accompanying me to all three salons this week, *and* the exhibition opening. Oh, Mademoiselle St. James, I must tell you about this artist I think you'd adore. . . ."

CHAPTER TWELVE

ST. AMIE AND SUITOR RESCUE
CARRIAGE DRIVER
AMELIE ST. JAMES IN ACCIDENT WITH
AMERICAN MAN
WHO IS DR. BENEDICT MOORE?

Amelie set the papers down at the breakfast table, satisfied. The articles contained no hint of scandal, accepting her statement later that day that she and Ben had met "through mutual acquaintances." The pictures accompanying the stories were too dramatic for her taste—even in black and white, the blood on her dress and Benedict's suit was rather lurid—but they would do.

The carriage driver would live, barring infection. Ben had returned the evening prior and found him awake and being pestered by a reporter who'd snuck in disguised as an orderly. After evicting the reporter and checking on the patient, he'd been kind enough to write Amelie a message updating her on the man's condition.

"Morning." Honorine yawned, stumbling into the room.

Amelie quickly flipped the newspapers over, still deciding what to say.

"What are you hiding?" Apparently even half-clouded with sleep, her little sister's eyes were sharp. "Oooh, did you get a bad review? I want to see!"

"No," Amelie said, snatching the papers out of reach.

Honorine rolled her eyes and sat back down. "All the bad ones say the same thing anyway. 'Amelie St. James, the so-called Saint of the Parisian people, performed with her usual technical virtuosity and astoundingly dull purity of spirit last night,'" she said in an officious, nasal voice.

"It's not a bad review. It's—oh, I need to talk to you about something."

Suzanne came into the room bearing coffee and toast. Amelie stretched the moment out by pouring herself a cup of the deliciously scented coffee, breathing in deeply before her first sip. Coffee was one of life's luxuries, one of the things you didn't take for granted if you'd ever had it taken away. Her sleep had been interrupted by dreams of furious, red-eyed dancers again, and the coffee helped chase the last remnants away.

"Well?"

Honorine was staring at her. "You're going to see some stories in the newspaper today, and likely hear talk at school. Yesterday I was . . . A friend of mine and I, we were going to lunch. He's a doctor, this friend. And, um, there was an accident."

"You were in an accident?"

"No! No. There was an accident *ahead* of us. And like I said, he's a doctor, so he—"

"There's a lot of *he* in this explanation so far."

"*He* went to help the people who'd been hurt, and I went with him, and there was this driver who . . . who was quite badly injured, and—"

"Did he *die*?"

"No! Ben—the man—my friend—saved him. Well, he and his friend did."

"And a lot of friends."

"As we were leaving the hospital—"

"When did you go to the hospital?"

"Um, an ambulance came, and we went to the hospital and they operated on him—"

"Did you get to see his *guts*?"

"Honorine!"

"What? I just think it would be quite interesting to see guts, that's all."

Amelie frowned at her little sister. "If his innards had been visible it would have been very bad for him," she said. "As it was, he lost a leg."

"A leg? Did it come off in the accident?"

"No, they cut it off later. *Honorine!* What kinds of questions are these?"

Her sister looked unrepentant. "We're studying anatomy in school."

"Oh," Amelie said. "Well, that actually sounds quite interesting. I'd like to hear more about it later. But what I'm trying to tell you—"

"Is that you have a beau." Honorine took a bite of toast and chewed it. Amelie closed her eyes. Her head was hurting. It was seven in the morning and her head hurt.

"I'm trying to tell you I have a friend, who the papers think is my beau."

"But he's not?"

"No," Amelie said. She'd spent a lot of time turning this decision over in her head, and she'd decided to be as honest as possible. "His name is Dr. Benedict Moore. He's an American."

"An American? Like Alva?"

"Yes. In fact, he's her brother-in-law."

"*Ohhhh.*" This fact made everything slide into place satisfactorily, apparently. "Well, you made such a fuss about it, I thought he must be something shocking." The matter dealt with to Honorine's satisfaction, she took a large slice of the omelet Suzanne had just placed on the table and dug into it. "May I borrow your hairpin again today? Only Marie Collette said how much she liked it, and Bernadine looked practically sick with envy—"

Amelie waved a hand. "Yes, yes. Who am I to stand in the way of you bringing illness to your enemies?"

"Oh, thank you!" The important matter of the morning dealt with, Honorine turned easily to school gossip. Amelie ate her omelet, making appropriate responses when called upon and feeling more than a little exhausted. She poured herself a second cup of coffee.

"Alright, I'm heading out," Honorine said, as Suzanne came back to the dining room with her apron off, prepared to walk Honorine to school. "Try not to amputate any legs today."

"You're so funny," Amelie said flatly, making her sister cackle delightedly. "Have a good day. I love you."

"I love you, too," Honorine said, the door closing behind her, leaving Amelie in the sudden quiet of her apartment.

Amelie finished her coffee, took her dishes to the kitchen, and walked back into the sitting room. Her body was stiff and sore this morning—well, it was stiff and sore most mornings, but yesterday's excitement had transformed her muscles into lead. She sighed, put on her ballet slippers, and padded to the barre.

Easy motions first, some leg swings and ankle circles, to get a trickle of warmth into her body. She looked out the window as she moved, her limbs needing no guidance to follow the motions they'd been doing for twenty-five years.

Yesterday's rain had stopped in the night, leaving an unusually clean Paris behind. The morning sun glinted off shiny sidewalks and orange and red leaves, promising a beautiful October day. Her eyes drifted up Montmartre to the construction site of the new basilica, and away.

Ben saved that man's life, she thought, as she began the first series of hip stretches. Another doctor would have helped the wealthy man first, as a matter of course. Ben had helped the person who was most injured, like the status of the patient didn't matter.

He'd grown into something rather wonderful.

And oh, she wished the warmth that came with that thought didn't have an edge of bitterness. She was so glad for him. But she wished—

She glanced at the cleared land on Montmartre Butte again, an ugly reminder of what had come before. No. She wished for nothing but survival.

"That's not very nice," Lise said, leaning against the wall. "You should extend the line more."

Amelie frowned, looking down at her body. She'd been sketching something out while she thought—she couldn't remember what. Lise was right, it wasn't attractive. Her arms resembled a mangled doll's. She lengthened immediately, turning the motion into a graceful extension, and closed in fifth.

"That's right," Rachel said, from the couch. "God forbid you do something unattractive."

Oh lord, they were all here. Violette was looking in the mirror over the fireplace, patting her extraordinary wig. Today's wig theme was nautical—there were little ships tucked into the curls of the hair, and a stuffed seagull perched atop, looking smugly satisfied with its afterlife.

"Have you figured out how to change your clothes yet?" Lise asked in silky-sweet tones.

"Have you figured out how to—"

"Ladies, good morning," Amelie said. Her head still hurt. Until this matter was solved, she was going to have a perpetual headache. "How are you?"

"Good," Lise said.

"Dead," Rachel said.

"Just fine, dear, just fine," Violette said, wandering over to the windows. "Pay me no mind, I'm only having an outing. Oh my, you ought to put something on these balconies. Look at your neighbors! They even have a potted rose over there. You ought to buy something like that, these look terribly bare. I don't think I've told you how smart this new apartment is, and when I think about your last one—well, you surely have come up in the world, my girl, and I couldn't be more proud."

"It's a monstrosity," Rachel said, looking at the older woman like she'd lost her mind. "It's a decorated box. Do you know what used to be here? A neighborhood. People used to live here, people like me and you—"

"I know that very well," Violette said, with a hint of tartness. "I was one of them. Lived about ten minutes south of here, for a good long while. I wasn't any happier than you about getting pushed out, but I can still be happy one of ours has made it big enough to live in a place as fancy as this, can't I?"

No one had anything to say to that. Amelie felt the familiar guilt opening a hole in the bottom of her stomach. She lived on bones—the bones of dead people and dead neighborhoods.

"Rachel's right," Amelie said. In the silence that followed, she crossed to the pile of correspondence Suzanne had left on the entry table, picking it up and flipping through it idly. Letters from admirers, a bill—and a white envelope with crisp black handwriting from Ben. She dropped the rest on the table, tore it open, skimmed its contents, and began reading aloud.

Dear Amelie and Lise,

I visited the morgue after our conversation yesterday, as part of our inquiries. Lise's body is still being held there, as she has no living kin. I'm writing for two reasons—to request Lise's permission to examine it, and to ask what arrangements you would like to have made for it. I believe determining Lise's cause of death would be helpful to our investigation, but I also understand it may be a matter of some sensitivity. Please let me know what you'd like to do.

Your humble servant,
Benedict Moore

The note was respectful but blunt, like him. Amelie looked at Lise questioningly. "Well, Lise? What would you like to do?"

"Oh," Lise said. "It's so thoughtful of him. Yes, of course. Please write him immediately and give my permission."

Amelie nodded. She sat down at her writing desk to write a reply, but before she'd written a word Lise spoke again.

"I shall also attend," she announced.

Amelie put the pen down.

"Oh no, I don't think that's wise," Violette said, into the stunned silence.

"I agree," Amelie said slowly. "It seems a bit . . ."

"Dramatic," Rachel said.

"Risky," Amelie finished. "It could . . . upset you."

"And then you might go insane and kill someone, again," Rachel said. "Not that it wouldn't be amusing—"

"You've killed *triple* the people I have," Lise said.

"Yes, *in combat*. I didn't 'dance them to death,' my god."

"Girls, let's simply agree you've both killed people," Violette said. "Now, Lise, Amelie's right. Why would you want to do such a thing? It's morbid, that's what it is. You don't need to see your body, my goodness. Who knows what might happen?"

"Nothing would happen," Lise said, flinging her arms wide. "And who better than me to be there while *my* body is being examined? Benedict asked for my permission, after all. *He* understands."

"Lise, I don't know that he meant it as an invitation—"

"My body, my terms."

"It's only the meat, you stupid girl," Rachel said.

"You're just jealous because your body got thrown into a mass grave somewhere," Lise said. "Who knows what it looks like now."

Well that was an upsetting thought. *I really need to stop associating with dead people.*

"I'm going," Lise said. "That's my final word."

Amelie closed her eyes. Maybe when she opened them, they'd be gone.

No such luck.

"I can't imagine they'll let me in the examination room," she said. "If I accompany Ben inside the building, will that get you close enough to go on your own?"

Lise nodded enthusiastically. "*Yes*," she said. "Thank you."

"I need to write Benedict," Amelie said. "I suppose we're going to the morgue."

The Paris morgue was open seven days a week to the viewing public, and the viewing public had rewarded it by making it the tourist attraction of the decade. Fashionably located behind Notre-Dame on the Île de la Cité, mere feet from the river from which it pulled so many of its occupants, it was an absolute must-visit for tourists and locals alike.

The main attraction was the curtained Exhibition Room, where unidentified bodies, often attractive young girls clad only in a simple white sheet, were displayed behind a window. The morgue claimed this was for "identification purposes." The guidebooks simply said it was the place to be seen.

The perfect weather of the morning had held, giving the area around the morgue a festive feel. The line for the Exhibition Room wove along the back gardens of Notre-Dame and vendors walked alongside it, hawking gingerbread and oranges and lemonade to eager sightseers.

Amelie sat on a bench slightly removed from the crowd, waiting for Benedict. The ghosts had disappeared, wherever it was they went—into her head or back to . . . she didn't want to think about that. She assumed Lise would show up at the appropriate time.

She saw Ben before he saw her. He was easy enough to spot, towering over most of the people he passed. When he spotted her, he lifted a hand, and a little warm spot blossomed underneath her ribs.

But as he approached, she saw he was frowning.

"Amelie, I'm not sure this is a good idea."

She lifted her hands to stave off argument. "Me neither," she said. "But Lise is quite insistent, and you have to agree she has a right to be present if she wishes."

He frowned more deeply. "Lise, I— Wait, is she here?"

"I have no idea," she said. "She can probably hear you."

"Lise, this could be quite upsetting."

Lise appeared to Amelie's left, between her and Benedict. "Tell him I thank him for his concern, but I'm hardly going to miss my own medical examination."

"She says to thank you for your concern," Amelie repeated. "But she's going to be there."

"Amelie, and I'm only talking to you right now, are you certain you're ready for this?"

"We've discussed it," she said. "I'll wait outside. I need to make funeral arrangements for her anyway."

"I'd like pink silk for my coffin lining," Lise said. "I've been thinking about it. And white roses. And the priest . . ." Suddenly her face clouded. "Amelie. What if they decide I'm a suicide? They won't bury me. They won't bury me! I won't be allowed in hallowed ground, and—"

"It's alright," Amelie soothed. The hair on her arms was standing straight in the air. "*Shhh.* They'll bury you."

"But what if I did do it?"

"Then I'll bribe the priest," Amelie said, condemning herself to further time in purgatory without a second thought. Suddenly there were shadows, and it was noon. "You'll be buried in sacred ground. *I promise.* Go take . . . whatever the ghost equivalent of a breath is."

After a long, tense moment, Lise disappeared. So did the shadows.

"Good," Amelie said. She turned to Ben. He had an odd look on his face.

"That is . . . very strange to watch," he said. "Did you know that you don't say all the words in your sentences?"

"I don't?"

He shook his head and bent, taking her chin in hand, doing that thing where he stared at her eyes. "I got the general idea," he said. "But I'd guess you're only saying every second or third word. You're skipping the connectors."

Well, that was unpleasant to think about.

"How do you feel?"

"Fine," she said. He held her gaze, and she saw the worry in his eyes. "I'm fine. Let's go."

She stood, giving him no more time to argue, and started walking toward the morgue. The crowds were thick, but once he caught up, they parted easily enough.

"You'd think they'd have seen enough dead bodies," she murmured.

Ben steered her toward a side entrance, the one for "official business," and pushed open the heavy, blocky door.

It was cold inside. She blinked in the low light, making out a tall desk in front of her and a young man in a white coat behind it.

Condensation dripped from the ceiling onto her shoulder. She startled.

"They use water for cooling," Ben said, his warm, low voice calming her. "It creates an unpleasant atmosphere, but it's quite efficient. Good afternoon," he said in French to the man behind the counter. "Is Director Fauré available? Please tell him Dr. Benedict Moore and Mademoiselle Amelie St. James are here to see him."

In the darkness, Amelie almost missed the way the young man's eyes widened. "Of course," he said. "Immediately."

"The man I dealt with yesterday," Ben said quietly. "When I was here gathering information."

There was a bustling at the doorway behind the counter, and a thin, middle-aged man with gray hair and another white coat entered. "Dr. Moore," he said. "Mademoiselle St. James?"

"It's nice to meet you, Dr. Fauré," she said. "I wish it were under better circumstances."

"Er, yes," he said. "Dr. Moore, I'm afraid there's been a change of circumstances."

Did he look nervous? Amelie watched him through carefully pleasant eyes as he rattled on. His muscles were quite tense.

People often didn't realize that the first rule in lying was to relax your body.

"I was mistaken about our policy," he was saying. "Your medical degree is American, and it appears we can only allow French accredited doctors examination privileges."

"You're the director of the morgue," Ben said. "How could you be mistaken about your own policy?"

"Er, yes, well, it's been quite a while since— I mean, we aren't often visited by foreign doctors—but when it was brought to my attention—"

"By whom?"

"I beg your pardon?"

"As I said, you're the director. Who brought it to your attention?"

"A—a colleague," the man replied.

"I see," Ben said. "Will a letter from the Minister of Health do?"

"I—I'm sorry?"

"I imagine he has the power to override whatever rules your colleague reminded you of," Benedict said, smiling politely.

"You— The Minister of Health is a very busy man—"

"Very," Ben agreed. "He complains about it constantly. Fortunately, I'll be seeing him tomorrow for supper."

Silence fell in the room, punctuated only by the drip of condensation from the ceiling.

"Perhaps . . . perhaps a very brief examination . . ."

"Alright," Benedict said. "While I do that, you can discuss funeral arrangements with Mademoiselle St. James."

"Funeral—no. I'm sorry, that won't be happening. I can't release her body to you."

"What do you mean?" Amelie said, startled. "She has no living relatives."

"I'm so sorry, Mademoiselle St. James. And may I say, I'm such an admirer of yours. It's so like you to want to do something kind, to extend your dignity over one who was unworthy of it."

"I'm afraid I don't take your meaning," she said, putting every bit of ice she was capable of into her words.

"But you are not her relative," he continued. "And I may only release her body to her kin."

"But . . . she doesn't have any," she repeated. "She was part of the corps de ballet. In the absence of family, she's the responsibility of the Paris Opera Ballet. I am here as their representative." That last part was a lie, but then, she was a very good liar.

"I'm afraid it's impossible," he said, shaking his head. "I wish it were different!"

"What—what will happen to her?"

"After Dr. Moore's examination, she'll be buried."

"You'll put her in a mass grave, with no marker, when I'm standing right here—"

"No, he won't," Ben said, quite comfortably. He leaned easily against the counter. "Director Fauré is not that foolish."

"I'm not? I mean, what do you mean?"

"You're a career man," he said. "You don't want to risk offending the wrong people. I understand, you're being careful here. And we'll play along, for now. But I'd advise you to have a long think about power tonight, and who has it. It may not be the people you expect."

"I don't like what you're implying," Director Fauré said stiffly.

"I'm not implying anything," Ben said with another pleasant smile. "Now, if you'll show Mademoiselle St. James to a room she can wait in, I'll conduct my examination."

Director Fauré looked as if he had changed his mind about

allowing any examination at all, but he nodded crisply. "Follow me," he said. "You may wait in my office, Mademoiselle."

They followed him to an oddly plush office. Every chair and settee was heavily upholstered, and a thick maroon rug covered the floor. There was even a tapestry hanging on one wall.

"Please make yourself comfortable," he said. "I will return with Dr. Moore in a quarter of an hour."

Fifteen minutes? That was all the morgue was going to allow? She opened her mouth to protest, but Benedict shook his head, and the two men left.

What *on earth* was going on here?

"Lise," she whispered. "You'd better hurry if you don't want to miss them. And *do not* get upset."

"I won't," Lise said, standing by the doorway. She held a white veil in her hand, the one the Wilis wore when they first appeared onstage. With great import, she shook it out, placed it over her head, and drifted through the door.

"Rachel has a point," Amelie muttered, sitting down in a soft chair. "She really is *very* dramatic."

A grandfather clock ticked loudly in the corner. Amelie crossed her ankles, uncrossed them, recrossed them in the opposite direction. The room had a muffled quality to it, likely the result of all the fabric and padding.

Director Fauré had been nervous. Perhaps he'd overpromised to Benedict earlier and someone had reprimanded him? And now he was embarrassed and being unnecessarily strict?

She uncrossed her ankles again and stood, idly looking around the room. The wooden desk was large and ornate, standing before a large wood and glass cabinet containing the morgue's files behind its locked doors. There were windows on one wall, but the curtains covering them were heavy and embroidered, and only a soft, mild light filtered through.

Amelie tapped her foot and glanced at the clock. She looked inside her purse to see what she'd brought with her, then she patted her hair, taking out a hairpin.

She looked at it, pursing her lips. It was the one with the pearl on the end that Honorine so coveted. It was a very nice hairpin.

The thing about growing up in Montmartre was that sometimes you learned things a gently reared girl would not. For example, how cheap most furniture locks were, and how easy the mechanism usually was to wiggle open. It had been years, of course. Idly, she wondered if she still had the knack.

Before she could talk herself out of it, she was behind the desk, delicately inserting the hairpin into the cabinet lock. She'd barely moved the pin before the lock opened—it was practically a prop. She didn't waste time looking over her shoulder before she opened it, running her fingers over the files and carefully noting the first letters of the last names until she came to *M*.

It was harder from there. She had to read the full names quickly and accurately, and she was a slow reader. Finally, she saw it—Lise Martin. A quick glance at the clock. The men had been gone ten minutes. Panic crawled up her chest, but she forced it down. She crouched on the floor and opened the file, carefully moving her finger line by line, until she understood.

Oh, she thought. *Poor Lise.*

She closed the folder, put it back, and relocked the cabinet. She'd sat in her chair and was just crossing her ankles when the door opened and the men walked in, followed by a gently drifting Lise. She took off her veil, holding it vaguely in her hands.

The men did not appear to be speaking, tension boiling between them. She and Ben left the morgue, Lise trailing behind them.

"She didn't drown," he said quietly. "They're covering something up. I confronted him, once I'd confirmed she was dead before her body went in the river. He denied knowing anything, but—"

Amelie nodded, leading the two of them to a secluded area by the cathedral fence.

"I broke into Fauré's files," she said. "Lise—"

How to say this? How to break the news of someone's death to them?

"Lise, I'm so sorry," she said. "Fauré *was* bribed, and he did falsify the report. He kept the original, though. I suspect it was possible blackmail."

The girl in front of her was so very young.

"Tell me," Lise said. "I can handle it."

"You died of a morphine overdose at an apartment near the Champs-Élysées," Amelie said. "The man you were with—unnamed—believed it to be accidental. We can assume he didn't want to be found with you, so he . . . moved your body to the river."

There had been a man, after all.

Lise shook her head, her brown eyes confused. "No," she said. "He wouldn't have—"

"Will you tell me his name?" Amelie asked, her voice gentle.

Lise took a step back, still shaking her head. "The file was wrong," she said. "A morphine overdose—alright, yes. That's possible. We—I used it occasionally. But he wouldn't have—he wouldn't have just *dumped* me—"

"Lise—"

"He *wouldn't* have, Amelie," Lise said. "He couldn't have. It's wrong. You'll look into it more. He didn't. No."

"Lise—"

But the ghost was gone.

The crowds of merrymakers seemed very far away now, their laughter and babble floating in as if from another world.

"I understood most of that," Ben said. "Are you alright?"

"No," Amelie said, looking at the space where Lise had been. "He just threw her in the river, Ben. Like she was nothing."

"Did she tell you his name?"

Amelie shook her head. She didn't tell him it wouldn't make a difference anyway. "At least now I can blackmail Fauré into releasing her body," she said, sitting heavily on a bench.

He sat next to her. "Let me do it," he said. "Blackmail's a little out of character for St. Amie."

She didn't know why the statement made her laugh, but it did. She closed her eyes and tilted her head back, feeling the autumn sun on her face. They sat quietly, the noise of the crowd swirling around them. After a few minutes, the cathedral bells began to toll the hour, pulling her back to the present.

"I have to go to rehearsal," she said, standing. "Oh, I heard back from Bonnet. We're invited for lunch next week."

"That was fast," Ben said.

"If he wants to see you, he'll arrange it quickly enough," Amelie said, only half paying attention. Her hip had stiffened while they'd sat and standing had ignited a sharp line of pain running down her leg. "He's cantankerous and eccentric, but, well, decent enough. I'll accept?"

"Yes," he said. "Thank you. I'm really incredibly grateful."

"Aid for aid," she said. The pain was fading slowly to a manageable level.

"How long has it been like this?"

"Bonnet's reclusiveness?"

"You know what I'm talking about," he said. "Your hip. How long?"

This was the problem with associating with doctors. She thought about lying, but—she didn't like to, not to Ben.

Instead she shrugged, made her voice casual. "It's an old

injury," she said. "I've had some version of it for probably half my career. That's part of being a dancer. We all have something."

"This is more than just something," he said. His voice was quiet, calm. "Have you spoken to a doctor?"

"No," she said. "I can't risk the gossip. If word got out, I'd lose my place. It only has to last another two years. I can retire then."

"Amelie," he said, slowly. "It's not going to."

"It will," she said. "It will because it has to. I have to go, Ben. Thank you for today."

She hurried away, leaving him on the bench, and hailed a cab. As they rolled away, she turned to see him one last time. He was still sitting, writing in his notebook.

The panic his words had sparked, the grief and anger for Lise, all pressed against her throat and chest. She needed to push it away, collect herself for rehearsal.

But she was so tired. She leaned against the carriage wall, and as they crossed the river, she simply stared out the window, watching the crowds along the banks enjoy the beautiful weather.

CHAPTER THIRTEEN

Amelie woke stiff and cold the next morning. She'd dreamed of bizarre, unsettling images: broken limbs and white silk tutus and horses running through bright pink water. All she wanted was to roll over in bed, cover her head in a blanket, and go back to sleep.

But she couldn't.

Tonight was a performance night. She needed to get up, make sure Honorine got off to school, warm up, go to class, fine-tune some steps, sit for an interview, warm up again, and then dance a two-hour ballet on a hip that currently felt like it belonged to an eighty-year-old woman.

Lise hadn't come back.

Amelie forced herself to move. She sat on the side of the bed, carefully testing her hip. It was bad—her fault, she'd been paying less attention to everything since the ghosts. She should have put in two more hours of practice yesterday, and she'd barely managed the most perfunctory stretches before collapsing into bed.

She was so tired.

Her head descended into her hands of its own free will. It was as though every muscle in her body had gone stiff and every bone had turned to jelly.

"Oh, stop feeling sorry for yourself. At least you *have* a body."

Amelie dragged her head up and found Rachel leaning in the doorway, triumphantly—and rather ostentatiously—smoking a cigarette.

"You figured out how to conjure things," Amelie said, her throat hoarse. "Can you taste it?"

"No," Rachel said. "But I feel more myself with it."

Amelie pushed herself up.

"Your little friend is mad at you," Rachel said.

The messenger really does get shot.

"Do you remember that time I put sand in your pointe shoes?"

"Yes." She was still mad about it. "I never got it all the way out."

Rachel laughed. She took a long drag of her cigarette before dropping it to the floor and grinding it into invisibility with her heavy boot.

"You don't go back," she said. "To the old neighborhood."

"I see you've been helping yourself to my thoughts," Amelie said.

"Don't delude yourself," she said. "They aren't that interesting. It's mostly *My hip hurts* and *How much will that cost* and *Ben really is awfully pretty, isn't he?*"

Amelie narrowed her eyes. If the woman had been corporeal, she would have thrown a pillow at her. "Death did not improve your personality," she said.

Rachel grinned. "Well that's hardly saint-like," she said. "Anyway, I'm not here to fight."

"That would be a first."

"I never liked you," Rachel said, sitting next to Amelie on the bed.

"You're not very good at this whole no-fighting thing."

"I never liked you. But I respected you."

"The bourgeois doll?"

"The dancer," Rachel said, lighting another cigarette. "You worked hard. Maybe I was jealous sometimes, that you had something you loved that much. The way your mother loved you. My brothers—there were so many of us, and not enough food or clothes or attention, and the two of you always seemed like you were in this better world, one all your own."

Amelie looked down. The wood floor was still new, barely scuffed. "We were," she said, after a moment.

"I was sorry she died," Rachel said.

"I didn't know you knew."

"That Leonie St. James had died of syphilis? Everyone in Paris knew. Even revolutionaries."

"Yes. I suppose they did."

Rachel herself would have died only a few months later.

"Does your sister remember? How she died?"

"I don't know," Amelie said. "I hope not."

Rachel nodded. "I hope not, too."

Abruptly, Amelie remembered she *had* gone to see Rachel's parents, after the boys had died. The memory was cloudy with grief—Rachel's brothers had all died on the battlefield in the last desperate weeks of the Franco-Prussian War, within a month of Leonie's death. Amelie hadn't known what to do, but she'd gone, after the Siege was over. She hadn't had anything to bring—she remembered feeling vaguely embarrassed, looking around the empty garret for the food she didn't have. She'd gone, and sat with Rachel's mother for an hour, and then she'd left.

"I'm sorry about your brothers," Amelie said. "I never got the chance to tell you."

"Yes," Rachel said. "Well."

"They were good men," Amelie said. They had been, mostly. "Boys, I suppose."

"Boys, killed in a war waged by wealthy old men, for nothing but unearned pride and glory," Rachel said, and Amelie nodded, because it was true.

The Franco-Prussian War had been an extravagant folly. The French Emperor had fancied his forces a match for the enormous, disciplined Prussian Army. He had thought to buttress his support and influence; instead, his troops were massacred, Paris spent months under siege, tens of thousands of people died, and in the end, the Prussians spent a week in the city and went home, leaving behind a government that looked an awful lot like the one that had come before. Paris was grieving and hungry and *furious*, and it was in that climate that the Commune arose.

"I'm not here to talk about the past, either," Rachel said. "I need a favor. I want you to go visit my parents. I need to know that they're alright. You don't see them anymore, so I can't pull from your thoughts."

Such a slight request. An hour of her time—she could fit it in before the interview. Silly to feel such resistance. She'd lived in that building almost her whole life. It wouldn't hurt her to go back.

She opened her mouth to agree, but the words refused to come out.

"I don't want to be here, Amelie," Rachel said quietly. "I don't know why I am. The longer I stay, the more I . . . oh, it's like I'm becoming part of the world again, but I don't fit anymore. There's no place for me. Two days ago, I barely remembered I had parents, and now I miss them. But I can't talk to them, I can't touch them. It's horrible."

"I'm so sorry," Amelie whispered. "I wish I knew how to fix it."

"Save your pity," Rachel said. "Just go see my parents."

"I'll go this afternoon."

"Thank you," Rachel said, nodding curtly.

"Wait," Amelie said, before she could disappear. "Rachel, do you remember how you died?"

"Every second of it," Rachel said. "Bastards."

And she was gone.

Amelie sat on her bed, feeling the chill from the window behind her. She could hear Honorine and Suzanne in the kitchen, starting their days.

So she was going back to the old neighborhood today. She'd gained so many lies, so many secrets since she and Rachel had been girls there. They weighed her down, made her stiff and heavy. She closed her eyes and imagined herself *before,* before the first one had landed upon her, prompting all the rest.

Well, she'd made her choices, and she still didn't see any better ones. Honorine was safe, and she'd continue to be so. She would sacrifice every single other thing to make it so.

She got up and went to the kitchen, pasting a smile on her face. She ate breakfast with her sister, laughed, listened to her stories. When Honorine and Suzanne left, she did her secret warm-up. She went to class, where for a few minutes she got warm enough that the pain in her hip faded. When it was over, the pain was back, and it was time to go to Montmartre.

She took the bus up the hill. She'd taken too many cabs recently—her two-year estimate was based on frugality.

The walk from the bus stop to the old building was in her bones. Little had altered in the last three years—a cafe had changed names, an apartment building had a bright new coat of paint, but the streets were the same.

She could feel her mother in these streets.

Amelie didn't know who her father was. Her mother had never said—Amelie wasn't sure she knew—but it hadn't mattered. Montmartre was matrilineal. Men came and went in those curvy, rustic streets, and women stayed. It wasn't uncommon for three or even four generations of women to live together under one rather shabby roof.

Amelie's mother had come to Paris at sixteen, an extraordinarily pretty girl who, like so many other extraordinarily pretty girls, came from the countryside to seek a better outlet for their talents. Paris was not the fertile ground it pretended to be in so many youthful imaginations, and most of these fresh-faced country roses faded quickly and almost without resistance into the general grime of the city.

But Leonie St. James had been more than pretty. She'd been brilliant, and ambitious, and . . . wonderful.

Amelie's first memories were beautiful: pictures of love and safety. No matter what job her mother had—first at a laundry, waiting at a cafe next, and then she'd caught the eye of a powerful man—there'd always been time for laughter and dancing. That kind of love was too easy to take for granted; you didn't even notice it until it was gone.

Here was the corner they'd passed every day on the way to the ballet school, and here was the cafe she'd worked in. She would have been younger than Amelie then.

You really do look like her. A memory of de Lavel's voice, his hands on her costumes, pushed its way into her mind.

He wasn't in these streets. Anytime he'd come to the apartment it had been in a shiny black carriage, not an uncommon sight in Montmartre. The nighttime brought plenty of them, up the hill from the Grands Boulevards.

She didn't want to think of him. She didn't want to think of those years at all.

And then, there she was, in front of the apartment building she'd spent most of her life in.

The building was three stories, painted the same faded pink it had been for as long as Amelie could remember. It was attached on one side to a brick building with a cafe on the bottom, and on the other, to an old stone house with a second-story addition of timber and plaster.

She and Leonie had lived in the attic apartment. When there had been money, neither had wanted to leave, and later, when there had not, they couldn't afford to. The roof sloped steeply, so you had to duck when walking into the single bedroom. The main room was long, with windows on one side and a very small kitchen at the end. The wood floor had been in a terrible state, but Leonie had managed to scrape together the funds to have a carpenter replace a small part of it and install a little barre, so Amelie could practice.

She wondered if the barre was still there.

The outer door swung open easily when she pulled. The lock had been broken for at least five years before she'd moved—apparently the landlord was still too cheap to replace it.

Inside, the building was dark, narrow, and smelled like mold. The stairs creaked as she climbed them.

Her throat tightened as she ran her hand over the familiar banister. Nothing had changed. She had left, and her old life, the one she'd lived with her mother, had kept going.

She missed it desperately, while also wanting to run away and never see any of it again. This building held the best and worst moments of her life, inextricably tied together.

Rachel's parents had lived on the second floor. As she lifted her hand to knock, she suddenly realized they might have moved—the two-bedroom apartment had been impossibly small for a family of six, but for only two . . . Well, even if they had, the current tenants might know where they had gone. She knocked on the door, and after a few seconds, it opened.

Rachel and her mother looked alike. The woman at the door had the same dark eyes and sharp nose, but where her daughter burned with intense, barely restrained energy, Madame Bonnard was simply tired.

"Amelie," she said, surprised, before she simply stopped speaking, as if it were too much energy to find words.

"Hello, Madame," Amelie said. "I was in the old neighborhood and wanted to pay you a call."

She hadn't thought how odd it would sound. She'd never been close with Rachel's family—likely hadn't been in this apartment since the death of Rachel's brothers.

"Oh." Rachel's mother blinked. "Come in, please."

"Thank you."

The Bonnards' apartment had always been a piece of crowded chaos—too much furniture, too many children, too much noise, too many chores to keep up with. Now it was quiet, and perfectly, immaculately clean.

"I'll get Monsieur Bonnard. He'll want to see you. Please, sit."

Amelie sat on their old sofa, looking around. Photographs of the boys in their neat military uniforms hung above the fireplace. They'd been older than her. Now they were forever in their early twenties, as the people they grew up with aged without them.

There were no photographs of Rachel.

The Bonnards came into the small room. Monsieur Bonnard was a tall man, broad-shouldered and bent. He'd spent most of his adult life as a builder, and his arms and hands were battered and scarred.

"Amelie St. James," he said, smiling at her. "I haven't seen you in years. We see your picture, of course."

"Monsieur Bonnard, it's good to see you. I—I was in the

neighborhood. I, um, I brought a cake." She pulled the cake she'd asked Suzanne to make from her basket and gave it to Rachel's mother.

"Thank you," Madame Bonnard said, staring down at the cake in confusion. "I'll . . . put it in the kitchen."

"Pull down that good wine while you're back there," Rachel's father said. "It's not every day someone famous comes to call."

"Oh, please—"

"No, I insist," he said, waving down Amelie's protests. "St. Amie, here in our sitting room."

She managed a laugh. "Monsieur Bonnard, you caught me hiding a frog in Madame Jessup's purse when I was six," she said. "You of all people know I'm hardly a saint."

"I know you're a good girl," he said. "You give a lot of people hope, my dear. Don't forget that."

Rachel's mother came back into the room, carrying a wine bottle and three glasses. Her husband poured.

"To your health," he said, and drank.

"How is your sister?" Madame Bonnard asked.

"Well, thank you," Amelie said, grateful to have something to talk about. "She's at St. Mary's Academy. The things they teach her there—I was at the ballet school, so I only learned the basics. She told me she's learning anatomy! I suppose that's what they teach these days."

Monsieur Bonnard nodded. "Felt like that when the boys were in school. I never had anything more than some basic math and writing, and they'd come home talking about numbers I swear I'd never heard of."

He laughed, and Amelie joined him. It was surprisingly nice to talk to someone who'd raised children. Few members of the ballet had children, and if they did, those children were usually very young. She didn't have time to socialize with the parents at Honorine's school very often, and she had no relatives she knew of.

"Yes," she said. "And the things she can do with them! She can cover entire pages with her figures. Actually," she said, smiling, "she reminds me a bit of Rachel. When we were about Honorine's age she won that prize at her school—the one for mathematics. She was so proud of it. I'm afraid I was terribly jealous."

It was as though the air had gone out of the room.

"Oh," she said. "I'm so sorry—"

Rachel's mother waved a vague hand. Her father stared at the floor, not looking up.

Grief was a hard and strange thing. Some people wanted to hear their loved ones remembered, others didn't. She'd assumed, when Rachel's father mentioned the boys, that the Bonnards were in the first category.

"The boys were good at math," Monsieur Bonnard said.

Amelie glanced at Madame Bonnard, unsure. The woman shook her head, ever so slightly.

"What are you working on now, Monsieur Bonnard?" Amelie said, choosing a question quite at random.

As he talked about the project he was on, one of the new, enormous "department" stores down the hill, Amelie surreptitiously scanned the room again. There were other pictures of the boys scattered around, in addition to the three over the mantel, but not one of Rachel. In fact, there wasn't a single thing in the room to indicate the Bonnards had ever had a daughter.

They talked a little longer, and when the clock on the opposite wall indicated she'd been there the polite half hour, she stood and thanked them. She'd seen enough to assure Rachel her parents were reasonably secure.

"No, thank *you*," Monsieur Bonnard said, as if the awkward moment had never happened. His tone was overly kind, and it itched at her skin. "I can't wait to tell everyone in the building who came to visit."

She nodded uncomfortably. "It was nice to see both of you," she said. "Um, if you ever want tickets to the ballet, please—"

"Really?" Rachel's father's eyes lit up. "You'd give us tickets?"

"Of course," she said, her discomfort increasing. She'd give anyone in her old neighborhood tickets, but no one had ever asked. Did they think she fancied herself above them?

"We'd love that," Monsieur Bonnard said. "Thank you, very much."

She nodded again, and after a few more awkward pleasantries, bid them goodbye and walked out of the building.

She paused outside the old, broken door, half-wondering if Rachel would appear. When she didn't, she squared her shoulders and glanced at her watch. She would have to hurry to catch the bus if she was going to make the interview on time. St. Amie was never late.

The Passage des Panoramas was a long, grand, covered alley, lined with shops and filled with food hawkers and street performers and throngs of people escaping the rain. Amelie had chosen it, saying the crowds made it a perfect location for a public yet private conversation.

"The more we're seen, the less people will gossip," she'd said.

Two days had passed since their trip to the morgue. Ben had another lengthy telegram from Sam in his pocket and an equally lengthy list of questions in his head.

"Lise thought the answer might be to find out . . . what happened to her," Amelie said, choosing her words carefully. No one was listening, and they spoke in English, but still they spoke only vaguely. "But she's still here. I feel her. And Rachel said she knows exactly how she . . . left, so even if that's part of the answer, it isn't true for all of them."

"It might be that Lise has to accept it," Benedict said. "She still hasn't reappeared?"

"Rachel said she's angry at me," Amelie said. "I can't blame her."

"You told her the truth," he said.

She laughed a little. "You're a doctor," she said. "You should know better than most that the truth isn't always easy to hear."

He inclined his head, acknowledging the point, and running yet again through what they knew. Rose de Boer, the ghost that Sam and Alva had encountered, had used people's fears as a way into their minds. She had lived a brutal, frightened life, and that fear had kept her fragmented spirit tethered to the mortal world for decades after her body had left it.

This was completely different. Rose had haunted multiple people, and had been tied to the house she was born in. The ghosts in Amelie's head were apparently tied to her, and with one exception—when Lise danced the man in the dressing room to his death—only appeared to her. When Rose had haunted people, they'd often fallen unconscious; Amelie could dance a two-hour ballet while hosting hers. Nor were Lise, Rachel, and Violette fragmented.

"You're scowling," Amelie said through her perfect public smile. She stopped to look at some paste jewelry laid out on a table. "People will think we're having a fight."

He blew out a breath and feigned interest in the very ugly brooches before him. "I'm thinking about your brain," he said.

"I don't know whether to be insulted or . . . insulted," she murmured. "Do you have any hairpins?" she asked the vendor in French.

He produced a tray for her to look at. Benedict shifted his weight and stared at Amelie's head, as though he could divine the secrets behind it simply by staring hard enough.

"I'll take this one," she said, deciding on a pin with a little purple crystal on the end. "My sister will love it."

"There's something odd about it," Benedict said, when they continued walking. "I wish I knew what."

"About my brain."

"Well, you can hardly think it's normal to be hosting . . . er, *visitors* around the clock," he said. "You have entire conversations with them. Plural!"

"I most emphatically do not think it's normal," she said. "Oh! Roasted chestnuts."

Still thinking about Rose, he took his wallet from his pocket and asked the vendor for two cones, handing one to her wordlessly.

"When Lise first appeared, what were your emotions like?"

Amelie's hand paused slightly on its way into the cone of chestnuts. "What does that matter?"

Interesting. "It could be relevant. Rose used people's fears as an entry."

"I suppose I was unsettled, both times," she said. "But I'd already calmed down."

"Hmm," he said, noting her shuttered expression. "You've grown very good at calm."

"Yes," was all she said. He moved on.

"I received official permission from the Minister of Health this morning, for a second examination." It hadn't been difficult to arrange—a brief mention at supper the night before, and a letter with a very important-looking seal had been waiting for him at the breakfast table. "And I arranged to have her released to us, as well."

"Did you—"

"Did I blackmail Fauré?" he murmured. "I did. An invigorating experience."

"Yes," she said, frowning. "You're having all kinds of those, hanging around me."

He touched the back of her hand with one finger. Startled, she glanced up at him.

"Let's play the game," he said. "A truth for a truth."

"That sounds to me like a very self-serving proposition," she said. "You want to know something."

"The things I want to know about you could fill an ocean," he said. "Honestly, you could stand to be less mysterious."

Hah! The corner of her lip twitched. "I'm not mysterious," she said, very quietly. "I'm a liar. It's different."

"You've never lied to me," he said.

"How on earth could you know?"

"I know."

She made a sort of *pshh*-ing, dismissive sound.

"I know," he insisted. "I know, because you go to an extraordinary amount of effort to avoid it. You change the subject. You flat-out refuse to tell me. And sometimes, you tell me the truth, even when it looks as though it hurts."

"Here is some truth for you," she said, pausing to sign an autograph for a little girl and her mother. She made small talk and smiled graciously at them before moving on. "You're annoying."

"*Pfff*," he said. "You say that as though it's a bad thing, when in fact, it's a carefully honed life skill that allows me to get the things I want. Now, let's play the game."

"Why don't you just ask what you want to know, since you're so sure I won't lie to you? What if I don't want to know anything about you?"

He grinned. "See, you couldn't even lie then. You phrased it as a question, 'What if I don't want to know anything about you?'

rather than a simple 'I don't want to know anything about you.' And the answer is, because you *do* want to know about me, but you're either too polite or too wary to ask."

"Yes," she said. "*Annoying* is certainly the word. Fine. I'll go first. Why aren't you married?"

Benedict winced. "Good god, woman."

"You asked for it."

He had, hadn't he.

"I blame my parents," he said. "They're nauseatingly in love, you see. It's upsetting. They'll start waltzing in the middle of the kitchen, with no music. They cuddle. If they're in a room together, they always know where the other one is. It's not like they need to be joined at the hip, but they sort of rotate around each other, like twinned planets.

"There are only so many people in a lifetime you like that much, right? It's rare. I suppose that's the answer . . . You're frowning."

Her expression immediately cleared, snapping back to its normal pleasant, slightly otherworldly cast. "But you might never find a person you like that much," she said.

He popped a chestnut into his mouth.

"Who says I haven't?"

A short intake of breath. "Ben—"

"My turn," he said. The rule was truth, and he'd given it. But neither of them would be served by lingering. "Tell me about the St. Amie business."

He'd expected her to stiffen, but she nodded, as if she'd been expecting the question. "Not here," she said. "The carriage ride home."

"Alright," he said.

They walked on, through the crowds of happy shoppers. Amelie was stopped several more times for her autograph, and every time she left the person with a smile on their face, as though Christmas morning had arrived two months early. They loved her, these people.

When they passed a bookshop, Benedict stopped, remembering a French text Victor had recommended on new surgical procedures. The store wouldn't have it in stock, but they'd be able to order it faster than he could. "Do you mind if we stop in?" he asked.

She agreed, and they stepped inside. The shop was paneled in dark wood and crammed to the brim with bookshelves. The aisles were only wide enough for one and the handful of people already inside felt like a crowd. "I'll only be a moment," he said.

He wove through the bookshelves—and the occasional pile of books that had apparently sprouted from the ground—to the counter and told the owner what he was looking for. As expected, the man had never heard of the book, but after a few minutes hunting through catalogues they found it, and Benedict arranged to have it ordered.

Amelie stood near the door, where he'd left her. She was craning her neck awkwardly to look at the books laid out in the window display next to her.

"I'm sure he wouldn't mind if you took one out," Benedict said.

She jumped. "Oh, I wasn't looking at anything particular," she said, with what almost looked like guilt crossing her face.

He picked up the small book she'd been looking at. "Hah," he said. "*Twenty Thousand Leagues Under the Sea*. That book is dangerous. I stayed up all night with it when it came out in America."

"You've read it?"

"There were vicious brawls over it in the Moore household," he said. "That's why I had to read it in a night. If I didn't, someone would have stolen it from me."

He flipped open the book to the illustrated frontispiece, which featured an enormous plunging whale and two tiny human figures standing in an underwater cave. Amelie edged closer to him, looking cautiously at the illustration.

"They look like they're out for a Sunday stroll," she said, her finger coming up to touch the little figures. "What are they doing there?"

"Having adventures," he said, grinning. "I'll not tell you more. You wouldn't thank me for sharing the ending."

He tucked the book under his arm and walked back toward the counter.

"What are you doing?"

"Buying this for you," he said.

"Oh, Ben, don't," she said. "It's so thoughtful, but I don't really have time for reading."

"Fine. I'll buy it for you, and it can look pretty sitting on a table in your apartment," he said. She kept looking at the book, like it was making her nervous. She wanted it, he was certain of it. There had been a covetous gleam in her eye.

"I don't want you to go to the expense," she said.

He lifted an eyebrow. "It's a book, not a diamond necklace," he said, as they reached the counter. He handed the book to the owner. "I'll take this, too," he said, and the man nodded, staring at Amelie.

"Besides," he murmured to her, as the owner wrapped the book in brown paper. "It'll hurt his feelings if we don't buy it."

She sighed in defeat. "Fine," she said.

Benedict slid a banknote across the counter and accepted the package in return. He almost put it in the bag he was carrying, but Amelie's fingers twitched as he made to put it away. He hid a grin and handed it to her.

"I suppose I should say thank you," she said.

"You're welcome," he replied, watching her smooth the brown paper with one tentative hand. He wasn't sure why such a small gift seemed so weighty, but it made him happy to see her place the book reverently in her bag.

When they had walked up one side of the Passage and down the other, properly seen by the Parisian public, they stepped outside into a gray, drizzly afternoon. Benedict hailed a cab, and they hurried into it.

"I owe you a truth," Amelie said, as the carriage began to move. Raindrops spattered lazily on the windows, as if unsure whether a proper downpour was really worth the effort. "You wanted to know how I became St. Amie."

Suddenly he felt guilty. It was rather churlish to force her secrets from her. "You don't have to tell me," he said. "It was rude of me to ask."

"You'll hear the story anyway," she said, shaking her head. "You'd just hear the version suited for public consumption."

She looked out her window, one finger tracing the path of a raindrop. "After the Siege and the Commune, things in Paris were very bad. We'd lost so many people—everyone had lost someone, whether to the war or the rebels or the French Army . . ." She stopped, started again. "After the Siege, it was only me and Honorine," she said, choosing her words carefully.

"Amelie," he said. He'd known she'd lost her mother, but he hadn't known when.

"We were so poor. Every day was about finding enough food. That was all that mattered. From when I woke up to when I went to sleep. Everything was expensive then, and it wasn't like the ballet was performing. I did everything, anything. I sold anything people would buy. I slept with men." She let out a little huff, almost like a laugh. "No one would believe that now, would they? Not very saint-like."

"You did what you had to do to survive," he said, as the guilt twisted through his limbs like a thorned vine. "For your sister to survive. But I'm so sorry you had to."

"I was desperate," she said. "And one day, when I was in a wealthier part of town, I passed a man playing a violin in the street. He was very good—obviously classically trained—and sometimes someone would throw a coin in his case. I thought, *I can do that.*"

She looked out the window again. "The next morning, I pulled out my old shoes, and I found a spot on one of the boulevards—an empty lot that had burned down during Bloody Week. And I started to dance. I didn't have a partner, or anyone to accompany me. I just . . . danced.

"People heard about it, I guess, and a crowd started to form. Sometimes someone would pull out a harmonica, or start to sing, and I'd dance along to that for a while. The bowl I'd put out filled up. That was the first night we'd had meat in a year. I should have saved the money, but we were so hungry. Honorine ate until she was full. It was . . . it was the best night we'd had in ages."

She was smiling, staring out at the wet streets and black umbrellas. Benedict's chest felt tight. He knew what it was like to be hungry, desperate. Terrified. It wasn't a feeling he'd wish on anyone.

"I went out the next morning, and the next," Amelie continued. "To feed myself and Honorine, you understand? But that's not how people took it. The crowds got bigger and bigger. They started bringing flowers to throw at my feet. They asked me to kiss their children. Eventually, they started calling me St. Amie."

"You brought beauty to their darkest moments," he murmured.

"But I didn't mean to," she said, softly. "I did it for the money, do you see? But they thought I was doing it for love. I suppose that's my foundational lie—I let them think it."

"Was it a lie? I don't think the two are mutually exclusive. You gave people joy. That's precious."

"I sold them joy," she corrected. "I still do. But somehow it got complicated. It was like the nickname created this person I needed to live up to. Before St. Amie, I was myself, dancing in the street. But when the name came along—suddenly I had to be someone else. Someone really *good.* At first it was little things. I'd dance in front of an orphanage and donate the profits. It felt good and I looked good, so more people would come watch me dance the next time. But," she shook her head, "I've never said any of this out loud before. It's hard to explain."

"Being good all the time isn't possible," he said. "It's not human. At least, not the kind of goodness that seems to be expected of you."

"That's it," she said. "At first it was just about *doing good.* Helping people. Things I liked doing. And when the city started recovering, the ballet company was re-formed, and suddenly it was about *being* good. Which meant being respectable. My mother was one of Paris's most famous mistresses. People remembered that, when the worst was over. Suddenly doing good wasn't enough."

"That's why you dance the way you do," he said.

She looked up sharply.

"I only saw you dance once, before, and it wasn't ballet. But it was like you felt everything when you danced. And now it's as though . . ." He trailed off.

"As though I only dance the emotions I ought to feel," she said.

"Yes."

She shrugged. "I do," she said. "And they love me anyway."

Oh, that had to hurt. To conceal so much of yourself and be loved for it.

"They would still love you," he said. "If you danced as yourself. They would have no choice."

"They would say I was like my mother after all," she said. "Wild. Oh, they'd still buy tickets to see me, but I've gotten rather used to respectability. Honorine goes to the best school in town, and she's the daughter of a fallen woman. She goes to parties with girls whose mothers would have crossed the street if they'd seen mine coming. She's not Leonie St. James's daughter anymore. She's St. Amie's sister."

"It must be exhausting," he said, thinking of the thinness of her face and the weariness beneath her skin.

She huffed out a laugh, and when she spoke her voice was brisk. "I made my choices," she said. "And we're safe and fed because of them. There are plenty in Paris who aren't."

"That doesn't mean—"

But she wasn't listening. They had stopped in front of her apartment building, and she was frowning out the window at the woman standing under the front awning.

"Do you know her?"

"That's Rachel's mother," Amelie said.

CHAPTER FOURTEEN

Madame Bonnard's face was pale in the dingy light. Her thin coat was damp, and her arms were wrapped around her chest.

"I'm sorry," she said, when Amelie got close enough to speak. The cab rolled away behind them—she'd asked Benedict to grant them privacy.

"Please don't apologize," Amelie said, hurrying to open the door. "You're soaked."

"I didn't think my plan through very well," the woman said, a stiff smile on her face. "I shouldn't be here."

"You're always welcome," Amelie said. She needed to get her near a fire, warm her up with a hot cup of tea. "I'm on the third floor. I'm afraid it's a bit of a climb."

They climbed the staircase silently, the only sound the squeak of wet boots on new wood. Amelie opened the door, quickly looking around for Honorine and relieved to remember she was at a friend's house that afternoon. They didn't have much time, though—Suzanne had already left to fetch Honorine home.

"Would you like some tea?" Amelie asked, after they'd removed their wet coats.

"Thank you," Madame Bonnard said, looking around the apartment. She'd grown thinner in the last several years.

"Please, sit. I'll only be a minute." She walked toward the kitchen, before pausing. Rachel's mother was standing in the middle of the sitting room, a lost expression on her face. "Actually, would you mind keeping me company while I make it? It's warmer in the kitchen anyway."

"Alright," Madame Bonnard said.

Amelie's kitchen was a small affair, though much sleeker and modern than the one she'd grown up with. Rachel's mother leaned against the counter while Amelie put the water on.

"Your home is lovely," Madame Bonnard said.

"Thank you."

"I'm sorry to . . ."

"Nonsense," Amelie said. "I'm delighted to see you."

Oddly enough, that was true. It was strange to see someone from Montmartre standing here, in her fancy new apartment, but nice.

She pulled down the teapot and two cups, measuring precious scoops of her favorite tea into the pot.

"Is everything alright at home?"

"Yes. I—" She exhaled, short and deep. "No."

The kettle sang. Amelie took it off the fire and poured the water, giving Rachel's mother a moment.

"I've been thinking about Rachel lately," she said, after settling the lid onto the pot. "Remembering her."

"Rachel," Madame Bonnard whispered. She looked down, running her hand nervously over the counter behind her. "He never says her name."

From the lack of pictures and the odd behavior of Rachel's

father, Amelie had put together an idea of what was happening in the Bonnard household.

"The boys, they're war heroes," Madame Bonnard continued. "We're allowed to remember them, honor them. But . . . Rachel—my husband acts like she never existed. Like I never had a daughter."

"Every family in Montmartre had a member in the Commune," Amelie said. "It's not shameful."

Madame Bonnard's hands twitched once, twice, in a sort of miniature gesture of helplessness. "He thinks she dishonored her brothers. They died for their government. She overthrew it."

"She grieved for them, too," Amelie said. "She did what she did *because* of them."

"But if she was right, they died for nothing."

The truth of that statement sat between them, dense and dark. It took the air out of the room.

And Amelie saw her, standing in the doorway. Rachel, dressed in her enormous brown coat, looking at her mother with love and sorrow and anger in her eyes. She met Amelie's gaze, nodded her head infinitesimally.

"I miss her," Madame Bonnard said.

"I do, too," Amelie said, realizing she spoke the truth. She hadn't liked her, but she'd *known* her, in the way you could only know the people you'd grown up with. And now that she was back, it was like a small emptiness Amelie hadn't even been aware of had been filled.

"You two didn't get along very well," Madame Bonnard said hesitantly.

Amelie chuckled, pouring the tea into cups. "Cream and sugar?"

"Just cream, thank you."

"No, we didn't get on," Amelie said, handing the cup across.

"We were quite different, weren't we? She was so smart, and passionate about *everything*. Intense. And I—the only things I cared about were dancing and my mother. And Honorine, when she came along. There were moments, though, when we almost had an understanding." She smiled as a memory struck her. "Actually, we were allies once."

"Allies?"

"Do you remember little Thomas Boucher? Lived in the building next door?"

"The boy with the limp? He's still around," Madame Bonnard said. "Does the books for a few businesses in the neighborhood."

Still alive, then. That was one of the perils of memories—the people in them might not be there anymore. The joy in her chest expanded.

"This must have been when he was about eight or nine, and Rachel and I were twelve or so. We'd both been walking home, but *not* walking together, you know? Very carefully keeping our distance. Well, we came across poor Thomas Boucher getting pushed about by some of the older children, even older than we were. Rachel tears in right away—you know that's not something she would have stood for. And she starts in on them, yelling at the top of her lungs, making such a scene."

A slow smile crept across Madame Bonnard's face. "I can see her doing that," she said.

"Now, I was terrified. I knew I had to go help her, because it was the right thing to do, so I sort of crept into the circle and helped Thomas up. But she didn't need my help. She wasn't scared of those boys. They scattered pretty quickly, with all the noise she was making, and the three of us were left standing there. She asked Thomas, *Do those boys bother you much?* and he said they did. She looked at me and said, *We're going to put a stop to this.*"

"What did you do?"

"She told Thomas the next time those boys bothered him he was to say he had protection. A terrible creature in the night that had sworn fealty to him. And if they bothered him again, the creature would come into their bedrooms at night and eat them."

Rachel's mother clasped a hand to her chest, her expression torn between amusement and horror. "She didn't."

"Oh, she did. She told me that we were going to be the creature."

"No."

Amelie laughed. "I'm not really sure I should tell you this," she said, glancing at Rachel. But she was smiling, hovering near the doorjamb.

"You should," Madame Bonnard. "Please."

"Well, those boys didn't even wait a day before they started bothering Thomas. So, he comes to Rachel and tells her. That afternoon, I was walking home from school, and there she was waiting for me. *Tonight*, she said. *Wear black*.

"We waited until past midnight," Amelie continued, looking back at Rachel. "Waiting for our parents—for you—to fall asleep. We met in the foyer of the apartment building. Rachel had a paper bag full of black feathers—I don't even want to know where she got them. She said we were going to visit the leaders of the group—there were two boys who seemed to be in charge. The first one was easy. His bedroom window faced an alley. We snuck up together and arranged some of the feathers outside the window, like an enormous bird had been standing there. Next, we took a couple of rocks, and scraped them against the window like claws. When we heard him scream, we ran. The second one was more difficult."

"How?"

"It was on the second floor," Amelie said. She and Rachel

were smiling at each other. "There was a tree that reached up to the window. I was *not* in favor. I was really conscious of injuries, you know? But Rachel called me a coward, and I sort of knew I was being one, so we climbed that damn tree and did the whole thing all over again. Scraped the hell out of our arms coming back down."

"I remember," Madame Bonnard said suddenly. "I remember those scrapes. I knew she'd been up to something, but she wouldn't say. I chalked it up to her usual trouble."

"Well, you weren't wrong," Amelie said. "But those boys never bothered Thomas again."

"I bet they didn't," Rachel's mother said. "I bet they didn't."

"She drove me up the wall, plenty of times," Amelie said. "She was smart, and brave, and intense, and once she decided something was wrong *that was that*."

"No, she wasn't much for nuance, our Rachel."

"No," Amelie said, glancing at Rachel again. "But she fought for what she thought was right. And there aren't many in the world like that."

"I loved her so much. I wanted a girl, after all those boys. And when she came along, with her little dark cap of hair—" Madame Bonnard took a sharp breath in. "I had a daughter," she said. "Even if everyone wants to forget her."

Tentatively, Amelie reached a hand across the table. "We remember her," she said quietly, and it felt like a pledge, not only to Rachel, but to all her ghosts.

"I'm sorry," Madame Bonnard said. "It was presumptuous of me to come here, without even sending a message. It's just . . . I suppose I wanted to talk to someone who knew her."

They fell into silence. Amelie wished she could do more than remember, to share a silly little story. She wished she could give this woman her daughter back. She wished she could give all the parents their lost children back, and all the lost children their parents.

There was something she could do, though.

"Wait here," she said, squeezing the woman's shoulder. She walked out to her desk in the sitting room and pulled out some sketches she'd done of the ghosts. She found Rachel's in the pile—a simple sketch of her face, but she thought she'd caught the confident, intense expression correctly.

When she entered the kitchen, Rachel was still in the doorway, her arms crossed over her chest, her dark eyes soft and far away.

"Here," Amelie said, handing the sketch to Madame Bonnard.

"Oh," the woman said. "Oh."

"I don't have my mother's gift, but she taught what she could," Amelie said. "I noticed you don't have any pictures of her up."

"He burned them," Madame Bonnard said absently, her eyes on the sketch. "How did you— This is so like her. You drew this recently?"

"I have a good memory for faces."

"I haven't seen her in so long." Tears, held back for who knows how long, ran slowly down the woman's face.

Maybe this had been a bad idea. "I'm sorry," Amelie said. "I didn't mean to upset you."

But Rachel's mother shook her head. "No," she said, almost fiercely. "I can keep this?"

Amelie nodded.

"Thank you. Thank you. I—" She clasped the picture to her chest. Rachel took a step away from the wall, as if to embrace her, and stopped.

Madame Bonnard used her handkerchief to wipe her face

and almost visibly drew herself back together. "May I come back?" she asked, when her eyes were dry.

"Any time you wish," Amelie said. "I'd be happy to have a friend from the old neighborhood."

Madame Bonnard nodded, still clasping the drawing, and walked from the kitchen to the front door. She carefully tucked the paper away in her bag and slipped into her still-damp coat.

"Thank you, Amelie," she said. "You're a good girl. Your mother would be proud."

The emotions of the afternoon almost overwhelmed her then. This woman had known her nearly her entire life. Had known her mother, in the good times and bad.

"Thank you, Madame Bonnard," she said. "I'll see you soon."

When she closed the door, she knew without turning that Rachel was behind her.

"Amelie St. James," Rachel said. "I never thought you'd be the one to give my eulogy."

Amelie didn't know what to say. She turned and looked at the young woman in front of her. They'd been the same age once. She realized for the first time that Rachel was younger than she was now. Her skin was unlined and fresh, there were no strands of gray in her hair.

"I'm sorry," she said.

"For what? I didn't just fight for what I thought was right. I died for it. I don't regret my choices. And now I can go."

"What?"

Rachel shrugged. "Something's changed. You released me."

"Rachel, I don't know what you're talking about," Amelie said, desperation rising in her throat. "I didn't *do* anything."

"You must have done something," Rachel said. "Listen, I can't stay here and talk all day. This requires effort, you know."

"I—"

"Oh my god, you're sad. Amelie, get yourself together. You don't even like me."

Amelie laughed a little. "Do you know, I actually think I might," she said.

Rachel rolled her eyes. "This sentimental streak of yours is nauseating," she said, sticking her hands in her coat pockets. "Well, I'm not sure what I'm supposed to say here. I already did the last words thing once. I guess this time I'll go with some advice. Don't take this sainthood thing too seriously, Amelie. They're not worth it. And—er—take care of yourself."

"Thank you," Amelie said. "You, too. Whatever that means."

"I'll be fine," Rachel said, her eyes far away. "Goodbye, girls," she said, over Amelie's shoulder. When Amelie turned, Lise and Violette were there, expressions grave.

"Goodbye," Amelie said, and Rachel was gone.

"What happened?" Amelie said, a few moments later. "What did— She's gone, I can feel it." It was as if there had been a place in her brain labeled *Rachel*, and it was empty.

She turned to the ghosts behind her. "Are you two . . . ?"

"Still here, love," Violette said. Lise looked away. "Don't know what changed. Maybe seeing her mother did it?"

"Maybe," Amelie said vaguely. It was so sudden—she didn't know what to feel. It was success and happiness and sadness and loss all wrapped up into one enormous, overwhelming package.

The door opened, and her sister breezed in, followed by a red-faced Suzanne.

"Amelie! What are you doing standing here?"

"I—I left something in my coat pocket," she said. When she looked over her shoulder, the ghosts had gone.

"You don't look good," Honorine said, slipping off her coat and hanging it carelessly on the rack.

"I didn't sleep well," Amelie answered automatically. "How was school?"

Honorine grinned and pulled a paper out of her satchel. "Highest marks," she said, handing it over.

"Oh!" It was the geography paper Honorine had slaved over the week before. "In the class? Highest marks in the whole class?"

Her sister nodded. "Bernadine is *furious*. What's the matter? Are you *crying*?"

And she was. Staring down at Honorine's beautiful, educated penmanship and the careful map drawings she'd made, and the teacher's glowing comments—this was worth it.

Maybe everything was going to be fine.

"I'm just so proud of you," she sniffled.

"You are *so* odd," Honorine said. "If the girls in my class knew *half* the weird things you do . . ."

"It must be terrible for you," Amelie said, pulling her little sister into a tight embrace. She rested her head atop Honorine's darker one. "Having a freak for a sister, who lends you her hairpins and buys cake for dinner when you get the highest marks in the class."

"Cake for dinner?"

"You have to have a proper dinner, too. So, I guess technically cake for dessert. I'll run down to the bakery."

"*Eee!*" Honorine clapped her hands, significantly more excited about the cake than the high marks. "Thank you, thank you, thank you!"

"You're quite welcome, Madame Scholar. Do you have studying to do tonight?"

"A little geometry," Honorine said, sticking her tongue out.

"Do it now," Amelie said, feeling abruptly giddy. "We're going to have a little party later."

She tossed her coat on, buttoning it quickly over her damp clothes and hurrying out the door. The rain was still spitting, but it was warm enough that Amelie didn't feel the chill. She went to the bakery and bought a beautiful, stupidly expensive cake, and then, buoyed by the outrageous purchase and the fizzy feeling in her chest, walked to the department store several blocks away where she found bright gold paper, perfect for party hats.

Supper was a quick affair, both sisters eager to get to the fun. When she was stacking the dishes in the kitchen, Amelie remembered the hairpin she'd bought earlier in the day and hurried into the hall to fetch it. As she reached into the bag, her hand brushed against the book Benedict had bought her. She pulled it out, turning it over in her hands.

Maybe she could read it. When things quieted down. Benedict had said he'd liked it—she smiled to think of the Moore siblings fighting over who could read it next.

It had been sweet of him to give it to her.

She laid it carefully on her bedroom dresser, leaving the paper on to take off later, when she had more time, and hurriedly wrapped the hairpin.

The cake was an enormous success, and Honorine's eyes when she unwrapped the pin almost made Amelie start crying again. They made paper crowns, and proposed very, very silly toasts, and then Honorine talked Amelie into teaching her the waltz, even though she was years too young for it.

By ten o'clock, her sister was rosy-cheeked and exhausted, her laughs turning into yawns. They collapsed onto the sofa, Honorine tucked against Amelie's side.

"Bedtime, I think," Amelie said.

"Mmm," Honorine said. "It was a very grown-up party."

Amelie, resting her chin atop Honorine's head, hid a smile. "Very," she agreed. "Soon you'll be going to all kinds of parties, I suppose."

"Ages from now," Honorine said.

"Yes, ages." There had been a time when twelve years old had seemed an age away, when Amelie had lain awake at night, terrified they wouldn't make it. She knew how fast an age could pass.

"I love you," she said. "Off to bed."

As her sister readied for bed, Amelie tidied the sitting room and did the supper dishes. She'd made a good place here, in this little bourgeois apartment Rachel had so despised.

She tucked Honorine in, kissing her forehead and turning off the pretty lamp she'd found used at one of the markets. "Night, little bean," she whispered, but Honorine was already asleep.

Amelie returned to the sitting room, energy bubbling through her veins like fizzy wine. Her curtains were open, the lights of Montmartre rowdy and familiar in the distance. The emptiness of the would-be basilica was like a bruise on the cheerful hillside, an aching reminder of damage that might never fade away.

A fragment of motion came into her mind, only a sketch of movement. Quick and sharp, nothing elegant or beautiful. Big steps followed by short, staccato ones, arms at right angles or aggressively straight.

She caught her reflection in the windows, illuminated by the low gaslight along the sitting room wall.

Ugly, she thought, balancing in *sous-sous.* Her arms were out to the sides and broken, her torso so far forward the balance was hard to hold.

For some reason, though, she didn't move. She kept staring at herself in the window. That woman was predatory, furious, vengeful. That woman was a bird of prey.

It shouldn't have felt so good to look at. So . . . powerful.

She came down off of *demi pointe* sharply.

But the restlessness hadn't left her; if anything, it had increased. She wanted to keep laughing, she wanted to dance, she wanted to scream and yell and kick something.

There was an old bottle of champagne in her larder, a housewarming gift she'd never opened. She walked to the kitchen and pulled it out, blowing at the dust on the label.

There was one more toast she needed to make.

CHAPTER FIFTEEN

Benedict stepped out of the cab in front of the Durands' building and stopped under a gas lamp to jot down a few notes in his notebook. The dinner with colleagues he'd just left had been pleasant, boisterous, and productive. He'd met a promising young scientist, a woman from the London Medical School for Women, who he thought might make a good addition to the institute—if she could be persuaded to cross an ocean, of course, but he had the budget to make decisions like that worthwhile.

At times, though, he'd found it difficult to focus on the conversation. He kept thinking about Amelie's story, the hunger and desperation in it.

He should have been there. Or rather, he should have gotten her out, somehow. Never mind that even now, eight years later, he couldn't see how it would have been possible.

"Hello, Ben."

He jerked his head up, squinting in the darkness. She was leaning against the building, a slight smile on her face.

"Amelie? What are you doing here?"

She lifted a bottle of champagne. "I'm here to kidnap you."

"Again?" he said, smiling back at her, a little ache in his heart. "You can't make a habit of this."

"Of course I can," she said, and the imperious tone of her voice worked exactly as it always had. "Well? Are you coming?"

"Yes," he said.

He didn't ask where to. The answer would always be yes.

The rain had cleared while he'd been at dinner, leaving a Paris of shining streets and glistening gaslight. He fell into step beside her.

"How was your supper engagement?" she asked, as though the two of them walking alone through the streets at almost eleven o'clock at night was a perfectly ordinary thing to do.

He supposed he'd play along. "I might have found someone to recruit," he said. "She's having trouble finding a position over here. I read some of her work beforehand—it's exceptional."

Amelie snorted. "You're such a pirate," she said. "You tried to infuse that sentence with righteous disapproval—*oh, how terrible people discriminate on the basis of sex*—when really you're delighted to have scooped her up."

"Unfair," he said. "They are not mutually exclusive. I can disapprove of the fools who overlook her brilliance because of her sex *while also* being delighted she's available to join my institute. Although it's not certain yet."

"She'll join," Amelie said. "She would be a fool if she didn't."

"You have a lot of confidence in an organization that has yet to open its doors," he said, laughing.

"I have confidence in you," she said simply. "How many people are you trying to recruit?"

"We need at least three more," he said. "I'd particularly like to find someone with successful surgical experience, but there aren't many out there. The ones who want a new job are mostly butchers; the ones who are good have no desire to move. It's one of the things I'm going to ask Bonnet about—if he knows any candidates."

"He might," Amelie said. "He's a recluse, but he still knows everybody's business."

They fell silent, walking through the quiet streets, the air crisp and clean from the rain. It was the kind of night that felt like an adventure.

"We're here," she said, stopping in front of a closed iron gate bordered by thick hedges.

He frowned, peering through the gate. "It's a cemetery," he said.

"Mmm," she replied, not paying attention. She seemed to be looking for something.

"It's a cemetery that's closed," he continued.

"Well, my plan was to bribe the night watchman, but since he seems to have left for the bar, we'll have to climb the gate."

He blinked at her. "I was afraid this would happen," he said. "The ghosts have addled your mind."

"Surely the American isn't afraid? I'd heard you were all strapping fellows, ready to wrestle a bear at any moment."

"A bear, sure," he said. "That's a rusty iron fence."

"Of course, if you don't want to—"

He sighed. "Damnit," he said. "Give me the bottle. And if we get caught you better put on the sainthood performance of a lifetime."

"I will tell them we were sent directly by God," she promised, handing him the champagne.

The bottle just fit inside his coat pocket. "I'll see if I can unlock it from the inside," he said.

"Very gallant."

He regarded the gate. It looked unpleasantly rickety.

She was watching him, though, so he was going to climb the damn thing, and he was not going to make a fool of himself doing so.

"This is the damn rowboat all over again," he muttered, finding a grip and hauling himself up a step.

"What's that?"

"Nothing," he said, waiting for the gate to fall over. It didn't. Heartened, he climbed another step.

There was a tricky moment at the top, when he couldn't find a good foothold on the other side and the whole structure wobbled ominously, but it didn't collapse. A few tense seconds later, he dropped to the ground on the other side.

"Amelie," he said, rattling the sturdy padlock on the chain around the gate, "it's not going to unlock, and I'm not sure you should come over. It was a bit difficult—Amelie?"

He peered through the gate, trying to see through the darkness.

"Amelie?"

The hedge next to the gate rustled, and she stepped out, brushing leaves off her skirt.

"You must be joking," he said flatly.

"I didn't know there wasn't a fence," she said innocently.

"I could have contracted lockjaw! Or fallen to my death!"

"What nonsense," she said, rolling her eyes. "You enjoyed showing off."

He narrowed his eyes at her. "You have most of a tree on your head."

"Oh, don't be like that," Amelie said, casually reaching up to pluck the single leaf off her hair. She walked past him, stopping briefly to lay a hand on his arm. "You looked terribly dashing."

He stayed completely still, feeling the echo of her hand on his arm, until she yelled at him to hurry up.

"Obviously I looked dashing," he said, catching up to her on a wide lane bordered by barren trees and tall stone crypts. "I'm a very dashing fellow."

"Oh no."

"Only last month I was credibly informed by a society matron that I'm one of the most eligible bachelors in Washington."

"I regret saying anything."

"A woman once offered me a thousand dollars just to kiss her hand."

"No, she didn't."

"Alright," he said. "It was two oranges and we were ten. Amelie, where on earth are we, and why are we here?"

"We are in Passy Cemetery," she said, stopping at the end of the lane.

Passy Cemetery . . . the name was familiar. He reviewed his mental files.

"Passy Cemetery is where Rachel Bonnard is most likely buried," he said. There was no way to be completely sure. According to his research, she had been arrested on the twenty-fourth of May, 1871, on suspicion of arson, and taken to the impromptu military court that had formed at the Parc Monceau. There was no record of a trial, but her execution was recorded later that same day, along with hundreds of other Communards. Most of the bodies had been taken here, buried in long trenches along the wall.

"The champagne, please," Amelie said. He gave her the bottle, and she opened it with a pop.

"To Rachel Bonnard," she said, lifting the bottle high. "She was fierce, and clever, and brave. She lived by her principles, and she died by them. She deserves to be remembered. She will be."

Amelie took a long swig from the bottle and handed it to Benedict. He followed her example, gave the champagne back, and lifted a single eyebrow. She gestured to a nearby bench.

"Rachel left this afternoon," she said, sitting down and taking another gulp of alcohol.

"I'm sorry?"

"She's gone. For good."

"My god," he said blankly. He took his notebook from his inside coat pocket. "I— How — I'm sorry, it happened this afternoon and you're only telling me now?"

"I wanted . . . this," she said, gesturing to the cemetery and the night sky. "I didn't want to talk about her like she was a problem, or a disease. I wanted . . ."

"A memorial," he said, closing the notebook. "Answer me one thing. Are you alright? Physically?"

"I feel fine," she said. "Better than fine. I feel like I've been buried under a pile of stones, and one of them has been lifted."

"Hope," he said.

"Hope."

He put the notebook back in his coat and took the bottle. "Then tell me about Rachel Bonnard," he said.

"She was a pain," Amelie laughed. "From my earliest memory—I don't even know how long I've known her—she was . . . oh, she could be hard on people. She saw things in black and white, you know? Even then. Her brothers were older than she was, and they hung together. I think she spent a lot of time alone.

"You know the kind of person who is always the first to say the unpleasant thing everyone is thinking? That was her. It takes courage to be that person," she said. "She had more courage than anyone I've ever met," Amelie said. "It was like . . . a duty to her. To tell the truth, no matter how unpleasant. To fight for it."

"You admire her."

She looked down, kicking her boots in the damp earth. "She was angry," Amelie said. "When her brothers died. Before, too.

Injustice made her furious. You're like that, too. The way you acted at that accident—she would have done the same thing."

"Anger can be strength," Benedict said. "And a privilege. And sometimes it sinks so low inside of you that you don't even know it's there. You taught me that."

Her gaze flew up to meet his, her eyes light and bewitching in the thin moonlight. "I don't see how I could have," she said. "Since it's not something I know myself."

"I was so angry after the war," he said, resting his elbows on his knees. He took a breath of the clean, rain-scented air, relishing the way it felt in his lungs. "But I *couldn't* be. We'd won. It was like . . . if I was angry, I was dishonoring the people who died, along with my country. I turned it against myself. Blamed myself."

"I remember," Amelie said, one gloved hand reaching out to rest lightly on his arm.

"I talked to you about it, and you . . . you were so sure I wasn't to blame. It was painful, how sure you were. I'd believed it for so long, even while I was in the field, and here you were saying this incredibly heavy thing I was lugging around wasn't even true. That I could put it down."

She shook her head, exhaling. "It seemed so simple then," she said. "My God, the arrogance of youth."

"But it was true," he said. "However you said it got through to me. I'm not saying things got better right away. But a few days later I talked to my parents. It was so hard, just getting the first words out. And over time, the burden got lighter."

"Lighter," she said. "Not gone."

"I don't know that the burden ever goes away," he said, leaning back and staring up at the sky.

"You know I research the brain," he continued after a moment. "It's been almost a decade and a half since the end of the war, and there's not a month that goes by without a middle-aged man walking into my office, waiting till the door is closed, and telling me they haven't had an unbroken night's sleep in fifteen years. Or they'll be out for a pleasant evening at the theater with their wife, and the smell of someone's wet wool cloak casts them so far back into war they can't even move.

"They've been to their regular doctors already. They've had shortness of breath explained away by the tightness of the packs we had to wear, any number of explanations that don't quite seem to fit. And now they want to know: Is something wrong with their brains? I don't know what to tell them. Because I think there is, but I don't think it's something I could find under a microscope. That's one of the reasons this institute is so important. If I have those kinds of resources, I can ask the questions other people aren't."

"Oh, Ben," Amelie said. "You really did turn out awfully well."

He looked down, wanting to say something flippant to turn the mood, but she was looking up at him with tears in her eyes, and without really knowing what he was doing, he put his arm around her, drawing her against him.

"You turned out pretty wonderful yourself," he said, pushing a tendril of hair away from her face. "Don't cry, Amelie."

She managed a wobbly smile. "Don't tell me what to do, Benedict," she said, resting one hand on the side of his cheek, and slowly, giving him every opportunity to move, she lifted her mouth to his.

The kiss was tentative, over as soon as it began, the tears on her cheeks wet against his.

"I'm sorry," she said, those bewitching eyes wide and abashed.

Instead of answering, he pulled her closer, and kissed her again.

"Ben," she murmured.

"Once more," he said, resting his forehead against hers. "One more time, for me to remember when you're an ocean away."

"Oh," she said. Her arms wrapped around his neck and they were kissing, and he didn't know who had leaned in first. The rosemary of her hair mingled with the smell of wet, dark earth. He ran a hand over it, marveling in its silky thickness, and down her back. He pulled her into his lap, or she climbed there, her legs straddling his in their layers of thin material.

"Why is it always like this," she whispered. "Why does it hurt so much, between us?"

Her hand wove through his hair, gripping it tightly, as though he might leave at any moment. She nipped at his bottom lip, and her mouth was against his, fierce and strong and a little desperate.

He pulled back, putting a bare inch between them. "What if it wasn't always like this?" he said. "What are we doing? I love you, Amelie."

"I love you, too." The words were easy, simple, like she hadn't even needed to think about them.

"Then why are we putting ourselves through this?"

She exhaled slowly, the energy leaching out of her body. "We need to stop," she said, standing up and straightening her coat.

"That's not what I meant," Benedict said, feeling frantic. "What if we didn't stop?"

"Don't do this, Ben," she said softly. "We've been here before."

"I remember," he said. "And I don't understand it any better this time. Come back with me. Bring Honorine, she'll love it in America."

"I can't—"

"Or I'll move here," he continued. "I can do my research wherever."

"No, you can't," she said sharply. "You've just finished telling me what you can do with your institute in Washington. It's beautiful. You're not giving that up for—for what? For a childhood dream? For a damsel in distress?"

"For you, who is neither of those things."

"No."

The word was absolutely, utterly final. "We're not doing this," she said. "It took me too long to recover the last time."

She took a long, deep breath. "You're not moving here," she said. "I'm not moving to America. My career is here. Paris is all my sister has ever known. My mother relied on men for her livelihood because she had no choice. I do."

It was as if someone had emptied a bucket of ice water over his head. "I see," he said.

She must have felt him stiffen beside her. "I don't—I don't mean you're like her lovers," she said. "But—I—I can rely on myself. I've built this—"

"Yes," he said. "You have. You've built a remarkable life for your sister. But what about for you?"

"I'm safe," she said, swallowing hard. "I'm never hungry."

"And you hate the falsehood of your dancing, and the gaze of your audience cuts you like knives," he said. "You've hidden yourself away so far you don't even know who you are anymore. You smile and spout sweet platitudes while you dance on a hip that must put you in agony every night. You're so afraid to trust anyone with the truth—"

"Yes," she said, and suddenly she was shouting. "I'm afraid to trust anyone with the truth. Am I wrong? If someone finds out about my hip, my career is over. If someone finds out about the ghosts, my career is over. If I make one single, tiny mistake, my career is over."

"But you hate it—"

"Do you know what happens if my career ends before I've earned enough? We aren't safe. We aren't full. We lose our apartment. Everything I've built—I could lose it all, because of one other person."

"I'm not that person," Benedict said, his voice scraping at his throat. "I would never hurt you."

"But you left," she said, tears running down her face. "You left and everything went to hell."

"Amelie," he whispered, taking a step toward her. She waved him back.

"I'm sorry," she said. "I don't mean it. I told you to go. You went. I don't—I don't know where that came from."

"I think it came from years of pain and loneliness," he said. His chest ached for her, for them, for the children they had been.

She took one breath, and another, visibly calming herself. She wiped her eyes. "There have been difficult times," she said. "But I've learned something important in them. I just haven't been saying it right. I learned I *can* depend on myself. I have to."

"And you have to depend on yourself alone?"

"I don't think there's another way," she said. "At least for me."

Benedict made himself take her words inside. They were incredibly sad. But she had a right to them.

"I understand," he said. A great emptiness had taken the place of his pain. He felt lightheaded and unmoored.

She sniffed, tucking her hands into her coat pockets.

"Are we— Do you—" She pursed her lips. "Are you still my friend?"

"I will be your friend until the day I die," he said. She looked so miserable and alone, standing there in the chilly cemetery. He desperately wanted to hold her; instead, he put his hands in his pockets as well.

But he couldn't do nothing. She was sad, and he didn't want

her to be. "Well," he said, aiming for rueful. "Obviously we can't be trusted with champagne."

A slightly sniffly laugh.

"I'm sorry for the things I said. The things you've achieved—the way you've protected Honorine—they're admirable."

"You don't need to do that," she said. "What you said was true. It just—"

"Doesn't change anything," he said. He took her arm and picked up the bottle. It was time to go home.

"Do you miss it? Dancing? Really dancing?" He didn't know why he asked. Maybe it was because he thought she'd answer.

"Every day," she said, leaning on him slightly. "Every day."

CHAPTER SIXTEEN

Stumbling into her darkened apartment, Amelie closed her front door and leaned against it. Benedict had walked her home, speaking only of light, friendly things. They'd fallen back into their pattern of tentative, cautious friendship easily enough.

But she'd kissed him.

She hadn't kissed a man since the Siege. And so many of those hadn't been— Well, it had been a very long time since she'd kissed someone for romance, or passion, or even just fun.

Her muscles were loose yet jittery, her lips tender and sensitive. Embarrassment crept in. He'd been talking about something serious, and she loved him. She loved him so much she'd wanted to kiss him. And something about the night sky and the cool air and the warmth of him next to her had made it possible.

Twelve years ago, they'd kissed for the first time, by the river on a hot summer night. She'd kissed him first then, too. He'd been shy and adorable, and she'd had to go up on her toes to reach him. He'd been surprised, and then—like tonight—he'd wrapped his arms around her and . . . well.

That kiss—that night—had been so full of hope and joy. She hadn't known then it would be the last time.

Now, twelve years later, she'd kissed him again. The pain had been there even before her lips had touched his—that she'd expected. But it had been twined around heat, and even more dangerous, happiness.

He kissed you back, a smug little voice whispered. *He loves you*.

It had been so long since someone had seen her. Had wanted *her.*

She shouldn't have done that, Amelie told herself, even as a flush of desire suffused her. It wasn't fair to him. And . . . it had been so long since she'd had a friend that she could be honest with. Even if she only had him for a month, she didn't want to ruin that. It was too precious.

Slowly, she unbuttoned her coat and hung it by the door. Then she padded down the hall to check on Honorine. She leaned in the doorway and watched her sister's breathing. They were fine, just like this.

Honorine was up and dressed for school when Amelie entered the kitchen the next morning, still bleary-eyed from anxious, frantic dreams. Her head felt as though she'd drunk five bottles of champagne instead of half of one.

"You look terrible," Honorine said.

"*Mmph*," Amelie said, gratefully receiving the coffee Suzanne handed her. The rich brew cleared her head slightly, and soon she was able to form proper words.

"Don't you have that history test today?"

Honorine nodded. "I'm ready," she said, with a complete

confidence Amelie envied. When was the last time she'd been completely confident about anything?

"Good," Amelie said.

She rested her head against her hand and closed her eyes—a mistake, because all she could see was Benedict's face right before she kissed him. His eyes had been half-closed, but the look underneath his lashes . . .

"Amelie?"

"Hmm?"

"I forgot to ask you last night, because of the party. Lucie Paquet's parents have tickets for the opera tonight, and they want me to go with them. May I?"

The request pushed her back into the present. She straightened, welcoming this little, mundane decision that reminded her who she was: Honorine's sister, ballet dancer, head of household.

"What did they have in mind?" Honorine wasn't usually allowed at performances because there was no one to go with her, but Amelie had met Paul and Ines Paquet, and liked them.

"Supper beforehand, and then the opening. They'll bring me home right after; I told Lucie you usually have to stay longer."

Amelie turned the plan over but couldn't find anything wrong with it. She knew Honorine found it rather hard that her sister was the prima ballerina of the Paris Opera Ballet and yet she wasn't allowed to go to the performances. "Alright," she said.

"Oh, thank you, thank you!" Honorine bounced up and down. "It's going to be *so* elegant. What should I wear?"

This was simple enough. There was a strict dress code for proper young women out in public. "Your white dress," Amelie said. "No jewelry. You could wear a ribbon around your neck if you wish."

Honorine nodded, happy to take her sister's advice on the

matter, and Amelie reflected ruefully that when she'd been Honorine's age, her taste had tended more toward yellow and violent pink.

"Take the dress out now so it can air," she said, tucking a bit of her sister's hair away from her face. "I won't be here to help you get ready, so have Suzanne assist with your hair. And . . . if you wish, and you think they might like it, you may bring the Paquets backstage afterward and I'll give them a tour. But send me a note first so I can make sure everything is as it should be."

"*Really?* Oh, Amelie, they'll love that," Honorine said breathlessly. "Oh, Lucie will be *so* impressed."

Well, that was rather nice. She could do something impressive.

"Hurry, now," Amelie said. "You'll be late for school."

Honorine dashed to her room to take the dress out. A few minutes of chaos later and she was gone, leaving Amelie with an empty apartment and a head full of inconvenient memories.

Her sister had left a book open on the sofa. Amelie found a bookmark and placed it, careful not to wrinkle any of the pages. She set the book reverently on a side table, thinking briefly of the still-wrapped novel sitting in her bedroom.

She could never read it. It would take far too long. She didn't have time to waste dreaming of far-off adventures.

She'd done rather too much of that lately. A memory of last night's kiss appeared, quickly banished. She needed to keep to the plan: two more years.

And what then?

The question startled her. She'd never asked it before. No morning class. No afternoon rehearsals. No performances. What would her life be, after ballet? What about when Honorine built her own life, and didn't need her anymore?

No more dancing.

She'd thought about retirement, and bank accounts, and the number of years Honorine had left in school, but somehow, she'd never thought, really *thought*, about what that meant.

She hadn't danced for herself in years. Ballet was a paycheck. It was pain. It was secrets and lies.

So why did the future suddenly seem so barren?

Friday night at the Palais Garnier was well underway. All of fashionable Paris was in attendance or was having dinner nearby and would be in attendance shortly. The building and the audience glittered, very pleased to be in the other's company.

The opera had started an hour ago. Amelie had been dressed and warming up in her dressing room for about an hour and a half when the ghosts appeared, Violette lounging on the sofa in a black-and-white-and-diamond wig concept, Lise sullen and quiet in the corner.

Amelie didn't know what to say. Lise hadn't spoken to her since the morgue.

"Good evening," she said. Lise turned away.

"Good evening, dear," Violette said. "Well, after watching you, all I can say is I'm glad I was a singer. This life is too hard on the body. Not that singing isn't. Hell on the throat."

Amelie mumbled an agreement, trying to return her attention to her feet. She'd felt off all day, scattered. Now Lise's presence—and Rachel's absence—distracted her further.

"It's awfully rude the way people don't even show up for the first part of the opera," Violette said. "Those are the best singers in the world, singing their hearts out, and these nobs can't even be bothered to fill the seats they bought! Just wanting to ogle the dancers."

"Mmm," Amelie said. Had her left *tendu* gotten a little sloppy?

"Mind you, opera was never my style," Violette said. "Standing up there, singing in whatever language, and the audience falling asleep because they haven't the faintest idea what's happening—"

"They do give them programs," Amelie said, vaguely feeling as if someone ought to defend the Paris Opera.

"—no, not for me. I like something that keeps the audience on its feet, if you know what I mean."

Amelie did not. She did a *tendu* to the right, and one to the left. Her stomach felt jittery, nervous.

"You need to point the left more," Lise said. Her voice was sharp.

"Are you . . . alright?" Amelie asked, feeling foolish as soon as she asked.

Lise shrugged. "I'm not going to kill anyone while you're onstage, if that's what you're asking."

"It wasn't," Amelie said, giving up. "But thank you for confirming."

"Don't mind her," Violette said, crossing the room to peek at her wig in the dressing room mirror. "She's been sulky ever since she found out what her man did. And then Rachel—"

"I'm not sulky," Lise said, a flash of red reflecting in her eyes. "And he *didn't*. And while you could be finding out what really did happen, so I can *leave*, instead you're spending all your time talking to Rachel's mother and kissing men."

"Lise!" Violette hissed.

Amelie flushed. "Please tell me you weren't there."

"We weren't there," Violette said soothingly. "But you *have* been thinking about it all day. . . ."

Amelie made herself stay calm. She was due onstage shortly.

"I understand why you're upset, Lise," she said, in her most reasonable voice. "And I haven't— I'm not ignoring you. If you tell me his name—"

"I don't see why that matters," Lise said.

"I could talk to him," Amelie said. "I could ask him—"

A knock sounded on the door. Amelie sighed, turning to Violette. "Would you mind?"

"Oh yes," Lise grumbled. "We wouldn't want to be in your way."

"Of course, dear. Come on, Lise," Violette said, and both ghosts vanished. At least they were getting the hang of that. Probably for the best considering they might be around for a while.

Another thing she shouldn't dwell on before a performance. Amelie sighed, putting it out of her head, and opened the door.

"Hello, Amelie," de Lavel said. He handed her an enormous bouquet of red roses. "I thought I'd better remedy my earlier mistake."

"Thank you," she said, crossing the room for a vase. The pain in her stomach turned knifelike.

"Of course, you have so many roses already," he said, drifting over to the bouquets crowded on her dressing table and the edge of her walls. "Who sends them to you?"

"I am fortunate to have many generous admirers with year-round greenhouses," she said, filling the vase with water and beginning to methodically arrange the roses.

"Do you? I rather thought your audience was on the poorer side. But I suppose there will always be wealthy men who wish to shower flowers on pretty girls." He laughed, and she squeezed the rose stem she held until the thorns bit into her flesh.

"In fact, I'm sure I heard of one such man," de Lavel said. "An American. He's in the audience tonight. The papers say he's *courting* you. They think you'll marry him and emigrate to America. Fools."

She needed to play this carefully. Her hand was bleeding; she picked up a rag and wrapped it over her palm. "Dr. Moore is a good man," she said.

He chuckled. "I'm sure he is," he said. "But are you a good woman?"

"I strive to be," she said. Her fingers closed over the towel, squeezing it hard. The tiny blossom of pain was welcome.

"My dear girl," he said. "You're bleeding."

She glanced down quickly. A trickle of blood ran down the edge of her hand. He moved closer, taking her hand in his and adjusting the towel.

The smell of his cologne was overwhelming. He was so *near* her, so large and so much stronger than her. He knew she wouldn't cause a scene. She was powerless.

She forced herself to speak. "What brings you here tonight, Monsieur de Lavel?"

"Oh, surely not Monsieur de Lavel," he said, stepping away. She fought the urge to gasp for breath. "We've known each other too long for that. How many years has it been?"

"Seventeen," she said. He'd met her mother when Amelie was thirteen, had been Leonie's sole lover for five years.

Leonie had loved him. And when she'd needed him, he'd abandoned her, without a backward glance.

"You've grown up in seventeen years," he said.

She looked down. The opera seemed loud in the silence.

"I miss her, you know."

"No," she whispered.

"What?"

"No," she said, a little louder. "You don't get to say that to me. Not after . . . not after. I don't know what you're doing lately, but this isn't the deal. This is pretend, you and I. We pretend to be polite. We pretend to forget, like the rest of Paris. You pretend you didn't do what you did, and I pretend I don't hate you."

"Hate me?" The words were slow and soft. "You don't hate me."

What was she doing? Terror shook through her, but something even stronger, black and stinging like acid, bubbled up through her throat.

"Honoré de Lavel," she said, the words soft and luscious on her tongue. "Sometimes, late at night, I think about you. I think about pustules opening up on your skin. I think about blood clouding your eyes. I think about rashes that itch and grow until you go mad. I don't know that there's anyone in the world I hate as much as I hate you."

"Well," he said, after a long pause. "That's going to make this a little awkward for you. But possibly more interesting for me."

"I beg your pardon?"

"I miss your mother, Amelie. I've never found anyone like her."

"Then maybe you shouldn't have left her," she said, and as soon as the words were out, she wished them back. No matter what had happened, she'd been glad de Lavel was out of their lives.

He inclined his head. "Maybe I shouldn't have," he said. "Maybe I only realized what I had once it was gone."

"Get out," she said. The pain in her stomach was all-encompassing; she could barely even think beyond it.

He ignored her. "I can't get her out of my mind, lately. Ever since I saw you two weeks ago. You looked so like her. No, that's not right. But something about you *felt* like her."

The nausea was rising. She took careful, measured breaths.

"Take her place, Amelie. Come be my mistress."

She leaned forward and vomited all over the roses.

She retched until there was only bile, until the physical

pain and emptiness drowned out the man in her dressing room. When there was no more left, she sat in her dressing table chair and wiped her mouth, staring at the mirror.

"Not the most flattering reaction I've ever had," he said.

"You need to leave," she said. "Because believe me, I don't care who you are. I'll have the stagehands throw you out."

"I'm afraid you're not thinking practically," he said. "You're concerned about your reputation, but it doesn't matter. I'll pay for everything. You won't need to—"

She stood up and opened the door. "If you don't leave here in the next three seconds I am going to scream. Reputation be damned, I will cause the biggest scene you've ever seen."

"Amelie, you're being ridiculous."

"Three, two, one." She took a deep breath and opened her mouth.

"Honorine."

Suddenly it was like all the air had left the room.

"Don't you dare say that name," she choked out.

"You say that word a lot," he said. "*Don't.* You'll learn not to."

She watched him. She couldn't stop shaking.

"I didn't want to do this—well, that's not really true. I didn't really care how we did this, and anger is passion, after all. We both know Honorine's mine. Your mother must have really loved me, to name her after me."

"You gave up any right to Honorine when you left while she was in the womb," Amelie said hoarsely. "And again, when you—"

"That was before," he said. "My wife is dead now. There's nothing to stop me from claiming her. I don't have a daughter and think how much easier that poor girl's life would be, if I acknowledged her."

"Her life is fine," Amelie said.

He smiled condescendingly. "To your standards," he said. "But I can do better."

"We don't need anything from you."

He rolled his eyes. "You're denser than your mother, but then, she was quite bright, wasn't she? I'm threatening you, my dear girl. Be my mistress, or I take the girl. The courts will see things my way, I'm sure, and I can make sure you never set eyes on her again."

She stared at him.

"Five minutes!" The call came down the hallway. The stagehand poked his head in the dressing room. "Five minutes, Mademoiselle St. James!"

"That's my cue to leave," de Lavel said, rising gracefully. "I'll give you a few days to cool down. I imagine you'll see things my way." He nodded at the dressing table. "I'd have someone clean that up, if I were you. It's starting to smell."

He left, leaving behind a choking blend of vomit and his cologne.

"Mademoiselle St. James, three minutes," the stagehand said, on his way back down the hallway.

She nodded blankly. She needed to be onstage. She ran down the hallway, slowing when she entered backstage. The lights were blinding. Someone said something to her, she said something back. She did a few leg swings to test her hip, but she felt curiously far away from her body. At least there didn't seem to be any pain.

The music swelled, and she went on.

She couldn't focus, all through the first act. She missed steps, almost lost a balance. The dancer playing the prince glared at her when she botched a lift.

"What's the matter?" he hissed, through his euphoric expression of love.

She didn't answer, already flying across the stage in a series of jumps that felt like madness.

Finally, intermission. She stumbled into the dark coolness of the wings, only to be confronted by a furious Director.

"What is wrong with you?" he asked, the redness of his face furious even in the low light. "They are *laughing* out there, do you understand? *Laughing*."

"I—" But there was nothing to say.

"Are you drunk? What *on earth* could justify this—this atrocity?"

"I'm sorry," she said.

"If you don't remedy this immediately, you're done. Do you hear me? I don't care about your contract. *You are done.* Nod your head if you understand."

She nodded her head, and he swept from the wings, the other dancers studiously not making eye contact.

Enough of this.

Emotions were luxury items. In the Siege and its aftermath, only the wealthy could afford them. Was she wealthy, now, that she could allow this?

The answer had just been given.

She walked to the temporary barre, placing two hands on the wood. She took all the fury and grief and sadness and disgust and put it into a ball, the biggest one she'd ever made. And she pushed it away from her, before going to change.

The music started as she returned, and the curtain opened. Giselle rose from the grave, surrounded by dead girls in white veils. She tried to save her duplicitous lover, because he was a man, and he'd been in a difficult situation, and her love was pure.

When she saw the first ghost, she thought it was an audience member, standing in the aisle. Until she made out the vivid red pants of the French Army, circa 1870.

She kept dancing, pleading for the prince's life. Back and forth, back and forth, begging Myrtha to spare him. She didn't miss a step.

The second was a woman, dressed in beggars' rags. She crawled onto the stage from the audience.

Three and four were Communard prisoners, who'd been shot in the head and still sported the wounds.

Six was the prop master, who had died the year before.

Seven was a little girl, hardly more than a skeleton.

Another group of Communards, in the wings. The Palais Garnier had been a prison before it was a theater. . . .

Her head was pounding, like someone was driving a stake through her temples. She heard a buzzing as she turned, flying down the stage.

She had to keep dancing.

They started coming up through the floor. One of the gas-lights along the stage splintered, casting sparks everywhere. A corps member screamed.

She had to keep dancing. She couldn't hear the music any-more over the pounding in her head; it was as though there was a whole other head being fit inside it—

Something red dripped onto her tutu. *The wardrobe mistress will be furious*, she thought, before she launched into her *grand jeté.*

For a moment, it felt like flying.

She landed, with a blinding, mind-searing pain. Her leg crumpled.

She fell heavily to the stage. The buzzing was deafening. Her partner ran to her, saying something she couldn't hear.

The ghosts were everywhere. She could see everything—the

beggar woman had frozen to death last winter on the steps of the opera house. That Communard hadn't even been eighteen when he'd died, not of a bullet to the head like so many of his associates, but of starvation. The French soldiers simply hadn't fed him. The woman gliding toward the Jockey Club members in the dress circle had been a prostitute who'd died of a disease one of them had given her.

Honorine was in the audience.

The recollection thudded into her stomach like an arrow. "No," she said, trying to stand. Her leg slid out from underneath her, and she landed heavily on her side. "No."

She saw a dark motion to her right and someone leaping up onstage. Benedict's voice, pushing through the crowd—crowd? When had a crowd gathered?—around her.

"Let me through," he was saying. "I'm a doctor. We're both doctors."

Then his face was over hers, along with Victor's. "Amelie," he said, his voice calm on the surface and desperate underneath. "You're going to be alright. We're going to get you to a hospital."

Could they not see them?

"The ghosts," she said, not caring who overheard. "They're in the audience. You have to—"

He looked confused. "Lise and Violette will be fine," he said. "They want you to be well, too."

"No—" She broke off as a fresh stab of pain cascaded through her skull.

It occurred to her for the first time that she might be dying.

"Ben," she said. "You have to get Honorine. She's in the boxes—box twelve. Get her and get out."

"She'll be—"

"Ben," she said, and she could feel the tears running down her cheeks.

He looked at her and nodded. "Alright," he said. "Victor will stay with you. I'll get her. I—I love you."

"I love you, too," she whispered.

It hurt so badly. Every nerve ending, every muscle, every inch of her skin was pain.

When he was gone, she looked at Victor, his face frozen in confused panic. "Sedate me," she said.

"What's wrong—"

She grabbed the sleeve of his coat. "*Make me sleep*," she said.

After a moment, he nodded and reached into his bag. There was a brief prick in her arm, and the blackness swallowed her whole.

CHAPTER SEVENTEEN

January 12, 1871
Seven years earlier . . .

Amelie stood outside the shabby Montmartre apartment building, hands clenching and unclenching in her coat pockets. The wind pricked needles in her cheeks, and mud sank into her stockings. The air smelled of urine and gunpowder, from the hundreds of Prussian shells hurled over the wall every night. There was a tiny, flickering light in the apartment window; Honorine had lit one of the few, precious candles. Good.

She'd left her five-year-old sister to take care of their dying mother so she could find more morphine. She'd left them for three hours, and her pockets were still empty. There was no more morphine in the city: no more morphine, no more opium, no more laudanum, not even any more absinthe, because Paris had injected and smoked and drank it all weeks ago, before the shelling had even started, before the zoo had been raided for meat. Amelie hoped Jean-Louise had had something. She had died of smallpox and hunger two months earlier, six months after dancing before the Emperor.

No more Emperor, of course. Amelie wondered where he

was, Louis-Napoléon. Likely well-fed and in good health—that was the way of people of power. Warm. Even if they executed him, he'd be warm right until the march to the guillotine. Did the Prussians guillotine people? Probably they shot them. Either way it was better than the final stages of syphilis, with or without the ameliorating effects of morphine.

Her fingers wouldn't stay still in her pockets, twisting the lining, tearing at it. Empty, empty, empty. No more doors to knock on, no more friends to beg or men to flirt with. She'd fuck someone for half a bottle of whiskey at this point, but no one had any.

A few months ago, Leonie St. James had been an artist, a beautiful, funny woman, one of the loves of Amelie's life. Her mother and her best friend. That woman was gone, sapped away in agonizing stages by an indifferent disease given to her by an anonymous man, leaving only a body in pain and a delirious mind. Until a few weeks ago, Leonie had broken through the madness, here and there. Amelie didn't know when the last time had been, only that she'd stopped expecting it to happen again.

And yesterday they'd run out of morphine.

She had to go in.

Her fingers were clumsy with the outer door, fumbling the key, and her feet were heavy on the stairs. Fifteen years of dancing had never made her as tired as she was today, hauling her useless body up five flights of stairs to the tiny garret. What good was dancing, in a siege? What good was beauty, in the face of the ugliest death?

She was out of breath at the top, shaking, so she paused, taking deep gasps in and out, ignoring the hunger pains in her stomach. When she thought she wouldn't frighten her sister, she opened the door and went inside.

It was cold; the fire had gone out. Her mother was curled on the floor, asleep, surrounded by drawings. Her long, auburn hair loose and tangled around her shoulders. They took turns brushing it, she and Honorine, and braiding it neatly, but it never lasted long.

The drawers had been torn out of the desk in the corner, their contents flung across the wooden floor. A surge of fear hit her chest, and she looked around for Honorine, but she found the girl sitting safely in the other corner. She walked over and bent to embrace her, feeling her sister's soft hair against her face.

"She wanted to draw," Honorine said. "At first I was scared. I didn't know what she was doing, but then she found the charcoals. She fell asleep a little while ago."

"Are you alright? Did she hurt you?"

"No, I stayed away."

"Good, good." She didn't know what else to say. She squeezed her harder, feeling her sister's warmth, and then walked to her mother.

Even Leonie's sleep was not peaceful, punctuated by incomprehensible mutters and violent jerks. Amelie crouched next to her, smoothing the sweat-soaked hair away from her mother's brow, and for a moment, Leonie calmed.

It wouldn't be long now. Syphilis was an unpredictable lover, but there had been blood in Leonie's stool for days, and rashes now covered much of her body.

Amelie picked up one of the papers scattered on the floor. It was covered in a mass of dark, writhing shapes, so far from the lovely, dreamy scenes Leonie had once painted. Amelie's hand shook as she stared at the drawing, desperately trying to find something of her mother in the heavy, angry swirls and slashes.

She put it down. "Put your coat on," she said to her sister.

"Why? We're not allowed to leave her alone," Honorine replied.

"I wasn't able to get the morphine."

"Oh," her sister said. Even at five, she understood.

"I can't leave you with her again. Not when she's like this."

"But where are we going?"

"There's one more place I have to try. Come on, hurry up."

Honorine grabbed her coat—bought last year, when things were still good. Now it was too small. Amelie doused the candle. It left the room nearly dark, only flashes of shells and the lights of Montmartre drifting through the window, but she wasn't going to leave her mother alone with an open flame. Leonie's only response was to grunt and push her paper closer to the window.

"Let's go," she said, making her decision. "We'll be fast."

It was almost ten at night. In the distance they could hear the shelling, but as long as they stayed away from the city walls, they should be safe. The bombs were more for show than destruction—the Prussians' real weapons were hunger and disease. They were content to wait outside the gates until Paris was forced to open them.

"You don't need to be afraid of them," she told her sister. Honorine shrugged.

"I'm not," she said.

They hurried down the winding roads leading away from Montmartre, and in about twenty minutes, they were off the hill. Her sister's cheeks were pink with cold, so Amelie pulled her, shivering, into her side as they walked. It was only another twenty minutes from here.

They passed the new opera house, a massive trifle of a building, still years from completion when construction had stopped. It was currently storing ammunition, the piles of lumber and stone heaped where they'd been stacked months before, waiting for better times that might never come. Amelie waited for the usual twinge, but nothing came. It didn't matter anymore.

From the opera they passed into the Grands Boulevards, some finished, some not. She was headed toward one of the oldest, completed almost a decade before.

As they walked, the night changed. Paris changed. The sound and smell of shelling was still in the cold, windy air, but light flooded from large windows, and bursts of laughter began to spill out onto the sidewalks. This was a Paris that still had parties, still had laughter.

And suddenly, the smell of meat cooking.

"Where are we?" Honorine asked, staring around her. Even in better times she hadn't come into this part of town often.

"The Boulevard Malesherbes," Amelie said, aware that wasn't what Honorine was asking.

Her sister didn't answer, continuing to gaze around with wide eyes, and Amelie pressed on, counting the numbers of the tall, white townhouses.

She stopped in front of number fifty-four: crisp white paint, neat black railing, still possessing that sheen of newness even four months of siege couldn't dim. There was light from every window, and the tinkle of glasses and clever conversation drifted into the dark.

Any hesitancy Amelie had felt evaporated when she smelled the meat. This was where it was, then. The poor of Paris were lucky to see rat meat once a week, and here they were cooking enough for a party.

"What are we doing here?" Honorine asked.

Amelie crouched so she and her sister were eye to eye. "There's someone here who should be able to help us get Maman's morphine," she said. "Whatever I do or say inside, play along, alright? You have to trust me."

"I trust you," Honorine said.

"Sweet girl," Amelie said, pushing Honorine's hood down

and planting a kiss on her smooth black hair before straightening. "Alright."

They walked hand in hand up the clean stone steps. Amelie knocked loudly on the door, and a servant in crisp black clothing opened it, obviously expecting more party guests. His face soured when he saw them.

"Beg somewhere else," he said, closing the door. Amelie threw her shoulder against it.

"We aren't beggars," she said, pulling Honorine into the golden light cast from the doorway. Her sister looked at her questioningly, the glow illuminating her dark hair and unusual amber eyes.

The servant stared at the child.

"I see he has a lot of people here tonight," Amelie said. "I'd hate to make a scene."

He looked up at her with pure dislike.

"But I will, if I need to," she continued.

He glanced behind him, weighing his options.

"Her name is Honorine."

"Fine," the man snapped. "Although why you had to pick the middle of a party to come here with your sordid business . . ."

"Be reasonable," she said, exhausted. "How else could I have ruined your evening?"

He stuck his chin in the air, gathering all the dignity a well-cut uniform and two francs a week could afford him. "Follow me, and if you even *think* about causing that scene, remember I can have the gendarme here in less than two minutes."

Amelie waited until his back was turned to make a face at Honorine. The fear left her sister's face as she stifled a laugh.

He led them to a small room off the entrance, sternly told them to wait, and left. The room was cold and quiet.

"Whose house is this?"

The inevitable question, the one she didn't have a good answer for.

"Monsieur de Lavel," she said.

But her sister was sharper than that.

"Who is Monsieur de Lavel?"

Footsteps sounded outside the door.

"Remember what I told you," Amelie said quickly. "Play along. And when I tell you to go outside, I want you to go, no arguments, alright? Go and wait for me at the lamppost in front of the house."

The door opened.

Six years had passed since Amelie had seen Honoré de Lavel up close. He hadn't changed—his hair hadn't been streaked by gray, his amber eyes, so like her sister's, still had that trick of pinning you in place. He walked in confidence and security, knowing nothing bad would dare befall him. He looked at Honorine, a quick, barely caring glance, and visibly dismissed her.

"Hello, Amelie."

"Monsieur de Lavel," she said, her breath short. She hadn't thought this out.

He sat down, carelessly crossing one perfectly clad leg over the other. "Well?"

"My mother is ill," she began.

"Your mother is dying of the pox," he said.

Honorine made a little sound in the corner. Amelie turned to her, trusting de Lavel had seen enough. "Go outside, Honorine. Keep moving so you stay warm. I won't be long."

She waited until her sister had left the room. "You know, then."

"All of Paris knows. Leonie St. James, dying of syphilis? Half the men in town are dousing their cocks in mercury."

"Are you?" She didn't think de Lavel was the one who had

given it to Leonie—it was probably one of the men after Honorine was born—but she hated him enough that she wanted it to be.

"No."

No, he wasn't dying of syphilis. That was her mother, the mistress he'd cast aside as soon as she'd gotten pregnant with his child.

"She doesn't have long," Amelie said. "She's in pain."

"I imagine she is," he said. "It's an ugly way to die."

His voice was bored, like he was talking about a nasty cold a second cousin once had. She plunged on.

"We're out of morphine, to manage it," she said. "I don't—She's dying, and I know there will be pain, but I can't bear—" She stopped, pulled herself together. "Morphine will make it easier for her. I can't find any more. I thought you could."

"Yes," he said easily. "But I won't."

"You . . ."

"You came here today to threaten me," he said. "You brought that girl with you, to remind me. Of what, I'm not sure, because what do you imagine you could do to me? I suppose you could parade her around this little gathering, embarrass my wife, but for what reason? Do you think anyone would be shocked to know I have a bastard daughter? I could have a dozen, for all I know. It wouldn't matter to anyone. I might have helped you, if you'd approached the matter differently. But I don't like being threatened."

"I'm sorry," Amelie said. "I miscalculated. I thought you wouldn't see me without her. But please, Monsieur de Lavel. You were with my mother for a long time, you cared about her, surely—"

He chuckled. "Care? You haven't spent much time in the world, have you? Do you think those men who rub up against you before the ballet *care* about you, Amelie? Have you gone home with one yet, or are you holding out for the highest bidder?"

"You were always with her; she made you laugh, I saw it," Amelie said. "You're right, I came here to threaten you, and it was wrong. Please don't take that out on her. You *can* find the morphine, you might have some in this very house; don't make her suffer when she doesn't need to. I'm begging you. *Please.*"

He stood, dismissing her. "I hope you learned a lesson here. There were better ways to approach this, your mother certainly knew that."

"*Approach?* My mother is *dying*, she is dying and hurting and once she called you Honoré and you danced together and laughed until morning, and sometimes when she drew, you liked to sit on our couch and drink a glass of whiskey and watch her. She was a person, *Honoré*, you knew her, you knew her and she's *suffering*—"

"Lower your voice," he snapped, as the door opened and the servant from before came in.

"I won't," she said. "This is my last chance and if I have to scream, if I have to embarrass your wife and every last person in this house, I will. Are you eating meat from the zoo, Honoré? I'd hate to disturb your guests' enjoyment of elephant. She's hurting. Some part of you must care—"

He left the room without a backward glance. The servant grabbed her by the arm and pushed her out of the room, toward the door.

"Honoré de Lavel, you are a coward and a villain," she screamed. "I hope when you're on your deathbed, you know her pain three times over, because death comes for all of us in the end, even you."

Another servant had her other arm, and she was screaming words and curses, the tears choking her, and then she was being flung out the door and down the steps, landing hard on her hip.

"Amelie?" Honorine ran to her side, helping her up. Her sister's worried face was like a slap.

"I'm alright," she said automatically, rubbing her hands over her face and staring up at the beautiful white facade in front of her. She was shaking and she didn't know how to stop. That was her last chance—she'd exposed her sister to this, and for what? To go home and watch their mother die in misery?

She couldn't bear it. She couldn't.

Sound began to filter in: another explosion in the distance, laughter and music resuming inside the house, a beggar somewhere in the distance. Her mind cleared.

"Did you get too cold?" she asked.

"No, I walked around like you said."

She'd told a five-year-old to walk the streets of Paris at night so she wouldn't freeze to death, while she tried to extort morphine out of her mother's former lover. How quickly things went wrong.

"You didn't get the morphine," Honorine said. "From the man."

"No."

Her sister didn't say anything, but her solemn face and big eyes told Amelie she understood, and if Amelie's heart could have broken any more, that would have done it.

"Come on," she said, standing up slowly. She winced as pain radiated through her hip. "Let's go home."

She took her sister's hand and started to limp away, when she heard the door open and shut quickly. She turned to see a youngish woman hurrying toward them, dressed in what had been the latest fashion, before the Prussians closed the city. She had a cloud of pretty blond hair. Charlotte de Lavel, Honoré's wife, and mother to his three legitimate children.

She pulled Honorine closer to her side. "Madame de Lavel," she said.

The woman stopped in front of them, her eyes on Honorine. "I can't be away long," she said. "I hope this is enough."

She pressed a handkerchief into Amelie's hand, and when Amelie opened it, she saw a bottle.

"If it's not, send a message to me. I'll find a way to get you more."

Amelie opened her mouth, but tears flooded her eyes before she could say anything.

"It's alright," Charlotte said, touching Amelie's shoulder. "I mean, it's not alright. It's terrible. But you will survive it, and someday you'll be able to remember her as she was, not like she is now. Like she'd want you to remember her."

"Why are you doing this?" Amelie whispered.

"I met her once, before Honoré and I were married. She was kind to me. I have to go back. Goodbye."

"Goodbye," Amelie said, feeling the blessed weight of the drug in her hand. She put it into her pocket.

"Home," she said. "Let's hurry."

CHAPTER EIGHTEEN

November 1878

The rehearsal room at the Palais Garnier was empty. The dancers were long gone, off to rest and stretch and prepare to do it all over again. Without Amelie.

The climb up the stairs had been hard. She'd regained much of her everyday motion in the three weeks since the catastrophe, but still every step had been agony.

You were lucky this time, Dr. Durand had said. *But if you have another injury like that one—forget about dancing, you won't be able to walk.*

It was the first time she'd been back to the Palais Garnier since that night. The room was dark, lit only by the reflection of the city lights off the clouds above. She took off her shoes and padded to the barre, feeling the cool wood floor through the soles of her feet. She'd already lost her callouses.

She stroked the barre. It was smooth, worn with sweat and use.

What about surgery? she'd asked. She hadn't been shocked by Durand's diagnosis. She'd known, perhaps had known long before the catastrophe. *I've heard they can sculpt new bones out of plaster these days.*

He'd shaken his head. As *long as you don't keep treating it like you have, there's no reason you can't regain perfectly normal function. Those surgeries have a 60 percent mortality rate. And you'd never regain your old abilities with the new joint.*

Benedict had sat quietly next to her, watching and listening. Always there.

Carefully, hands on the barre, she bent into a *demi plié* in first position, only a gentle bend of the knees with her legs turned out. The pain was immediate. Tears pricked her eyes as she straightened.

As is, I don't know how much you'll be able to get back, with care and rest, Durand had said. *Your training, your musculature . . . your body is more capable than most. That might be a benefit, or it might be a curse. You might be tempted to push harder than you should and reinjure yourself.*

But I might be able to get it back, she'd said.

Durand had frowned. She liked this man, with his careful mustache and his gentle eyes. *Forgive me,* he'd said. *I'm not an expert in your art. As I said, you have an incredible body. You might be able to force yourself back to the level you were dancing at before. But to do so would be to guarantee another injury, and next time, you won't be lucky.*

Benedict had leaned forward. *Amelie—*

She had cut him off. *I understand.*

The pain ebbed. Slowly she sank into another *demi plié.* The tears escaped her eyes and rolled down her cheeks.

One more. Not the grand *plié,* the full bend of the knee, but one more *demi.* She closed her eyes and fell into the pain, letting it surround her. She bent with it, rather than against it, feeling the way it intensified at the lowest point of the *plié.* A ragged cry escaped her, the sound of a wounded animal. It shamed her.

Finally, her legs straightened. She clutched the barre, her

vision blurred and gray at the edges, and sank to the floor, one hand still gripping the barre above her. She didn't want to let go. The wood felt like home beneath her fingers.

The first night. In and out of consciousness. They moved her, first off the stage, and then somehow, to her apartment.

Flitting between waking pain and a darkness that was more than the lack of consciousness. Girls in white veils, dancing across a blackened stage. Girls with dead eyes and impossibly high grand jetés.

When she had awakened, the ghosts from the Palais Garnier were gone. Only Lise and Violette remained. The sedative had put her to sleep in time.

She was so tired. Her arm fell to her side, leaving her in a huddled clump against the wall. She wasn't sure how she was going to get back down the stairs. Not that it mattered. She was useless.

They'd buried Lise two weeks after the injury. Benedict had brought a stool for her, had insisted she sit on it. He'd wrapped her in blankets, and she'd sat as Lise watched her own funeral with distant eyes. At least Amelie hadn't needed to bribe the priest.

It was cold in the studio. Somehow winter had crept up while she was in bed; it crawled through the windows and over her skin.

A pair of dead pointe shoes lay forgotten a few feet away. She reached for them, pushing her body along the floor until she had one in her hand, the pink satin faded and threadbare at the toe and still perfect along the sides. The sole was broken—the shoes had been used until they had no structure left. They'd never hold a dancer up again.

Footsteps sounded on the stairs, a gentle knock on the doorframe. She couldn't tear her eyes away from the shoes. They'd been perfect once, shiny and pink and full of possibility. Every pair was like that, at first. But they were disposable, meant to be destroyed.

Benedict sat down next to her, stretching his long legs out in front of him.

"I've never seen those up close," he said.

"What are you doing here?"

"I went to your apartment," he said. "You weren't there."

And Benedict, there, every day, never pushing, making sure things were as good as they could be. She didn't notice at first—she wasn't awake for more than a few minutes at a time—but someone was organizing her doctors' visits, and making sure Suzanne knew what medicines to give her, and when Durand had suggested morphine he hadn't asked why she'd refused it, but instead quietly shaken his head.

He was there in the darkness as well, flashes of golden lamplight on shiny, dark hair, a laugh, a dance on a summer evening. A kiss stolen in a cemetery.

She'd told him everything about that night, except for the conversation with de Lavel. He'd tried to ask her questions, to keep investigating, but it had become more and more difficult to see him. He was still fighting, when she had only defeat left in her. She'd started feigning sleep when he called. A coward's way out.

"There has to be a better way to do this," he said, taking the shoe away from her and squinting at it in the low light. "Is this—I'm sorry, is this entire thing *fabric*?"

"Yes," she said, thrown off-balance. "It's stiffened at the toes."

"I thought you were balancing on a wooden block or something," he said. "You're really dancing on your toes. But there's hardly any support."

"Taglioni danced on less," she said.

He looked from the shoe to her feet. "Your ankles must be inhumanly strong."

"I suppose so." How had she gotten into a conversation about pointe shoes?

"I should buy Sam a pair," he said.

"I don't think they come in his size."

"I mean to study," Benedict said, with a little smile. "He'd be fascinated."

Amelie shrugged. "Take those. They're dead. Someone left them."

"I will," he said, taking the other shoe and beginning to wrap them together with their ribbons. "Speaking of my brother, I had another cable. And by another cable I obviously mean volumes one through three of *The History of the Decline and Fall of the Roman Empire.* I left it at your apartment, so you can look at it when you want."

She nodded, staring down at the shoes in his hands. "I'm never going to dance again," she said.

"Amelie . . ."

"Am I?"

"Your injury is very bad," he said, not for the first time. "You could certainly dance again, if you give it plenty of time to recover, but not professionally. Not the hours and hours a week you do now."

It was so still and silent at this hour, here at the top of the Palais Garnier. This was her favorite hour to practice in—an empty room, and no one around to pretend to.

"I suppose it doesn't matter anyway," she said. "The ghosts have seen to that. I can't perform, knowing what might happen."

"You can still dance," he said. "It doesn't have to be professionally. And we'll figure out the ghost problem."

"It doesn't matter anymore," she said, turning away from him. She didn't know if she meant the dancing or the ghosts.

"You matter," he said.

"I'm useless, Ben. Pretty soon I'm going to have to sell the apartment. I have a little money in savings, but I—" She made herself pause, swallow the panic in her throat. "What does it matter if I can dance in my sitting room? I've lost everything."

He sighed and shifted, putting his arm around her. "I know it feels like that," he said. "I know."

"I've failed everyone."

"Who? Who have you failed?"

"Honorine," she said. "The company. The Director. My audience. You."

"That's a lot of power you have there," he said. She didn't want to admit it, but the warmth of his body next to her was nice. "I didn't know so many people were depending on you. You don't think you're being a bit egomaniacal?"

"Honorine—"

"Honorine is fine. A little worried about you, perhaps." She felt him smile against her hair. "She's as charming as you said."

Even in her lowered state, happiness bloomed in her chest at the praise for her sister.

"The company and your audience are fine. Also concerned about you. But you don't owe them anything."

"They made me."

"*You* made you," he said. "As for that piece of shit you call a Director, he can go hang for all I care. I hope you did fail him. He needs more failure in his life."

Someone had told Ben about the confrontation backstage. When the Director had come to pay a visit, complete with flowers and chocolates, there had been an unpleasant exchange.

"You certainly didn't fail me," he continued. "In fact, I don't really see how you could."

"We had to delay the visit with Bonnet," she said. "And I know you wanted to solve the ghost question. All I've done is make it worse."

He squinted at her. "So . . . you being haunted onstage by the ghosts of everyone who died near the Palais Garnier since it was built and then collapsing because of a hip injury is your fault?"

"I'm the common element," she said. She put her head in her hands. "I'm the one who's too stupid to figure out what I did to let Rachel go."

"You are *not* stupid," he said. "You are sad and overwhelmed."

"I've been avoiding you," she said.

He tangled one of her curls in his fingers. "I know."

"You're not angry?"

His fingers stilled. "It can be hard, after something terrible happens, to see the people you knew before," he said. "They seem the same, and you're so different. I suppose I hoped you'd wake up one morning and miss me."

"I missed you every morning," she said. "But this—our agreement—was for the hauntings, yes? I'm exhausted, Ben. I'm not sure I have the energy to fight them anymore. Maybe they aren't meant to be fought. Maybe there's nothing I can do, and Rachel left because it was simply her time to go."

"Maybe," Benedict said, playing with her hair again.

"You don't believe me."

"I believe you when you say you're tired," he said.

He was humoring her. "Ben—"

"No."

"You don't even know what I was going to say."

"You've let me down somehow, or you're going to. But I'm not interested in being another weapon you use against yourself.

It's alright if you don't want to see me right now, but I'll be here when you do."

He was so comfortable beside her—she felt better than she had since the fall, resting against his torso. If she didn't have energy to fight the ghosts anymore, well, she didn't have energy to push him away anymore, either.

"I can't get down the stairs," she said quietly.

He snorted. "Like a cat that's treed itself," he said. "Come on. I'll give you a ride down."

CHAPTER NINETEEN

Four weeks after Amelie's injury, the conference Benedict had supposedly traveled across an ocean for finally began. He presented a well-received paper on potential surgical interventions for the brain; attended several stimulating lectures; and finally persuaded Dr. Montgomery to move across the Atlantic. For the institute, the conference was a smashing success. But the best part of every day, after the presentations and before the rowdy, convivial suppers, was the few hours in the afternoon Benedict spent at Amelie's apartment.

The best part, and the worst part. He was so hungry for her that every moment in her presence was precious, but behind everything was the same, constant drumbeat.

You're failing her. Again.

She'd seemed better since the night he'd found her in the rehearsal room. When he went to visit, she was in the sitting room, or even moving about. She'd stopped avoiding him. Occasionally, she smiled.

But when she thought no one was looking, sometimes she

stared out the window toward Montmartre, and a terrible, aching expression came into her eyes. Grief, anger, and a sadness that ran bone deep.

As he walked to her apartment, the November wind biting through his coat, he thought through the problem again, for likely the tenth time that day. *Something* had released Rachel. And *something* had called all those ghosts at the Palais Garnier.

He couldn't do anything about her hip, or her dance career. But he was damn well going to make sure she didn't spend the rest of her life among the dead. If she didn't have the energy to deal with it, he'd deal with it for her.

It was frustrating that his family had chosen now to stop responding to his telegrams. This was not in itself unusual, but did they have to choose this precise moment for one of their ramshackle adventures?

He arrived at her apartment building, passing by the small crowd of ever-present reporters, and climbed the stairs to her door. The small lobby and narrow staircase always smelled like beeswax.

"Benedict!" Honorine threw the door open almost as soon as he knocked, and the frustration that had settled into his chest lifted.

"Hello," he said. "How'd the test go yesterday?"

It had been geometry, which she'd been reluctant about until he'd pointed out the subject's usefulness in mapmaking. After, she'd abruptly shown an unsurprisingly strong aptitude.

"It was easy," she said, sounding a little disappointed. "I overstudied."

"Oh well," he said. "We don't learn things for tests, anyway." That had always been the Moore family way, at least. Tests rarely bothered with the interesting bits.

"Sure," she said. "But I wanted to show off."

He nodded, feeling that was entirely reasonable. "I brought you something," he said, reaching in his coat pocket.

Amelie wandered in, carrying a book. "Honorine, don't you need this for tomorrow— Oh hello, Ben."

She smiled at him. He smiled back, noting the dark smudges under her eyes and the pallor of her skin.

"Benedict brought me a present," Honorine announced.

"How exciting," Amelie said, carefully setting the book next to her sister's school satchel and sitting on the sofa.

"It's nothing much," Benedict said, suddenly feeling a little sheepish. He held out the little compass he'd found used, at a street market. It was somewhat weathered, but well-made, and in excellent working order. He'd spent an hour the previous evening cleaning and polishing it. "If you're going to be a cartographer, you need equipment."

Honorine gazed at the small disc in astonishment, and then, ever so reverently, took it and opened it. "It's a compass," she said, in an awestruck whisper that seemed absurdly out of proportion to the size of the gift.

"To get you started," he said. He glanced at Amelie. She was staring at him, her eyes wide and . . . stricken? As soon as he identified the emotion, it was gone. She smiled again.

"What a lovely present," she said. "Don't forget to—"

"*Thank you,*" Honorine exclaimed. "Can we use it right now? Oh *please.* I know it's not perfectly precise, but I did learn about a mapmaking method—you only need a compass and a measuring tape—oh please, please, *please.*"

He looked at Amelie, lifting his eyebrow. She nodded. "Of course you must, if Ben has the time."

"I have until six," he said.

"That's three hours," Honorine said. "We can make a *whole map* in three hours! I'll go get my coat. Don't leave without me!"

With this desperate command she dashed from the room.

Amelie laughed. "Would you like some tea before your adventure?"

"No, thank you," he said, sitting next to her. Some of her curls had come loose from her bun, drifting lightly around her face. He wanted to touch them, brush them away. Feel her skin under his fingers.

Instead, he put his hands firmly in his coat pockets.

"Victor came by today, didn't he?"

"Mmm," Amelie said. "He said I'm recovering well, and that I should walk a little every day. Then he talked about the Impressionists for thirty minutes. I made a mistake, actually. I told him I'd met Edgar Degas, and he asked me for stories, and the only thing I could think to say was how much of a nuisance he is every time he comes to sketch. Always in the way. I think I broke Dr. Durand's heart."

"He'll recover," Benedict said. "Victor's heart breaks at least once a week."

She laughed right as Honorine ran back into the room, carrying a notebook and pen. Benedict hid a smile. She reminded him so much of Maggie—though she was significantly less likely to light something on fire. Or punch him. "Amelie," she asked, a little out of breath. "We have a long measuring tape, don't we?"

"In the sewing basket," Amelie said, standing and rummaging through the basket in question before producing the leather-cased measuring tape. "I don't know how long it is, though—maybe eight meters?"

"That's enough," Honorine said, taking the tape. "Thank you."

"But . . . what are you going to do?"

"Come with us," Benedict said. He'd caught the muffled curiosity in her eyes, that look that said she wanted to know something, and was afraid she couldn't.

"Oh, I—"

"Come on," he said. "I'll give you a piggyback down the stairs, and Victor said you ought to walk."

"Oh please," Honorine said. "We'll stay nearby."

"No, no, you go on," Amelie said. "The reporters will bother you if I'm there."

"Right," Benedict said. "You'd think they'd be sick of you by now. Alright, give me a minute. Honorine, get your sister her coat. And you should both wear scarves—it's cold out."

Honorine nodded and dashed off again.

"Ben—"

"A moment," he said, and left the apartment.

At least this problem could be easily solved. It was the afternoon, and the reporters were thin. There were only so many "Dr. Moore, a faithful constant at St. Amie's bedside" stories they could write, after all. Benedict walked to the main road, flagged down a cab with a large, muscular driver, and arranged to have him wait in front of Amelie's building. Then, with his most charming smile, he approached the reporters, complimented them on their hard work, and suggested they have a drink at his expense. The nighttime crowd would likely have become suspicious, but these were mostly the junior reporters, and it was cold outside. Half of them took his money and headed for the nearest bar.

He hurried back up the stairs. "I have a cab waiting," he said. "And there are only two reporters outside. They shouldn't bother you too much. We'll head straight out the door to the carriage."

"Well done," Honorine said. Amelie looked a little flustered but wrapped her scarf around her neck. He wondered if she'd been outside since her trip to the Palais Garnier a week earlier.

He knelt with his back to her. "Up you go. And no nonsense about it," he added sternly. "I know it's undignified, but you already did it once."

"Oh, fine," she said, clearly giving in to the adventure. She wrapped her arms around his shoulders, and he stood. She was lighter than she'd been the week before.

"Ready?" he asked Honorine.

"Ready," she said, and led the way out of the apartment.

Their exit was simple. He put Amelie down at the foot of the stairs, out of sight of the reporters, and they quickly entered the carriage.

"What do you want to map?" he asked Honorine.

"Not this street, it's too straight. It would be boring," she said, thinking.

"There's that alley, a few blocks away," Amelie said. "If you're looking for something with more angles."

"Yes! Perfect." Honorine leaned forward to give the driver directions.

The drive took only a few minutes. Benedict paid the driver handsomely to wait for them and helped the sisters down.

They were in old Paris. A narrow, twisting alley, no more than a few houses long. A house at the entry had recently been torn down, leaving behind a pile of rubble. Benedict pulled a large, sturdy crate out of one of the piles for Amelie to sit on. A chicken clucked contentedly by, looking for interesting items to peck at.

"Alright, Mademoiselle Cartographe, what are your instructions?"

Honorine frowned, thinking. "The method involves taking compass headings and using them to plot points on a map. We will pace off the distance, which is not ideal." She produced the measuring tape. "But we can at least take an average distance of our steps, to reduce some of the inaccuracy. That is what we must do first."

He gave her a brisk nod. He'd never done any mapmaking before—he didn't know if any of the Moores had. It was rather fun.

Honorine guided them through stride measurement: first they measured a straight section along a wall, before walking along it, counting their steps. After they each had a number representing the average length of their stride, Honorine rolled up the measuring tape. She handed it to Amelie, who was sitting there, wide-eyed.

"Since when do you know how to do that?" she asked Honorine.

"Now don't start gushing," Honorine replied, quite severely. "Sister Agnes mentioned it, and I read up on it."

Amelie looked as if she would quite like to gush, but she closed her mouth obediently, and watched as Ben and Honorine paced off the alley, taking a compass heading every time their direction changed. A handful of residents drifted out onto the street, pulling up crates and sitting next to Amelie. They recognized her—he heard *St. Amie* a couple of times—but seemed more interested in the bizarre actions occurring in their alley.

He stopped cold when he heard Amelie laugh—an actual laugh, the first honest one he'd heard since her injury.

". . . my sister," she was saying. He recognized the proud tone of her voice and smiled. Someone had brought out a bottle and they were passing it around. It appeared he and Honorine were the best entertainment the alley had seen in years. Satisfied that she was having a good time, he turned back to Honorine.

It took at least an hour to gather the compass headings for the short alley, and even then, he and Honorine were painfully aware they would be approximating the shape at best. When they finally finished, Honorine's nose was red from the cold, and someone in the group around Amelie had started a cheerful fire. She was taking a drink directly from the bottle when they approached.

"Have you finished already?" she asked, smiling.

"We just have to translate our data into drawing," Honorine said with a pleased smile. A woman scooched over on a crate so Honorine could sit next to her sister. "Hello," she said to the group at large.

"This is my sister, Honorine," Amelie said. "And this is Dr. Benedict Moore."

"The American," said a man across the fire. "We know all about him."

"Hello," Benedict said, bowing.

Honorine rummaged in her satchel and produced a protractor and ruler. Amelie watched her in awe as she began plotting the map points in her notebook.

"Heard you were a brain doctor," the woman next to Amelie said.

"That's why he's here," Amelie said, never taking her eyes off the map forming before her. "For a conference."

"It sounds very nice," the woman continued. "But mind yourself. Not everyone's good enough for our St. Amie."

"I know," Benedict said, smiling, because they loved her. They didn't just like the pale copy she showed them on the stage, they loved *her.* She was so afraid the people of Paris would turn on her, but suddenly, he didn't think they would.

"There," Honorine said, and everyone around the fire leaned forward to examine the final map. It was a very good representation of the alley, with a small compass in the upper corner, and the scale noted below it. Benedict felt the same little puff of pride as whenever Maggie or Sam did something extremely clever.

She handed it to her sister. "Will you illustrate it? Just roughly?"

"But it's perfect—"

"A map is not useful unless it tells you something," Honorine said, sounding like a professor. "I've marked out where the houses and trees are."

"Oh, alright," Amelie said, sniffing a little in the cold. She took the pen and notebook and looked down the alley in the dying light.

"She's very good," Honorine said to Benedict. "Our mother was a painter."

The group watched avidly as Amelie sketched, adding a few trees and nearby houses. When she'd filled in the close bits, she stood. Benedict hurried to offer her an arm, and they walked down the alley so she could see the last few houses. She drew quickly, producing loose caricatures that nonetheless conveyed the feeling of the place.

"There," she said with another sniff.

"It's cold," Benedict said. "We should go back."

She took his arm again. "I don't know when the last time I met new people was," she said softly.

When they reached the group, Amelie handed the map to Honorine, who nodded in approval and tore the page out. "I asked Madame Flaubert if she wanted it," she explained, handing it to the woman next to her.

"How wonderful! Thank you, Honorine," Madame Flaubert said. "But you must sign it."

"Oh!" She pulled her pen back out and signed the paper painstakingly. "There."

"I'm afraid we really must go," Amelie said. "It's almost time for Ben's appointment."

They said goodbye to the cheerful group and piled back in the carriage.

"It's my first autograph," Honorine said, her cheeks rosy. "And don't worry, Ben, I kept the data sheet. I can make another map. I'm sorry I gave away your art, though, Amelie. I should have asked."

"You did the right thing," Amelie said, running her hand over her sister's hair. "It's their alley, after all."

Honorine nodded. "Oh! It's been such a good day."

As the carriage drew up in front of Amelie's building, all Ben could think was that he didn't want to leave. Amelie was laughing, and she hadn't really laughed in so long.

They walked past the reporters, warmed from drink and full of questions. Once they were out of sight, Ben carried Amelie up the stairs, Honorine running up first to open the door. She was already out of sight when he set Amelie down in the sitting room.

She smiled, her face flushed. "Thank you," she said. "For today. And for the rides."

"You're welcome," he said. He needed to go. He knew he needed to—his meeting started in twenty-five minutes.

He turned to leave, then stopped. "Come to supper tonight," he said. "After my meeting. At eight."

"What? Don't you have some terribly important meal with your fellow scientists to attend?"

He shook his head. "Not tonight," he said. "Come out with me, you and Honorine. We'll go somewhere nice, where the press can't follow. Please. After all, we are still officially courting."

He was sure she would say no, was braced for it. Instead, she nodded. "Alright," she said.

"Alright," he echoed. He looked at his watch and jammed his hat back on his head. "I'll see you then."

He couldn't stop smiling all the way down the stairs, or during the cab ride, or even, quite inappropriately, through a combative meeting about new methods of dissection. As soon as he could politely leave, he did, almost running to the street to hail a cab. He had forty-five minutes to change before returning to Amelie's.

When the cab stopped at Victor's, he almost threw money at the driver in his hurry. He dashed up the stairs, burst into the Durands' sitting room, and came to a complete and sudden halt.

The Moores had come to Paris.

CHAPTER TWENTY

"I wish I could wear my pink dress," Honorine said, staring longingly into her wardrobe. They were standing in her bedroom.

"I know," Amelie said. She wished she could wear a pink dress, too. A lurid, bright, flashy pink that would stun passersby with its vibrance. "But we're going to be in public."

Honorine sighed and pulled out the white dress she'd worn the night of the accident. It was extremely respectable, the kind of dress the daughters of all the best households wore. Demure, polite. Just like St. Amie.

When had she started pushing Honorine into that role as well?

"Let me see the pink," she heard herself say.

Honorine glanced up in surprise and hurriedly shoved the white dress back in the wardrobe and pulled the pink one out.

The pink dress was adorable. It was a perfectly acceptable pink—a light rose color. And there were charming ribbons along the skirt. Honorine had talked her into buying it earlier that year and had yet to wear it, because of—well, because of this.

It was only noticeable because of how pretty it was.

"Wear it," she said.

"Really?" Her sister's face lit up.

She nodded firmly. "Yes," she said, and before she could change her mind, she left the room.

No one would gossip about Honorine because she wore a pretty dress.

"Quite right," Violette said, from her usual spot on the sitting room sofa. The theme for tonight's wig was apparently masquerade. Several ornate masks dotted the curls, along with black beaded tassels and bright white pearls. "She's young. Let her have fun. And what are you wearing?"

Amelie looked down at her simple, pale blue dress. "This?"

"Oh," Violette said. "Yes, of course. Very . . . respectable."

Amelie smiled a little. Violette sounded so disappointed.

Since the accident, she'd seen Violette often, and Lise hardly at all. She assumed Lise was still angry with her.

"Is Lise around?" she asked.

Violette looked up from the hazy fashion magazine that had appeared in her hands and nodded toward the windows.

"I'm here," Lise said softly, standing by the barre. Amelie hadn't taken it down yet, although she'd need to before they showed the apartment to potential buyers.

The ghost was staring at the floor, rubbing one of her pointe shoes back and forth.

"I haven't seen you very much," Amelie said.

Suddenly Lise looked like she was about to cry. "Amelie, I'm so sorry," she said.

Confused, Amelie looked to Violette for a hint. The older woman simply shook her head and went back to her magazine. "Why?"

"I was very rude to you—right before you fell—I'm so sorry—I caused this—"

"No! No, of course you didn't. Why would you say such a thing?"

"I distracted you, I made you upset. You couldn't concentrate on your steps, and you—"

Amelie exhaled. "Lise, I fell because there were ghosts coming out of the floor of the theater. Is that why you've been so scarce?"

"You can't dance anymore," Lise whispered.

"No," Amelie said. She wanted to touch the barre, to rest her hands on it. "But it's not your fault. Truly."

She supposed Lise, of all the people she knew, might know what it was like to have that taken away. What was dancing like, when you were dead?

"Oh, Amelie, what are you going to do?"

"Lise," Violette hissed.

Lise bit her lip. "Sorry."

What *was* she going to do? She had no idea. The tightrope had been cut from underneath her, and it felt as though she was still falling. Every time she tried to think about the future it skittered away from her. She could barely think to the next day.

There was a knock on the door.

"Have fun!" Violette sang out. Both ghosts vanished.

When she opened the door, Ben's face looked strange. Worried. Happy. Slightly guilty. A trickle of amusement cut through the gray haze that had settled upon her.

"Oh dear," she said. "What have you done?"

"I am very much hoping I've brought you a lovely surprise," he said. "And if not, well, there's nothing I can do about it."

He stepped aside, and behind him stood Alva Penrose Rensselaer Webster Moore. Her friend.

"Alva," she whispered.

"Amelie," Alva said, stepping through the doorway and taking

Amelie in a firm, no-nonsense hug. "Oh, what have you gotten yourself into?"

Amelie started crying.

"To be clear," Ben said, handing her a crisp white handkerchief. "I had no idea they were coming."

"Sam *said* he was going to send you a telegram," Alva said.

"You've been married to the man three years," Ben said. "You didn't think there was a strong chance that plan would go awry?"

Alva lifted her shoulders. "It didn't seem like my concern," she said.

Several years ago, Alva had briefly entered Amelie's life in Montmartre. She'd lived in rather more spacious accommodations in the building Amelie had grown up in, trying to put her life back together after her then-husband did his best to smash it apart. For three years, they'd been friends and neighbors.

"You're here," Amelie said, still half-entangled in the embrace. "I can't believe you're here."

"The whole herd is here," Ben said. "Except Henry, because he isn't insane. Listen, Amelie, I'm sorry about this. They're going to be absolutely hideous. If you want to cut my acquaintance I completely understand."

"Here? Your family is here in Paris?"

Sometimes, in the bad years leading up to the Siege, after de Lavel had left Amelie's mother and the money was getting tighter and tighter, Amelie would remember Benedict's stories about the Moores. She would wonder what Maggie might be doing or whether a lamp she passed on the street had been designed by John.

They had become a fairy tale to her, and then there had come a time she hadn't been able to think about them anymore. It hurt too much.

Now, after everything, they were here.

"Yes, I've just spent a week on an ocean liner with them," Alva said. She looked very smart—Alva always had, with her glossy dark hair and her dashing dresses. "It's a miracle we're all still alive."

"Alva?" Honorine stood in the doorway, looking perfectly adorable in her pink dress.

"Honorine? My god, the last time I saw you—well, that's a tiresome thing to say, isn't it? Come here."

Honorine ran across the room into Alva's arms. "You came back," she said.

Alva's smile was a little tight, and Amelie wondered what it was like, being back in the city she'd lived in with her monster of a late husband. She squeezed her friend's hand, grateful.

"Well, you both look very smart, and Benedict has informed me we've ruined your dinner plans, so I'm terribly sorry for that, but we're here to transport you to a family dinner."

A family dinner?

"Oh, we couldn't," she said. "You've only just arrived, you must be so tired—"

"Excuses won't help," Alva said. "They've come all this way to get a look at you. You can't let them down now."

Well. Now she wished she'd chosen a grander dress.

"Come on," Ben said, kneeling in front of her. "Hop on."

Apparently, his family had rented a house. The four of them hurried past the reporters—there were more of them tonight; perhaps they'd already heard about the Moores' arrival—and piled into the waiting carriage.

Alva, squished next to Amelie in the forward seat, watched out the window with interest as they made their way out of Amelie's neighborhood. "It's changed," she said. "I've only been gone three years and I hardly recognize it. Not the traffic, of course. That I recognize."

"We made a map this afternoon," Honorine said. "Ben said he'll help me make a map of the whole city."

"He did?" When had Honorine secured that promise?

"Paris is in desperate need of better maps," Ben said, as though it were in no way unusual for a celebrated doctor and scientist to begin a mapmaking project with an eleven-year-old. Amelie hadn't realized the ongoing nature of this enterprise. "We looked at a few while you were ill and were appalled."

"They have no consistency of measurement," Honorine said, in the disapproving tone of a forty-year-old. "And most of them are already outdated."

"We need to figure out how to measure more accurately," Ben said.

Honorine nodded. "I'll ask Sister Agathe," she said. "But I suspect we'll need to do more research."

Amelie met Alva's gaze. Her friend was watching the pair with a sort of grim amusement.

The night was foggy outside their windows, and a little icy. It was warm inside, though. Amelie couldn't stop looking at her companions in the flashes of hazy, golden gaslight. Ben and Honorine were laughing about something map related. When had they become so close? And Alva, her real, proper, actual friend, was there in person. She'd missed her terribly, she realized. She just hadn't let herself know it until now.

The carriage turned down a narrow lane, lined by tall hedges. The plantings muffled the sound of the city, shut it out, giving the impression of entering a different world.

"How did you talk them into renting a house, Alva?" Ben asked.

"I told them the French were rather less understanding of explosions than Americans."

The carriage stopped. The Moores had managed to find a

little piece of the country in the middle of Paris. Buildings had been thrown up all around it—in fact, even the hedge-lined lane was sandwiched between two apartment buildings—but somehow, hidden in the middle of them was an old country house, surrounded by trees.

Amelie stepped out of the carriage, staring in wonder at this secret refuge. A handful of lanterns dotted the drive, casting a golden light over the two-story house and the small greenhouse standing next to it.

"How does this place exist?"

"Beautiful, isn't it," Alva said, standing next to her. "I suppose someone forgot to tear it down."

Even the air felt cleaner, sharp and cold in her lungs. She heard Honorine and Benedict clamber out behind her.

"Hello!" The voice came from the dark lawn, underneath a tall, bare tree.

"Sam?" Alva asked, as the large (and *extremely* handsome) man stood up. "What are you doing out here?"

"Mother and Father are fighting," said the small woman next to him. That must be Maggie. Amelie couldn't believe she was seeing them. She almost couldn't believe they really existed.

Ben came around to her side, standing close enough that she could feel his warmth. "They want the same room for their labs," he predicted.

"Mother and I ought to have the downstairs," Maggie said. "It's better ventilated. And the wall color is charming."

"But that's not completely fair, Mags," Sam said. "Father has a lot of heavy equipment."

"Which he insisted we drag across the entire Atlantic Ocean," Alva muttered.

"I don't see why he can't share the library with you!" Maggie said.

"You know he can't," Ben said. "Sam's too messy for Father."

"So don't be messy!"

"I'm not messy!" Sam protested. "It's my process!"

Amelie glanced at her sister. Honorine's mouth hung slightly open, her eyes wide as she stared at the Moores.

"That's a bit cheeky coming from you, Rags," Ben contributed. "You're messier than any of us."

"I *have told you* not to call me that! And we're having the downstairs!"

"There are more than enough rooms for all of you," Alva said.

"Oh, I secured the morning room for you," Sam said. "Father was looking at it in a very acquisitive manner."

Amelie caught Alva's small smile. It was extremely smug.

"It's cold," Ben said. "And I don't hear any shouting."

"They're probably making up," Maggie said, in a disgusted voice. "Alva, you go first. Hello, you must be Amelie and Honorine. I'm Maggie. This is my brother, Sam. He's an idiot."

"Hello," Amelie said, Honorine echoing her in an awed tone. They shook hands.

"I've been wanting to meet you both," Sam said, shaking her hand enthusiastically. "Honorine, Ben's been keeping me apprised of your mapmaking interest. I brought some books you might find interesting—" He offered one arm to her sister, the other to his wife, and swept them into the house while maintaining a constant stream of excitable chatter. Maggie rolled her eyes and followed.

Benedict had been keeping his brother apprised of Honorine's mapmaking interest? Amelie stood rooted in the cold, her hand resting against the tight ball of emotion in her chest.

"They can be overwhelming," Benedict said fondly.

She shook her head. She could barely speak.

"Well, I suppose you'd better meet my parents," he said, taking her arm. They strolled slowly up the stone path, underneath trees gilded by the cheerful light streaming from the windows. The yard smelled of herbs and woodsmoke and good, rich soil.

Inside, the house was a hodgepodge of styles, dating back at least a hundred years. The battered old floors gleamed with polish, though, reminding Amelie of a well-loved dance floor, and the walls were a cheerful yellow.

It was also *loud*. She could just make out her sister's happy chatter in the cacophony. Ben was grinning. "I can't believe I finally get to introduce you to my family," he said. "Oh, I told them not to talk about the ghosts in front of Honorine."

That reminded her of other secrets. Did they know she and Ben had met all those years ago? What did she need to conceal?

But before she could ask, he was already pulling her into the sitting room, and there they were, John and Winn Moore.

"Mother," he said, "Father, this is Amelie St. James. Amelie, these are my parents, John and Winn Moore."

"Hello," Amelie said, suddenly feeling shy.

"Doesn't she have a hip injury?" John said to his wife, in what he apparently thought was a whisper. "Should she be standing?"

"Yes, certainly she should sit down," Winn said, standing and crossing the room to shake Amelie's hand. "Thank you for coming to see us, Miss St. James. Won't you sit?"

"Thank you," Amelie said. She felt rather stupid and dull, dressed in a simple blue gown, distinguishable only because of how remarkably ordinary it was.

It was clear where the Moore children had gotten their looks from. John was tall and silver-haired, with the same kind, twinkling eyes that Sam and Benedict had. Winn and her daughter looked a great deal alike, both short and soft, with tumbling reddish-brown hair a few shades lighter than Benedict's.

"Now," John said, turning those eyes intently upon her. She shrank back. "Is this nonsense Benedict is saying true? Are those shoes you dance in really only fabric?"

"Er—"

"Oh, I stopped by Victor's and got them," Benedict said, handing over the pair he'd taken from the rehearsal rooms.

"I don't see how these work," John said, taking them and peering inside. "Surely you can't stand in these."

"Well, er, those are softer than usual," she said. "We wouldn't use them in that state. You can go through two or three pairs in a performance."

John continued to regard them, the small shoes looking impossibly delicate in his large hands.

"Who won the laboratory fight?" Ben asked, stretching his legs out comfortably before him.

"We came to an agreement," Winn said. "In exchange for use of the downstairs, your father will bake us five batches of sugar cookies."

"Five batches! Mother, that's extortion."

Winn shrugged.

"Are you looking at shoes?" Maggie drifted over. "Amelie, come to the greenhouse with Alva and I. Supper's running late because *somebody* wanted to improve the stove."

"And I have," Sam said, from the corner he and Alva were chatting in. "You can't expect someone to cook with inferior tools. Food is very important."

Maggie sighed dramatically. Sam shrugged, as if to imply some things were simply out of his control.

"Come on," Maggie said, taking Amelie's hand. "Alva, are you coming?"

Maggie pulled Amelie out of the room, Alva following. The

last thing she heard was Benedict's voice asking about the map-making books.

They went out the back door, crunching along a gravel path until they reached the glass greenhouse Amelie had seen on their arrival. It was warm and humid inside, glowing in the light from the house. Amelie took a deep breath in, luxuriating in the way the heat spread through her muscles.

"Now then," Alva said, examining an orange tree. "How do you and Benedict know each other? Because the papers seem to believe *I* introduced you, and I'm quite certain I didn't."

"Um—"

"Oh, she and Benedict have known each other forever," Maggie said.

Amelie froze.

Alva lifted an eyebrow. "They have?"

Maggie hummed an agreement. She seemed to be considering a corner of the greenhouse quite intently. After a moment she came to a conclusion, stepped forward, and began dragging a small table out of the way.

"The first time we came to Paris," she said. "After the war. They met then. I believe we can fit our lab out here."

"You can't put your lab in a glass building," Alva said. She turned to Amelie. "Is that true?"

"Yes," Amelie said. She cleared her throat. She couldn't imagine lying to these people, so she didn't, but it felt dangerous, this truth. "Yes," she said, her voice stronger. "How did you know?"

"He wasn't subtle," Maggie said. "We knew there was a girl here. And as soon as we got back to the States, he developed the most bizarre fascination with ballet."

"What?"

"He did," Maggie said. "Every time a traveling company came within a hundred miles of us, he'd go. He even read books about it. It was fairly clear whoever she was, she was a ballet dancer."

"Sam's never said anything," Alva said.

"I doubt he ever thought about it. You know Sam, he probably thought developing a fixation with a dance form barely even represented in our country was a perfectly ordinary thing to do. Anyway, when we started getting letters from him talking about a ballet dancer he seemed abnormally attached to—" Maggie shrugged. "It was hardly a mystery. Why can't we have our lab in a glass building?"

"Shards," Alva said. "Why isn't Henry here? The first explosion, you'll look like a glass porcupine."

"We won't have an explosion," Maggie said.

"You've burned down your last three labs," Alva said. "You need to start building explosions into your construction design."

"Hmm," Maggie said. "You really are awfully clever, Alva. Oh, I hear supper." She strode out of the building, pulling a notebook from her skirts as she walked and beginning to write.

"Three weeks ago, that young woman discovered a new chemical element," Alva said, watching her sister-in-law walk away in fond bemusement. "So. How bad is the hip?"

She'd forgotten how blunt Alva could be.

"They say I won't dance professionally again," she said.

"Oh, Amelie, I'm so sorry," Alva said.

Amelie sighed, playing with a leaf growing over the edge of a shelf. They should go in. "I don't know what to do with myself," she found herself saying instead. "I've spent my life going to class, to rehearsal, to performances. I suppose I need to get a job. Maybe teaching."

"You need to let yourself heal first," Alva said. "But I understand what you're saying. Those few weeks right after I left Alain—I was alone, in this new apartment, no friends, no routine. You helped me then. You brought a bottle of whiskey, knocked on my door, and told me that I was going to go outside the next day."

"Good advice."

"It was. It helped."

"I've given a lot of advice, over the years," Amelie said, smiling ruefully, "and now I'm in the terrible position of having to take it."

"How awful," Alva said, laughing. "What's the phrase? 'Tis better to give than to receive. Come on, let's go eat."

Inside, the smell of roast duck and the sound of laughter were in the air. Maggie was showing Honorine something in a fashion magazine, Ben was talking with his mother, and Sam and John had disassembled a clock and were happily involved in putting it back together. Amelie eyed the mess warily, but no one else seemed concerned, so she decided she wouldn't be, either.

After supper, Honorine began to yawn. The newly improved clock said it was almost midnight, so Benedict sent for the carriage. While they were waiting, Honorine dozed off on the couch, and the adults huddled together quietly at the dining room table.

"Do you think they'd talk to me?" Sam whispered. "Violette and Lise?"

"Yes," Amelie said. "I rather suspect they'd enjoy that."

"Marvelous," Sam said. "Will you come back? When we can speak more openly?"

She nodded, feeling rather bleary-eyed herself. Benedict fetched her coat and helped her into it.

"Your family is everything I imagined," she said.

"Is that a good thing?" His voice rumbled across the back of her neck, and she took a quick breath in.

"Mmm," she said, stepping away and buttoning her coat. "They're wonderful, Ben."

"Well, *I* think so, but that's rather the definition of bias, isn't it?"

"By the way," she said, "Maggie knows. About us."

"What do you mean?"

"She knows I'm the girl, from all those years ago. You never told me you developed an interest in ballet, Ben."

And then the most wonderful thing happened. He blushed.

"She's one of the most important scientific minds of her generation," he said. "It's a shame she has to die."

"I think it's sweet."

He narrowed his eyes at her. "Oh look," he said. "Here's the carriage. Honorine, time to wake up. Your sister's in a terrible hurry to get home."

She laughed, and let him hand her into the carriage, followed by her sleepy sister. "I'll see you tomorrow," she said.

"See you tomorrow," he replied, and she didn't realize until after the carriage was moving that they hadn't made any specific plans—she'd simply assumed she'd see him tomorrow.

Oh, Amelie. That way danger lies.

Honorine fell asleep again on the ride home, her little body curling against Amelie's side. Amelie rested an arm around her, watching the night streets pass by in a blur of black and gold.

Honorine woke just as the carriage stopped before their building. A flashbulb went off. "Are we home?"

"Yes, don't go out yet," Amelie said, frowning out the window. "Don't they have more interesting people to follow?"

"You should show some ankle when you get out," Honorine said through a yawn that ended in a sudden giggle when Amelie swatted at her. "Have a heart, Amelie, they've been waiting all night. It's cold!"

"I hope they freeze to death," Amelie said.

The Moores' driver opened the door. "I'll help you into the building, mademoiselles."

"Thank you," she said.

The journalists crowded around her as she descended, keeping Honorine close by her side.

"St. Amie! How's the hip?"

"Are you planning a comeback? Did you hear ticket sales have fallen since you left?"

"Where were you? Seeing that American doctor?"

"I heard he's out, and she's taking after her mother now—"

Amelie froze.

Her sister tugged at her sleeve in confusion.

"Go inside," she said, pushing her gently through the door the driver held open.

You know better. Don't engage.

"What did you say?" She turned in the general direction of the speaker, blinded by the cameras.

"Well, you need a new source of income, don't you?"

The words rose quick and hot in her mouth. *My mother was worth ten of you,* she wanted to say. *You reduce her to the men she slept with and the money they paid her. Well, fuck them and fuck you, too.*

She closed her mouth so tightly her teeth hurt. "Good night, gentlemen," she said, turning to go inside.

"Ah, come on, Amelie," the anonymous man said, grabbing at her arm. "Give us one good quote."

"Let me go," she said, yanking her sleeve out of his grasp and stumbling backward, unused to the weakness of her leg. She slammed her hip into the brass railing lining the stairs.

Spots of color appeared in her vision, and she couldn't breathe. The pain radiated everywhere. She couldn't think through the fog.

No one noticed. The noise, the cameras, the questions—they pressed in on her mercilessly.

Then the driver—she didn't know his name, she needed to ask—was back, taking her arm and forcing his way through the crowd and into the building.

The door closed behind them, shutting the worst of the noise out, and she could breathe again.

"Thank you," she said. The pain was fading. "Monsieur?"

"Girard, mademoiselle."

"Thank you for your rescue, Monsieur Girard."

"It was my pleasure," he said, bowing before heading back out. "Good night."

"Are you alright, Honorine?" Amelie turned to her sister.

"Fine," she said, slightly confused. "Why did you stay out there?"

"Oh—they asked me to comment on something and I misheard." She hadn't heard it, then. Good. "Come on, let's go to bed."

The climb up the stairs was agonizing. She felt panic rising. Had she reinjured it? Had she made it worse? She pushed the thoughts down. She couldn't let Honorine know something was wrong.

A few flower boxes lay in front of the door.

"I wish they'd send something useful," Honorine said, as they pushed them into the front hall.

"Oh yes? Like what?"

"Candy," her sister replied.

"Ah," Amelie said, trying to sound calm. "The most fungible currency."

Her sister replied, but Amelie didn't hear. She had opened a box of bloodred roses and lying atop the thornless stems was a message. *Thinking of you,* it said. *With love, Honoré de Lavel.*

She waited until her sister had gone to her bedroom. Then she picked the box up, flowers and note and all, stepped out of the apartment, and, shaking, threw it down the garbage chute.

CHAPTER TWENTY-ONE

The Moores were working. Well, they were working and talking and occasionally knocking things over and somehow, in the single day they'd been in Paris, his father had acquired a stray kitten. Ben could already see they were going to have to smuggle it back on the ocean liner. It was a straggly little gray and white thing, currently sleeping off a very full belly on his father's thigh while John sketched in a chair near the window. Sam was somewhere, probably the kitchen, if he knew his brother, and his mother and sister had meant to go shopping but had gotten sidetracked when Winn had "a thought" about their newest alloy. They really were the most ramshackle family.

Ben couldn't remember when he'd been happier.

He was giving another presentation at the conference tomorrow and was reviewing his notes in a worn, squashy chair by a bookcase. Every so often he'd glance up and watch them. It had been several months since they'd all been together, and he'd missed it terribly.

Amelie liked them, he thought, smiling at his notes. She'd said they were wonderful.

Seeing her with them, after all these years, had been surreal. She'd been stunned at first—most people meeting the Moores for the first time were—but within the hour she'd been discussing choreography with John and arguing about theater gaslights with Sam and asking questions about the alloy and—it wasn't that she fit, exactly, so much as she was excellent, and they were excellent, and together they all . . . shone.

A small, slight, almost nonexistent flame of hope lit in his chest. What if . . .

Before he let himself finish the thought, Alva sat in the chair next to him.

"Good morning," she said, in her crisp, contained way. She set a cup of coffee on the table between them and opened her newspaper—St. James Yet to Regain Consciousness? the headline read—by all appearances settling in for a calm morning read. So why did Benedict suddenly feel nervous?

"Oh, is it time?" Maggie said. "Mother, Father, it's time."

Ah, that was why. It was a trap.

"Time for what?" Winn asked, looking up from an equation. "Oh, *time*."

"Is it time?" Sam popped out from the kitchen. "Did I miss it?"

"No," Maggie said, pulling chairs toward Benedict's corner. "We're just starting."

"Oh good," Sam said, with what could only be described as a malevolent smile crossing his face.

Alva folded the newspaper and frowned at her assembled in-laws. "Really," she said sternly. "We agreed I would be in charge of the plan."

"But you gave the signal," John said, a chair in one hand and a kitten in the other. "You opened the newspaper."

"The newspaper was not the signal," Alva said. "There was no signal. The newspaper was to put him at ease."

"I also understood the newspaper to be a signal," Sam said. The rest of the Moore family nodded in agreement.

"Would you like us to start over, dear?" Winn asked.

"No," Alva said. "I suspect we've lost the element of surprise."

"Oh, *military* tactics," John said. "Still, there's usually a signal."

"You deserve this," Benedict said, crossing his legs and taking a sip of his coffee. "Traitor."

Alva lifted an eyebrow. "What's going on with you and Amelie?" she asked, bluntly.

Benedict grimaced.

"She's wonderful," Sam said, apparently to the room in general. "Don't you think she's wonderful? Did you see that? She simply cut right to the heart of the matter."

"Quite wonderful," Winn agreed, settling in one of the chairs that had been drawn into a semicircle around him.

"Could have been clearer about the signal," John muttered.

Alva closed her eyes. "I miss Henry."

"Yes," Ben said, grabbing the distraction. "Why isn't he here?"

"Business," Winn said.

"Love affair," John and Sam said.

Maggie looked up sharply. "What?"

"If I murder them," Alva said, "will you mind?"

"Yes," Benedict said. "It's just getting good. Love affair with who?"

"We are not talking about this," Alva said. "It is not our business."

"I agree," Winn said hastily.

"Of course it's our business," Sam said. "She's the widow of a merchant—"

"*Signal*," Alva shouted, her cheeks pink. "This is the signal! Signal, signal, signal!"

"I believe Alva has given the signal," Benedict said.

"Oh, right. Come, Lumiere." John sat down, settling the kitten on his shoulder. It took out its fury at being moved by biting his hand. Then, having vented its spleen appropriately, went back to sleep. Sam and Maggie joined in sitting, and five sets of eyes were pinned directly on Benedict.

"Amelie," he sighed, resigned.

"Very impressive woman," John said. "Ought to write a book. Told her so."

"I wonder if she's ever thought of starting her own ballet company," Winn said. "Of course, I don't know anything about that world."

"I liked her," Maggie said. Benedict thought her voice sounded a bit muted, but when he looked at her, she was smiling. "She should burn that dress, though."

"Maggie!" he said, protectively.

"She's not wrong," Alva said. "That's gotten worse, hasn't it? The hiding."

He'd forgotten Alva had known her during the in-between; she had a piece of the puzzle that was Amelie St. James.

"I don't know," he said. "I knew her before it started. She used to wear pink."

"You admit it, then," Maggie said triumphantly. "She's the girl."

"You already know," Ben said. He sighed again. Better to tell them and get it over with. "I met her on our last visit here," he said. "After the war."

After the war. He felt the memory reflected in his family's eyes.

"She was . . . she was life. I fell in love with her. I'm still in love with her."

"Oh, Ben." His mother came to sit on the arm of his chair, wrapping her arm around him. Briefly, he let himself lean into it, the warm, familiar love.

"I don't know what to do," he heard himself admitting. "I just—all I can think is to help her, and I can't even do that. She saved me, and when she needed it, I couldn't save her."

"Her hip wasn't something you could fix," John said, his voice slow and grave. "You should know that better than any of us."

"And the ghosts—we'll help with that," Sam said. "We've some experience, after all."

"It's not just you," Maggie announced. "All last night, she couldn't stop looking at you. Honestly, it was a little revolting."

Alva said nothing. He met her gaze and saw understanding. His family lived in a world where if you tried hard enough, you could simply *make* good things happen. They weren't as oblivious as they sometimes seemed—they had all lived through the war, and now, so many years away from it, he suspected they had each lost some part of themselves during it. For the first time he wondered if that was part of why they did try so hard.

But Alva had spent most of her life in a world where good things did not happen, and he could see the awareness, the doubt in her eyes.

His mother laid her head on top of his.

The kitten woke up, climbed down John's enormous frame, stretched elaborately, and announced its desire for a second meal.

"I love you," Winn murmured. He didn't know why that made him want to cry.

"We all do," Sam said stoutly.

"Sometimes," Maggie said.

"All the time," John said.

Alva patted his hand.

"Thank you," he said, trying to find his composure. "I love you, too. Now, have you interrogated me sufficiently, or is there more to the plan?"

"Honestly, we thought it would be more difficult," Maggie said.

"In hindsight the plan was perhaps overly elaborate," John said.

Alva huffed. "The plan was for me to sit down next to him and bring up Amelie," she said. "That's it."

"I remember more moving parts," John said, Maggie and Sam nodding.

"Next time," Alva said, "I'm going to run the plan myself without mentioning it to any of you."

She picked up her newspaper. His family stayed where they were, so she looked over the top of it. "This is the signal the plan is concluded."

Nodding, his family stood up and began moving the chairs away. His mother kissed the top of his head and slid off the chair, turning to face him.

"Ben—"

"I'm alright," he said, squeezing her hand. "Really."

She frowned, as if she'd like to say more, but a knock on the door interrupted her.

"I'll get it," Maggie said, opening the door. A messenger handed her an envelope. "It's for you, Ben. I think it's from Amelie."

The whole family watched as she crossed the room to hand the letter to him.

"Don't you all have work to do?" he said, opening it.

Ben—

I wrote Bonnet this morning to set a new date for your meeting, only to discover he's leaving town tomorrow. Or, as he puts it, "fleeing the hideous noise of this new, churning city."

If we want to see him, it has to be today, hence the emergency messenger. Write me back and tell me what you wish to do?

Best regards,
Amelie

"It's Emile Bonnet," Ben said. "The anatomist. Amelie convinced him to meet with me, but it has to be today apparently. Will you wait for a reply?" he asked the messenger.

The young man bowed. Ben quickly scratched out a message confirming he would be at her apartment within the hour.

"Thought he didn't see anyone," John said.

"Amelie's mother—" he paused. He didn't know how much Amelie would want him to share. "Knew him."

Alva lifted a brow but stayed silent.

Ben hurried to find his hat and coat and rummaged through his satchel to find the notes he'd written several weeks before in hopes of exactly this meeting. He took a few moments to refresh himself on the man's work, and of the questions he wanted to ask. Meeting Emile Bonnet was a coup. If his map of the cerebral cortex existed, if it was anything as detailed as the rumors made it out to be—they could be performing brain surgeries within a year. If, that is, he could be persuaded to share it.

He jammed his hat on his head, bid a hasty goodbye to his family, and hurried out the door.

Amelie was waiting for his knock, already dressed to leave. She ushered him inside. He looked unusually rumpled.

"Those journalists! Don't they have anything better to do? They're getting worse."

Amelie grimaced. The fall the night before had left an ugly purple bruise on her hip, making it harder than usual to walk. Dr. Durand had already visited that morning and assured her she'd done herself no lasting damage, but she was still favoring the leg. Thank God Honorine hadn't seen.

"I don't know what to do," she said, honestly. "I can't imagine the public still cares."

"The mountains of flowers left outside your apartment every day indicate otherwise."

She didn't want to think about flowers.

"I told Bonnet we'd be there at three," she said. "If you're ready?"

Getting through the journalists was easier this time. Benedict had hailed a cab before coming up, and before she knew what was happening, he had pushed through the crowd and handed her inside. More flashes went off. Benedict cast one last stern look out the window.

"My family interrogated me about you this morning," he said, grumpily.

"Oh yes?" She felt her lips curve.

"The real betrayal was Alva."

"Ringleader?"

"I never would have expected it of her," he said, and Amelie snorted.

"You don't mind?"

"Mind what?"

"My family . . . discussing you. You're so private."

"On the contrary," she said. "They're interested in me because they see me as a romantic possibility for their son. You're a catch, so it's flattering to be considered."

"Sweet-talker," he said, grinning.

She rolled her eyes and ignored him.

They fell into a comfortable silence. Ben pulled some papers out of his bag to read, while she leaned against the carriage wall and stared out the window. It had been a difficult night between the hip and the flowers. She didn't know what to do about de Lavel. Why was he even still interested, after her injury? He liked his women high-profile, and she was officially a has-been. Between the worry and pain, she'd only dipped in and out of sleep, dancers in white waiting for her every time she closed her eyes.

The Moores had talked about her that morning. She probably shouldn't feel so flattered.

Sometime in the middle of the night, between the dreams and the worry, she'd found her thoughts drifting to Ben's mother. Winn Moore was so sure—not only of herself, but of her *purpose*. She was a brilliant chemist, and she was in no doubt about it. How many women were allowed to have that sense of drive? Of sureness?

Leonie St. James had. Every time she picked up a paintbrush.

The carriage stopped.

Emile Bonnet lived in the same grand apartment building he had when he and her mother had been together. Her mother had always left her lovers' addresses, in case something happened and Amelie needed her. Leonie had never lied about her actions, but until de Lavel, she hadn't allowed Amelie to know too much about them, either.

De Lavel had been different. *She loved him*, Amelie thought. *He wasn't only her lover. She thought he was her partner.*

She pushed the past away. She was doing this for Benedict. And she was helping him do something very important indeed.

A smartly dressed doorman greeted them, nodding when she gave their names and showing them up the stairs. Bonnet had the entire top floor of the building. She supposed it was easier to be a hermit when your family money allowed you to command such prime real estate.

Rather a sharp thought. Really, she bore Emile Bonnet no ill will. He'd been perfectly fine to her mother.

The door was opened by a young man with neat blond hair, dressed fashionably but conservatively in a brown suit. "Good afternoon," he said, in careful English. "I am Monsieur Bonnet's secretary, Pierre Dubois. He is waiting for you in the library."

Also easier when you had staff.

"Thank you," she said. They followed the young man through the apartment, which was lavishly decorated in the style of two decades earlier. He led them to a large, welcoming library. A fire crackled behind a marble mantel.

A tall, thin man with long white hair stood up from an armchair as they entered. "Well," he said. "Leonie's little girl."

"Hello, Monsieur Bonnet," she said.

"It's been a long time," he said. "I was sorry to hear about your mother."

"Thank you," she said. He'd sent a note, afterward. It was short and formal, but he'd been one of only a handful of Leonie's vast acquaintances to do so. "May I introduce Doctor Benedict Moore? Doctor Moore, Monsieur Bonnet."

"It's an honor," Ben said, in his increasingly excellent French.

"The American," Bonnet said, looking him up and down. "I've read your work. It's interesting."

"Thank you, sir."

"So, you two are—"

"Friends, sir," Amelie said.

"Ah, *friends*," he said. "Well, there aren't many people I'd open my doors to these days. But I liked Leonie. You look a little like her. She was prettier."

"Yes," Amelie said.

"Beautiful woman, Leonie St. James." Bonnet sighed. "Alright, young man. I imagine you want to discuss brains."

"I'll be over here," Amelie said, excusing herself. She wandered to the other side of the room, only half-listening to the rumble of conversation behind her.

Idly she browsed the books, tracing her fingers delicately over the leather spines. She didn't dare take one down. A room filled with books—an unimaginable expense. The thought had a touch of spite to it. Why was she in this mood? Bonnet was one of the few decent ones. It wasn't her business what he put in his home.

She reached the end of the bookshelves and found herself looking directly at one of her mother's paintings.

All feeling left her body.

It was a pretty scene. The seaside. Waves. A handful of people bathing.

Dr. Durand would like this, was her first, bizarre thought.

The brushstrokes were slightly rougher than the style at the time. Leonie had painted quickly. *To capture the moment*, she had said. *Else you'll miss it*.

Brushstrokes. Her mother's hand. Her mother's moment.

Was she still there? Standing by a beach, the smell of salt in the air? If Amelie reached out and touched the sea, would she find her mother's hand waiting?

Slowly she reached out. Her fingers drifted over the waves, feeling the dry, rough paint. No, not there. Not anywhere, not even a ghost to haunt her.

Her hand fell.

"Amelie?" Ben's voice, concerned. How long had she been standing here?

"Oh," someone said. Bonnet, they were in Bonnet's library. "Her mother," she heard him murmur.

She needed to pull herself together. *Can't be coming apart in public,* she reminded herself. *Find the words. Tell them it's alright.*

She opened her mouth. Nothing came out.

Benedict's arms came around her. Not appropriate, embracing her in public. Nothing to be done about it, she supposed, since her limbs weren't working.

Say something. Tell them you're fine. Be fine.

"I've been to this building before," she said instead.

"I don't think so," Bonnet said, in the careful, kind voice one used with children and the very old.

But she had. She hadn't remembered until now.

"When my mother was sick," she said. "During the Siege. She needed morphine, and we ran out. I took her address book, and I went to every man she'd ever listed. I came here. You were gone. No one was here."

"I left during the war," Bonnet said, very slowly. She didn't want to look at him. "I was in England."

"Yes," she said, though she hadn't known. "Many of you were."

The old man—he *was* old, older than Leonie by twenty years or so—flinched. She should feel sorry for him. She'd caused him pain. He wasn't a monster; he cared that Leonie had suffered. He wasn't de Lavel.

"I should go," she said. "I—I'm not feeling well." That was the truth, at least.

"Yes," Ben said. "The cab is waiting for us downstairs."

"No," she said, turning. "You stay and finish your conversation. I can go alone."

"We've finished," he said. "Thank you for meeting me, Monsieur Bonnet."

"My pleasure," Bonnet said, looking grateful to have the visit concluded. He rang the bell, and his secretary entered. She must be looking very ill indeed, given the speed with which the man hurried them to the door.

"You weren't finished," she said, as he led them down the stairs. "The map—"

"He said he'll send it to me," Ben said, his arm around her as he helped her down the stairs. "He wasn't even difficult to persuade. I think he just wants to do the work and not bother with the publication part. If it's anything like what he described . . . it could change the field, Amelie. You did this. You made it happen."

"No," she said. "I got you the meeting. You did the rest on your own."

Marvelous, how she was able to speak normally while most of her person sat frozen. She got into the carriage, Ben exchanged the necessary goodbyes, and they were moving.

As soon as they were out of sight of Bonnet's secretary, Ben switched seats, putting his arm back around her.

"I'm sorry," she said.

"No," he said.

"I—I couldn't push it down."

"Don't," he said.

For twenty minutes, neither of them moved.

When the carriage stopped in front of her building, she pulled herself away, feeling as if she was leaving a warm bed after being awake for days.

"Thank you," she said. When he didn't say anything, only stared back at her with that intense look in his eyes, she shifted. "I really am sorry. I didn't expect to see one of her paintings. I haven't—" No, that was too bruised. Better to leave it. "Anyway. Thank you."

The press crowded around the carriage door, and she sighed, preparing herself for battle. Her muscles refused to engage.

"Why are you limping?"

She looked at him, seeing him through a sudden fog of exhaustion. "Because I have a very serious hip injury?"

"No," he said. "It's worse today."

"Oh." She tried to smile. "I tripped, yesterday. One of the journalists made me mad, and I stayed when I shouldn't. When I tried to leave there was a bit of a tangle. Stupid of me. I banged it on the railing."

"Did Victor look at it?"

"Yes. It's fine."

"Which journalist?" His voice was mild, his expression perfectly pleasant.

"Who knows."

He nodded, staring out the window. "Come home with me," he said.

"What?"

"Well, not home. To my family's rental. And not with me. I'll be staying with the Durands obviously."

There were many things she should say. The only one her brain could muster was, "Why?"

"Because you can't get any rest here," he said. He had that look in his eye, like he was really *seeing* her. "Because you look exhausted, all the time. Because you can't go outside without the press hounding you. Because last night you got *into a tangle* with one of them and fell, and you could have reinjured yourself badly."

His voice was so calm, but something lurked beneath it. "Are you angry with me?"

"No," he said, but his voice softened. "Think about it. There's a yard. Trees. Even a kitten. Honorine would love it. When was the last time you had a holiday?"

She'd never had a holiday. Was it as simple as that? Could she just . . . leave?

This was the sort of thing she absolutely should not do.

But she was considering it.

There were benefits. Her sister *would* love it. The press had mostly left Honorine alone, but it was awful she had to walk through them every day. It had only been luck that had prevented her from seeing that nasty little argument the night before.

And Honoré de Lavel wouldn't know where they were. Maybe he'd forget them, like he had before.

And she didn't know what else to do, and Ben was offering her a way to run away.

Ben was still talking. "Even if the press did find you, it'll all be proper with me at Victor's. You'll be getting to know my parents—perfectly appropriate for a courting couple."

She thought about the trees.

"Won't they mind?"

He laughed. "My parents? No."

There was such certainty in his voice that it removed the concern from her head.

She kept turning it over. There must be something wrong with the idea, but she was so tired, and she simply couldn't figure out what.

"Alright," she said.

"Alright?" He sounded shocked.

"What, are you taking it back?"

"No!" He said. "I thought this would take longer."

"I'll have to pack and speak to Honorine. Not that she'll

mind, I imagine she'll be as excited as if we were visiting you in America."

He looked out at the horde waiting for them. "What if we send a message asking Suzanne to pack for you?" he said. "You could meet Honorine after school."

It was her turn to laugh. Could she really—yes, she supposed she could. She didn't know what else to do, so why not try running away?

"Fine," she said, laughing when he looked at her suspiciously. "I mean it."

"Good." He tapped on the window separating them from the driver and gave him the new address. The carriage lurched to a start, and Amelie experienced a strange jolt of pleasure watching the startled expressions on the journalists' faces as they faded into the distance.

"Ben," she said.

"Yes?"

"Since when does your family have a kitten?"

CHAPTER TWENTY-TWO

The Moores were delighted to have her, which apparently in their world meant greeting her enthusiastically, finding her and Honorine unoccupied rooms in the large rental house (a slight difficulty, as each Moore seemed to need two to three rooms for themselves, their clothes, and their equipment), and then leaving her alone to do whatever she wanted. There was a genial, and entirely incorrect, assumption that she knew what that was.

She met Honorine after school. As expected, her sister was overjoyed by the news. Ben left after making sure she was settled, but he came back for dinner that evening. Afterward, he and Honorine devoted two hours to their map, their dark heads bent over protractors and rulers and pens. Amelie sat by the fire, feeling, as she did most days lately, that she ought to be doing something, and having absolutely no idea what that was.

Alva sat next to her, her dress a luscious marvel of burgundy wool. "They've gotten close," she said, looking at Ben and Honorine.

"Mmm," Amelie replied, surveying her friend. Alva wasn't

an expressive woman, but where a quiet, fierce desperation had lurked once there was now a quiet, fierce happiness.

"She's grown so much since I saw her last," Alva said. "Three years didn't seem like that long."

"It was long," Amelie said. "I missed you."

"First tears and now blatant expressions of feelings," Alva said. "Honorine is not the only one who's changed. Though, regrettably, I see that dress has not. I hated it three years ago, Amelie, and I hate it now."

Amelie laughed. "Me too," she said. "Shall we burn it?"

"Yes," Alva said, grinning. John came by bearing a plate of sugar cookies. Alva took two and handed one to Amelie.

"It's so odd being back in Paris," Alva said, after eating hers. "When I left, I didn't know if I'd ever return. And now I'm here, and it's not just that the city is different. I'm different."

Something in Alva's expression reminded Amelie of Ben. They had both survived impossible darkness and had crawled back into joy.

"Is it hard?" She didn't know exactly what she meant. Alva interpreted it as a response to her previous statement.

"A little," Alva said, shrugging. "Yesterday I passed Père Lachaise Cemetery. It was—it was odd to be so near him again. Even if he's only bones now."

Père Lachaise was where Alva's late, unlamented husband was buried.

"But mostly . . . it's nice. I have so many good memories here. Even more than I realized. I took Sam to Montmartre yesterday."

Amelie laughed. "I imagine it suited him," she said.

"He designed a new easel," Alva said, her tone flat, her expression adoring.

Yes. She was happy.

They kept talking, Alva telling her about her various projects, the latest funny stories from New York, and the problems with the printing of her latest book. Eventually Maggie and Winn joined them, Maggie chattering about what she'd bought that afternoon at the shops. Amelie found herself watching Winn through the evening; the way she laughed at her daughter's anecdotes, talked about her work, touched her husband's shoulder.

When it was time to retire, Winn walked next to her up the stairs. At the entrance to Amelie's room, Winn put a hand on her shoulder and squeezed it. "I'm glad you're here," she said, simply. "Sleep well."

When Amelie closed the door behind her, she felt like an old teacup that had been washed too many times. Worn out and brittle, like she might crack at any moment. There was so much easy love in this house. It pushed at her, stealing her breath away.

The room she was staying in was all worn boards and soft linens. There was one window, with a small, scarred desk in front and a large tree just outside. She lit the lamp on the desk and sat down.

She wondered what kind of tree it was. It was wide and mostly bare, a few leaves clinging despite the cold. Through its boughs she saw the glow of the city, reflected off the low clouds hanging in the night sky. When she'd been a girl, there had been stars in Montmartre. You could look up at night and see the constellations, look down and see the city.

Was there anywhere in the world where you could still see stars?

"I remember them, too," Lise said. She stood by the windows while Violette bounced on the bed, the mattress moving not at all. "At least, I think I do. When I was really young."

Lise was nineteen—had been nineteen; how did you measure age when someone had stepped out of time?—and most of her life would have been during the massive renovation efforts.

"Ah, you're both too young," Violette said. "When I was a girl, you could stand on the Île de la Cité and see the clear night sky."

Amelie doubted it.

"Well," Violette said. "You've landed on your feet, that's for certain. You should marry him."

"Violette," she hissed, looking at the door as if someone could overhear the ghost's words.

The ghost, who had switched her wig to one with an animal theme, made a dismissive gesture. "You need to think with your head, girl. It's what I should have done. When I was your age—well, I had any number of men wanting to marry me. There was even a viscount! He was sixty years old, of course, though honestly, even better. But I thought youth and fame and my legs and my voice would last forever." She shook her head, causing the giraffe on top to list dangerously to one side. "I'm not saying I had a bad life. But plentiful food and heat would have made the end of it a mite more pleasant."

"Didn't help me much," Lise said, fidgeting around the room. Amelie looked up—it was the first time Lise had alluded to the way she had died since the accident.

"Did you—did you remember something?" Amelie spoke cautiously, watching the room for suspicious shadows.

"No," Lise sighed. "But . . . he has a terrible father, you know. Just a terribly harsh man. R—he wanted to live in the city and experience life, you know? And his father was always writing him awful letters about responsibility and decorum and propriety. I think . . . I think what happened is that his father found out and arranged to have my body moved."

"I see," Amelie said slowly.

"Because *he* wouldn't have done anything like that," Lise said. "He loved me."

Amelie and Violette exchanged a look but said nothing. Amelie was very familiar with wealthy, young men who simply wanted to experience life in the city. Sometimes the fathers writing the letters had a point.

"Will you tell me his name?"

"Why?" Lise looked out the window, rising nervously up and down on her toes. "What could you say to him, *Oh, your lover is dead but I can still talk to her*? He should move on. He should find love again."

Amelie pressed her lips together. Suddenly she wondered what Rachel would say to that. Something very harsh indeed, probably.

"We should let you sleep," Violette said. "Come on, Lise."

The ghosts vanished, leaving Amelie alone in the lovely, unfamiliar room. She sighed and began her evening toilette.

She slept fitfully, the same dream haunting her sleep. This time she walked amongst the dancers, trying to see their faces, but their veils were too thick. Finally, she snatched the fabric away, only to find nothing but a blank, fleshy oval behind it.

That was when she woke up for good.

Light was drifting through the lace curtains. She lay in bed for several minutes, her heart pounding. Slowly her breath came back, and she sat up. She glanced at the clock; it was seven in the morning.

She got out of bed, tested her hip. Better. Scrupulously she did the exercises Dr. Durand had suggested.

After, she got dressed and went to find her sister. Honorine didn't have school that day, but she needed to make sure she was dressed and fed and so forth.

Honorine wasn't in her room.

Amelie wandered down the stairs to the kitchen, and found her sister sitting on the counter, next to a shocking amount of metal parts. Sam Moore was kneeling on the floor with his head in the oven.

"Amelie!" Honorine shouted. Amelie opened her mouth to scold her—sitting on counters and shouting!—but her sister giggled, slid off the counter, and ran to her with such a delighted expression on her face any remonstration dried up immediately.

"There's no breakfast," Honorine said. "Sorry. Sam had another idea about the oven, and he let me be his assistant"—she gestured vaguely to the pile of parts, which Amelie realized had once been an oven—"and we really did *think* we could have it done in only a few minutes, but then Sam had *another* idea—"

Sam popped his head out. "The question is how to get it hotter," he said. "I believe if we just realign this valve—hand me that wrench?"

Honorine ran back to the counter, rummaged through a pile of grease-covered tools, and confidently handed him one of them. How did Honorine know what a wrench was?

"Madame, I completely understand your concern," Ben said, coming into the kitchen on the heels of an elderly woman Amelie imagined was the cook. "It is intolerable to have your kitchen so disturbed. Particularly for a person of your talent. But I beg you—"

"They told me you were all famous," the woman said, in furious French. "Not that you were criminals! Americans, yes, I was willing to overlook that! But you *cannot* simply barge into this house—a respectable house, sir!—and begin taking it apart!"

A small bang sounded upstairs. Ben winced. Sam and Honorine carried on.

"What was that?"

"No doubt someone knocked over a piece of luggage," Ben said.

There was a clatter on the stairs, and Alva hurried into the room, her hair uncharacteristically askew. "Everyone's fine," she said. "Nothing happened."

She ran back up the stairs.

The cook narrowed her eyes. "You may have a lease on this house," she said. "But you don't have a lease on me."

"I'll double your rates," Benedict said.

The woman paused.

Sam took his head out of the oven. "You're not leaving, are you, Madame le Blanc?"

"Young man, how am I supposed to work like this?"

"I promise it will be much better when we are done," he said. "Come see—what I didn't think of this morning was that if I just change the way this valve is connecting, the whole thing will heat up much faster and cook more evenly."

She sniffed. "What I see is a pile of wreckage where my oven used to be."

"Oh, that'll only take an hour to put back together."

"Sam," Ben said in English. "If you don't have that oven back together in fifteen minutes, I am going to personally set you on fire and use *you* to cook breakfast. Good morning, Amelie."

"Good morning," she said.

"Sam, Amelie's hungry."

"I didn't say—"

"Look at her, how pale she is. She's going to faint."

"I am not!"

He ignored her. The cook had peeked over Sam's shoulder, and was hesitating in the middle of the room.

"Triple," Ben said.

Amelie saw an apple on the counter. Maybe she *was* hungry. She snatched it up and bit into it.

Madame le Blanc said nothing. She was eyeing the oven.

Three times her pay, with the possibility of better kitchen equipment than anyone else on the block? It had to be tempting.

"Tell them the next time it happens the rate goes up four times," Amelie heard herself say. "And so on from there."

Honorine giggled as Ben turned to her with a dramatic expression of betrayal.

Madame le Blanc smiled. "Yes," she said, nodding. "That's fair."

Ben muttered something that sounded like "highway robbery" but extended his hand. The cook shook it. "And until my oven's fixed, you're paying the Golden Rooster down the way for part use of their kitchen," she said. "Unless you fancy cold meals."

He reached for his wallet, counted out some bills, and thanked the woman. She left the room with a determined stride.

"You know he's going to do it again," Benedict said.

"Yes," she said, taking another bite of her apple. "That's why I told her to gouge you."

He looked at her, fighting the grin on his face.

"There!" Sam stood up, and suddenly the oven was miraculously intact. When had that happened? "Where did Madame le Blanc go? I want to show her!"

Ben threw an apple at his brother's head.

"There's tea in the sitting room," he said, offering Amelie his arm. "I boiled the water on the fire. Let's leave these miscreants to wash the grease off, shall we?"

Sam lobbed the apple back. "You know, from a man who dissects brains for a living—"

"Yes, see, the key is not dissecting the brains of the household staff," Ben replied. "And *particularly* not before breakfast!"

John poked his head through the doorframe. "Good morning," he said. "Is there breakfast?"

"Now," Ben said to Amelie. "We're leaving now."

She put her hand on his arm and allowed him to lead her from the room, hearing her sister's laugh behind her.

"Is every morning like this?"

"Well, normally they're in their own home," he said. "And we pay our staff . . . a lot. So, there are fewer threats of quitting. But yes. Traveling is particularly bad. You didn't seem particularly shocked."

The smile was back, lingering at the edges of his mouth.

"It reminds me of being backstage on opening night," she said. "Everyone dashing here and there, props being lost, costumes being sewn, the choreographer yelling at someone and three of the girls from the corps crying in the corner."

"That sounds much worse," Ben said, handing her a warm cup of tea.

She laughed.

"Honorine's happy," she said.

"Yes, she was upstairs with the women, but I didn't know how you felt about explosions—"

"I beg your pardon?"

"—so I suggested she help Sam." He glanced at his watch. "I should have left for the conference ten minutes ago. I hid some bread in the linen closet on the second floor. You'll be alright?"

"Yes," Amelie said. "Of course."

He looked at her, his beautiful smile blooming slowly on his face. "I like seeing you here," he said.

Then he was gone. Amelie sat down with her tea and looked at the clock. It was seven forty-five.

She had no idea what to do.

Honorine ran in from the kitchen. "Madame le Blanc is back with breakfast," she announced, dashing out before Amelie could reply.

There. Eating. That was something she could do.

But breakfast only took twenty minutes, and the Moores drifted off to whatever it was they did, and Alva had a meeting with a French publisher, and Madame le Blanc didn't want any help cleaning up, and Honorine had been invited to a friend's house for lunch but didn't need any assistance getting ready . . . no one needed Amelie to *do* anything.

She went up to her room, deciding to put away the rest of the stuff Suzanne had brought over. She'd hung the clothes the day before, but there were still a few things in the bag. Her cheque-book, some cosmetics. Some smelling salts she was fairly sure she didn't recognize. The little book Ben had bought her that day at the promenade, before her accident, still wrapped in brown paper.

She sat at the desk and carefully unwrapped it. The frontispiece was as outlandish as she remembered, with its illustration of people walking on the bottom of the ocean.

"*Twenty Thousand Leagues Under the Sea*," she said aloud. She touched her finger to the little people, and looked up abruptly, sure someone was watching her make a fool of herself.

But no one was. She turned the page.

"*The year 1866 was signalised by a remarkable incident, a mysterious and puzzling phenomenon, which doubtless no one has yet forgotten*," the book began.

The year 1866. The year she and Ben had met. A remarkable incident, a mysterious and puzzling phenomenon, which indeed no one involved had yet forgotten.

She laughed, the sound startling her in the quiet room. Apparently, idleness made her ridiculous.

But there really did seem to be nothing that she needed to do, so she kept reading.

Sometime later, she noticed the wooden desk chair was cutting into her legs. She took the book downstairs, stopping by the linen closet to eat a piece of bread.

"So that's where he hid it," Sam said, reaching around her to get a piece. "There's lunch downstairs. Oh! *Twenty Thousand Leagues*!"

He drifted away, holding a spool of wire, and she continued on her way. Lunch had indeed been set out on the dining table. It had already been picked over—what time was it?—and she was alone in the room. She fixed herself a plate, wondering if it was rude to read over a meal if you were the only person at the table and deciding she would allow it. Reading while eating turned out to be rather pleasant.

But the problem with dining chairs was that they were also wooden, and eventually developed the same digging-into-the-thighs problem as the desk chair upstairs. She set out in search of a softer chair.

She found it in the sitting room, next to a small table and a conveniently placed lamp. It was an old, deep armchair, upholstered in thick, soft fabric that had likely once been some kind of patterned gold brocade, but was now the mild color of sunshine on a winter morning. There was already a fire going, and a blanket was draped across the chairback. Amelie looked around, but there was still nothing for her to do, and she really had abandoned the book's characters in a perilous spot, so she sat down and opened the book.

People drifted in and out of the room, always occupied by their own business. At one point, John's kitten strolled up, looking at her passingly before jumping onto the back of the chair and falling asleep.

Honorine brought her books in and sat on the sofa. Amelie put *Twenty Thousand Leagues* down long enough to ask if she needed any help.

"Are you reading?" her sister asked.

"Yes?"

"Huh," Honorine said. "No, I'm fine. Thank you."

That was that, apparently. A little while later Maggie interrupted to ask her opinion about a choice of fabrics. One was cream, with a pleasant pattern of lilies of the valley, the other a luscious striped brown velvet.

"It would go with this sort of lavender silk," Maggie said, dropping both fabrics in an attempt to find the third swatch. "Ah, here. See?"

Amelie was so startled by *anyone* asking her opinion about clothes it took her a moment to answer. The cream was something she would wear. She hated it.

"The velvet," she said.

"Yes, I thought so, too," Maggie said. "The woman at the shop said pale fabrics with floral motifs were very in right now, though—"

Amelie nodded. "Yes," she said. "But that's dull, and you aren't. Have the brown." She struggled to find the right English word to convey her feelings. "Dashing," she said, pleased with herself. "Like you."

"Oh," Maggie said, flushing pink and smiling. "What a lovely thing to say. *Hold on, Sam, I'm coming.* Brothers! He's taking Alva to dinner tonight, and he can never decide what to wear. Honestly, I'm not sure how he gets dressed in the morning."

And then Maggie was gone, and still no one needed her, so she sat back down and continued reading. Honorine finished her studying and announced her intention to go outside. Amelie opened her mouth to tell her to bundle up, only to discover her sister already had.

Later, Winn stopped by with two cups of tea. "I'm going to pry," she said plainly.

Amelie put her book down, pulse speeding up. She'd been waiting for this. Winn would want to know what she was doing here, what her intentions were with Benedict.

"You've known Benedict a long time," was what Winn said instead.

"Yes," Amelie replied. It wasn't a secret anymore, but it was strange to hear out loud.

"I don't think about that time very often." Winn took a sip of her tea. She was dressed beautifully in midnight-blue wool, her brown-red hair swept up in the latest style. She set the cup down in its saucer. "I thought he was going to die, in the hospital."

With those words, Amelie's tension left her, replaced only by sympathy. She thought about Rachel's mother. She thought how she would feel if something happened to Honorine.

"I can't imagine," she said. "Or rather, I can, a bit, and even that small portion is almost too terrible to look at."

Winn nodded. "I knew it might happen, when he left. He was so proud, and excited to be helping, and I knew I might never see my son again. So many mothers didn't."

"I met Benedict before the Prussian War," Amelie said slowly. "I didn't . . . I had a lovely life, then. I thought I understood what he'd been through, and now I look back and I think, *how foolish*."

"Maybe it helped that you didn't," Winn said. "After, we were all so . . . *worried* about him. Desperate to help, to make it right. But none of us were alright. I don't know what happened between the two of you then, but when he came home, he talked to us again. I have you to thank for that."

Tears sprung in Winn's eyes; they were echoed in Amelie's throat.

"I took him dancing," she said.

"Ah," Winn said, smiling a little. "Dancing is a cure for a great many things."

Amelie's expression must have stiffened, because Winn leaned forward and touched her arm. "There are many ways to dance," she said.

That was slightly confusing, but Amelie's lips curved up anyway.

"I also made him row me around a lake," she said.

Winn wiped her eyes and laughed. "Tell me," she said, so Amelie did. All about that sunny day, and the bright pink boat, and how grumpy he'd been when she hadn't let him pay for the sandwiches.

"And he complained and complained, all because I thought he must be penniless, given the way he dressed."

"One day! I leave the house dressed badly *one day* and she tells my mother about it a decade later." Amelie looked up to find Benedict lounging in the doorway. How long had he been—well, long enough, obviously. She pulled away from Winn, embarrassed. She shouldn't have been sharing this without his permission.

But he was smiling down at her, those dear lines around his eyes crinkled, and he flopped down on the sofa with pure, good grace.

"You looked like a crow," Amelie said, trying out a little teasing.

"Well, you looked like—"

"I *happen* to know I looked perfect that day," she said. "It was a very nice hat."

"You're right," he said. "It was."

He gave her the sort of look he had no business giving her in front of his mother. It wasn't particularly heated—it was much worse. It was an expression that spoke of understanding, of belonging. *I am yours*, it whispered. *I always will be.*

She cleared her throat and tried very hard not to blush.

Fortunately, Honorine chose that moment to hurry in through

the front door. "It's snowing!" she declared, as if nothing more exciting had ever happened.

They turned toward the window. It was snowing, hard, the ground already coated white.

"Well," Ben said. "That's quite bad news for all of you, isn't it?"

"Benedict," Winn said, warningly. He shrugged and leaned back.

"What?" Amelie asked, as Sam strolled through the door.

"Did someone say it was snowing?" He looked extremely sharp in his evening suit.

"Yes," Honorine said, with *very* wide eyes. "Look."

"Too bad," he said.

"Sam!" This from Winn.

"Sam, if you rumple that suit before you go out—" Maggie hurried into the room. "Oh."

And she cackled. Well, Amelie didn't exactly know what a cackle sounded like, but Maggie went *hehehe* and tapped her fingers together.

"Fine," Winn said, standing elegantly. "But you know your father and I are world-renowned scientists, yes?"

Maggie, Sam, and Ben looked at one another and shrugged.

"I mean, *world-renowned* is going a bit far, don't you think?" said Ben.

"Getting on a bit, though, aren't you?" said Maggie.

"Nothing to explode here, Mother," Sam said.

She looked down her nose at her children. "If you think I can't blow up snow, Samuel Johannes Moore, you don't know me at all. John!"

"I already set up the catapult, my love," he said, from somewhere near the landing.

"Good luck," Ben said to Amelie. Moores scattered everywhere.

"With me," Winn said commandingly, sweeping Amelie and Honorine up the stairs. She looked a bit martial. "We've secured the high ground, but we'll have a problem with the supply chain."

Amelie was beginning to understand how the Moore family operated. "We're having a snowball fight, aren't we?" she asked as they reached the top of the stairs and walked into a small attic. "This is a snowball fight."

"Wrong," Winn said. "We're reminding our children that we are stronger, smarter, and better in every way. Now, John, what is our situation?"

"You're looking very pretty," he said, glancing up from his position next to what appeared to be a makeshift catapult situated in front of a window.

"John! Concentrate!"

"Right. As soon as I saw the snow was going to stick, I laid a canvas cloth down on the ground and attached it to a lever system here. When I heard hostilities commence, I pulled the cloth up, giving us a large—though melting—initial snow supply."

"Excellent work, dear," Winn said.

"This is the best thing we have ever done," Honorine whispered to Amelie. Her sister was still wide-eyed, her face glowing with excitement. Amelie hid a smile.

"Do you need ground reinforcements?" she asked.

"Hmm," Winn said, looking at them carefully. "Honorine, are you capable of great secrecy and stealth?"

"Yes," her sister breathed.

"Then I have a plan."

Later, standing outside a window she and her sister had crawled out of, Amelie wasn't sure it was a good plan. There were three geniuses somewhere out there in the dark. And she was bait.

According to Winn and John, their children were likely spread over three levels, one on the second floor of the house with an already formed but melting supply of snowballs, one in the tree by her window, and one monitoring the ground. Anywhere, inside or outside, was considered fair play. Amelie was still unclear what "winning" looked like. Her job was to draw the siblings' fire, identifying their locations, while her sister snuck snow from under their noses. Honorine, armed with a large pot, was slightly overcome by the prestige of her position.

"Alright," Amelie whispered, gathering a few snowballs. "Ready?"

"Ready," Honorine whispered.

Amelie thought about her targets. The two in the tree and house were at least fairly stationary. It was the roaming one, on the ground, that should be her priority.

She took a deep breath and started walking.

Was that a sound?

She stopped. Yes, there was someone nearby.

"You're the bait," Benedict said, from somewhere in the darkness. "Which means Honorine is somewhere around here, getting snow."

She'd known it was a bad plan. It was so dark she couldn't even see where Benedict was standing.

"That would be a bit obvious, don't you think?" she said.

"My parents are not the deep military thinkers they believe themselves to be," he said. Somewhere to her right, she thought, edging around.

"Well?" she asked. "Aren't you going to throw a snowball at me?"

A pause. Honorine should have one load up. "I don't know," he said. "I don't want to hurt you."

She developed a new plan.

"It's so dark out here, Ben," she said. "I'm a little frightened."

Another pause. "No, you're not."

"Fine," she said. "But I am cold, and I don't want to be covered in snow. Where are the others?"

"I'm not telling you that!"

"But if you tell me, I can avoid them!"

"I don't think you're understanding the concept of a snowball fight," he said. He was closer.

"Just tell me what side of the house to avoid," she said. "That's not giving anything away."

"It's dark," he said. "You can't use your eyes on me down here."

He was quite close now; she could make the shape of him out. She wrapped her arms around herself and looked miserable.

There was only one thing that had ever bothered her about her reviews. She expected them to call her passionless, restrained, tragic, beautiful, sweet, or dull depending on who was reviewing. But what they all failed to mention, good or bad, was that Amelie St. James was an incredible actress.

"Oh," Ben said, hurrying the last few feet and wrapping his arms around her. She dropped every snowball but the one hidden in her pocket. "You are cold. Poor thing. Go back inside, wait it out."

She looked up at him, tilting her face so the light drifting from the window would catch her lashes. "I can't," she said. "I don't want to let your parents down."

"Alright," he said, rubbing his big hands up and down her arms. "Maggie's in the tree. Sam's on the second floor, in the library. Avoid those spots and you'll be fine."

"Thank you," she whispered before she smashed a snowball on his back.

"You did not just do that," he shouted, as she hurried away as fast as she could without jarring her hip. A snowball landed on her shoulder as she headed for the back door, but it was too late. He was marked with a white spot, visible from the attic, and the snow began to fly.

"Sam's in the library," she said to her sister as soon as she got inside.

"I'll tell Winn," Honorine replied. "We got Maggie. She and Ben are pinned down. Winn said we need to cut off their retreat. Here." She handed Amelie a bucket of snowballs.

"Yes, ma'am," Amelie replied smartly, and went back out.

The air was white and filled with taunts and laughter. Missiles flew from the attic window with shocking speed and accuracy—the two siblings below couldn't hope to match the barrage, but it didn't stop them from screaming with laughter and throwing snowballs in the general direction of their parents. Ben's black coat was entirely white.

They didn't see her cutting around behind them, but after all that effort she forgot about Sam. Three snowy projectiles hit her, one after the other.

"Behind you!" Sam cried to his siblings, and Ben turned. More snowballs from the second floor followed, until there was a great cry and they stopped. Sounds of a desperate and hilarious fight rang out from the library.

"We've got your man in the library," Amelie said, as Ben stalked toward her. "You should surrender."

"Ah," he said. "But I have you cornered. *You* should surrender."

She looked behind her. Somehow, he'd turned her around, backing her toward the house. She looked wildly from side to side.

"Ben—"

"There's no point in pleading," he said, reaching down to scoop snow. "I'm on to your tricks."

"But—"

He stepped forward and dumped an enormous pile of snow on her head.

She screamed.

He rubbed it in.

She called him several very strong words in French, grabbed some snow from the ground and smashed it into his face.

They were both laughing uncontrollably.

"You look ridiculous," Amelie said.

"You don't," Ben said, gently dusting snow from her cheek. He was quite close, his face bathed in golden light from an upstairs window.

Her laughter faded.

The air smelled of woodsmoke and ice. The sky was overcast, the glow of Paris turning the clouds gray and gold. Snow clung to Ben's hair and shoulders, shimmering a little in the gaslight from above.

She reached out to brush some from his coat. The precious cashmere was soft beneath her fingers. Her hand slowed, lingered on his shoulder. She felt him go still beneath her touch.

His hair was wet. Her fingers barely grazed the edge of one damp curl. She glanced up, meeting his eyes.

An entire world was held in his gaze. Understanding, and love, and desire. The kind of desire that lit an echoing flame in her own body and sent it racing through her veins. It was a gaze that said the moment was in her hands: that wherever she led them, he would follow.

For one light-headed breath she let herself wonder. If she could be the woman that he deserved. Or if she could have him, damn the consequences.

And then Maggie and Honorine ran by, screaming and

laughing and pelting each other with snowballs. The noise of the fight trickled back in.

She let her hand fall. He smiled wryly, a quick flash of awareness and understanding, and stepped back.

"Want to go steal some cookies?" he asked.

CHAPTER TWENTY-THREE

A week later . . .

"That's it," Camille Durand said, snapping her newspaper shut. "You're driving me mad."

Startled, Benedict looked up from the paper he was revising, wondering what on earth he'd done to offend his hostess. "I beg your pardon," he said. "Tell me what I've done so I may remedy it immediately."

She stared at him with such serious disapproval he found himself sitting straighter.

"Camille! What have I done?"

"You have been glancing at the clock on my mantelpiece every three minutes for the past hour and a half. Every three minutes *exactly*."

"Oh dear," he said, restraining his smile.

"Indeed," she said. "Furthermore, if you tap that pen one more time, I will pound it through your eye."

"Completely understandable," he said.

"I am not devoid of sympathy," she said. "You want to go see her, propriety says you must wait, frustration, impatience, so forth."

"God," Benedict said, dropping his pen and rubbing his hands over his face. "It's that obvious?"

"Painfully so," she said. "Let's go riding."

He couldn't stop the smile this time—horses were Camille's solution to most things—but he really had been staring at the same page for . . . well, an hour and a half, so he might as well give Camille's way a try.

Besides, she'd already left to change. He followed her example.

Camille kept her horses in some very smart stables at the outskirts of town. "This is Louis," she said, stopping in front of a box stall roughly the size of Amelie's apartment. A large white horse looked imperiously over the gate. Ben held a hand out and was rewarded with a dismissive huff.

He chuckled. "Royalty, are you?"

Louis ignored him—very proper, who was Benedict Moore, after all?—and looked to Camille. She gave him a piece of apple.

"And this is Cabbage," she said, moving to the next stall. An enormous chestnut munched docilly at some hay, looking up obligingly when they stopped in front of his gate. "Yes, you're a sweetheart, aren't you? Half Brabant," she said. "He'll hold your weight, and he won't bolt if you turn out to be terrible in the saddle."

As her voice implied this would be a significant moral failing, Benedict sincerely hoped he would not disappoint her further.

A groom led the horses out to tack them, while Camille introduced Ben to the three other horses she housed there. That completed, she proceeded to summarize the major pieces of stable gossip and cast aspersions on the horsemanship and general character of most of the other owners until Louis and Cabbage were saddled. He tried to give this the attention it deserved.

Camille was a funny and intelligent conversationalist who he'd already offended this morning, and it was certainly not her fault he wasn't able to keep Amelie out of his head for more than three minutes at a time.

The day was cold and clear. Once they were mounted, Camille led the way through a small wood to the open meadow beyond. The snow of the week before had long turned to slush in the city, but here small streaks clung to the ground.

The past week had been difficult.

Seeing Amelie with his family was wonderful. She liked them. They liked her. Honorine fit in as easily as if she were a long-lost relative. Amelie was finally eating well again, and she looked more rested than she had the entire time he'd been in Paris.

But it was temporary.

This wasn't anything new, or so he told himself, over and over again when he couldn't sleep at night. He and Amelie were always temporary. He'd postponed his return ticket, but there would come a time he and his family had to go back to the United States. This was a false peace, and the longer and more comfortable it became, the more he dreaded its inevitable shattering.

But, he argued with himself in the night, *what if it didn't have to?*

It was a question he wasn't sure he had the right to ask. But their—her—circumstances had changed.

She wasn't performing anymore. She was likely going to have to leave Paris anyway; she couldn't afford to stay without a salary. Why not leave with him?

Why not marry him?

He had more than enough money for her and Honorine. They could start a new life in New York, together. This was simple, straightforward. Three times in the last week he'd opened his mouth to suggest exactly that.

And every time he'd realized he was suggesting something like paying for her. A hip injury didn't change what she'd said in the cemetery, it only made it more difficult. So, he said anything else instead, and the thing between them, this hot, complicated, disastrous, unsaid thing, kept growing.

But this was exactly what Camille had brought him out here not to do, and he was being a bad guest. He focused on the horse below him, on finding his rhythm. The cold air felt good on his face. Camille must have approved of his riding, because as the sun began to set and they turned back she suggested a gallop. When they arrived at the stables, he felt sweaty and loose, like he could have gone on for hours.

"Not bad," was Camille's assessment, on the way back in the carriage. "And look, now you can go see her. I believe Victor had an appointment with her today."

It had been six weeks since the accident. She was moving much better. Benedict was hopeful Victor would confirm progress had been made.

"I'm sorry I've been such a trial," he said.

"You went riding with me, so you're forgiven."

"Thank you," he said.

Camille rubbed her hands against her skirts. "Is she really never going to dance again? I can't ask Victor, because it would be wrong for him to tell me. But the papers say terrible things one day and declare a comeback the next."

"I don't think she'll dance the way she did," Ben said, slowly. "Performing. Significant work in pointe shoes. That's done with."

Camille turned to look out the window. "I don't know who I'd be if I couldn't ride," she said.

The sentence stayed with him as he washed and changed,

as he drove over to his family's house for dinner. The look on Camille's face when she'd said it.

He found Amelie sitting in a chair in the front room, reading. She looked up hastily when he entered, putting the book down quickly.

"You're reading it," he said, looking at the title. He was absurdly pleased.

"Yes," she said.

He sat across from her. "Well? What did Victor say?"

"He said I've healed."

"That's wonderful," he said, jumping to his feet. Relief rode through his body like a tidal wave.

"Yes," she said. Her voice was calm, pleasant. Off. She looked out the window. "And I've had more good news. The Director wrote me this afternoon. He wants me to take a position teaching. Of course it's mostly for the press—St. Amie returns to the Opera Ballet."

"Oh." He sat down again. "That's . . ." *Good,* he should say. "Are you going to accept?"

"I ought to," she said. "I didn't expect the offer. The pay will be lower. I won't be able to retire as quickly. But I won't have to sell the apartment, either."

"But you'll still have to be her," he said. "The saint."

She looked down. "I'm still thinking about it," she said. "I have a few weeks. But . . . I don't know what else to do. While I was dancing, the ghosts were the threat. I thought they'd end my career. But now that it's over—" She shrugged. "I'm more worried about Honorine's tuition. So long as Lise restrains herself, this is something I can do. It's a path I know how to walk down."

Marry me.

He didn't say it. He knew what the answer would be.

Instead, he nodded. He looked down, too. Something was pressing at his chest—sadness and anger and frustration and guilt. He needed to say *something.*

"Before all this happened," he said slowly, "I asked you if you ever missed dancing."

She pressed her lips together.

"You said, *Every day.* I know you can't perform anymore. But you're an artist. Doesn't it . . . doesn't it hurt to hide that?"

"I'm not an artist, Ben," Amelie said. "My mother was. I know the difference. I am a tool for artists. A broken one."

"That is a rather grotesque thing to say."

"It's the truth. I was chosen at a young age because my body was unusually well-suited for achieving the vision of other people. I am not the hand of the painter; I am not even the brush. I am the canvas. People paint on me what they wish to see, and I accomplish it."

"I have seen you dance," Benedict said. "You think people love you because you're a blank canvas. But I think they love you because of the little bit of you that creeps out around the edges."

Amelie shook her head.

He took a breath. He was getting angry, and he shouldn't be.

One of her fingers traced the lettering on the front of her book. "The other day. With the journalist. He said I was 'taking after my mother.' He meant prostitution."

"What?"

She shrugged. "I realized, in hindsight, he was baiting me, hoping to get an interesting quote. But—" She sighed. "I don't know how to say this."

He made himself relax. "I'm listening," he said.

"My mother was many things. She was smart. Perhaps extremely so. She was a very gifted artist—you saw the painting at

Bonnet's apartment. She was charming. She walked into a room and suddenly that room was better. And she also had relations with men for money, which we badly needed. She died because of that. Because of how she made money. And I'm supposed to be her opposite."

She pursed her lips, looking out the window again.

"But—the thing is, anyone would be lucky to be like Leonie St. James," Amelie said quietly. "She was wonderful. All the way down. You say an artist can't stop being an artist? That was her. Oh, not just the painting. The prostitution, the art, it's all the same thing in the end. Just *her*. Wonderful."

"I did see the painting," Benedict said, thinking of the ways Amelie had just described herself. "She was remarkably talented."

"I stole her a set of paints, once," Amelie said.

Benedict laughed. She needed him to. "I should probably find that harder to believe."

She smiled. "It was Christmas. This was before she found a more permanent situation. Long before Honorine. Her previous lover had a financial setback and left her. She'd spent the last bit of her waitress money on ballet lessons for me, and she was down to around three colors in her paint box. She pretended it was fine, a challenge. She painted a lot of skyscapes and Paris at dawns that month. But I knew. So, one Saturday I walked down the Butte—I wanted to go to a store where I didn't know anyone—and I saw the most remarkable set of paints in one of the really expensive places near The École des Beaux Arts. I sat outside and watched through the window for several hours, to understand how everyone moved inside, and then, when I understood, I walked in, took it, and walked out."

"This is a deeply shocking tale."

"It was a stupid risk," she said. "But she created so much

beauty with those paints. It's not bad to be the paint or the canvas, Ben. It's an honor."

"Yes," he said. "I just think you're more your mother's daughter than you think you are."

She jerked her head up, closing her lips tight. She tried to smile, failed.

"I can't talk about this anymore," she said.

The frustration that lived under his skin lately twitched. "Alright," he said. It was not her fault she couldn't see herself. She was not responsible for . . . for this desperate need he felt for her to be safe and happy and well.

He left her in the sitting room. When he was in the hall, out of sight, he leaned face-first against the wall, closing his eyes.

He wanted to whisk her away, to take her somewhere she had choices. Where she could laugh and dance as she liked. It was all he'd ever wanted, and what he'd never been able to do. Was this what his family had felt like, during his recovery? Just waiting and hoping the person you loved could find their way out?

He was angry at her, he realized. Angry at how she belittled and held herself down. He was angry at himself, for everything he wanted to do and couldn't.

And none of that was remotely useful. He had to do something, find something to sink this anger into. He took a deep breath, pushed himself off the wall, and walked outside.

The air was bracing. It was already dark. He wrapped his arms around himself and stared into the black hedges before him as he thought.

Artists needed places to create.

Would she thank him for making her one? Probably not. But he very desperately needed something to do.

Walking back inside, this time with purpose, he examined the first floor of the house. The kitchen was out for obvious reasons. The dining room didn't really have enough space. He went up the stairs. The second floor was all currently in use.

He climbed the small ladder leading to the attic.

The owners of the house used the room as storage. There was a small, empty space in the center, which was reasonably clean, but the walls of the room were lined with what was probably a hundred years of accumulated trunks and broken furniture and oddments that had lost their place below, all covered in dust and cobwebs and probably rodent droppings.

It was perfect.

He returned downstairs for supplies and got to work.

First, he needed to clear more space. The people who had put things up here hadn't thought about doing so efficiently, they'd simply wanted them out of the way. For an hour, Ben stacked and pushed and scraped and shoved. Sweat got into his eyes, he wiped it away with a dust-covered hand.

Sam popped his head around the corner. "Dinner's ready," he said. "What are you doing?"

"Not going to tell you," Ben said, breathing hard as he tried to move an enormous three-legged china cabinet from its place in the middle of the room. Sam came over to help.

"Why not?"

"You can't keep a secret," Ben said.

"Oh." Sam nodded. "That's fair. But do you want me to install one of those rod things along that window?"

Finally, the cabinet shifted. They half lifted, half dragged it to the space Benedict had cleared along the wall.

After he caught his breath, Benedict narrowed his eyes at his brother. Sam blinked back innocently.

"Why would I want you to do that?"

"This is a lovely space for a studio," Sam said. "That's what you're doing, aren't you? Making a studio for Amelie?"

"I don't know." Benedict sat down on a trunk he had not yet moved. "I don't know if she'll want it."

"Might as well have it ready for her if she does," he said. "Do you think a ballet studio would let me in so I could look at the rod things?"

"They're called barres," Benedict said. "And probably."

"I'll go look and get the supplies tomorrow morning," Sam said. "We can have this done in a day. Oh! Dinner!"

Benedict pushed his damp hair off his forehead. The tight knot in his chest wasn't gone, but it was better. "I'd better change first," he said. "Tell them I'll be right down?"

Sam nodded and turned to leave.

"And Sam? Thank you."

CHAPTER TWENTY-FOUR

A week and two days after Amelie started *Twenty Thousand Leagues Under the Sea*, she finished it.

It was the first book she had read for pleasure in her entire life.

When she closed the back cover, she simply held the book in her hands. It was *hers* now. She hadn't understood that before. When you read a book, and you loved it, it transformed in your mind. It became a thing you possessed, that couldn't be taken away. For the last two days, she hadn't thought about anything else. She'd told herself she would think when she finished the book.

Now she had.

It was still morning. She'd walked Honorine to school, come back, sat down, and read. The house was quiet and empty, the Moores off to pay a family friend a visit.

Amelie stood up, taking the book with her, and walked outside.

Now it was time to decide what was next.

She was healed. Or at least so said Dr. Durand. She'd stared at him when he said that, thinking, *This is what it feels like to be healed*? And then the Director's letter had come. Offering a way back. A way out.

She could go back to the Palais Garnier. She could pay Honorine's tuition. Everything, with the exception of the ghosts, could go back to normal. And even the ghosts had been quiet lately.

That was a good thing. It shouldn't make her feel itchy and restless and . . . angry when she thought about it.

And then there was the note Ben had left her that morning, tucked into the pages of her book. Waiting.

Amelie,

I'm not really sure how to say this, as I've realized it was possibly an incredibly presumptuous, terrible idea, but I've already done it, and it might be equally presumptuous and terrible not to tell you. So, I'll simply say, the attic has been cleared, and there's a barre underneath the window.

Yours,
Ben

He'd said she was an artist. He'd said she was her mother's daughter. Such easy words for him. And now he had done this thing, this sweet gesture.

She wanted to rip his note into pieces.

Why did he keep *pushing* her? She was already off the tightrope, and it was as though he was tempting her over a huge cliff, where she couldn't see where she would land, and something terrifying lurked in the darkness.

She pulled the note out and looked at it. She hated it.

And still, she wanted to see the studio.

Every morning, she woke up and missed dancing. The slow warming up and the smell of the wood and the way her breath felt in her chest when she was near the end of her stamina.

There was a barre in the house.

She would just go look at it.

So, she went inside and climbed the stairs to the attic. And when she opened the door, she froze.

Her whole life, Amelie had thought there was something magical about a studio. It didn't matter if it was new or fancy or exclusive, if it was at the top of the Palais Garnier or an attic with trunk-lined walls. With a little empty space, a barre, and a mirror, you could become art. Perhaps the magic was in the emptiness itself.

Whatever the element was, this space was filled with it. The room was in a corner, so there were four medium-sized windows spread out over two walls. The other two had furniture and trunks and boxes organized neatly against them. Four floor-length mirrors had been installed in the room, two on each wall, between the windows.

She looked at the floor. It was old and uneven and scarred. She couldn't do pointe work on it, but she likely would never put pointe shoes on again.

She set *Twenty Thousand Leagues* down carefully on a wooden bench Ben had put in a corner and walked to the barre.

It was smooth and beautiful, with firm metal supports attaching it to the wall. She put her hands on it, took a breath, and went up onto *demi pointe*. It didn't hurt, so she turned to the side, with her left hand on the barre, carefully found first position, and sank into a *demi plié*.

That didn't hurt, either. She dropped her hand.

Her chest and throat were tight. Her arms were shaking. She

didn't know what to do next. Leave? Stay? What did it mean if she stayed?

It doesn't need to mean anything, she told herself. *It can just mean that your muscles ache from disuse and this is the best way to loosen them up.*

Slowly, she led herself through a barre. Anything she thought was too hard she simply didn't do. She didn't push herself. At the end, nothing hurt.

All those years of pain, erased. Like they'd never been. She could live her life without ever feeling that pain again.

She shouldn't resent that.

Did any of it matter? The years of pain, of hiding, of pretending, of working. All gone, now, and no one mourned it but her.

Amelie sketched out a few turns, nothing difficult. Her balance was completely off. The stability of her torso, built over years of training, was gone. It was strange, watching her reflection move. She didn't look the same anymore.

St. Amie was gone. Could she be her again?

Hazily, she sketched out a familiar motion, one caught somewhere in the back of her mind. She bent her body, swinging her arms to the side like broken wings. The position was reminiscent of a bird of prey. Hideous.

Going up onto *demi pointe* made a cleaner line. Pointe shoes would be better. For a moment she almost fell into self-pity, but it would be hard to be *en pointe* and judging the position at the same time. *Imagine it* en pointe, *then. And what if the dancer* bourrée'*ed from side to side, perhaps a few inches in either direction, but very rapidly . . .*

She watched herself in the mirror. When she realized what she was doing, she came down abruptly.

It was the dream.

Or rather, it wasn't the dream. The dancers in the dream were angry, but their choreography wasn't—mostly it was *Giselle.*

No, this was the choreography the dancers in the dream *wanted.*

It was anger. It was grief no one thought was important, loss no one noticed.

It was the thing lurking in the darkness.

There was a knock on the attic door. She knew it was Ben before she answered.

"Come in," she said.

The door opened, and he entered the room, taking his coat off and dropping his satchel by the entrance. She met his eyes in the mirror.

His face was flushed from the cold, his nose a little red. He looked a little tired. And he was so achingly beautiful.

"Are you speaking to me?"

"Yes," she said, watching him. Soon he would leave. Soon she would go back to her life. Soon, she would never see him again.

She should say *thank you.* For making her this studio. For everything else.

She didn't want to.

Ben's lips quirked. "It sounds like you're speaking to me begrudgingly. Where is everyone?"

"Your family went to visit someone," she said. "And Honorine's at school."

He nodded as he strode across the room. She watched his reflection, the long, loose, powerful way he moved, and she felt something tight and hot settle across her skin. Something like anger. Something like desire.

"I'm sorry," he said. "I didn't know what to do, so I did this.

And once I had, I thought it would be equally wrong to conceal it from you."

She didn't say anything for a moment. "Don't apologize," she said, finally. "You made me something beautiful. It's just that . . . I don't know. I don't know what's wrong with me."

He sat down against the wall, stretching his long legs out. After hesitating, she sat next to him.

"I'll miss you," she said.

He nodded slowly.

"I'm so angry," she whispered. "At everything."

He nodded again.

"I want to break things," she said softly. "I want to scream."

He nodded a third time. The moment stretched between them, taut like wire, before he pushed himself off the floor. He walked across the room to the neat stack of accumulated detritus, and deliberately selected a chipped, dusty plate. He held it aloft.

And dropped it.

She jumped.

He chose another plate and held it out to her. His eyes were focused on her, the challenge simmering in that bright, blazing blue. He was daring her. She didn't move.

"No?" He dropped the second plate. It shattered into four pieces, the crashing sound racing through her blood. "You should. It's quite satisfying."

His anger reached out to hers, meeting it, thrumming in harmony. It was delicious.

He held out a third plate.

She felt fate settle upon her. For twelve years, their paths had been crossing and diverging, crossing and diverging. Tonight, here, they were going to cross again.

The knowledge felt like freedom and fire and a little like regret.

She stood, took the plate, and dropped it.

"Well?" he said, his scrupulously polite tone at odds with the tension in his body.

"You're right. Satisfying," she said.

"Scream, if you want to," he said.

She looked up, deliberately held his gaze, and took the final step. "I want you to make me scream," she said.

His nostrils flared, a quick, sudden intake of breath.

"Alright," he said.

"I want to climb on top of you and tear your shirt off," she continued. "I want to leave claw marks down your back."

"Fine."

"Promise me we'll still be friends afterward," she said.

He met her gaze. "I promise," he said.

"I don't have protection."

"I'm a doctor," he said. "I don't leave the house without it."

Anger and lust were coursing through every vein, but that made her laugh.

"What?"

"The image of you pressing French letters on unsuspecting patients," she said.

"It's my ethical duty," he replied, crossing the room and pulling a small container out of his satchel. He locked the door. "Amelie," he said. "Are you sure—"

"Yes," she said.

"You didn't promise *you* would still be friends with *me* afterward," he said. "Given our history—"

"I promise," she said. "Whatever happens. I haven't done this in a long time, Ben."

"Take your dress off."

His voice was husky, firm. She stood up, unbuttoned the top of her dress, and slipped it off.

A muscle in his jaw pulsed.

He was handsome, and he was hers, and she loved him, and she was so, so angry, and at the moment she could think of no better way to solve that problem than by pushing him against the wall and kissing him.

She crossed the room, dressed only in her chemise, her hands rough at his chest.

Immediately his hands were at her waist, holding her against him, his kiss echoing her own aching desperation. He flipped their positions, pressing her back to the wall and his body against hers. She could feel his cock stand against her stomach.

"Tell me what you're angry about," she gasped, as he lifted her up and braced her against the wall. She wrapped her legs around him, her chemise riding up her thighs.

"You," he said, kissing her neck, the bristle of his beard making her gasp. "I am furious about you. I am furious at the things that happened to you. I am furious I couldn't stop them. I am furious you didn't come to the States twelve years ago. I am furious at the way you treat yourself. I am furious that I want you *so much, all the time*. I'm furious that I love you, and that you love me, and somehow, for some stupid reason, we are not getting married right now, and instead I'm about to fuck you in an attic."

"Stop pushing me," she said, ripping his shirt off. The cloth tore with a satisfying clatter of buttons. "You think I like this? You left. You were gone. I missed you." She bit his shoulder, not hard, but enough to leave a mark. "Now you're back, and you're looking at me with that stupid loyal expression in your eyes, and you make it *so tempting* to give it all up. And I can't, Ben! You have to stop asking!"

"I. Never. Have." He growled the words, moving with ease across the room and plopping her onto an abandoned desk. "No matter how much I want to. I've almost asked you to marry me three times *this week*, Amelie, and every goddamn time I've swallowed those words right back down my mouth because I don't want to seem like I'm trying to buy you."

He took her chemise off in one gorgeous motion that sent warmth all the way down her body. He stepped back; the simple white cotton fabric balled in one large hand.

"Don't. Fucking. Move."

She hadn't worn a corset that day. She rarely did, a habit from years and years of dancing. She sat before him wearing nothing but drawers.

"I'll be honest," he said. "It's really hard to have this argument while I'm staring at your breasts."

"They're small," she said.

"They're yours," he said. "Do you know how many times I've stroked myself, wondering what you look like under your clothes? And now, you're half naked, right in front of me, and your breasts are so much more glorious than I have ever imagined."

Well, then. She looked down at them.

"May I touch them?" The anger was gone from his voice, and if she was honest, it had drained from her as well, replaced only by need.

"Yes," she said.

He moved his thumbs over her breasts, gently, a whisper across her nipples that she could feel all the way down her body, and then his hands were there, too; slowly, agonizingly, drifting over her. She was mesmerized by the way they looked against her body.

And at how he was looking at her. His expression was almost worshipful.

"Amelie," he said. Only her name, said in a way no one had ever said it before. Like she was the most precious thing in the world.

"I want to touch you," she said.

His laugh was hoarse. "Thank god."

She reached her hands up and pushed the torn shirt the rest of the way off his shoulders.

"I thought about you," she said, leaning back and drinking him in. He was long and lean and pale, his stomach flat and his shoulders—those beautiful shoulders—wide and strong. She touched him, laying her hands on his chest. The strength of him under her fingers—she wanted to map every centimeter of those long muscles.

He made a shivery choking sound. "Tell me," he said.

"When we were younger," she said. "And last week. And—" This part was harder to admit.

"Tell me," he said, with a smug smile. He pulled her closer, so her legs were around him and she could feel the length of him against her drawers. His hand stroked down her side, along the edge of her breast to her waist, just above her waistband.

"I didn't admit it," she said, quickly. "But . . . I rather think you've been the man. When I close my eyes, you're who I imagine."

More growling. Such a delicious sound, his growling. She reached for his belt, yanking him still closer as she undid it. She threw it to the side, undid his pants, and—pushing him back a step—slid them to the ground.

He swore.

His drawers followed. He kicked them off, along with his shoes, and tried to step closer. She stopped him with a hand on his chest and knelt.

"Amelie," he said, "you—uh—"

His cock was gorgeous. Long and straight and a little smug, like him. She took it in her hand; he made another satisfying noise.

"Yes, Benedict?" she said. "You wanted to say something?"

Then she licked him, from his testicles to his tip.

"No," he said. "Nothing."

She licked him again. That same strangling noise.

"I really think you did. Probably something about me not needing to do this." Another lick.

"You don't," he said, his eyes closed. "But I really fucking hope you will."

She took him in her mouth.

The feel of him overwhelmed her. She needed to touch him more, her hands roaming over his stomach and his cock and his thick, beautiful thighs. This was so *intimate*, the most intimate thing she could think of. It wasn't always, of course, but with this man—

"Amelie," he said. "You need to stop. I'm close."

Tempting not to, but there were still the claw marks to get to.

She reached her arms up to him, pulling him to the floor. He stretched out next to her and kissed her.

Slowly, as if he was prolonging his pleasure, he slid his hand up her leg until he reached the waist of her bloomers. He pulled them down, sliding his fingers over her skin, making her tremble. It had been so long since she'd been touched, and to be touched with such reverence and desire . . . her emotions ripped through her. She wanted to scream, to lick him from top to bottom, to cry; she wanted to straddle him and fuck him until he begged for release.

Benedict's dark brown hair was mussed—her fault—and his normally pale face was flushed with need. He was staring.

"So beautiful," he said. "God, I can smell you. I want to taste you. May I?"

She couldn't speak. She nodded.

His hands were on her thighs, firmly pushing them farther apart, his tongue making one long stroke between her legs until she let out small gasp.

Benedict seemed to take this as an encouraging sign, because he did it over and over, his mouth switching to different but equally intriguing things, until a moan escaped her and there was nothing in her world but his hands on her thighs and his tongue and the waves of sensation flooding her. When she came, his fingers stroking inside her, it was all she could do to muffle her cries.

He did not give her a chance to recover.

"With your permission, I'm going to have you now," he said, reaching for his container of French letters and pulling one on. She couldn't speak, but she nodded, and before her muscles had finished spasming he pushed inside her.

She peaked almost immediately, or perhaps she had never stopped.

"That's it," Benedict said, his hand reaching down to caress one of her breasts, his fingers playing with her nipple. "Scream for me, Amelie."

Suddenly, she didn't want to. There was no one at home, no one to hear her, but—the idea was so uncomfortable.

Benedict chuckled, leaned down so his cheek was against hers, his mouth against her ear. "I can do this all day, sweetheart," he said, nipping at her ear. "You wanted to scream. You're going to scream."

He hitched her knees up, his cock plunging deeper inside. Her head fell back against the floor as her reply evaporated.

She felt the pressure mounting again. He was everywhere, he was inside her, on top of her, his hands at her breasts and cunny, his eyes firm on hers. He enveloped her.

And inside him, she was safe.

She let go.

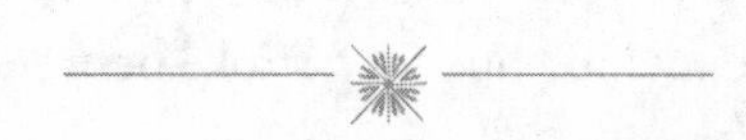

It had been afternoon when Benedict had climbed the attic stairs; now, as they lay entwined, her body resting on his, the room was turning the gray of winter twilight. They were slick with sweat. After a few minutes of breath and silence, she started to shiver. Carefully, he rolled her to the side and walked to the trunks. He found a blanket in the second one he looked in.

"I came back," he said, not looking at her. "But I couldn't get to you."

He heard her shift behind him and made himself turn around and hand her the blanket. She was sitting up, her expression confused. She pulled the blanket close.

"What are you talking about?"

He didn't know why he was telling her this. He'd kept it in for so long.

"I left you," he said.

She frowned. "I told you to," she said. "I know I said that—I *am* angry, Ben. Of course I am. But it's not your fault. I wish—"

"I left, but I came back."

A pause. She wrapped the blanket tighter. "To Paris?"

"I got on a boat three weeks after war was declared," he said. "I didn't know your last name, but I didn't think you'd be hard to find. I was right," he said, shrugging. "As I discovered later. But in 1870, I couldn't even get into the city. The Prussians got there first."

She was shaking her head. "I don't understand," she said.

"I was thirty miles outside of Paris when France surrendered," he said. "You'd told me to go. I wanted . . . I wanted to respect that. I hired a private detective to find you, to make sure you were alive. And I left. I didn't see the Commune coming, or how brutally the government would respond to it."

"You came back?"

"I failed," he said. "If I'd stayed longer, or thought about the social forces in play—"

"Sorry, are you blaming yourself for not predicting Bloody Week?"

"I—"

"Stop." She held a hand up. "Stop talking. I need to think."

She stood, gathering her garments in silence and slowly putting them back on. After a moment, Benedict followed suit, at least as best he could with most of his buttons missing.

"You came back," she said. "Four years had passed, and you still came back for me."

"It didn't help," he said.

To his astonishment, she laughed. "Benedict Moore, you are a very impressive man, but even you cannot defeat the entirety of the Prussian Army."

"If I'd been faster—"

"No," she said. "You're not going to do that. Bad things happened to me. None of them are your fault. You have only ever been lovely. You say that I helped you, back then. If I did, if I'm any part of who you are today, then you're the second-best thing I've accomplished in my life, only Honorine above you. This guilt—" She threw her hands up. "It is not appropriate."

Despite everything, he wanted to smile. "Appropriate?"

"I assume you are familiar with the word," she said, looking exactly like the girl from the park. "It means suitable. Your guilt is ill-suited."

He didn't know what to say—he wasn't sure he should have told her. He appreciated her absolution, but it didn't change his conviction that somehow, someway, he should have protected her.

She was cleaning up the plate shards, lifting the larger pieces and stacking them atop one of the trunks. He found the broom and pan he'd left earlier and began to sweep.

She set the last piece on the pile, crossed her arms over her chest. "I don't know what to say."

"About our wild afternoon of passion or my confession?"

"I had plenty to say about your confession," she said, smiling a little. "Maybe it's truer that I don't know what to think. About any of this."

"I do," he said. "It's very straightforward. You should marry me, and you and Honorine should move to New York."

"Oh," she said, faintly. She looked down at the broken plates. "I don't know who I'd be."

"I said something like that to you, once," he said.

"I'm sure I had something terribly clever to say in response," she said.

"I said I didn't know who I was anymore," he said. "You told me I was a Ben."

"A Ben, who brought me walnuts after rehearsal," she said, her eyes far away.

"You'd be an Amelie. You'd be Honorine's sister." He paused, took a breath. "You'd be my wife."

"I am only just realizing something that I do have in common with my mother," Amelie said. "People defined her by who she was to others. She was *Emile Bonnet's mistress*, or *Gabriel Charpentier's mistress*, or *Honoré de Lavel's mistress*. I'm the people's saint, I'm Honorine's sister, I was the Paris Opera Ballet's prima ballerina, and you want me to be your wife. But what is an Amelie, on its own?"

"A dancer," he said, his chest tight. "An artist. A woman who's passionate and funny and more than a bit bossy. A talented actress. And yes, a good sister and friend. And the rest . . . let me give you the space to find out."

"You deserve better than being the *space*, Ben."

"Do you love me?"

"You know I do, but—"

"Then don't do this. Not again," he said quietly. "I have not stopped loving you, not for twelve years. We do not have to be this complicated. We do not have to keep suffering. It can be simple."

She was perfectly still, staring down at the wooden floor. "I need—I need time, Ben. I can't think."

"Let me protect you this time," he said. He knew the words were wrong as soon as he said them; he watched her stiffen.

"You can't," she said. "Ben, you can't. God knows you tried." Her eyes were wet. He wanted to run across the room, to take her in his arms. "*I* protected myself. I protected Honorine. That's who was there. And I will continue to do so."

"You don't have to do it alone."

"The thing about relying on other people's protection is that they leave," she said softly.

"Damn it," he snapped. "I'm not your mother's lovers."

"I know," she said. There was a long pause, and she shrugged. "She left, too."

"Oh, Amelie," he said.

"I'll give you this, Ben," she said, beginning to cry in earnest. "You're the only one who ever came back."

He couldn't help himself. He crossed to her, held her. She tried to push him away. He didn't let go.

"Do you know how she died?" she asked. "Did anyone tell you?"

He shook his head.

"She had syphilis," Amelie said. "I don't know who gave it to her. She died during the Prussian Siege, and there were so many bodies I don't know exactly where she's buried. When I tried to summon her, I had to guess."

Dead bodies, one atop the other, covered in snow.

Somehow, they'd sunk to the floor. Ben held her tighter. He knew what it was like to see the dead become nothing but a disposal problem.

"Why didn't she come, Ben? I called and called. Why didn't she come?"

"I'm sorry," he said. Her agony was physical, sobs shaking her in his arms. He kissed the top of her head.

"She was my best friend," Amelie said. "I'll never have another conversation with her. I don't even know when the last one was, or what we talked about, because I didn't know it was the last. She just . . . slipped away. No. That sounds peaceful. She was ripped away. Day by day, for months, I saw that disease steal parts of her. And I didn't know it would be forever, I didn't know *that day* was the last time I'd see my mother staring out of her eyes. I . . . if I could just talk to her, to *her,* the real her, one more time. If she could sit down at our old table and drink a cup of tea with me and tell me the latest gossip about Marie at the cafe. I *miss her.*"

He held her tighter, wishing he could take half her grief and hold it, his memories blending with hers. "I know, sweetheart," he said, because there was nothing else to say. "I know."

"I don't even know who gave it to her," she said, dully. "After Honorine's father left, things got bad. We didn't have money. She loved him. She thought he'd always be there. And when she got pregnant, he *blamed* her for it and left, and we had nothing but the little I made at the ballet. She went from man to man. For a while. It was one of them."

Benedict closed his eyes.

"If I knew," she said, "I would kill him. She had less than four decades on this earth, because of him."

Her sobs were slowing. She looked empty. Slowly she pulled away.

"I love you," she said. "But I can't say yes to you."

"Because you think I'm going to leave you like she did? You won't marry me because I might die? Amelie, that's—"

"Insane," she said, letting her head fall forward so her forehead rested on his. "And that's why this is over."

"What?"

"You crossed an ocean for me, even after I sent you away," she said. "This time, don't."

"This is wrong," he said. "We love each other. We can get over this. I'll wait. I'll—"

"*No.* You're not waiting for me anymore, Benedict Moore. You're going home to your institute. You are going to live your damn life. You are not going to spend *one more minute* on me. I am done crying on your shoulder."

"I said I would help you with the ghosts," he said, panic crawling up his throat.

She shook her head. "They've been so much quieter lately. And with your permission, I'll correspond with your brother."

She doesn't need me, he thought. Somewhere he knew that wasn't right, that it wasn't about whether she needed him, but it had been his last, desperate hope.

"You said—you said we would still be friends."

"I will *always* be your friend," she said, almost savagely. "If you need me, *I* will cross the ocean for *you.* But we can't do this anymore. I'll move out tonight."

"So, it's going to be like last time, after all," he said.

She flinched. "Yes," she said. "It's going to be like last time. I'm sorry."

And, without looking back, she walked away.

CHAPTER TWENTY-FIVE

June 1866
Twelve years earlier . . .

It was hot that summer, in a glorious, eyes-closed, greenhouse sort of way. The kind of heat that puts a haze over the day, turning every moment into nostalgia. The smell of roses and earth hung in the air as she walked toward him.

He was waiting for her beneath a tree in the park, leaning carelessly against it. His hair needed a trim, it was falling in his eyes again. There, he saw her, he was smiling at her. There he was, the boy she loved. She wanted to remember him like this, smiling. When she was done, she didn't think he'd smile at her.

Last night, they'd kissed for the first time.

"Amelie," he said, loping toward her. He'd filled out some that summer, but still he was all bones and awkward angles.

"Hello, Ben," she said, stopping short of him.

Last night, he'd walked her home, and she'd gone up the stairs dreaming of today.

"I—I'm happy to see you," he said, his expression slightly confused by her distance. He took her arm, guided her to a bench.

He took a deep breath, his hand going into his pocket. His face was red. "You know I'm leaving tomorrow," he said. "Or I'm supposed to, at least. But last night—" He broke off, cleared his throat. "Let me start over. Amelie, I lo—"

"Don't, Ben," she said. "Please don't."

"Amelie," he said, his confusion turning into an awkward laugh. "You don't know what I'm going to say."

Last night, she'd found her mother, her beautiful, perfect, laughing mother, sobbing on the sofa. Last night, she'd discovered she was going to have a little sister or brother. Last night, the love of her mother's life had left her.

She looked him directly in the eyes. There was no point in dragging this out. "I'll miss you," she said, very clearly.

"But—"

"I'll miss you, Ben. This summer has been wonderful. I have to focus on my dancing now."

His face paled. "But—"

"You've been a bit of a distraction," she said, making herself laugh. "It's probably best you're leaving."

His hand left his pocket.

Last night, she'd decided it was time to grow up.

"Oh," he said.

She wanted, so badly, to take his hand. She made herself stay perfectly still.

"I'm sorry," he said. "I—"

"No," she said. She couldn't bear for him to be sorry, to think any of this was his fault. "Please. This summer has been wonderful, hasn't it? Can we just . . . let it be that? It can't be more. Let it be a beautiful memory, that we'll always have."

"I see," he said.

"We did have fun, didn't we?" She supposed she was pleading, begging for it to be alright.

"Yes," he said, swallowing.

"I—I'm sorry, Ben."

He didn't understand—how could he?—but he gave her a sweet, lopsided smile. "Don't be sorry, Amelie. You're right. It's a beautiful memory."

She stood before she'd be tempted to do things like ask his last name, his mailing address. It was over. Things were going to be different, harder, going forward. Honoré de Lavel had paid their rent, their bills. Now Amelie would need to. Her mother had given her everything, and it was time to do the same for her.

"Goodbye, Ben," she said, and before she could stop herself, she leaned over and kissed him one last time.

"Goodbye, Amelie."

She walked away as quickly as she could. She did not look back.

CHAPTER TWENTY-SIX

November 1878

She left that night.

Benedict gathered she'd done so with the necessary propriety—thanked his parents, arranged to correspond with Sam about the ghosts. He wasn't present. He stayed in the attic until he saw a carriage come to take her away. As usual, his last view of Amelie St. James was of her back.

He wondered what she'd said to Alva.

There was a lamp in the corner, but he didn't bother to light it. He simply sat, watching as the room turned from cold brown to gray to black.

The worst part—oh, there were so many worst parts—the worst part was this was always how it was going to end. He'd known that, and he'd fallen in love with her again anyway.

The worst part was she'd told him, over and over, that she would stay, and he would leave.

The worst part was she didn't need him.

The worst part was he couldn't follow her.

The worst part was she'd told him not to cross an ocean for her again, but if she called, he would. That was true, every atom in his body agreed. He *would always* come for her, which perhaps was really the worst part, because she didn't want him to.

The worst part was he'd failed her.

The worst part was she didn't love him enough to try, to risk.

The worst part was she was in pain.

The worst part—oh, the worst part was that he would do it all over again.

He couldn't regret it—any of it. Regret helping her? Never. He always would. Regret loving her? The same. Regret knowing her as a woman, steel and porcelain and pure, dogged stubbornness? No. He hadn't regretted her the first time, and he didn't now. Amelie St. James was never a regret.

But it had felt easier, the first time. When she'd walked away from him twelve years earlier, his love had been that of a boy. He'd been in love with summer, then—and oh, how he'd needed it. He'd had a ring in his pocket that day, bought at a little jumble shop that had surely been demolished. A simple silver band. He still had it, in a little box back in America.

Really, he needed to stop trying to marry her. That was always where it went wrong.

He was getting confused. The point was—he'd recovered. She'd given him his life back, and he'd proceeded to live it with joy. He didn't remember this *loss*.

Why is it always so painful between us, she'd asked. The truth was that it wasn't. It was only painful at the end.

A knock on the door, followed by a triangle of light cutting across the floor.

"Ben?"

His mother slipped through the door, blinking in the dark.

"I'm sorry," he said, making himself stand. "I was—I got lost in thought. I'll be down soon."

She embraced him.

She was small, his mother, though she didn't seem like it. His chin rested easily on the top of her head.

All his life, his parents had been there. They'd patched his skinned knees and nursed him through fevers and even, on one very painful occasion, set a broken arm when a snowstorm had prevented a doctor from reaching their home. During the war, they had very literally saved his life after their arrival: his father actually throwing the doctor who had been administering too much arsenic out of the room. He would have died of arsenic poisoning long before the malaria finished him off if not for them interceding.

And there had been the long recovery, during which they'd helped and waited and worried. He didn't want them to have to worry ever again.

He kissed his mother's head and pulled away. "I'm fine," he said.

"Don't lie to your mother," she said.

He laughed. "Alright," he said. "I *will* be fine."

She looked up at him, the light from the hall falling across his face. Her expression was strangely grim. "Come with me," she said.

"I'm—"

"Benedict!"

When Winnifred Moore spoke in a certain tone of voice, you listened.

"Yes, ma'am," he said, and let her pull him out of the room.

She led him down the attic stairs to the second-floor library, where his father was messing around with a battery and some wire filament. "John," she said. His father looked up and immediately turned off the battery.

"Hello, son," he said.

So, this was to be a two-parent situation. "Really, I'm fi—"

"I wouldn't," John said, patting him on the shoulder. "Let's go downstairs."

Benedict resigned himself to the situation. They needed to know he was alright. He'd talk to them, reassure them. And when he went back to wallowing, he'd do so where no one could find him.

His parents led him to the kitchen. He'd missed dinner, he realized. No wonder they were worried.

"I'll make the tea," John said. Benedict and his mother sat down at the kitchen table. She took his hand.

"Is there anything to be done?"

Benedict shook his head. "I don't think so," he said. "I asked her to marry me. She said no. It's not the first time."

His father made a disgruntled sound from the stove.

"John," Winn said, a warning in her voice.

"I'm sorry," he said. "I liked the woman, but she must be an idiot."

"Father!"

"*My son* asks her to marry him, and she turns him down? Hmph. She can't be that bright."

"John," Winn said, and Benedict had the distinct impression she was trying hard not to laugh. "I don't think that's helpful."

His father shrugged, pouring tea into the pot. "Helpful, not helpful. It's true, all the same. Look at him! Brilliant, handsome, kind. Any woman would be lucky."

The good news was that the embarrassment might soon kill him, and his suffering would be at an end.

"Well," Winn said. "He's not wrong. But I think Amelie already knows that."

He shrugged. "It didn't work out," he said. "Really, I'm fine. You don't need to worry about me."

His parents exchanged *a glance*. He resisted the urge to squirm in his chair.

"Benedict," his mother said. "We need to talk about that."

"About what?"

"You know it's alright not to be fine, right? With us?"

"I—"

"Because talking to Amelie made me wonder if perhaps you don't. Because of the war."

This wasn't relevant. He opened his mouth to say so, but she cut him off.

"You never told us about her," she said. "And I wonder if that's because you didn't want us to know how much you needed her, that summer. How sad you were."

"That's ridiculous," he said. "You knew. I could see it every time I looked at you. All of you, Sam and Maggie, even Henry. The worry in your eyes. You must have worried enough for a lifetime. But then I got better."

His father came over with three cups of tea, setting them down on the table.

"We *were* worried about you," Winn said. "That's love. There's no lifetime worth of love, or care. There's not a limit."

Benedict shifted. He felt itchy, like fleas were crawling over his skin. "There's a limit to how much you can hurt the people you love, though."

His mother frowned. "*You* weren't hurting us, Ben. We were hurt. *All of us.*"

"I—I got better. I came back, and I got better. You helped me, you let me talk to you, over and over again. It's not wrong to want to . . . to extend that forward. So many people saved me. I decided—"

"You decided you would be the one doing the saving," Winn said.

"I—"

This time he stopped himself.

That was true. But somehow, hearing his mother say it, it didn't sound noble, or honorable. It sounded scared.

"Is that wrong?" he asked.

"It's never wrong to want to help other people," Winn said. "But that's not your sole value. I worry that somehow, after the war, you slipped into thinking it was."

He knew it wasn't his sole value. Didn't he?

"You can't spare other people the pain you went through," John said.

Benedict Moore, you are a very impressive man, but even you cannot defeat the entirety of the Prussian Army.

Was that what he was doing?

"It's normal to want to protect the people you love," he said.

John and Winn exchanged a rueful smile. "Of course it is," Winn said. "But sometimes, you have to remember it goes both ways. The people you love want to protect you, too, and they want to be there for you when they can't. For example, we couldn't protect you from a broken heart. But we'd like to hold your hand and listen to you now."

"I— She said something like that, too."

"See, John? I told you she wasn't an idiot."

His father responded with another *hmph*.

"I'm scared for her," he said. "I'm furious at her. I love her. And I think I'm never going to see her again." He looked down at the table. "I feel like I let her down."

"Do you think Amelie believes that?"

Did she? Well, she had her own troubles in that department.

She didn't expect anything from anybody. "No. She doesn't. But maybe she should." He paused. "Maybe you should."

"*Benedict Moore*," his mother gasped. "You'd better be retracting that statement."

"But I did let you down," he said, the words coming from some deep, buried cavern inside of him. "I was the problem, after the war. We all had problems. I was the only one who crumbled."

"No." His father thumped one massive fist on the table. "Don't you *dare* say that. You didn't crumble. You didn't let us down. You were hurt, Benedict."

"But after I recovered from the malaria—"

"You were still *hurt*. And you needed to heal. Maybe you still do."

"I'm angry at you, that you could think that," Winn said.

He didn't know he had. It was out in the light, and there was something wrong with it, something warped. Of course he'd been hurt. Of course he'd needed to heal. It was like Amelie, with her hip, but also with everything else. He'd told her she'd needed time to rest. So had he.

"I'm sorry," he said, reaching his hands out to his parents. They each took one, and suddenly, he felt a bit better.

"Good," Winn said.

"I think—if you want to hear about it, I'd like to tell you about that summer," he said.

"We have nowhere else to be," Winn said.

CHAPTER TWENTY-SEVEN

Amelie walked Honorine to school the next morning. The morning was blue and cold, sunshine sparkling off icy sidewalks and giving the dead leaves still clinging to their boughs one last chance to glow orange and fiery. Honorine was barely visible beneath her coat and hat and chunky scarf, only her pink nose sticking out.

Her sister was angry with her. "I don't understand why we had to leave," she said, for the fourth time that morning.

"I know," Amelie said. "But it's time to go back to our lives."

Honorine did not answer. Amelie had the distinct impression she didn't think their kind of living compared favorably to that practiced by the Moores.

She walked her sister to the school's gates. "Have a good day," she said, straightening Honorine's scarf.

Honorine grunted and walked away.

Amelie stood, her arms wrapped around herself, until her sister walked through the wide, wooden double doors of St. Mary's. Safe.

There had been no letter, no more flowers waiting from de

Lavel. Amelie hoped he'd forgotten them, but in those last painful moments with Ben, she had made her plan. If de Lavel tried to take Honorine, they would disappear. She had enough money, between the apartment and her savings, for them to live a quiet life in the countryside.

She would keep them safe.

She didn't *feel* safe, though. She felt . . . wounded.

The city was already bustling as she walked to the opera house. She was recognized a few times, and signed some notebooks and handkerchiefs, smiling her St. Amie smile for the first time in two months. It felt strange on her lips. Like it had claws.

She missed him.

She missed him so much her body felt it physically. Her breath hurt.

She'd known this was how it would end. Why hadn't that protected her?

And oh, she'd hurt him again. She'd hurt both of them, just like the last time, but worse.

She didn't regret walking away, twelve years ago. She'd done what she'd needed to, protected her family. If she hadn't stayed, if she hadn't been there when her mother got ill, Honorine would likely not have survived the Siege. She'd made the best choice she could in the circumstances that had been forced upon her.

That decision had been forced upon her, like so many afterward. There had never really been a true *choice*.

But was that true of last night? It hadn't felt like a choice, but what if it was?

The thought was knifelike.

We do not have to keep suffering, he'd said. *It can be simple.*

In the moment that had seemed . . . not wrong. But foreign, a lovely thought from a faraway world she could never visit. In her world, it was never simple. And she always had to suffer.

For the first time, she wondered if that was true. She remembered something Dr. Durand had said during her recovery: "If something hurts, stop. Pain is your body warning you."

She'd thought, last night, that she was avoiding pain. Now, with that damned smile on her face and needles in her lungs, it felt as though the fear of loss had created the loss itself.

Amelie reached the Palais Garnier. She had the Director's letter in her pocket. Her intention had been to accept his offer. But as she stood in the cold shadow of the magnificent building, she hesitated.

The Palais Garnier was the most famous building in Paris. It was hated and beloved. It had lived a lifetime long before its completion; it was a symbol of decadence, violence, wonder, sin, and triumph.

But when Amelie remembered the last twelve years, it was another building she thought of. One still unfinished, rising day by day at the top of Montmartre.

During the Siege, the pious folk outside the city had decided the Prussian Army was God's way of punishing Paris for its decadence, as symbolized by the new opera house. And so, while the people of Paris were trapped and starving, while Leonie St. James had been dying, they'd raised money for a church to atone for the city's sins.

Months later, after the surrender and the Commune and Bloody Week, when tens of thousands of Parisians had been killed, it was time to find a place for this new basilica. It would be pure and simple, unlike the extravagances of the Palais Garnier. And it would sit where the rebels had executed two generals at the beginning of the uprising, on top of Montmartre Butte. A warning, overlooking the neighborhoods where the revolt had been born.

Don't do it again.

When she'd looked for a new apartment, she'd chosen the one she now owned for its view. Every morning, drinking her coffee, she saw the warning. And remembered who had power, and who did not. Who usually lived and who usually died.

A man bumped into her shoulder as she stood before the entrance. He bowed briefly and apologized, before continuing through the doors. She nodded politely in return.

He looked a little familiar: fashionably dressed, of medium height, with curly dark hair. She watched him hailing someone and laughing as the door closed.

"It's him," Lise said softly, suddenly appearing next to her.

Amelie turned to her. "Your lover?"

Lise nodded, her eyes on the door he'd walked through. "Can we—will you follow him?"

Amelie didn't respond, simply pushed through the entrance. The man was only a few steps away; he'd stopped to talk to a group of men she recognized as Jockey Club members. His camelhair coat was easy to follow as he jogged up the marble steps, past the statue of Psyche, and down a long, red-carpeted corridor.

She followed him quietly, a few meters away. The building was still—the dancers would have just left their morning class, and there were no rehearsals onstage. It was hours before an audience would enter, if there was a performance tonight. She realized she didn't even know if there was one.

The man walked with purpose, a spring in his step, and then turned into a small side room. He closed the door casually, and it bounced slightly ajar. Amelie softened her footsteps even further and crept close, until she saw through the crack into the dim room.

Where he was passionately embracing a girl dressed in the white rehearsal dress of the Paris Opera Ballet.

She stepped away quickly, but it was too late.

"Lise—" The ghost stood behind her. Nothing of her moved; all the little ways Lise had simulated life were gone. She was nothing more than a still image, standing in a hallway. And the shadows along the baseboards were lengthening.

Lise flickered, and then, suddenly, she was in the room.

"*Merde*," Amelie said, pushing the door open. The man glanced up.

"What— *Lise*?" He stumbled back, falling against the wall. The girl he was with—Amelie recognized her from the corps, a girl just out of the Opera Ballet School—looked around in confusion, staring right through the ghost. She didn't see her.

"What— Mademoiselle St. James? Oh, it's not what you think. Um, this gentleman and I—"

"You should go down to the dressing room," Amelie said.

"Er—" The girl looked at her lover, who was still paralyzed against the wall. "Alright. Just—you won't say anything, will you?"

"I won't say anything," Amelie said. "Hurry now."

She left, closing the door behind her.

"You're dead," the man whispered.

Slowly, as if a puppet master had only now remembered to tug the strings, Lise nodded. "I am," she said. "Raoul, I heard—I heard the strangest rumor—"

"You're dead," he said, pressing himself farther back, as if he could put the wall between himself and her. "Brun said he moved your body. He said he put it in the river."

Ah. So it had been as brutal and thoughtless as Amelie had feared all along. Lise went still, as though she had forgotten everything else.

"No," she said. "No. You wouldn't—"

A sharp pain exploded in Amelie's head. It was just like the night of the accident. "Lise," she said, hissing as she put a hand to her forehead. "Whatever you're doing, it *hurts*."

"I'm going to look in his head," Lise said.

Amelie crumpled to the thickly carpeted floor. She could *feel* the ghost pulling from her this time—the physical limit Ben had always been worried about.

And then it was gone. Amelie blinked, staring at the flower pattern beneath her hand. Her nose was bleeding, the blood warm against her skin.

Lise stepped back. The white veil appeared in her hands.

"He gave me the morphine. The first time. He likes keeping his girls a little desperate, you know? It's a good way to keep us dependent on him, always needing a little more. That day, I took too much." She twisted the fabric of the veil. "He thought it was such an inconvenience. He had to arrange for my body to be moved, and he had to bribe people. It took up almost half his day. He was really irritated about it. He had a supper engagement later and . . . and he almost didn't have time to change."

The man—Raoul, Lise had called him—whimpered.

"I was nothing to him," Lise said. "I was . . . a pleasure. And then a chore. An inconvenient body." She put the veil on. "I'm going to kill him."

Tears flowed down his face. His mouth was open, as if to scream, but no sound came out. His eyes were unfocused.

"Dance," Lise said.

He didn't dance. His muscles twitched, like a dog that was dreaming. Sweat mingled with his tears.

Amelie stood and watched.

She possessed no mercy for this man. She could watch Lise kill him and not shed a tear. But did Lise deserve to have another murder on her conscience? Didn't she deserve another choice?

His skin twitched. A low moan filled the room.

And then, suddenly, Lise tore the veil off. Her eyes were bright red.

"I can't do it," she said. No tears fell from those eyes, but in her voice was anguish and loss and fury and betrayal, and Amelie felt every one of those echoing inside herself. "Amelie. *Amelie.* I can't do it. I can't—"

The man sagged to the floor, sobbing. Amelie watched him. This man had thrown the body of his nineteen-year-old mistress into the Seine, and he'd had his hands on another girl, even younger. And no one would stop him. No one cared, or at least no one who had the power.

But that wasn't entirely true, was it?

"You don't have to," she said to Lise. "We'll find another way."

"But how—"

Amelie couldn't look away from him, this pitiful pile of a man, who gave young girls drugs and treated them like last night's leftovers. He wasn't so much, at the end of the day.

For years, she realized, her very existence had protected men like this. She had been the saint, so they could be the sinners.

And he was so very not worthy of her protection.

"Let's go home," she said.

She walked into the sitting room of her apartment and observed the space. The furniture belonged to another woman, one who had never really existed. That silly, stiff sofa she'd purchased because it was a good price, and no one would ever notice it. Setting her weight against it, she pushed it until it was along the wall. The coffee table was next, and the inoffensive armchairs. Finally, she rolled up the rug, shoving it in front of the line of furniture. Now she had a floor.

"There," she said, standing in the middle of her new emptiness.

Lise looked at her in concern. "I think you might be in shock again," she said. The veil and the red eyes had disappeared on the walk home, and now there was only Lise, a little sweet, a little nervous, and a little sad. "I must have frightened you."

"You didn't frighten me," Amelie said. "You gave me an answer I didn't even know I was looking for. I'm going to cast you."

"Cast me? What are you talking about?"

"I need a dancer," Amelie said. "And you're the only one who will do."

"Amelie," Lise said, looking around nervously. "I'm dead."

Amelie almost laughed. "I haven't forgotten," she said. "Can you still dance?"

"Not so other people can see," Lise said.

"Do you mind if I'm the only one?"

The girl stared at her. "No," she whispered. "I don't mind."

"Good. Get out of that ridiculous costume, and let's get to work."

Lise flickered, and when she returned, she was dressed in her practice costume. Her hair was in a neat bun, and she'd traded her pointe shoes for ballet slippers.

"Right." Amelie looked at her. She had no idea what she was doing. She walked to one of the chairs along the wall and sat. "I need to watch you move," she said. "*Giselle*. Act two, scene two."

Lise moved into the center of the room and began to dance.

Every movement was perfect, implausible. There was only music in Amelie's head, and Lise hit every count. Her balances were only constricted by the choreography—she came down when it was time for the next step. Her extensions had the brittle quality of memory; Amelie suspected she was lifting her leg exactly as high as she had in life.

It was deeply, deeply unpleasant.

She finished as the last note played in Amelie's mind.

"Alright," Amelie said. "I'm going to show you a few ideas. Watch me."

It turned out that the ugly dance from the attic had only grown over the last day. Amelie sketched out the motions, explaining the pointe work where she couldn't demonstrate it.

"You must be joking," Lise said.

"No," Amelie said.

"It's disgusting."

Amelie shrugged.

"It's immoral."

"How refreshing."

"All I can say is, I'm glad no one will see me dance it," Lise muttered, but she moved back to the center of the room, indicating she was ready to continue.

"Let's mark it," Amelie said. "And then I need to watch it."

Lise simply nodded. Amelie danced the section again, this time counting out the beats as she went. Lise marked the section with her, mimicking her steps. Amelie wondered if she needed to, or if she already knew it, but when she glanced over, her face was creased in concentration. So, whether or not Lise needed the practice, she might need the ritual and process.

After marking, Amelie leaned against the wall as Lise ran through it.

"Extend a little longer there," she called out. "I know you can. Hold that line. Yes. Now hunch your back, really curve your spine—yes, I know you don't want to. Think rag doll, think vulture."

When the section was over, Amelie walked over to her desk and found an empty notebook.

"You once told me you might dance Myrtha," she said. "You're about to."

"That is *not Giselle*," Lise said.

"It's what *Giselle* ought to be," she replied.

The vision was coming clearly. The Wilis were women who had been betrayed in life and died because of it. They were murderous, out for vengeance. There would be no prettiness here, no silly wings, no restraint.

This would be about rage.

It was hard going. Amelie had never choreographed anything before, there were things she could only guess at. Communicating movements that you couldn't demonstrate was hard. If there was a right way to do this, she didn't know it.

They worked for several hours, until Amelie faded. Her head was beginning to hurt again. Lise, of course, could dance forever.

"It's good," Amelie said.

"It's awful."

Amelie smiled. "It's good, Lise. How does it feel to dance?"

"I don't know," Lise said, repeating a motion they'd been working on. "It's strange not to feel it in my body. I have to imagine every movement. It's a different thing. How do I look?"

"Powerful," Amelie said. "You look powerful."

CHAPTER TWENTY-EIGHT

Amelie? Amelie, where are you?" Honorine banged through the front door a few minutes after Lise disappeared, urgency in her voice. She stopped short in the sitting room. "Are we moving?"

"No," Amelie said, standing. "I was—"

She stopped. She'd been about to lie, and she wasn't sure why.

"I was working out an idea for a dance," she said. "How was school?"

"Is Honoré de Lavel my father?"

Amelie sat down.

"Yes," she said.

"Oh," Honorine said. Her sister's braid had come loose, like she'd run up the stairs, and one chunk of hair hung in her face. She looked uncertain.

"I'll answer any questions you have," Amelie said. "But there must be a reason you asked."

Honorine's throat worked. "They were talking about it at school," she said.

"Who was?"

"Some girls. Daughters of—"

"De Lavel's set," Amelie finished. Honorine nodded.

This was a message. He hadn't forgotten them.

She thought of her plan to take Honorine and run to the countryside. The time for that was over. Now . . . now it was time to be powerful.

She hadn't forgotten Honoré de Lavel, either. And that should frighten him.

"They were saying I was his bastard," Honorine said, trying to sound nonchalant. "I don't know why it matters. They know I don't have a father. You don't, either. Shouldn't matter if I'm de Lavel's bastard or not."

"They were being cruel," Amelie said. De Lavel could wait. She needed to talk to her sister. "Specifics make it easier, I suppose."

"I look like him," Honorine said.

"You have similar coloring," Amelie said. "You have his hair, and his eye color, which is quite striking. But I've always thought you resemble our mother a great deal."

"Really?" Her sister looked at her for the first time. "I do?"

"Yes. You have her face. Come here." Amelie pulled her sister close, touching her cheek. "She had this line of cheekbone. You have her nose, and her chin, and the shape of her eyes, too." *And her laughter, her brilliance, her joy.*

"I barely remember her anymore," Honorine whispered. "Was it . . . was it my father who gave her . . ."

"No," Amelie said. "I don't know who did. But it wasn't de Lavel. Their relationship was over."

"That's good," Honorine said. "I mean—"

"I know what you mean," Amelie said. Honorine didn't want

her father to be the person who'd killed her mother. It was reasonable.

"We went to his house," Honorine said, slowly, as if she was pulling the memory from a faraway place. "Near the end."

"Yes," Amelie said. "She was in pain. We were out of morphine. I hadn't been able to get any, and I knew he'd be able to. I took you with me to blackmail him."

Once, there had been shame at the memory.

"But he didn't give it to you."

"No," Amelie said. "His wife did. Charlotte. And she gave us more, three days later, when I sent her a message asking. She was a very brave, very kind woman."

"I remember her," Honorine said. "Why did she help us? No, that's not . . . Why didn't he?"

"I don't know why he didn't help us that day. Maybe I approached him the wrong way. Maybe he didn't want to be linked to her. Maybe he didn't care. I don't know." She paused, trying to decide how to say what she needed to. "He's not a good man. I'm not telling you this to upset you, or frighten you, but there may come a time when he wants to be in your life, and it's important you know the truth about him. He's cruel and petty. He enjoys having others in his power."

"Amelie," Honorine said. "He didn't help our dying mother when you asked. I already know everything I need to."

There was nothing to say to that. Amelie stroked her sister's back.

"Why didn't you tell me?"

Why hadn't she? Why were there so many secrets in her life? "Honestly? Maman didn't tell you when she was alive—you were so little, there was no reason for you to know then—and for a long time after she died, I didn't think about it. It was you and me. We were the only people who mattered. Are you angry at me?"

"I don't think so," Honorine said. "Maybe."

Amelie smiled into her sister's hair. "You don't have to decide now. I'll be here if you get mad later."

"Do you know who your father is?"

"No. Maybe someone from the village she came from. She never talked about it."

"Do you wish you did?"

"Hmm." Amelie set her chin on Honorine's head. "You know how happy the Moores seem?"

Honorine nodded.

"Sometimes I wish I had that—all those people to love. But I'm also very happy with the family I have."

Honorine stayed silent.

"What?"

"You miss her," she said.

All the time, Amelie thought. *So much so, I turned away the best man I've ever known, the only man I've ever loved.*

She'd spent all these years thinking about the next step. How to survive. She'd never let herself stop to grieve.

"We never talk about her," Honorine whispered.

Oh.

"I'm sorry," her sister said immediately. "I shouldn't have—"

"*Yes,*" Amelie said hurriedly. "You should. I'm the one who's sorry."

"I know you don't like to talk about her."

It wasn't that she didn't like to talk about her. She could say her name, reference her casually. But deeper than that—going deeper felt a little like going twenty thousand leagues under the sea. You didn't know what monsters were going to surprise you.

Maybe, though, maybe she could now.

She took a breath. Her sister wanted to know about the mother who'd died when she was five.

"What do you remember about her?" Amelie asked.

"She laughed. A lot."

Amelie smiled, trying to let the memory be a good one. "She did. You and she used to laugh together. I'd come home from ballet and the two of you would be in stitches about something."

"She always left in the evenings, and you stayed with me."

"You understand what she did? For money?" Over the years Amelie had at least tried to explain that, to give her sister some context.

Honorine nodded.

"Some people will say she was wrong, to live that life, or selfish, or . . . worse things I don't want to repeat. None of that is true. There aren't many ways for women to take care of their families, but she made us a life. She was brilliant, actually brilliant. Like you or Benedict. Brave and beautiful. And for a few years, Paris sat in the palm of her hand."

She ran a hand over her sister's hair.

"Do you remember her drawing?"

Honorine shook her head and paused. "When she was sick. At the end," she said.

A stab to the stomach. Another careful breath.

"She was very talented," Amelie said, standing. "Wait here."

She walked to her bedroom, closing the door behind her and leaning against it. Again, she waited for panic. Again, it didn't come.

How could she have kept their mother from Honorine like this? She hadn't meant to—hadn't even thought about it—but she had all the same. Oh, she'd made sure her sister knew the facts, but she hadn't shared the woman. She hadn't been brave enough to think about her. It had been selfish.

She pulled a dusty portfolio from under the bed. Amelie hadn't looked inside it since the day her mother had died. She left the other, smaller envelope, the one that contained the drawings from those last, bad days, where it lay.

She held it close as she walked back to the dining room, laying it carefully on the table. "This is her portfolio," she said. "I imagine we'll find some portraits of you in here. She was always drawing you."

"She was?" Honorine was looking at the portfolio with desperate eagerness.

Amelie unwound the stiff string. She opened the flap and drew the thick stack of paper out, and because sometimes there is grace in the world, the picture on top was of them.

Honorine had been about two, Amelie remembered, and realized this was the kind of thing she had to start saying out loud.

"This was when you were around two years old," she said, clearing her throat. "It was the very beginning of summer. I had the day off, and we took a picnic to the top of the hill. You chased butterflies, and I chased you, and Maman sketched us. We had lemonade."

Amelie glanced at her sister. Honorine was spellbound by the drawing, a soft smile on her lips. Reverently, she turned it over. "Our old apartment!"

"The window that never opened," Amelie said, sitting next to her sister.

Honorine turned the pastel over and inhaled sharply. "She looked like you."

It was a charcoal self-portrait, and Amelie started to cry.

It had been eight years since she'd seen her mother.

"Oh, Amelie—"

"No, it's alright," she said, pulling Honorine against her side. And in a way, it was.

She'd been afraid of the thing—of the *fury*—in the dark for so long. It was *wrong* that Leonie St. James had been taken, too soon, and by such a cruel disease. It was wrong that people had laughed about it, made jokes. It was wrong that Honoré de Lavel had abandoned her, twice, when she needed him most.

Looking this rage and grief in the eyes, she knew too why she had hidden it down so deep. There was a reason she couldn't get the Wilis, those furious, vengeful ghosts, out of her mind. She'd been afraid she'd become one.

With her sister pressed against her side, finally, she let that fear drift away. She didn't need to punish every person who'd participated in her mother's downfall. But she didn't need to protect them, either.

"She looks like both of us," she said, her voice hoarse.

Honorine turned the painting over, moving to the next. It was a strange scene, one Amelie hadn't seen it before. The brushstrokes were wild, a little clumsy; the paint formed small ridges to the touch. The colors were extraordinary shades of pink and green. She didn't understand what she was looking at, or why it unsettled her.

"It's the Camargue," Honorine said.

"What?" As far as she knew, the Camargue was a seaside region. This didn't look like the seaside.

"The salt makes the water pink," she said. "Look. That's the grass. And this is the water. Do you think that's where she was from?"

She tilted her head. She could see it. "She never said," Amelie replied, slowly. Was that strange? It had never seemed odd. Leonie never had much to say about life before Paris. She had lived in the moment.

There was something white, in the water—

"I think that's a dead body," Honorine said.

Amelie startled away, dropping the painting.

Honorine looked closer. "Yes, see, there's the head—but there's something above it—"

A ghost. She was looking at a ghost.

Amelie seized the painting, desperately searching for more. Turning it over, she saw her mother's handwriting. *Aigues-Mortes,* it said. *1848. Lorette Sourd. The first one. Three months, four days.*

"My God," Amelie whispered, crossing herself.

"Amelie?"

Her mother had seen them, too.

Frantically, she pulled the paintings out of the portfolio, spreading them on the floor. There were so many, but it wasn't hard to find the ones with ghosts. They were always wilder. Desperate.

And they had writing on the back.

Aigues-Mortes, 1848. Matildhe LeClerc. Second. Old Age. Two days.

Aigues-Mortes, 1849. Jacques Poulin. Third. Horse accident. Three days.

Paris, 1849. Marie Roche. Fourth. Murdered. One day.

Paris, 1849. Emile Fabre. Fifth. Dead in winter storm. One day.

And on and on and on.

Leonie St. James had seen ghosts. And she'd known how to release them.

"Amelie?"

She sat back on her heels. If her mother had seen them, and she saw them, then Honorine . . .

It was a day for truth telling.

"I am going to explain all of this," she said, standing. "But there is one thing I need to do first."

She knew the ghosts would be waiting before she opened her bedroom door. Lise stood by the dresser, nervously fidgeting. Violette was on the bed.

"Excuse me," Amelie said, reaching under the bed and pulling out the dusty package that contained her mother's last, syphilis-crazed work.

Violette moved over, making space on the bed, and Amelie pulled the drawings out.

They were all black and white, messy and desperate and mad. She'd thought them the meaningless scribblings of a dying woman.

"I never looked at them before," she whispered. "I couldn't throw them away, so I . . . I crammed them in here and hid them. But look."

There was a ghost in every drawing.

"It's the work," she said. "I don't know how, but she released them through her art. After 1849, she never had a ghost who stayed longer than a day. Why didn't she tell me?"

Violette's hand hovered over hers. "Maybe she thought it was only her," she said. "Maybe she ran out of time. Maybe this *was* her way of telling you."

Yes, Amelie thought. There was so much of her mother in this work. She could see her, working frantically, emotion boiling out of her onto the page. Even in the end, her mother had been there, trying to protect her.

"It's not about the ghosts at all," she said.

"There you are," Violette said.

"It's the anger, isn't it? And the way I never faced it. You came when I was angry, so angry I couldn't even look at it, so I pushed it away. Lise, you came right after I saw Benedict again. I remember, I was in the rehearsal room, and I was so upset. And I couldn't be, so I balled it up and shoved it away and—there you were. Violette, right before you and Rachel came, Honoré de Lavel visited me in my dressing room. He never had before, we always pretended there was no history between us. And suddenly he was *there*, in my room, and he was talking about how I remembered what he liked to drink. I was furious, and again, I couldn't be. When I came back from performing, there you were."

"He senses us, a little," Violette said. "Explains why he suddenly started sniffing around."

Amelie couldn't stop the grimace. "Urgh," she said. "And when he asked me to be his mistress . . ."

"The ghosts came out of the floor at the Palais Garnier," Violette said.

"And you're still here because *I'm* angry about what happened to you. What happened to all of us, I guess." She sat down heavily on the edge of the bed. "I'm sorry."

"Well, you don't need to apologize to me," Violette said. "I'm happy to be here."

"You've given me the chance to dance one last time," Lise said.

"It's still wrong," Amelie said. "Of all the things in the world, your deaths, your afterlife, those should be about you."

"It's about all of us," Violette said. "You saw us. You couldn't be furious for us if you didn't."

"Rachel," Amelie said. "She didn't want to be here."

"You found a way to let her go," Violette said. "How?"

Amelie stood, pacing the room. "She shouldn't have died. Not that she was falsely accused—we all know what she did during the Commune. But none of it should have happened. Her brothers shouldn't have been killed in a stupid war. The people of Paris shouldn't have been left to starve. My friends shouldn't have died of disease. I shouldn't have had to beg for drugs to make my mother's death less painful. And most of all, after it was over, something should have *happened.* But nothing did. Our government changed, but it was the same people. We were supposed to go on like nothing had happened. Rachel did something, and they killed her. They won, and we're supposed to forget. It's more than she shouldn't have died. It's that she should have been remembered."

"She was," Lise said. "Her mother."

"Yes," Amelie said. "She was."

They were all silent.

"It's that simple, isn't it?" Amelie asked, staring at the floor. "I have to find a way to settle it in my head."

"That's where we all live," Violette said.

"I know what I need to do. But first, I have to talk to my sister."

CHAPTER TWENTY-NINE

January 1879, New York City

There was something poking Benedict in the stomach, and it wouldn't stop. He batted at it, grumbling in his sleep. It stopped briefly, then resumed, this time with sound.

"Ben," the poking said. "Ben. Ben. Ben."

"Samuel Moore, if you poke me one more time, I will break that finger off and feed it to you."

"See?" Sam said, delighted. "I told you he was awake."

"Go away," Benedict said, rolling over and taking the blankets with him.

"That would be rather wasteful," Sam said. "Especially since Henry went to all the trouble of picking your lock."

"Henry *did what*?" He threw the covers off and glared at the room's inhabitants.

Sam stood next to Henry Van de Berg, unofficial adopted brother and neat, brown-haired lawyer. Sam wore his usual—and in this case, extraordinarily annoying—expression of charm and good humor, while Henry looked on calmly.

Benedict had a headache.

"*Et tu,* Henry?"

Henry shrugged. "If I had to be woken by this idiot pounding on my door at seven in the morning, I don't see why you shouldn't suffer as well."

"So, you *picked my lock.* Aren't you supposed to be an upstanding citizen these days?"

Henry looked unmoved. Sam shook his head. "How can you say that, Ben? Look at Henry's suit. It's practically an upstanding citizen all on its own."

"I would like to remind you that I was promised breakfast," Henry said. "And coffee."

"Well, don't look at me," Sam said. "Benedict's the one who's lying around in bed."

"I have never loathed anyone more than I do in this moment," Benedict said. Sam tore the covers off him and rolled him onto the floor. He lay there, staring at his ceiling. "No, I was wrong. It's *this* moment. This is the one."

"Come on," Sam said. "Can't you see Henry's hungry?"

"If I get dressed, will you promise to be absolutely silent until I finish my first cup of coffee?"

"I second that request," Henry said.

Sam huffed impatiently, closing his mouth dramatically.

"Fine," Benedict said, standing and pulling on some trousers. His head protested, and he tried to remember what time he'd fallen asleep the night before. His couch was covered in papers, so apparently, he'd nodded off while working.

Since he'd been back in America, he'd thrown himself into the institute. He'd found the location, recruited more staff, even begun organizing the first teams and their projects. Dr. Montgomery had moved across the Atlantic. And Emile Bonnet had finally, after several weeks, sent his research, which was every bit as groundbreaking as it had been rumored to be.

He'd seen his family at Christmas, making the train trip to Ohio with Sam, Alva, and Henry, all of whom were currently based in New York City. He'd returned exhausted from pretending it didn't bother him to see the way his parents chattered together, or how Alva's eyes followed Sam around the room.

Apparently, everyone was back in the city.

He threw on some respectable clothing and a coat, brushed his teeth, and ran a comb through his hair. "What," he snarled, when he saw Henry's lifted eyebrow.

Henry shrugged.

Sam took out his notebook, wrote something, and showed it to him.

"Interesting," Henry said.

"Both," Benedict said. "I loathe you both."

Sam and Henry, unmoved by Benedict's fury, simply led the way out of his apartment and into the early morning city.

It was winter in New York. Snow dusted the sidewalks, and cold bit through Benedict's coat. He swore under his breath as they hurried toward the cafe two blocks away.

Warmth welcomed them as they pushed through the door into the small restaurant. It was a tidy place, already busy, with a good cup of coffee and reasonably priced breakfasts. They were shown to a table, and Benedict slumped into a chair.

Coffee was poured, and Sam fidgeted while waiting for Henry and Benedict to finish their first cups. Benedict was tempted to draw the last sips out, but his desire for caffeine outweighed his need for revenge.

"Alright," he said, setting the cup down. "You can talk."

"I've *had a letter*," Sam announced emphatically.

Benedict groaned.

"Sam, you said this was important," Henry said. "Is it important like the time you had a thought about the way caterpillars are like trains, or is it important like the time you redesigned the electrostatic generator?"

Sam looked down his nose. "Both were equally important," he said, in a very dignified tone.

"Please," Ben said. "For my sake. For the sake of everyone around us who might be eavesdropping. Get to the point."

"Fine," Sam said, with one last miffed glance at Henry. "The letter is from Amelie."

"Stop," Ben said. "I don't want to hear it."

"You do."

"I know you're corresponding with her, Sam. It's the only thing that allowed me to leave that damned country. But she's made it very clear she doesn't want me involved in her business, and I'm trying very, very hard to respect that."

"And well done, you," Henry said, waving over the proprietor for another cup of coffee.

He still hadn't fully absorbed what his parents had been trying to tell him, but since his return he'd done a lot of thinking. There had been so much guilt tangled up in his relationship with Amelie—it was like he'd thought the only way to her heart was to save her.

I protected myself. I protected Honorine. And I will continue to do so.

He'd thought about that a lot. Amelie saved herself. Perhaps, with her help, and the help of his family, he had saved himself, all those years ago. In the end, she'd asked him to stop trying to save her, and he rather thought he needed to listen.

"Well, I *know* that," Sam said. "And I haven't told you loads of things, even though she never asked me to keep them secret. For example, I never told you her mother saw ghosts, too, and that she might be a spirit medium of some sort, a real one—"

"What?" Benedict exclaimed, making neighboring diners look at him in discomfort. A spirit medium? He should— No. "See, this is why I don't want to talk about this," he said, and realizing he didn't have to, he stood, took his coat, and walked out the door.

Damn Sam and his letters and his meddling. And damn Henry for going along with it.

It was over. He had to figure out a way to go on. Sitting in a cafe rehashing ancient history wasn't going to help.

It took them a block to catch up to him.

"Leave it alone," he growled.

Sam fell into step beside him. "Ben," he said.

"I can't, Sam. It's too hard. All I want to do is run down to the docks and board a ship back to her, and it's the *one thing* she expressly told me not to do."

The wind picked up around them, whirling snowflakes between the three men.

"That's what I'm trying to tell you, you blockheaded donkey," Sam said. "She asked about schools for Honorine. In New York."

"She's—she's coming to New York?"

It didn't mean anything. Sam could have misunderstood, or Amelie might simply be starting over in a new city, maybe she'd forgotten he lived here, or—

Or she could be coming to him.

This time, he understood he had to let her.

"Oh," he said. "Alright."

"Unexpectedly muted response," Henry said. "Frankly, a bit suspicious."

"Well?" This from Sam.

"Well, you should look into schools for her. Actually, you should ask Henry to look into schools."

"That's it?"

"That's it," Ben said.

Sam sighed, throwing his hands up in the air. "I despair of you," Sam said. "Both of you."

"I don't know what I've done," Henry said. "Other than wake up two hours too early to commit a crime for you."

"You had an entire love affair and you're not moping *at all*," Sam said. "Where's the heartbreak! The drama!"

"Our priorities are different," Henry said. "Ideally, my love affairs end without either."

"That's so dull."

"Also, Ben has plenty of heartbreak and drama," Henry said. "Even now, he's *nobly pining from afar.* You're not giving him his due."

"Nobly pining?" Sam looked at his brother curiously, while Benedict tried his very best not to murder him.

"*Nobly pining*," Henry said.

"Hmm. I suppose. Oh, look, there's one of Mother's lamps!" He hurried on ahead.

"I hate you," Benedict said.

"Don't be ridiculous," Henry said. "You need me to compile a list of appropriate schools, investigate appropriate properties for a three- to four-person family in the city, and find out what wealthy philanthropists are most likely to fund a small ballet company. *And* accompany you when furniture shopping, because we both know you don't want to greet her with that sofa in your sitting room."

Benedict considered Henry's proposal. He supposed all of that fell into the category of *preparing*. If she was coming for him. If.

"Fine," he said. "*But that's it.*"

He walked back to his apartment with a much lighter step.

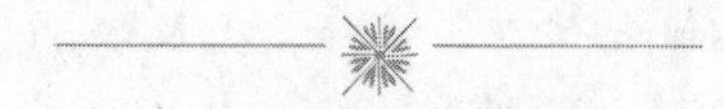

The little lot where her career as St. Amie had begun, almost exactly eight years prior, was still empty, but not for long. By the time the leaves returned to the trees, it would be a smart, modern building, with a restaurant on the ground floor and apartments on the upper three levels. The owner had been more than happy to lease it to her in the meantime.

She'd had it cleared, and a temporary stage and canopy built. She'd had posters made, with the words *A New Ballet by Amelie St. James* printed in large letters. She'd invited the press to the ballet and an interview period after.

The last two months had been good. Hard. She missed Benedict, especially at night, when there was nothing to distract her. But she had to finish this first, and so, in the meantime, she simply had to hope he would want her when she was done.

An easy sentiment that sounded absolutely ridiculous at two o'clock in the morning.

Honorine had taken the news about the ghosts surprisingly well.

"I know this is overwhelming," Amelie had said. "Especially since you just learned about your father."

Honorine had stared at her with wide eyes. "I know this isn't a joke," she'd said. "Because you don't play them. But . . . are you sure someone isn't playing one on you?"

"It's the truth," Amelie had said.

Honorine had taken a long breath. "So, you're telling me, at some point in my future, I'll be able to communicate with the dead. Like a spirit medium!"

"Maybe," Amelie had said. "I can, and our mother could. I'm not an expert in the subject."

"I'll be a spirit medium," Honorine had said.

"If we're calling it that . . ."

"I'll be *famous*!"

Oh no. Amelie had tried to stop it, but the laughter had come anyway. She'd been so worried about her sister, and here Honorine was imagining her debut on the spiritual stage.

"I thought you wanted to be a mapmaker," she'd said, once the giggles had subsided.

"I could be both," Honorine had said with a gleam in her eye. "I could travel the globe talking to ghosts!"

Since, she'd developed strict lists of questions for Amelie to ask Lise and Violette, had set up her own correspondence with Sam, and had apparently continued her mapmaking. She had even asked Amelie for permission to correspond with Benedict, and Amelie had cautiously agreed. Her romantic entanglements, or lack thereof, shouldn't interfere with her sister's education.

Honorine had been excited about America, as well. Whether or not Benedict would take her back, they were done with Paris. She would always love it, but she needed to see new horizons, to make new things in new spaces.

"Mademoiselle St. James," her hired stage manager said. "It's time."

She gave a nod from her position behind the makeshift stage.

"I'm nervous," Lise whispered, next to her.

"You'll be perfect," she said. "*Merde*."

"*Merde*," Lise replied, and hurried to the stage.

The crowd quieted as Amelie walked out. She'd chosen a bright pink for her gown, far more fashionable than anything she'd worn in the last eight years, and it was hard to tell if the gasps from the crowd were from the smoothness of her walk or the vividness of her gown.

It had turned out to be a rather large event. Most of Paris seemed to be trying to jam into the small lot. She was glad she'd notified the police ahead of time, as they'd had to shut down a street.

"Good afternoon," she said. "And thank you for coming. The performance you are about to watch is my first choreographic attempt."

Murmurs, confusion, eagerness, and some derision ran through the space.

"It is dedicated to a dancer named Lise Martin. Lise was a part of the corps de ballet of the Paris Opera Ballet. She was nineteen years old when she died of a morphine overdose at her lover's apartment. He supplied her with the drug, and when she died, he had his servants dump her body in the river. He did not kill her, and he was hiding no crime he would be prosecuted for. He simply wanted to avoid having his name linked to hers."

The crowd was buzzing. Confusion continued to run high. Choreographers did not usually introduce their ballets with salacious stories. Fortunately for Amelie, she knew her audience.

"That name is Raoul Fabre," she said, with a small smile.

Chaos. A little shouting. Oh yes, this was about to be the event of the season.

"You see," she said. "For many years, I have pretended to be something I am not. I am not a sweet, demure, respectable curtain to be drawn across disturbing acts. I have many secrets, and tonight, I am going to share a few."

This was surprisingly fun.

She gestured toward the crowd. "But for now, enjoy the performance."

She stepped offstage as the first notes of a violin hummed

out. In the end, she'd settled on simple music, working with a violinist and a cellist she knew from her time at the Opera Ballet. Plain, staccato notes, against the low hum of the cello. Beating hearts and thrumming blood.

The hired stagehands pulled the curtain back.

The piece had been choreographed for seventeen dancers, sixteen alive and one dead. Many less than the Opera Ballet could command; slightly more than could comfortably fit on Amelie's makeshift stage. In the middle, Lise.

Amelie had worked with the dancers both with and without Lise. She knew what the piece looked like without her dancing in the center, but . . . she wondered. As the dancers began to move, in their twin lines like huntresses, or hawks, and Lise twisted and leaped around them, the audience almost seemed to follow her. Not exactly, but as if they could sense *something*.

With only the empty space, the ballet was unsettling. There were moments that were lopsided, limping, like a piece was missing. With the feeling that *something* was there you couldn't see. Amelie smiled. It was even better than she could have hoped.

The piece was short, only twenty minutes. When it ended, there was no applause. She had not expected any. The ballet was angry, ugly, and horrifying. It could only be called a ballet because it used the steps of the discipline; it certainly resembled nothing she had ever danced.

This was the burning of her bridges. If she chose to stay in Paris, she would not have a career.

Strangely, though, there was no heckling, either. That she *had* expected. This was an audience who loved her because she was everything the ballet they had just watched was not. Surely, they would reject her.

The curtain parted once more. The dancers stared at the audience. The audience stared at the dancers.

As the dancers bowed, the crowd began to react. There was a smattering of applause, and a cluster of Jockey Club members in the front recovered themselves enough to get a small jeer together and throw two apples.

"Awful, isn't it," she said, climbing back onto the stage. The crowd quieted, shifting uncomfortably, almost warily. Was she frightening them? Did she want to?

And then she saw it. Scattered through the audience, a handful of people were crying.

Oh.

This had been the part where she was going to make a grand speech about vengeance. She had a list of names. And she was going to share them, because she had the power to. She was leaving, they couldn't reach her across an ocean. But suddenly, her anger had dissipated, leaving only sadness.

She sat down on the edge of the stage. "Some of you, I believe, know how that feels," she said. "Tonight is about the people who have been forgotten. I have a few I want to tell you about. After, I'm very much hoping you'll share some of your loved ones with me."

She sat there, and told them about Lise, not her death, but her life. She told them about Rachel's fierceness. Then, Violette sat next to her and told a very bawdy story about her days on the cabaret circuit that Amelie repeated to the audience verbatim.

She told them about Jean-Louise. She told them about her mother, the painter.

When she was done, it was dark. She'd arranged for portable lanterns, and as they were lit, they cast a strangely intimate glow over the crowd.

"Tell me, if you're willing," she said. "Tell me who you haven't forgotten."

For a moment, no one responded. Amelie waited, easy in the silence.

An elderly man stood up, three rows back. He'd gotten there early, to get that seat. "My son, Roland," he said. "Wanted to be a painter, like your mother. Died in the war. Twenty-one."

"I'm sorry," she said. "What was he like?"

"Impudent," the man said, and there was a light ripple of laughter. The man smiled. "Loved his mother." He looked down at the woman next to him. Amelie thought he might have squeezed her hand. "Never met a chore or a job he wanted to do, but he wasn't bad at the painting. Might have made a go at it."

There were more, after he sat. Dozens more. It was like a polluted wound had been lanced, and the infection was draining out, until there was nothing but clean red blood. It wasn't all war deaths, or those who had died on one side or the other or no side at all during the Commune. More often it was just people who were missed.

"Bertrand Tailler," a woman said. Amelie squinted in the low light and saw a tall, brown-haired woman standing. Next to her she recognized Dr. Durand. His wife?

"He was the son of a stable master on my family's estate," she said. "Died during the war. Signed up for it, when he should have known better. He was good with horses."

She nodded and sat down.

And on it went. There were those in the crowd who left—the small group from the Jockey Club among them. Amelie waited until the lanterns had burned down low before she stood.

"Thank you," she said. There were tears on her face. She didn't know when she'd begun to cry; perhaps a long time ago. "I'm—I'm so grateful. Thank you for sharing this with me, and for letting me tell you about the people I love."

The applause came. It wasn't thunderous, she'd had much louder and more impressive, but it went straight to her chest.

"Thank you," she whispered again.

She'd hated these people sometimes; thought they'd kept her trapped as St. Amie. But some of them had been with her since the first time she'd danced in this empty lot. Some of them loved her, and she found she loved them, too.

When she walked offstage, she gestured for her stage manager. "Tell the press I'm ready," she said, her voice hoarse. She'd been looking forward to this part, but now she was only tired.

It was her insurance policy against Honoré de Lavel: she was going to give the press every last thing she had on him, the way he'd acted during her mother's death, the proposition he'd made her, and perhaps most damningly from the press's perspective, the evidence she'd uncovered in her mother's things that de Lavel had, at least between 1865 and 1868, engaged in significant manipulation of the Parisian financial markets. Denying a dying woman morphine was shocking, but not criminal. Market manipulation was a different matter entirely.

Only a little bit longer. Talk to the press, ride out the interviews, and then there were two tickets to New York, waiting on her desk.

As she walked to the small area they'd arranged for this purpose, she saw Lise out of the corner of her eye and changed direction.

"Oh, Lise, congratulations. You danced beautifully. I think a few people even sensed you."

"Thank you," the ghost said. She was dressed in the costume they had settled on for all the dancers: a simple, dark gray bodice and tutu, with a long veil. The veil was currently pushed back.

"You did all the work."

"No," Lise said. "*Thank you.*"

"Oh," Amelie said, understanding. This had been the goal of the ballet after all, at least in part. But somehow in the work and practice and fuss of mounting the production, she'd forgotten. "You're leaving."

"I'm mostly gone already," she said, and it was true there seemed less of her. She flickered. "There's not much time."

"I'll miss you," Amelie said, feeling the tears in her throat. "God, Lise. I'll miss you.

"Now, aren't you glad I haunted you? You didn't even know me before."

Despite everything, Amelie laughed. "It made it all worth it," she said. "Do you know—"

"Where I'm going? No. If I ever remembered, it's long faded. But it's nowhere bad. I know that for certain."

She needed to be strong. It was just that she'd grown so used to Lise, to Violette, even to Rachel. They were part of her.

"We'll still be part of you," Lise said.

"I thought I told you not to read my mind."

Lise shrugged. "Honestly, I never really followed that rule," she said, and with a very cheeky smile, she was gone.

Lise Martin, nineteen years old, a talented and ambitious dancer, Amelie thought. *Funny. Killed a man once by dancing him to death, claimed he deserved it. Dearly missed.*

"Mademoiselle St. James? They're ready."

Forcing the tears down, Amelie nodded. "I'll be right there," she said.

CHAPTER THIRTY

They traveled from Le Havre by steamship, Amelie, Honorine, and Violette.

Violette had asked, very politely, if she might be allowed to stay "a little longer" to see America. Amelie thought she was beginning to understand how to release her ghosts, and with that she had gained a very small amount of control. Because she could let Violette go when the ghost wanted, she could also let her stay. She had agreed, and Violette had immediately donned her nautical-themed wig. Over the course of the voyage, she had also accumulated luggage. Fortunately, it carried itself.

Now, they stood on the deck of the steamer, waiting to disembark. Amelie stared at the new city, so unlike the one she had left and yet so similar. Here, too, nothing stood still. She could see the half-framed buildings in the distance.

She hadn't told Sam or Alva when she was coming—she'd known Alva would want to meet her at the dock, and she needed a little more time.

The ship had arrived in New York City at six in the morning.

By the time Amelie and Honorine had disembarked, passed through customs, found a cab, and checked in to their hotel, it was almost suppertime, and Violette had long disappeared. "Call me when something happens," she'd said.

"I can't believe we're here," Honorine said, staring out the window of their small hotel room. They were traveling on a strict budget.

"Neither can I," Amelie said, coming up behind her and putting a hand on her shoulder. "How are you feeling?"

"Excited," her sister said. "Scared."

"Me too," Amelie said. "Come on. Somewhere out there, probably on this very street—which certainly has quite a number of very tall buildings on it!—there is a place where we can buy some supper. Let's go find it."

"Don't forget to call Violette," Honorine said. "She'll be sad if we don't invite her to our first meal in our new city."

"Violette, we're going to supper," Amelie said obediently, and the ghost was there, sporting a brand-new, New York–themed wig.

"Too much?" she asked.

"Never," Amelie said.

That evening, eating unfamiliar food in a small cafe, and later, in bed, listening to the unfamiliar sounds of an unfamiliar city, Amelie felt afraid. What if Benedict didn't want her? What if she'd pushed him too far? What if he'd found someone else?

I'll go on, she reminded herself. She hadn't left Paris for him. She'd left for herself, for new spaces, and for Honorine, who shouldn't have to grow up in a place that would always judge her by her parentage. They were going to be happy here, Benedict or not.

But she really, really hoped he hadn't found someone else.

The next morning, Amelie put on her new pink dress, and a hat she'd refurbished with a dashing bow. "I know you want to explore," she said to Honorine. "Please don't. I want you to wait here for me, and when I get back—"

Honorine rolled her eyes. "I know you're going to see Benedict," she said. "And I'm hardly going to go out wandering in a city I don't even know yet."

Amelie narrowed her eyes.

"Alright, fine. I promise not to leave."

"Better," Amelie said.

When she stepped out of the modest hotel, she wished she had half Honorine's urge to explore. The city was overwhelming, and she didn't know a single brick of it. She set her shoulders. The new Amelie—the old Amelie, too—was brave. She hailed a hansom and gave the driver the address, grateful for the months she'd recently spent speaking English.

Benedict's apartment building was pleasant and built of pale stone. She hesitated outside the main door. Should she have sent a letter first? It was a bit much to simply arrive at his doorstep, after months of not speaking. What if he had a woman inside? What if he didn't want to see her? She stood frozen in the middle of the sidewalk, until she was very properly shoved out of the way by passersby.

She'd never thought she'd be one of those idiots, gawking at their surroundings and clogging up the sidewalk.

Get ahold of yourself. He probably won't even be home.

That was it. She'd go in, ask the doorman for him, and when she was told he wasn't home, she'd simply leave him a note. Very appropriate.

He was home.

This was it, then, appropriate or not. She followed the doorman up the stairs.

Should she have brought flowers?

Thanking the doorman, she knocked. And he answered.

He was so . . . *Benedict*. Right there, in front of her. Real.

He sucked in his breath when he saw her. "Amelie?"

"I thought, this time, I should be the one to cross it."

"What?"

"The ocean." She was doing this wrong. "I told you not to cross it for me. So, I crossed it for you. That doesn't sound very romantic, does it?"

He leaned against the doorway. "Is it supposed to?"

"Yes," she said. "It's supposed to be a proposal of marriage."

"Ah," he said. "Yes, I'm also very bad at those. Would you like to come in?"

"Would I—"

But he had already vanished into his apartment, leaving her to follow. He hadn't said no. Then again, she wasn't at all sure she'd actually managed to propose to him. And she was curious about his apartment. So, she went in, shutting the door behind her.

And frowned. "This is properly furnished," she said. "I was led to believe you only had a sofa. That you'd found on the street!"

He sat against the back of his actual sofa, which looked *very* smart and not at all as though it had been abandoned by its previous owners. "See, I also made this mistake. When proposing marriage, you aren't supposed to start an argument."

"Right," she said. "Very fair. May I begin again?"

He gestured his consent. She took a breath.

"Benedict Moore, we have had an exceedingly long courtship. It has encompassed wars, revolutions, disease, ghosts—are you *smirking* at me?"

"No."

"I believe you were."

"It's only that you're worse at proposing than I am," he said. "It's not at all common to begin by listing the extremely dire events that occurred over the course of your romance."

Amelie crossed her arms, deciding to ignore him. "*And* it turns out, after all that, and—oh, Ben, I'm just going to talk to you."

She sat down on his very smart sofa. He joined her.

"I've missed you terribly," she said, to his knee. "After you left—"

"Amelie?"

"Ben, how am I supposed to get through this if you keep interrupting me?"

"I'm going to say yes. To the proposal. I want to hear everything. But I strongly suspect I'm going to want to put my arm around you or kiss you during it, and that might be derailing if you were still waiting on an answer. So, it's yes."

"Oh," she said. "Good."

He did kiss her, then, and it took a few moments for her thoughts to gather themselves back together.

"I burned a few bridges, when I left," she said. "Well. Exploded them, more like—"

"See? You're a Moore already."

That was rather lovely. "Before I tell you about all that, I need to apologize. I— It took me a while to see I was holding on to the wrong things and hiding from the right ones. And when I did realize, it took me even longer to set it right."

"Hence the exploding bridges, I assume."

She nodded, and then she told him everything. About de Lavel, and Raoul Fabre, and Lise, and the ballet, and all the other things she'd kept secret that she didn't have to anymore. "I got so in the habit of hiding things, I forgot how to tell the truth," she said, twisting the fabric of her skirt. He was the only person left to whom she owed the truth, and now that she'd told him, she was nervous.

But when she glanced up, he was looking at her with understanding and love and something like amusement.

"I'm still working on it," she said. "I'll probably get it wrong sometimes."

He kissed her.

"I learned a few things, too," he said, after a while. "And I will tell you about them. But first, I want to show you something."

"Alright," she said, standing and following him obligingly. He stopped at the dining room table, on which there was a neat stack of papers.

"This is the Amelie pile," he said.

"I beg your pardon?"

"I may have had some advance warning of your arrival," he said.

"Sam."

"You'll learn quite quickly not to trust him with a secret," he said. "It's not malicious, it's just he has no sense of social mores."

He pushed the stack toward her. "I knew I had to let you be the one to come. Last week I *may* have walked to the docks to buy a steamer ticket, but I definitely ripped it up afterward. Anyway, I couldn't come to you, but I *could* hope. So, that's what this pile is. Hope."

She sat down, flipped through it. "Oh, Ben."

It was all the information she could possibly need to move to a new city. Schools. Homes of various sizes. There was even a list of properties suitable for conversion to a studio space.

"Benedict Moore," she said, through the thickness in her throat. "I would very much like you to row me around a lake."

"In January?" he asked, grinning.

"Yes," she said. "Consider this a kidnapping."

EPILOGUE

1880, Hudson River Valley, New York

The day was green and warm and golden. Sunshine drifted lazily over the rolling landscape of the Hudson Valley, kissing Amelie's skin. Honorine stalked dragonflies by the nearby pond, evidence of her recent fascination with entomology.

Amelie stood before the small wooden stage Ben had built for her, watching the small company she'd spent a year and a half building finish their warm-up. There were only six dancers, four women and two men, but given that ballet barely existed in the United States, they might well be the largest company in the nation. They also boasted a violinist.

"Let's start with the *pas de deux*," she said. "I'm not sure about the *attitude* turn, Sarah, let's run it through to there."

As dancers cleared from the stage and Abe the violinist played the first notes, she felt Ben come up beside her.

"You're back," she said, smiling. She kept her eyes on the stage.

"Mmm," he said, snaking his arm around her waist. "That's pretty."

"Yes," she said. "Sarah, let's try that in *arabesque*. How did the surgery go?"

"We got it all," he said. "He's recovering well."

She nodded, the flush of joy and relief that accompanied every one of his successful surgeries blooming in her chest. The institute was thriving, and Ben had performed his first successful brain surgery the year prior.

"There's a band at the pub in town tonight," she said. "Violette wants to go listen."

"Sounds nice," he said, kissing the top of her head. "I'm going to change and reply to Maggie's letter. She says she was arrested at a suffrage march again."

That took Amelie's attention from the stage. It was the fourth such arrest for Maggie, who led the family in jail time. Ben was in second place. "Is she alright?"

"Henry got her out again," he said, rather blithely in Amelie's opinion. "He *also* sent a letter. Sounds a bit cross."

"Yes," Amelie said. "I imagine he might." She returned to watching the dancers. They finished, waiting for her comments.

"I'll see you tonight," he said, kissing her hair again.

Later that day, when the sky had turned violet and rehearsal was over, she walked back to their house. Fireflies sparked alongside her, and crickets sung heavily in the long grass by the pond. She stood for a moment, watching the light stream from their windows. She could hear Ben and Honorine laughing inside.

Three more ghosts had appeared since her move. Each had been quickly released, but they were still learning what she was, and how it worked. Honorine persisted in calling her a spirit medium; Amelie had no word for it.

But standing there, on a summer's night, with the first stars peeping out above her, she didn't feel any hurry. Every day she woke up next to the man she loved. Every day she did the work she loved. And every night, she could look to the heavens and see the stars.

She was happy.

ACKNOWLEDGMENTS

This book came to life at around five o'clock on a jet-lagged Saturday morning, as I sat in a quiet apartment, the only one awake, and watched the sun reflect pink and golden off the dome of Sacré-Coeur. Two years later, as I write these acknowledgments eight months into the COVID-19 pandemic, that moment seems very far away. I find, thinking back over the writing of this book, that it is the people in my life who connect those two points with memories of shared joy, sadness, love, anger, laughter, and support. They are all so precious to me.

Rachel Paxton has been my critique partner for seven years. She is a beautiful writer, a wonderful friend, and a plot whisperer (an extremely convenient trait in a critique partner).

Patty and Tim Billings have shown me so much love and warmth over the years. They let me belong with them. Brianna Billings is the closest thing I have to a sister, and she shows me every day what grace and strength look like.

I'm so grateful for Rose Savard, Isaac Skibinski, Morgan Smalley, Hilary Richardson, Martha Reynolds, and Kaitlyn

Sullivan, all of whom bring beauty and joy to my life. I'd also like to mention the choreographers who have inspired me with their work, particularly Crystal Pite and the legendary Twyla Tharp.

My agent, Amy Elizabeth Bishop, is talented, fierce, and brilliant. I'm so happy we're on each other's teams.

This book is my heart, and because it is my heart it was a struggle to translate to the page. Certainly I would not have been successful without my editor, Vicki Lame, whose clarity of vision, calm reassurance, and infectious laugh lit many a dark day for me. I'm also thankful for the many talented people at St. Martin's who worked on this book, including Angelica Chong, Devan Norman, Danielle Christopher, Marissa Sangiacomo, Kejana Ayala, Melanie Sanders, Joy Gannon, and Kelly Moran.

One of the best things about being an author is making author friends. I'm so grateful for the many lovely people I have met over the last several years, and I hope that eventually I'll even get to meet some of them in person!

My dog, Valentino, and my cat, Giselle, are a hugely important part of my writing process, in that they frequently sleep near me, and occasionally vomit on the carpet in my office.

Finally, to my husband, Timothy Savard, who loves me, laughs with me, and holds me when I cry: thank you, and I love you.

ABOUT THE AUTHOR

DIANA BILLER is the author of *The Widow of Rose House* and *The Brightest Star in Paris*. When she isn't writing, she enjoys snuggling her animals, taking "research" trips abroad, and attending ballet class. She lives with her husband in Los Angeles.